THE DOOR WAS LOCKED

He felt like crying, but he was incapable of it. It would take too much strength to cry. He took a deep breath. Told himself, it's okay, it's all right.

He sniffed the air. There was a cloying smell; a rotting flower stink. As if the rosebuds in the wallpaper were rotting.

There was also—somehow a function of the cloying stink of rotting petals—laughter, from somewhere; sticky, shriveled laughter, and foreign-sounding music, sort of Arab and sort of Oriental and sort of American. Played on what sounded like a malfunctioning stereo.

The noise came through the room's single window. A big bay window all veiny with shadows and fragmented with light. It made him think of a biology class where he'd dissected a lizard and the teacher had him hold its bellyskin up to the light and you could see all the veins picked out in a rosy glow. . . .

Roses. Big fat ones, he saw, as he hobbled up to the window. He'd never seen roses this big before. And the veiny shadows were made by thick rose vines, some as big around as his wrist, and all dinosaur-spiny with large thorns.

The window was nailed shut.

WETBONES

JOHN SHIRLEY

LEISURE BOOKS   NEW YORK CITY

A LEISURE BOOK®

June 1999

Published by

Dorchester Publishing Co., Inc.
276 Fifth Avenue
New York, NY 10001

ISBN 0-8439-4525-7

The name "Leisure Books" and the stylized "L" with design are
trademarks of Dorchester Publishing Co., Inc.

Printed in the United States of America.

For Micky Perry, who qualifies for the following job descriptions:

> *Excellent Wife (not experienced but willing to learn—and to teach)*
>
> *Patient and Affectionate Editor (experienced and qualified)*
>
> *Beacon of Faith (patience a plus)*

She's hired. Position is permanent, retirement plan included.

The author wishes to thank . . .

Mark Ziesing for his patience and supportiveness

Nancy Collins for her Sympathy for the Devil

Bob Frazier for his exacting implementation of my edits— sorry for the headaches

Micky Perry again for her editorial help

Julian for restoring some of my innocence

WETBONES

You can rot here without feeling it.
—John Rechy, on Los Angeles

Los Angeles, California

They slid her body out in a long aluminium drawer on small, well-oiled rollers in a room that was sterile and cold, so cold he could see his breath: a little cloud steaming out over her, dissipating, pluming again, vanishing.

She was under a plastic wrapper, like something in a supermarket meat department. The morgue orderly peeled the plastic wrapper back so Prentice could see her face; her torso down to the sternum. Blue gray. Wasted. That's the word the doctor had used. The *wasting* of her.

She looks like a fucking mummy, Prentice thought.

Less than a day dead and she looked like a mummy, gray skin clinging to her skull, sharply outlining her jawbone, her collarbone, her ribs. Her eyes – it was as if someone had plucked out her eyes and replaced them with peeled grapes. Lips skinned back, flat and blue, as if painted on, exposing her teeth in a grimace. Gums so receded you could see the roots of her teeth. Long, thick white scars braided her right arm, rope-like scar tissue that pinched the sections of flesh together, and a jagged reddish-white scar bisected her right breast, just missing the shrivelled blue nipple.

1

Self mutilation, the doctor had said. The body was barely recognisable as Amy, but there was the grinning-bat tattoo above her left breast, a breast flattened, now, to an old woman's droopy pouch.

Faintly, he could smell her. Acid splashed up into his esophagus. "Okay," he rasped, and the orderly slammed the drawer shut with a clang.

Prentice wanted to belt the guy for not showing more respect; but it would have been absurd. Respect? Life and death had already shown Amy its fullest contempt. Prentice turned and walked out. He went looking for the L.A. sunlight.

Hollywood

"Look," Buddy was saying wearily, "I've been pitching you heavily to Arthwright, telling him you're not one of these Hollywood hacks. Tom, you're a screenwriter. An *A* writer fuh Chris' sakes. This guy is special, I'm telling him. He hears that stuff a lot from agents, how's he supposed to know it's true for Tom Prentice? You don't show up, he's gonna think you're a flake."

"Look – if you'd seen her –" Prentice began, his knuckles white on the hotel phone. "She was all . . ." He broke off not knowing how to explain it in a way that wouldn't make him seem, yes, flaky. A whiner. Buddy was his agent, not his therapist.

"I know how you feel," Buddy told him. "But you can't cancel on Arthwright. Isn't done. Especially not you and not now." Buddy's telephone voice had the distant cave-echo quality that meant he was using his speaker phone. He almost always used the speaker; fussing around his office, scribbling notes and signing papers or maybe mixing a drink while he

2

yelled across the room at the phone's remote mike.

"I don't want to cancel," Prentice said. "I want to postpone." He was sitting tensely on the edge of his bed, in his hotel room.

"It's the same. He isn't gonna have time for you whenever you're damn ready."

"Come on, Buddy. He'd understand if you told him about Amy."

"He'd understand, but that don't mean he'd find time for you later on. You know? He'd promise but would he do it? Not very fucking likely."

Prentice nodded to himself. In the back of Arthwright's shrivelled little producer's heart, the son of a bitch would feel that appointments with him were more important than anything else in your life. Including grieving for the dead who, after all, were not consulted in movie marketing surveys.

And, really, Prentice had known what his agent would say about cancelling the meeting. He knew Buddy, though he'd only actually met him twice, both face to face meetings quite brief. Prentice had told himself he was going to cancel the meeting anyway. But now, pressing the phone against the side of his head so hard it hurt, Prentice felt the shaky feeling that meant he was weakening, was probably going to give in. *Especially not you and not now*, Buddy had said. Like putting a rubber stamp on Prentice's forehead: He was on the Out List. He had to get back in. It was just too good a gig to lose. He couldn't handle the humiliation of going back to the only other work he knew how to do. Bartender. Maybe end up serving a cocktail to Arthwright. *"Well Hi, Tom . . . Prentice? Right, how are ya, doin' a little moonlighting from scripting huh? Hell, Tom, I may be in here washing dishes or something myself, if I don't jumpstart some*

3

*box office rentals here. We'll have to talk sometime. Ummm
– I'll have a margarita and this lovely young lady here takes,
I think, a tequila sunrise? Great. Thanks Tom. So anyway,
Sondra . . ."*

"Tell me something, Buddy," Prentice said now,
venting some steam. "How do people get to be on the
Out List in this town anyway, huh? There are all these
guys, they write films that make no goddamn money,
they get no critical recognition, but they still get con-
tracts. Just because they had something *produced* once?
Then I get one bomb and I'm supposedly on the Out
List. How's that happen, huh?"

"Look, don't get pissed at me, how the fuck do I
know, Tom? It's pure caprice, right? It's gossip or something, probably. Some guys, when things go sour, they
don't get talked about, they don't get blamed. Some do.
I don't know. Maybe it's because you're out of town until
now, you're not here networking, you didn't make
Warner's season-opener party, you're not at the Golden
Globe receptions, people notice who's there and who
isn't, you know –"

"I tried to rearrange my schedule so I could fly out
for the Globes reception, but I had this thing –"

"Prioritize, Tom, you know? Got to prioritize.
You've got to be here hustling close to the bone, schmooz
any time you can, keep the relationships going so people
stay loyal. They're always looking for somebody to back-
bite. If you're not around, it's your back that gets
bitten . . ."

"Okay, okay, you're right. I'm here now. But Buddy
– when I saw Amy's body today–" His voice broke. He
swallowed, and got the masculinity back into it. "The
guy said she lost fifty pounds in two days. Without lipo-
suction, without surgery, and it wasn't losing blood and

it wasn't losing water weight. It was – It was just *her.*"

"Fifty fucking pounds in two days? Bullshit! Somebody screwed up, clerical error in the hospital records, you know? Couldn't have been that much. She lost some weight, well the woman wasted herself on drugs, *you* know than–" A double *peep* in the background as Buddy's secretary informed him someone was on the line for him. "Just a minute, Tom. Lemme–" A couple of dry clicks. Static. Another click. "Tom? I gotta go here, I've got to call somebody back. But uh... Well, hey, about Amy: She was probably doing crack or crystal or something. You can't feel responsible."

"She was my wife, Buddy, dammit."

"Not for years, not really. You were divorced, and let me tell you, I know – my therapist, he put me on to this: the secret is, you got to let go. Let go of resentment, responsibility, after a divorce. Just write the checks and write it off." Again, the background *peeps* of Buddy's secretary, letting him know he had another call. This time there were three *peeps*, a signal that let Buddy know it was someone important, a key client or a major player. Prentice knew Buddy's phone habits the way another man knows his partner's facial expressions. "Hey," Buddy was saying, "I got to take that, Tom. Look, show up for Arthwright. Pitch him. *Then* do your grieving, what have you. Work is therapy. And you can't afford not to take that meeting. Got to go–"

"Buddy –"

Click. Buzz. Gone.

Prentice banged the phone down on the receiver. *Pitch Arthwright, then do your grieving, what have you.*

"What *have* you?" he muttered. "Christ." Prioritize, Tom, prioritize.

Prentice stood up. Wobbled for a moment on his legs

5

as the circulation shivered painfully back into them. He put on his sunglasses, thinking: Go ahead, get self righteous about the way people are in L.A. But you know you're relieved Buddy talked you into going to the meeting . . .

Amy. Was there someone he should inform? Her dad had abandoned the family when she was little. Her mother was dead. Cirrhosis. Her brother was a biker somewhere. Where, was anyone's guess. Prentice could call his own parents, but they'd never liked Amy, they'd been glad when she'd left him. His Mom had bugged him about finalizing, getting a divorce, settling down with "someone more stable. God knows, you *need* someone more stable."

He looked at the paper sack that held Amy's effects. Now he knew why she'd sent his last two checks back; why she'd burned her bridges with him. She'd been getting money somewhere else. Even a Gold Card. The card was in the sack, along with her wallet, a gold chain ankle bracelet, an address book. No addresses in the address book, just cryptic scribbles and two phone numbers. It was like her: she kept most of her addresses on little scraps of paper in her wallet. Used to drive him crazy. He was fanatically methodical about addresses. Rolodexes, black-leather-bound planners. Now he even had an electronic address book that looked like a calculator.

If he didn't click with Arthwright, he might have to hock that calculator soon. Prentice looked once more at the detritus of Amy's passing on the bed. Like the nest of a dead pheasant, the American peacock, found in the tall grasses, after the hunter's downed the bird. Nothing left but a handful of feathers and dead grass.

He went downstairs, jangling his hotel and rental car keys together in his hand.

Alameda, California just Across the Bay from San Francisco

Ephram chose a girl he saw working at the cash register, in Dresden's Hardware Store.

She was at Cash Register Three. Maybe it was the faint pattern of freckles on her cheekbone, the same configuration as the negative constellation. The constellation Kali, that no one saw but him: Ephram Pixie, who saw so much, ha ha, that no one else saw.

The girl was plump but pretty. Soft brown eyes with a little too much eyeliner. Tammy Fayeish eyelashes. White gloss on lips that carried on the Zaftig theme of her slightly oversized body. Full breasts for a girl, oh, sixteen or so. Her honey-blonde hair charmingly ruined by being up in one of those strange do's that teenage girls were affecting lately, a "pump", it was called: a little ridge of hair jutting straight up above the forehead, like a radar scoop of some kind, yet delicate and bound in place by lots of big blowzy curls. The esthetic blindness of it fascinated him. Here was real innocence.

And she wore a little charm bracelet made of small gold hearts about one wrist. He counted them: there were seven little gold hearts. Seven of hearts: his omen card in the Negative Deck. Another sign.

About her neck was her name in gold, hanging from a necklace. C-O-N-S-T-A-N-C-E. Constance? Oh, really? Ha ha.

She wore a raspberry coloured dress, with a frilly collar; raspberry Adidas tennis shoes, that looked gauche with the dress, but again she was unaware of that. The sneakers weren't gauche with her dress at her high school after all, ha ha.

Ephram was buying a coil of rope when he spotted

7

her. He felt a warm, sweet tingle when he saw the girl and at the same time became sharply aware of the rope's texture in his hands. The delicious coincidence of it . . .

The rope was quarter-inch soft white synthetic fibre, and it would do very well.

"Hi, how are you today," she said, automatically, not quite looking at him. Looking at the price tag on the rope and ringing it up.

"I'm glad you don't use those machines to read the – what are they? – those atrocious little bar-symbols that computers read," Ephram said. Just to get her to say a few more things to him. To dawdle there as he got a fix on her.

"Hm?" she said, blinking at him, "Oh, those computer price reading things? Bar codes, I think, it's called. I wish we *did* have theme A nervous little laugh like a trill on a toy piano. "– because, um, like, they're faster. The lines get long in here and everybody gets, you know, they want to get in and get out . . . . That's three-ninety-five."

"Here you are. Yes, well, that's a shame. I like . . . lingering here, myself. This is a charming hardware store. So cluttered and old fashioned."

She looked at him, to try to decide if he was serious. People didn't talk like that, in her little world, with words like *lingering*, describing a hardware store as charming. He smiled broadly at her. Not hoping to interest her in him, no, ha ha. He was a squat little man, with a soft wheel of fat at around his middle, his oversized head mostly bald, a few colourless hairs slicked across it. An astrological glamour just barely visible, if you looked close, in the back of his deep-set green eyes. And if you looked closer . . .

But all she saw, he knew, was a funny looking little

8

fat guy grinning at her from the other side of the counter. She stared at him, beginning to feel the feather antenna of his first probe in her brain. And then another customer came up and she turned gratefully to him: a black teenager with an earring and a Mercedes Benz hood ornament hanging on a chain around his neck. He was buying spraypaint. Fairly obvious, Ephram thought, what the boy was going to do with that, the vandal. Inexplicably, the girl squirmed with pleasure when the boy said something vaguely flirtatious, and shook her head, saying, "I'm *sure*."

The boy really ought to be arrested, Ephram thought, for stealing that Mercedes ornament off someone's car.

Carrying the rope out to the car, Ephram found himself thinking of calling a cop on the little son of a bitch . . .

And then he laughed aloud at himself. *Absurd that I of all people should be thinking of calling the police on anyone . . . Ha ha.*

When Garner saw Constance coming up the walk, he found himself looking to see how steadily she walked, and if her eyes were glazed.

There was no reason at all to suppose his daughter was on drugs. Really, there was none. She stayed out too late sometimes, she didn't take school seriously – she worked in spurts to maintain a C average – but she was a careful girl, in most ways, and she didn't smoke or drink. As far as he knew.

Probably unrealistic to think she'd never had a drink It was fucking 1990, man. The kids drank or were scorned.

But when your old man is a drug counsellor – three days a week, when he wasn't doing pastoral work – you probably didn't get into drugs. Did you?

Easy does it, Garner counselled himself. Let go, stop obsessing. This is Alameda. She's all right.

Alameda, after all, is an island. An island of safety and an island geographically, neatly packed with houses and parks, with San Francisco Bay on one side and an estuary on the other. There were big signs just this side of the bridges onto Alameda: *DRUG FREE ZONE. This Community mandates double penalties for drug violations.*

There weren't any drug free zones in America. The signs stood at the ends of the bridges to warn ghetto gangsters who drifted over from Oakland.

The town was mostly an enclave of upper-middle class safety, tough cops, a big Navy base, half a dozen marinas, a 25 MPH speed limit. The local kids were fairly straight, and stuck to their own community. There was no open drug dealing at all. But there were lots and lots of liquor stores and bars, thanks to the military, and just a mile across the estuary was Oakland's East 14th, and anything could be had, there . . .

Stop stressing out, he told himself again. She's all right.

"How was work?" Garner asked, when Constance came in. Knowing how she'd answer.

"Okay, I guess," she said. As always. What was there to say about working in a hardware store for the summer?

Without pausing as she bustled by, she slid her purse onto the hall table, making the vase of dusty silk flowers rock. It was a clumsy blue and pink ceramic vase she'd made for him in a sixth grade art class; he grabbed it just before it toppled, turned to ruefully watch her walk into the kitchen to get herself the inevitable Diet Coke. Singing a George Michael song absently to herself. He thought about telling her that her skirt was too short. He stopped himself, amazed, not for the first time, to find

10

himself turning into his own father. In the late 60s, when Garner came of age, Constance's skirt would have been prudishly long.

Garner went to sit on the living room couch, looking out the picture window at the sunny suburban yard. July in California.

Somewhere above, in the province of passenger jets, fighter jets from the base's carriers, and the birds that choked on the jets' exhaust, a cloud drew itself over the sun. Far below, the cloud shadow spilled slowly and inexorably across the lawn.

Clunk, clunk, Constance kicking off her shoes in the hallway. "Hey, Daddy Dude," she said, coming in with her can of Diet Coke, sitting in the easy chair across from him, feet tucked partly under her. She had those awkward little white socks they were wearing now, and a thin gold ankle bracelet. In the 60s she'd have had white go-go boots. At least she hadn't got one of those ugly fanny-paks yet.

Garner was wearing jeans, sneakers – real Converse sneakers, which were hard to find – and his Oakland Street Ministry t-shirt. He knew the trappings of the Ministry embarrassed her a little, but she liked the t-shirt because its graffiti-style design was at least marginally hip. He knew she was proud of him, too, because he was cooler than some other dads. He let her stay out later, let her watch the movies she wanted, was tolerant of profanity up to a point, let her go to rock concerts alone, never said a word about loud music, though he couldn't stand most of the bands she liked. What was that band? Bon Jovi . . .

She liked her father being politically liberal; it was hipper to be P.C., because MTV was mostly slanted that way. They both liked the Beatles and the Stones. He

11

wished she'd known her mother. For one thing, her mother would know how to tell her she wore too much makeup...

"Daddy Dude," she began, smiling sweetly.

"Let me guess. The car. Had your license two months and you think you get to wheedle the car."

"I'm sure, it's not like the only thing I ever talk to you about is wanting something, I mean –"

"Not the only thing, no. But when you call me Daddy Dude, in that sweet voice, it's a dead giveaway."

"Whatever. Daddy... Daddy Dad. We just want to go to the mall and the arcade."

"I'm staying around here this evening because we're having a counselling group here. They're painting the Volunteer Centre in Oakland so it's got to be here. So yeah, okay. But if you hurta my car I breaka you face!"

She laughed. Then her expression went ludicrously earnest. "Did anyone call for me?"

"No, hon, he didn't call, whoever he is. What's his name? Is he in puberty yet? Does he have pubic hair?"

"*Da*-ad!"

Ephram thought about doing away with Megan. He thought about it as he drove his '88 Porsche to the condo he'd rented near the beach, in Alameda. On the way, he drove through a neighbourhood of Victorian and Queen Anne houses, most of them prettily restored and trimmed, ostentatiously gardened. The matronly old houses seemed to wear the lush foliage of the street's many oaks and maples like fir stoles. He would have preferred one of the fine old houses to a condo. But anonymity was better, and you were more anonymous in a condo.

He left the old town neighbourhood, drove into the area of housing projects and condos and beach front apartment buildings; an area of town rather glaringly open to the sky. It was a sweet summer evening for a drive by the beach, a few clouds strikingly purple against the lemon glow of the horizon. It was an evening to savour, an epicurean's evening, and Ephram regarded himself as the last word in epicureans.

A nice night to do away with Megan. She was mostly used up. There wasn't much left but the sticky, impure stuff at the bottom of the bottle that was her brain.

He always thought of it that way: *Doing away*. It was such a pleasantly euphemistic expression. It made him think of the way Valentine Michael Smith had rid the world of unwanted people in that novel, that bit of silliness from the 60s. *Stranger In* ... something. Valentine Smith would simply think them out of existence.

He couldn't do that with Megan, just think her out of existence when he was done with her. And having to *do away* with them physically, personally, was his least favourite part of the whole process. Well, the actual killing was all right, but the disposal – the away of it – was a bore and a mess. Literally, a mess. There was no truly pristine doing away, he thought. Not even incineration. There was always a mess of some kind. A cadaver leaving its mutely insistent signature on the scene, if only a little grease and ash.

Nothing for it but to roll up his sleeves ...

Ephram arrived at the cluster of two-story security condos and pressed the door signaller that would let him into the parking lot. The gate lurched a little, then rolled aside. He drove through and neatly into his parking place. He was not a man to waste movements.

He went into his condo without bothering to check his mailbox. There shouldn't be anything in it except bills and trash. No one knew he was here. And, of course, there was no one alive who would write him a letter, anyway, ha ha.

Megan was right where he'd left her, under the sink in the bathroom.

Part of her naked, pale, pinkwhite body was set aglow by a long bar of light that expanded from the hall when he opened the door. She had her back to him, lay on her side, curled up around the sink pipes like a snail around a stem. Her long red hair – now matted and oily – fanned across the bathroom tiles. Freckles across her back. He often chose freckly girls, or girls with birth marks. Marks on the skin were signs to him.

She groaned when he switched on the bathroom light, but of course she couldn't move. He hadn't given her leave to move. She was still cerebrally locked. He reached oat with an exploratory impulse, the probe making her shudder and gag a little as it passed through her skull. He tasted the pleasure centres of her brain. The *reward receiver* of the brain, as Ephram thought of it. There was some capacity left. Some cells not yet wrung out. More than he'd thought. Best use her once more before the doing away. Waste not, wanton. Ha ha.

He first had to unlock her brain. He reached out mentally and undid the partial paralysis. She spasmed like a sick dog and defecated thinly and wetly on herself, then flopped onto her back. Ephram wrinkled his nose at the smell and switched on the bathroom's ventilator fan; he took a little can of air freshener from the glass shelf over the sink and sprayed it around a bit. Honeysuckle.

He put the can away and inspected her. The marks he'd made were scabbing over, but rather badly. Some of them were purulent. This definitely did have to be the last time with Megan.

She tried to speak, managed to croak, "Listen . . . just once . . . listen . . . I can't believe you don't . . . you can't . . ."

"You should believe it," he said, sending a probe into her cerebral punishment receiver. She gave out a cawing sound that was all the scream she could manage anymore and arched her back. Ephram felt his penis harden. It hardened a bit, anyway.

He moved to stand beside the bathtub and said, "Come over here and get in the tub. Facing me."

The look on her face. Her eyes going dully to the door. Thinking about pushing past him, running. Not having the strength – and knowing he'd never let her get a step toward the door, anyway.

He savoured the completeness of his triumph over her. She had fought him all the way. She was better than some, who'd capitulate in some kind of role reversal madness, beginning to identify with him, losing their grasp on identity. That was a bore. But Megan fought to the last breath, bless her.

All she could do was say, emptily, "No.".

Psychically, he speared her again. She writhed and tried to weep, but the tears were long since dried up. Her lips were cracked from dehydration.

She struggled to her feet. She swayed.

Ephram reached over and turned on the water, started the shower going, lukewarm. He didn't want any steam to obscure his view. Then he said, again, "Get in the tub."

She took a wobbly step toward it. She might not make it . . .

His mental probe encircled her reward receiver; grasped it, almost squeezed it like a sponge. His use of her this past week made the extra exertion necessary.

15

She struggled, but the pleasure rippled through her, prompted by Ephram's control of the master switch in her brain, the nexus of all biological switchboards . . .

Raspily sobbing, she struggled across the floor to the tub and, with great effort, climbed over its rim, stood miserably in the shushing water. He waited till her fouled thigh was rinsed, then bent to the portable cassette stereo he kept on the floor – what people called a "ghetto blaster", ha ha – and Mozart unreeled sweetly from its speakers, the music bouncing tinnily from the tiles in the little room.

Ephram closed his eyes and listened. He took a deep breath, refining his senses, and opened his eyes.

He grabbed Megan by the hair, turned her about in the shower to lubricate her. He unzipped his pants. His psychic probe found the last pleasure receivers that could still be stimulated in her . . . She wailed and commenced involuntary humping motions with her hips. He put a hand around her throat and forced her to her knees, directed his semi-erect penis into her crusted mouth . . .

His hand closed slowly around her neck; as the crispy tissues of her throat collapsed under his strong, practiced fingers, his penis briefly hardened to something like complete tumescence.

A minute after the Mozart cassette ended, he withdrew from her, mentally. Withdrawing with excellent timing: just as she died. He dared not experience her death more closely, with the psychic probe. That would set up etheric repercussions and the Akishra would hear. They would find him again. The soulworms would find him. His freedom from them must be scrupulously guarded.

He wasn't sure if he'd killed her with the choking, or if she'd simply died from being used up, from exhaustion.

She was rather emaciated. It didn't matter.

Now he had to clean up the mess.

There was always a downside, in life.

"Did Constance come back there, Mr. Garner?"

"What? Isn't she with you, Terry?" Garner told the cold, clutching hand of his imagination to let go of his guts. Constance's friend Terry phoning from the mall – he could hear the video arcade going bing, bam, bong in the background. The girl was looking for Constance. Who, dammit, was supposed to be with this girl Terry. But there could be a lot of explanations. "Terry . . .?"

"No, uh, she was with me, but, it's like, she goes, 'I'm gonna go to the restroom', you know? And I'm like, 'Okay but hurry up because you have to drive me home before eleven or my dad'll get really gross on me, you know?' And she's all, 'I'll be right back'. But then she doesn't come back and doesn't come back and –"

"She hasn't shown up here, either. Did you check for her car?"

"No. You think she'd, you know, actually *ditch* me at the mall like that?"

"No. I just want to make sure she's still in the mall somewhere. Can you check and call me back?"

"Um . . . Sure. Bye."

They hung up and Garner went back to the group. Nothing he could do till Terry called back. Just get on with the group and try not to think about it. If you freaked out every time your kid misplaced herself for a few minutes, you'd get some kind of chronic stress syndrome.

Group was in the living room. It smelled of stale coffee and cigarettes. It went on for ten minutes more, with Mrs. Wineblatt wallowing in self pity about her shambling marriage; the others struggling bravely to keep their interest in Mrs. Wineblatt's share, though they'd heard it all a half-dozen times and generally felt she was playing out some heavy denial about a necessary divorce...

Garner shook his head, thinking that his attitude toward Mrs. Wineblatt was slanted by his anxiety about Constance. He'd had a bad feeling about Constance all day and it made Constance's losing touch with Terry at the mall seem more important than it probably was.

The minutes dragged by. Mrs. Wineblatt was snivelling, Harry Dugan seemed an irritating old cynic, James seemed a pouty, self-indulgent college sophomore. Damn Constance. This kind of thing was just not on. She had to be responsible, because *he* had to be responsible...

Or maybe she...

The doorbell rang. Garner jumped up, announcing the end of group though James wasn't quite done with his share yet. Garner could see the boy's pout deepen, the kid taking it as a personal rejection.

Tough. Garner nearly sprinted to the front door, expecting to find a cop with a long face on his doorstep.

But on his doorstep was a twenty-five-year-old white woman, six months pregnant. Aleutia Berenson. He'd been counselling her for three months, on and off. She was a crack addict.

"Come on in, Aleutia," he forced himself to say. Looking up and down the street, before he closed the front door.

He escorted Aleutia into his study. She smiled at him, her eyes wet, the skin under them looking bruised. She was working up some kind of manipulative addict trip to pull on him. She sat on the sofa.

This wasn't her appointed counselling day, but he

18

made time for pregnant women with drug problems. You help a pregnant drug addict get clean, you've scored a twofer.

His face may have been a little wooden, though. Waiting for the phone to ring. Terry to call back. What was taking so long?

From the Journal of Ephram Pixie, "for 5 January 1987".

... Number Seven is responding more readily than Six did and I am convinced that the difference is in me. Getting free of the Akishra is no doubt part of it. Without their sucking, sucking, sucking at me all the time, my talent flourishes. And Number Six responded more readily than Number Five did.

The Divine Vision is quickening in me. It is emerging and strengthening. Whatever spirit put this Talent in me (I do feel that it is Spiritual Power of some kind, intended to elevate me to the Transcendence I have always known is fated to me, known even when I was bowing and scraping to get tenure as a Professor trying to teach Nietzsche to the television-stunned cattle of this generation). I feel the Spirit is beginning to merge with me, to take part in my celebrations. Without the Akishra to interfere with our communing, I feel the Spirit's enjoyment the way a great solo violinist senses the rapt attention of the audience at a recital. Indeed, I can feel The Spirit participating, sharing with me all that I experience when I employ this Celestial Gift. Although I have never seen this Presence with my physical eyes, I felt it sharply last night as I used Seven on the deserted pebble beach and, in the course of things, I looked up at the stars and saw the unseen stars between the bright ones, the Negative constellation, the secret Zodiac that guides the lives of the world's secret masters . . . Zodiac signs no one but me and, perhaps, a few others, have seen . . . The Sign of the Lamprey. The Sign of the Cobra. The Sign of the Judge. The Sign of the Spider. The Sign of Kali. The Sign of the Sow. The Sign of the Hangman . . .

"I mean, if you really wanted to help me," Aleutia was saying, with elaborate innocence, you'd give me maybe fifty or a hundred in cash so I can get a room for a couple days –"

"So that's it. I can arrange shelter," Garner said wearily. "I can arrange a hotel room. I can arrange food. But no way do I give crack poofers a dime. I know better."

"You're a minister. Liberal Methodist or whatever, it don't matter, you're just another Minister, Rev Garner, and I should know you can't trust ministers anymore than cops!"

"So don't trust me. I don't give a fuck. Trust God, and that's enough."

"I just don't see how you can expect me to believe in God, with all this shit coming down on me in the world," Aleutia said. She was thinner, except for the pooch of her swollen stomach – and there were bruised hollows under her eyes. The backs of her hands were flecked with small, crusted sores; more of them scored her cheeks.

"You've been using again," Garner said.

20

She said, "Uh . . ." as she tried to decide whether it was worth the effort to deny it.

He went on, "You've got tweakin sores on your arms and face. You've been picking at cocaine bugs."

She started to cry, with a ratchety sound in her throat, and a bubble of phlegm appeared at a nostril. He gave her a tissue from the box on his desk, and she wiped her nose awkwardly, her fingernails getting in the way. They were six-inches long, painted gold, curling like the nails of a tree-sloth. Her brown hair was razor cut into wave patterns along the sides. She was a white girl, but these were the emblems of ghetto culture, Garner knew, which probably meant that she was living with Donald again. He decided to ask her point blank. Theological issues were for later. (Why didn't Terry call?)

"You're back with Donald, aren't you?"

"And you think that's bad, right, because he's a black man."

"Hell no, not because he's a black man, because he's a fucking crack addict, Aleutia, and he's got you back on the shit."

She broke down, then, and he put his arm around her and patted her. She said she was sorry, she knew it was hurting the baby, but she just found herself at the rock-house at five in morning, looking for Donald.

"You were looking for the cocaine, girl, you know? At least as much as Donald."

"So I'm a fucking addict. I didn't ask to be no addict."

I hear you. I was – I'm an addict too." He hadn't done dope of any kind in years but you were supposed to never talk about being an addict in the past tense, because that led to complacency, and somewhere inside, the addict was waiting for complacency. "I've been there. People who say, 'It's your fault because you started and you should have known better', those people are full of shit. We all had a direction in our life, a momentum, see, that carried us into addiction. Your stepdad raping you, your Mom beating you up *because* your stepdad raped you – the shit you went through goes on and on. You felt like you had to hit the streets. I can see that. But once we know what's happening, we can take responsibility and get the fuck off the streets, Aleutia. You know?"

She shook her head. Shivering. She was having a strong craving now, he knew. A spooncall. Or, in her case, a pipecall. She put her hand to her mouth and he could imagine a crack stem, the glass coke-smoking pipe, in her fingers.

Looking at her, he saw a little girl. Not much older than his own kid. It made him ache with worry about Constance. He thought: I'd better call the cops, tell them Constance is missing . . .

No. He knew what they'd say: It hadn't been long enough. Give her time. And if they picked her up when nothing was wrong she'd be so mad at him . . .

He forced himself to concentrate on Aleutia. "Look, Aleutia – you had a cocaine relapse, that's all. It's easy to do. We haven't had a chance to talk much and there's some stuff – Listen, Crack gets you two ways. One, getting off is a way of escaping from all the shit, right? Addictive personalities. We've talked about that. Second – and this is important, Aleutia – it gets to you neurologically. Meaning it messes with your brain chemistry. It pushes your brain-buttons, so to speak. You ever see that film of the white rat that's got a wire running into its brain? The rat pushes a button to stimulate the pleasure centre of the brain and it becomes this little

22

furry button pushin' machine. That's all it can do, it doesn't eat or sleep, it just pushes that fucking button till it *dies*, girl. It reprogrammed itself that way."

"Oh God, that's fucked up." Her face crumpling. "What're you saying, we're like robots? Programming and shit?" Tears streaking her makeup.

"Only up to a point. You get trapped. Neurologically trapped."

"It's like a fucking roach motel," she said miserably, reaching for a clean tissue.

He nodded, thinking about the baby in her belly: trapped in the trapped. He took a deep breath. "But if you get off the shit, and give yourself a whole new system of rewards, well, eventually, you can get free. It takes time for the brain to get normal. And holding on till then takes help from outside the trap. What you need to do, maybe, is think about going to a halfway house. Inpatient recovery home. For six months, say . . ."

Aleutia just shook her head. After a moment she said, "Can I smoke a cigarette?"

Before he could answer, the phone rang. Aleutia was startled as he lunged at it. "Yeah?"

"Mr. Garner? This is Terry. Um – her car's there. But I swear – Constance's just not at this mall. And all the stores are closed now . . ."

Ephram was sitting in his living room at the desk, writing in his journal. The old fashioned rolltop was the only piece of furniture in the room, except for the LA-Z-Boy recliner by the CD player. He was listening to Franz Schubert.

Ephram wrote in his journal to soothe himself, after the irritation of his labours over Megan's body.

He wrote, 'For 18 July 199 – ':

23

... found that the large wire clippers worked very well to remove her fingertips, and I disposed of the fingertips quite confidently off a pier, finger food for the crabs, ha ha. Disposed of the clippers off the pier also.

The body presented another problem. The sea cannot be trusted with a cadaver. As planned, tied it to the underside of a train. This had to be carefully timed in order to avoid discovery of the body by railroad workers before the train should begin its work. All went well, thank the Spirit. The train dragged the body a goodly distance, face down on the cinders, making shreds of the face and many other identification details and of course providing a reasonable explanation for the death, if no coroner chooses to look too closely. After the ropes broke, it dropped the body. I removed the ropes. Some drugged girl wandering across a railroad yard ... I of course used the blowtorch to remove body hair ... Perhaps a full incinerator would be ideal after all and when I find another wealthy subject I will shore up my bank account and look into the purchase of an incinerator big enough to do the job ... After disposing of Twenty-six I traced Twenty-seven by her pscent, ha ha, finding her outside one of those dreadful arcades at the Southshore Mall ...

★   ★   ★

Garner almost collapsed with relief when he saw Constance coming up the sidewalk. He didn't think about the odd, drifty way she was walking, didn't think about it consciously at first, till she came into the kitchen with him. Then he was hit by one incongruity after another.

"Where's your necklace?" She was never without that tacky gold-letter necklace that spelled out her name.

"Hm?" She looked at him from the other side of a fog bank. "Um - I don't know." Indifferent. Normally she'd have run around like a decapitated chicken, looking for the necklace.

She looked tired, too. She didn't smell like crack smoke or pot, but... all the other signs were there. She was wobbly on her feet. Not meeting his eyes. Distancing. Indifference to what used to be important to her.

How could it happen so fast? It just didn't happen that way overnight.

"What is it, hon?" he said gently. "Was it cocaine or what?"

"What do you mean?" Her voice dreamily monotone. Normally she would have said, *Da-ad! I'm sure! Gross!*

"Where's the car, Constance? I didn't see it outside."

"Car?" She blinked. Twice. "Oh. God. I left it at the mall. I'm sorry." She smiled distantly. "Happiness comes in places you never expect, didn't you say that once, Dad?"

"Uh - yeah."

"You were right. I would never expect... a guy like ..." She shut her mouth. Rather abruptly.

"A guy like who, Constance? Hon - did someone give you drugs?"

"No." Soft-spoken conviction. Convincing understatement.

"You fall in love?" That was a kind of drugging. "Falling in love" released hormones, endorphins, made you feel drugged. He knew it was grasping at straws but he grasped at it anyway.

"Sort of."

"Sort of? Who with? Some guy you met at the mall?"

"Yeah. His name's ... Michael. And he's leaving town." And I can't stand to stay around this summer without him. So ..." Suddenly she got all chirpy, sitting up straight and beaming at him as she asked it, as if to say, *How could you say no, Dad?* "Could I go visit his family in Los Angeles? They'll chaperone us."

She was explaining all this with uncharacteristic verbal clarity. Maybe it was just an infatuation drunkenness, after all.

"This is pretty sudden," he said. "Can't I meet this guy before you take trips with his family? I mean, you only met him yourself today, sweetie."

"Um – sometime. You can meet him sometime. I better go pick up the car, okay?"

"I'll go with you," Garner said, watching for her reaction. She frowned, but didn't argue.

They went. They took the last bus and picked up the car. It looked abandoned in the midst of the vast parking lot. In silence, they drove home. Garner cooked dinner; she ate her food mechanically but thoroughly. She continued to deny any drug use; quite convincingly, though with a weird detachment. Normally an accusation of that sort would have made her first outraged and then sulky.

She went up to her room, to go to bed early.

Garner finally dropped off to sleep about three a.m. He woke at six, knowing something was wrong.

Knowing, with a cold-sweat certainty, that Constance had gone.

26

Los Angeles, a Day Earlier

Prentice drove the rented Tercel down Sunset to Highland, made his way to Barham, bypassing the freeway where sunlight lanced off the thick metallic flow of traffic. He followed the curving road through the hills, past condos and ranch homes, and down into Burbank. His eyes burned as he drove into the valley. The palm trees looked gray as dead skin here.

Arthwright had a development deal with Sunrise Studios and they gave him a little bungalow office on the old studio lot. Sunrise had bought the lot from MGM; somebody else had recently bought Sunrise, Prentice had forgotten who. A soft drink company or an oil company. Or possibly a soft drink company owned by an oil company which was maybe owned by a plastics conglomerate. The Security guard at the gate's little Checkpoint Charlie – a black guy in cop-style mirrored sunglasses – scanned a clipboard list to be sure Prentice really did have an appointment with Arthwright, then directed him to Parking Area F.

"F for full," Prentice muttered, looking at the rows of Porsches and Jags. There was only one empty space,

27

where the tarmac was stenciled *LOU KENSON*. The erstwhile star had lost his deal with Sunrise and was now on the actor's Out List. Kenson could be relied on not to show up to claim his parking place and Prentice was on the verge of being late. He took Kenson's place, but with a twinge: thinking maybe it was bad luck

You could be as rational as a mathematician, but working the film industry you eventually came to believe in good and bad luck.

Prentice got out of the car and looked around. The studio looked like a series of overlarge warehouses and overgrown barns with oversized doors. The sunwashed buildings were old, mostly dull green, their paint peeling. On the other side of the lot, just visible between the interior-shoot buildings, there were a few generic tenement-facades, false fronts used for shooting generic inner-city street scenes in generic cop movies.

Prentice glanced at his watch, hurried out onto the little studio road. He found Building E and Zack Arthwright's office.

Arthwright could have had a spacious suite in the big mirrorglass skyscraper that Sunrise had built adjacent to the old studio, but he affected the air of a Colden Era traditionalist – 'Arthwright Pictures' was printed on the door – and he stuck to the old-fashioned office bungalows with their wonky air conditioners and cracked green walls.

This particular air conditioner was working too well, and noisily, thrumming rheumily to itself from a corner window behind a secretary who probably no longer heard it. The room was almost refrigerator cold, making Prentice think of the morgue. Amy in the file drawer. He'd worked hard at not thinking about that and he'd almost succeeded for half an hour.

28

Arthwright's secretary was busty but otherwise scissor-thin; gold mascara around eyes glamoured by blue-tinted contact-lenses.

She had a gold streak in her feathered blue black hair and a New Age crystal on a gold chain around her slender neck.

"Hi, I'm Tom Prentice..."

She glanced up from her work station with a brief but professionally sunny smile. "Go right on in, Tom, he's expecting you."

Tom, she said, though she'd never met him before. Fake intimacy. Welcome back to Hollywood.

Arthwright was, of course, using a speaker phone. He sat tilted back in a swivel chair with his faded black cowboy boots on his antique, leather inset desk, his brown leather suit jacket buttoned up in the excessive air conditioning. His long, curly brown hair was tied with rawhide strips into a small ponytail; his sharp-featured boyish face didn't tan very well, so his nose and cheeks were always a little burned. Lines at the corners of his eyes, and the beginning of a double chin, told the truth: he was no more the *enfant terrible* journalists had made him out to be just a few years before. But he was hot with a string of hits, taking first and third place in the Summer Box Office, rentals going strong on the new release. Everyone wanted into see him, everyone had a pitch for him, and Buddy probably had to use up a favour to get Prentice the meeting.

Prentice felt like he had been smuggled in, like a spy. *The Spy Who Came In From The Out List*, he thought.

Arthwright winked, gestured at a chair. Prentice sat stiffly, trying not to be obvious about wiping his damp palms on his jeans.

29

It was wrong to be here.

"If your client doesn't want to deal, he doesn't want to deal," Arthwright was telling the phone, not missing a beat. "I'm not going to give him control. Whenever I give up creative control the damn thing just doesn't work. He can have an extra fifty out front. That's the best I can do."

Prentice was embarrassed. Made to wait out a negotiation carried on in front of him as if he weren't there. But in fact part of it was probably Arthwright flashing power at Prentice. It didn't matter that Prentice was a relative nonentity. The demonstration would be something Arthwright did compulsively.

Prentice tried to look interested in the office decorations. Framed movie posters on the walls, going back fifteen years to some of Arthwright's earliest: *The Hellmakers*, an old Lou Kenson western vehicle; *The Grafters*, the expose that had given Arthwright a veneer of respectability; *Warm Knife*, his mega hit thriller. The teaser read: *Keep the knife under the pillow. It'll be warmer that way . . .*

Prentice stared at the poster for *Warm Knife*. Thinking: We're a sick bunch of flickers, all of us.

"Creative control stays right here," Arthwright was telling the speaker phone. Turned sideways from Prentice, looking as if he were talking to the air; like Jimmy Stewart talking to Harvey. "If I need to, I can get Hagerstein. She's damn good."

Arthwright took his long legs down and spun his swivel chair around once, in an absently playful way, as he waited for the ultimatum to sink in.

"Zack, get real" A crackly female voice on the speaker phone. That'd be Doll Bechtman, Jeff Teitelbaum's agent. Prentice and Jeff had gone to NYU

Film School together; had chased girls and made pretentious 16 millimeter student films together. Prentice decided he was going to have to look Jeff up.

Evidently Arthwright was arguing with Doll Bechtman about Jeff. Prentice had met Doll once; a middle-aged woman with a look like Betty Crocker and a style like Roy Cohn. A barracuda, Jeff called her gleefully. The tougher she was, the better he liked it. It appeared she'd met her match in Arthwright. But she kept on: "I'm telling you, Jeff has good instincts. This Hagerstein woman cannot write an *action* picture. It'd be a joke."

Jeff, Prentice mused. Arthwright was fucking Jeff Teitelbaum out of creative control on a movie? So what else was new.

'Then tell Jeff to compromise a little, work with us, Doll. Look, I got someone here. You talk to Jeff."

"I'll get back."

"Sure, okay."

Arthwright swivelled to the phone and hit the disconnect. He cocked his head impishly, grinned at Prentice, and said, "Tom. Long time no see."

"Yeah. I've been holing up in New York." Prentice had only met Arthwright once, briefly. Arthwright probably didn't really remember the occasion.

Prentice toyed with the idea of asking what Sunrise had cooking with Jeff. But, even though he was undoubtedly supposed to hear Arthwright throwing his weight around on the phone negotiation, he wasn't really supposed to listen to the details. He didn't need to ask, anyway, when he thought about it. Arthwright was co-producing *A Cop Named Dagger II* for Sunrise; Jeff had conceived and written the first *A Cop Named Dagger* picture. Chances were, he was supposed to do the screenplay again but was holding out for creative control. Something few writers got till they became a "hyphenate" – writer-director, a writer-producer. Usually he had to be a Player, a guy who could command points of the gross profits. Jeff wasn't there yet.

Why the hell did Jeff want to hold out for creative control over an action picture? But come to think of it, Jeff thought action pictures could be high art.

Arthwright checked out his watch, and said, "Glad to see you back in town. What have you got for me?"

Arthwright wanted the pitch *now*. It was do or die. "What I've got is . . ." Prentice spread his hands – and then stepped off the cliff into space. ". . . a comedy with a strong drama backbone, a twist on buddy pictures." He could see Arthwright's eyes glazing already. Another buddy picture. Prentice went on hurriedly, "A lady cop walks a beat in San Francisco. She walks it alone, in a tough neighbourhood. One day she gets a new partner – a rookie, a kid who ignores her eight years on the force and thinks he's hot shit, compared to her, because she's a woman and he can't take a woman seriously as a street cop. The humour'll come naturally. She's going to learn he's not the asshole he seems, deep down; he's going to learn she's a good cop and that he's got a lot to learn."

It sounded stupid to Prentice in his own ears, just now. It sounded vague and fatuous.

"Uh huh." Arthwright managed to seem half interested. "Might be a little predictable. Familiar."

Come on, you son of a bitch, Prentice thought. *All* your fucking movies are predictable. Out loud he said, "It's a question of how it'll be carried off. They're on foot, they're part of the neighbourhood, and walking a beat is different to being in a cruiser, gives them a feeling of family with the people they protect. And there'll be some plot twists. I've got an outline right now, hasn't got all the plot points but it's basically there. I see it as having the appeal of *Alien Nation* – only it's funnier, and it's men and women. Men and women are alien to one another when they're thrust into this kind of situation. We play it for laughs." *Alien Nation?* A pretty dumb comparison. Get your shit together, Prentice!

Prentice waited. He'd shot his wad, he decided.

After a moment of staring glaze-eyed at a Grammy on a shelf of otherwise mostly minor awards – he'd started out in record production – Arthwright nodded sharply, but contradicted the nod by saying, "*Broken Windows* didn't work out too well. That was a cop thing too. Might be hard for me to sell you after that."

Meaning sell him to the Studio. Convince them to do it. Which was bullshit. Arthwright could do what he wanted, now, if he really wanted to do it.

What had he said? *A cop thing too.* Like *A Cop Named Dagger*, like *Broken Windows.* Cop Things, everything seemed to be Cop Things.

"*Broken Windows* was a straight ahead drama," Prentice pointed out, hoping he didn't sound desperate. "Not my forte. I shouldn't have tried it. I can't pull it off without comedy in there too. That's where I shine. I had two hits." And a flop, and one so-so. "And you might point out to the studio that *Broken Windows* wasn't really a cop thing. It was about burglars, it was mostly from their side, so it was a problem of anti-heroes. This wouldn't have that problem."

His back was sticking to his shirt with sweat. When you had to apologize and explain, backing and filling, it wasn't going to fly. Shit.

Arthwright said, "Okay, well, have Buddy messenger the outline over to me and I'll take a look. Has this baby got a name or are you just calling it Junior?"

Prentice laughed nervously. "I'm calling it *Tenderloin Seven* right now. It's set in San Francisco."

'You're from San Francisco originally, aren't you?" Arthwright asked abstractedly, standing. Standing up was a way of telling him he was expected to leave without actually having to say it.

They shook hands. Prentice said, "I grew up in San Francisco. How'd you know I was from there?"

"The *49ers* shirt might have done it," Arthwright said, letting his hand drop, grinning.

"Oh yeah. I forgot to change back to the Clark Kent suit."

Arthwright faked a chuckle. He was checking his calendar, as he added, half to himself, "And Amy mentioned it."

Prentice stared. "Amy? My wife Amy?"

"Uh huh. I –" Arthwright looked up at Prentice blankly. Hesitation. Just a fraction of a second. Arthwright hadn't meant to bring this up, apparently. "She was out at a party in Malibu. Judy Denver's place. I talked to Amy a little. She had a high opinion of you. She was a sweet girl."

So Buddy had told Arthwright that Amy had died. Unless he'd heard it somewhere else.

Had he got the appointment out of charity, because of Amy's death? Christ. I'm climbing on Amy's body.

And Amy had met Arthwright. And Arthwright was working with Jeff. The world wasn't just small, it was cramped.

"Yeah. Yeah, she was... a sweet girl," Prentice managed.

"Yes. Well. I've got a late lunch..."

"Right. I'll ask Buddy to get that outline to you. Take it easy."

"Whenever I can. Talk to you later, Tom."

Prentice hurried out, as Arthwright left instructions with his secretary.

Outside, the day seemed brutally warm after the over zealous air conditioning. But he strolled round a little, thinking. Suppose the deal with Arthwright didn't come off? What then? Arthwright had been discussing Jeff Teitelbaum. By God, Jeff might just be able to help him.

Prentice paused to frown up at one of the tenement facades. All the sets looked familiar – but this one seemed to jump out at him for recognition. Maybe it had been used for *A Cop Named Dagger*. Jeff had sent Prentice a polaroid, a shot of Jeff posing on the set of *Dagger*, peeking around the edge of one of the false fronts; the fake bricks on the front were spraypainted with equally fake graffiti. But the polaroid's angle revealed the raw-wood supports holding up the false fronts from behind, and in the picture Jeff was crouched in the shadows, peering around from the real world into the make-believe world, leering at the female lead, Zena Holdbridge.

A couple of months earlier Jeff had sent Prentice a postcard from Maui. Jeff was the kind of guy who sent you post cards from Hawaii of topless girls stretching out in the sand, under a printed caption that read, *Great View From My Hotel!* Jeff getting off on the baldfaced kitsch of it all.

The sun was beating on the back of Prentice's neck

as he made his way back to Lou Kenson's parking place. By the time Prentice reached the car he had the start of a good, strong headache. Inside, the car was a vinyl-reeking cauldron of heat from having baked in the sun, trickling an instant sweat down Prentice's back.

"Fuck it, I'm gonna punch another hole in the ozone layer," Prentice murmured, turning on the air conditioning.

Driving out of the studio, Prentice tried to evaluate the meeting and came to exactly no conclusion. Arthwright hadn't jumped for it, but that didn't mean it wouldn't go anyplace. He'd been sort of encouraging – but as people said at WCA parties, Hollywood was a place where you could die of encouragement.

As usual, after a meeting in the Industry, Prentice had no idea where he stood, at all.

Los Angeles County Juvenile Detention Facility

Cutting himself worked best. That's what Mitch had found out that morning.

It wasn't a store-bought knife. It was a shiv made out of a shiny metal piece torn from the frame around a steel mirror, some alloy of tin and aluminium maybe. The mirror was metal instead of glass to keep them from breaking it, but working at the frame, day after day, Mitch's room-mate, Lonny, had bent the frame section, creaking it back and forth, till finally it snapped off diagonally. Making two blade-shaped pieces. Lonny'd sharpened them on a rough piece of iron pipe in the bathroom fixtures; kept one shiv, gave Mitch the other, for protection. The base of each blade was wrapped in multiple thicknesses of torn towels to make a knife grip.

Mitch was in Juvie Hall, sitting on the floor, in the

room he shared with Lonny. He was in for possession of one little vial of hubba. Crack cocaine. He was alone in the room; Lonny was out in the exercise yard. Their room looked like a small dormitory unit, with two-tone walls, orange brown near the bottom and light orange above shoulder level. Tube lights in unbreakable ceiling fixtures. Thick metal mesh over the window. Chickenwire-glass observation window centred in the door. The door was closed and Mitch was on the linoleum floor just to one side of it where they couldn't see him if they just glanced through. They'd think he was out playing basketball with the others.

Maybe he should have gone down the hall to the bathroom to do this because of the blood. Drip it in the toilet. But he couldn't. He had to do it now. He dug the crude knife deeper into the meat of his upper arm. It didn't hurt at all. He could feel their happiness, and the sweetness, the reward syrup, in his groin and spine and head.

Blood runnelled down his arm and pattered onto the floor. It wasn't a knife, to him, it was a probe; a sensor.

Mitch Teitelbaum was seventeen, tall and lean like his brother Jeff; with quick, dark eyes like Jeff but without Jeff's vulturine face. His nose was smaller and his cheekbones flatter. Jeff had a small beard; Mitch had tried to grow a mustache, but what came out was about twelve long, curly black hairs with nothing in between them. "Looks like dog whiskers," Eurydice had said, so he'd shaved it off. He'd shaved it off about two days before he met the More Man and he wasn't sure how long it had been *since* he'd met the More Man.

Six weeks? Two months? Since, anyway, a day after the last time he'd seen Jeff. Long time since he'd seen Jeff. Long time since he'd seen Eurydice and her brother, Orpheus, too. She had a little sister named from another myth, Aphrodite, maybe one of the ugliest little girls he had ever seen. But Eurydice, she was the prettiest girl he knew personally, and sexy – and when a black girl is sexy, Jeff used to say, she was sexier than a sexy white girl, and Eurydice could make you breathe hard just by shifting her weight from one foot to the other. And he'd gotten some off her, too, that was the unbelievable thing. When the More Man was done he was going to have to go and find her. She'd been real patient with him. "Everybody got to have a first time," she'd said.

His thoughts drifted on a slow current of the head syrup, teetering and turning like the wax cups he and Jeff used to launch on the culvert-wash that was the so-called "Los Angeles River". The head syrup was not a drug. It was just his name for a feeling. He had tried to tell Lonny about it, and Lonny had thought it was a drug because the words "head syrup" sounded like it. But no: it wasn't, no way. It was more like a radio station.

He had peeled off his *Iron Maiden* t-shirt – it lay beside him with the iron-masked face of the metal band's symbol all wrinkled up and horribly distorted with its crumpling. He stared at it as he began on his left pectoral. He thought he saw the face on the t-shirt cock an eye at him and move its mouth like it was giggling. After a minute he looked back at his chest, watching as he methodically dug the knife into himself, observing as coolly as a man shaving or squeezing a pimple, that kind of half focus and meditative distance. All the while plowing the ragged blade-edge into the soft white skin, wishing he'd built himself up more so there was more muscle to get into. Push, push, the skin and muscle and fat tissue of his pectoral resisting the blade, it was like trying to cut open a package that was sealed in heavy plastic, the stuff stretching under your letter opener. Push. *Punch.* It broke through, the blade jabbing out under his nipple, red blood arcing and – *for a moment he felt some pain.*

Oh, shit, how did I get here and what am I doing?

But then the head syrup came back, the pain vanished, and he relaxed. Jerked the blade loose, and jabbed it through his jeans, deep into the meat of his skinny thigh.

He was not on drugs. He was not insane. He felt no pain at all.

Culver City, Los Angeles

"I haven't seen ol' Mitch for, oh, six or seven weeks," Jeff said, around a mouthful of Doritos.

Tom Prentice and Jeff Teitelbaum were watching the Dodgers get their asses kicked by the San Diego Padres. They were sitting on a sofa-futon in Jeff's second story apartment, near the open French doors onto the balcony. The room smelled like stale cigar smoke; Jeff had trotted out the cigars when Prentice showed up. Jeff liked smoking cigars with his friends because it was playing at "Guy Stuff." Guy Stuff was a joke and very serious with Jeff, both.

In the background were laughing squeals and taunts from the swimmers in the complex's swimming pool; the sounds of splashing, a teasing underscent of chlorine. It was a high security "singles" apartment complex, with security guards at the gate and TV cameras and its own hot tub spa and weight room and sauna and game room.

Jeff's living room was undecorated except for a Norman Rockwell print of a small, rosy-cheeked boy with a fishing pole proudly holding up a string full of fish, only Jeff had cut out small men's magazine photos of naked girls and pasted them on over the fish: a small boy proudly holding up a string of naked girls. On TV, a couple of baseball players drank Budweisers with Phil Collins, and then the game came back on. Fernando was on the mound, but his arm was cold today: Martinez was up to bat and *whack*, he drove a line drive out past third base for the eighth goddamn Padres run of the game and it was only the top of the fourth inning. Prentice was doing his best to space out completely on sports and Tecate beer, because it was the way he got out of his head. Amy was in his head, and it was too crowded in there for both of them.

He didn't want to hear about Mitch, either. Jeff's little brother, nine years younger, always screwing up. Jeff's parents divorced when Jeff was ten and Mitch was one, and Jeff had gone to live with his dad, who worked for the NRA lobbying against gun control, and Mitch had gone to live with his mom, who was "a whiner," Jeff said, "and a sponge." Prentice had never heard Jeff say anything good about her. She'd been the one to leave; maybe Jeff was forever mad at her for abandoning him when he was ten.

Jeff hadn't seen Mitch for years, because his parents hated each other and his mom ducked out on the visitation rights. Then Mitch turned up at Jeff's door, two years ago, run away from their mom's new boyfriend. "A real asshole" was the extent of his report on the guy. So Mitch had moved in with Jeff, and Jeff had taken care of him through various traumas, most of them drug-related, for two years, "Trying to straighten the kid's head out", and then, bingo, he'd disappeared. Phoning to New York, Jeff bent Prentice's ear endlessly about Mitch; Prentice had heard all the Mitch stories. He didn't feel like hearing any more, especially now when he was trying to think about nothing but baseball. The stately jumble, the clunky Zen of baseball.

It wasn't working very well. He couldn't keep his mind on the game. He was remembering the first time he met Amy. The experience summed her up...

He was in a New York cafe on a wet October day, lunching with Gloria Zickurian, a book illustrator. Cabs the same yellow as adult bookstores rippled as they passed the rain-streaked window. Prentice and Gloria drank cafe lattes and ate salads and cheese croissants. It was a date, more or less. More for Gloria, Prentice thought, and less for him. Gloria was pretty in a wistful, slightly weak-chinned way. She had big, dark eyes and curly black hair allowed to tousle wispily around her red beret. She wore a rust-coloured, gypsyish dress with a gathered bodice that displayed her cleavage in a way that made him think of bread dough.

She was proud of the little cafe she'd picked on Central Park west, a yuppie coffee shop with Santa Fe style decor, specializing in salads, or "salades" as the menu had it, and she talked of *discovering* it until Prentice dutifully said, "Yeah, it's a great little place." Then she launched into an interminable complaint about having been asked to illustrate a line of science fiction books, a field she knew nothing about, resulting in her attendance at science fiction conventions, "where a lot of married fat guys with homemade swords and wide belts and medieval hats" made clumsy passes at her. She bitched about the abysmal taste in cover art at the paperback house she was working for. She droned

41

a bit, when she was nervous, nasally stretching out the syllables; afraid of gaps in the conversation. The gaps, Prentice thought, were his favourite part, at this point.

That's when Amy slammed through the cafe doors, wearing a Walkman and the only miniskirted raincoat Prentice had seen this side of 1968. Amy was willowy, with a kind of blueblood prettiness that would only have been blurred by makeup. Her hair, hennaed cedar-red in those days, was pinned up so you could see the sweep of her long neck. Her earrings were little onyx bats.

Amy paused just inside the doorway, looking around with quick movements of her head, taking her time putting the Walkman in her pocket, closing her umbrella, letting everyone get a good look at the sweep of long legs in their dark purple pantyhose.

Spotting Amy, Gloria stiffened, looking as if she wanted to bolt, then sagged with a kind of polite despair when Amy spotted her and made a bee-line for the table. "Glorie-uh!" Amy chirruped, going on with machine gun rapidity, "I knew you'd be in one of these grotty places, where everything costs at least two dollars too much. Gloria, I have great news."

"This," Gloria said wearily to Prentice, "is my roommate Amy Eisenberg. Amy, this is Tom Prentice."

"God it took you long enough to introduce me, ooh he's a big one isn't he, I didn't think you liked big ones, big men I mean, I mean big physique"

Gloria stammered, "Amy – did you, uh, need something?"

Amy kept her eyes on Prentice as she talked, looking him up and down. He smiled as neutrally as he could. Her wet umbrella was leaning against his chair, dripping on his pants leg. "Your address book, sweetie. I need Polly Gebhart's phone number, I lost it –"

Gloria snatched up her purse, yanked it open, muttering, "Why don't you get an address book and *organize* yourself, Amy?"

Amy took the address book. "I going to, I *have* to now, that's my news, – there's a producer who's hot for me, for me as an actor I mean –" She made a conscious policy of pretending to stumble over sexual innuendoes, Prentice later learned. "– and he's having me do a call-back, it's for an off-Broadway show, a really happening show that half of Hollywood is trying to get the rights to –" She turned abruptly to Prentice, as if thunderstruck. Looking at Prentice but speaking to Gloria. "Hey is this that screenwriter you told me about that you were –?"

"I'm only barely a screenwriter," Prentice said modestly. A kind of pseudo modesty that was really a way of confirming his status. "Just one credit." He'd just had his first script produced, *Fourth Base*. First script? First one he sold. Fifth one he wrote.

"Amy, if you've got what you need," Gloria said, brightly "we –"

"Don't you listen to her," Amy said to Prentice, "it's her quaint way of asking me to join you. But only for a minute." She pulled a chair from the next table, and sat herself on it with the air of a guest on a talk show who's just been asked to sit and tell the host what her newest project is. "This is my first real break, this part in *Sweet Fire*, but I did that thing at Summer Stock with Julie Christie, you remember that, Gloria?" Gloria, who had sullenly lit a cigarette – she was one of those people who saved smoking for expressing anger – nodded briskly and blew smoke at the window. A waitress caught Gloria's eye and shook her head, and Gloria stabbed the cigarette out in her coffee cup. Amy hadn't

43

waited for Gloria's answer. She went breathlessly on, "– And I think the Connecticut gig got me this job because Ervin – Ervin's my agent, Tom – Ervin got this producer a videotape of me working with Julie Christie, who played my mother... Maybe I'll just have a capuccino." She grabbed the waitress's apron as the woman sped by, smiled sweetly into the glare this got her, and said, "Could I have a capuccino with lots of chocolate sprinkles? I'd be infinitely grateful. Thanks."

Gloria groaned and didn't bother to muffle it. Prentice shrugged and winked conspiratorially at her, as if to say, We'll wait her out and then we'll get back to our lunch.

But Amy stayed for an hour, giving a sort of informal resume of her bit parts and commercial walk-ons and her part-time gig as a back-up singer in a rock band (surprising Prentice by mentioning that she played the accordion with them, too). She was too amusing to be tedious, but then Prentice's viewpoint on that might have been muddled by the sheer erotic magnetism Amy gave off. She could be quite funny, too, and despite everything, he was glad she'd showed up.

Finally Gloria had to go to a meeting with the director of an art department. Prentice paid the check and they put on their coats; Prentice opening his mouth to offer Gloria a drop-off from his taxi, when Amy said, as if just thinking of it, "Tom, I have to walk through Central Park to go to my agent's office and – and I'm kind of scared –"

"You scared you might hurt someone?" Gloria said, with savage sarcasm. "Amy, it's broad daylight, Central Park is perfectly safe now."

"It's never safe, don't give me that. I thought if Tom wanted to walk me –"

"We could drop you off in the cab," Prentice said. "It's too rainy to walk."

That wasn't the graceful way out after all, because once they were in the cab Amy and Gloria jockeyed to see who would get dropped off first. Gloria had to give in: her office was on this side of the park.

When she got out of the cab, she slammed the door. "Gloria takes life too seriously," Amy said, and laughed.

By the time Prentice had dropped her off at her agent's building, he found he'd asked her to go to a jazz club with him that night. And he'd begun to suspect that she was loaded on something.

When he picked her up to take her to the club, she offered him some of the drug. She called it "X", which was short for Ecstasy, also called MDMA, a neurotoxin variant on speed that produced animated friendliness in people. In Amy it only made her more the way she already was when she was in her hypomanic stage.

Amy was manic depressive. She preferred the term "Bipolar". Something the hospital in Culver City had completely failed to diagnose.

Now, remembering that wet day in New York, and her astonishment the same night when he'd told her he didn't take drugs and didn't want any X, he thought: Yeah, it was probably drugs. Some other drug, like Buddy said, probably crack, methamphetamine, or some new designer drug that ate her up. Left a mummy in a file drawer.

But there was something else, too. Some*one*. Who gave her a Gold Card and two hundred dollars. She hadn't been working, he knew that for a fact. Someone. Some son of a bitch. Some bastard.

Probably some goddamn producer.

LA. County Juvenile Detention

Lonny went yelling for the supervisors, the first time he ever went to them for anything, trying not to cry and trying not to be sick, bringing them back to the room, swearing at them for their slowness. Showing them Mitch.

Mitch was just sitting there. Sitting awkwardly, legs out-thrust like a baby, his face infant-innocent: a baby sitting in a pool of blood. Red strings hanging out of the ragged openings in his left arm – pieces of muscle. Leg sawn open and in one place you could see the bone. Mitch shaking and still working at himself, the knife carving his right thigh, working its way up, getting close to his groin. Mitch smiling distantly, as his eyes went in and out of focus, pupils widening and shrinking, widening and shrinking. And then he saw Lonny and the guard and his connection was broken and he stopped cutting himself, and said, "Oh. Oh. Oh. Oh fuck it's starting to hurt. Oh no."

But he didn't take the knife out of the wound.

Culver City, Los Angeles

"God DAMMIT did you see that!" Jeff shrieked, making Prentice jump half out of his seat. "He had it, he HAD the motherfucking ball and he DROPPED it!"

Prentice slumped back in his chair, and cracked another beer. "Yeah. He probably feels bad 'cause he can hear you at Dodger Stadium, too, Jeff."

Had the ball and he dropped it. It was beginning to sink in to Prentice: he blamed himself for Amy's death. He'd dropped the ball.

He'd known the relationship was going to go

somewhere the third time he dated her. The first date had been convulsively sexual; the second time a bit rocky, both of them defensive, unsure, her manic jitteriness making it worse.

After the second date, parting with a brittle politeness, Prentice didn't think they'd see each other again. He'd told her she was childish to talk about herself all the time; she'd said his conversation was nothing but jokes, and she had to talk about *something* real.

But two days later she surprised him, again, by inviting him over for dinner. Very sweetly. Another mood swing maybe. Get into a relationship with a girl prone to wild mood swings and you were, to paraphrase President Bush, in deep doo-doo.

But he went. She was a good cook, though afterwards her kitchen looked like hurricane wreckage. And she left the mess for two days. The stir fry was great, her raspberry mousse was exquisite, but before he'd quite finished it she pushed the little table aside, strode across to him, and straddled his lap facing him. Reached down for his zipper. He could taste mousse and brandy on her tongue. She wasn't wearing panties.

The first time they made love, that particular night, was a prolonged spasm, starting on the chair and ending on the rug. But when it happened again, in bed, it began languorously, and veered into an ecstatic mutual searching. He quickly learned to maintain a steady, pistonlike rhythm, once he was inside her, to counterbalance her bucking and thrashings. It was exactly what she needed, his rigid organ the axle for her wild torquing, and it brought them to that rare confluence of desire, mutual orgasm. In the moment of orgasm, the timing was right: they both flung their

47

emotional doors open; they opened their eyes and saw one another. Knew fleetingly that until that moment, their skilled and very modern sexuality had been only a way of using.

Suddenly, all the pretenses were dropped, and isolation was gone, and they embraced for the first time: the first time it was real.

"Jesus Christ," he breathed, amazed at the intensity of his feeling.

After that, she didn't have to talk about herself, her outsized ambitions, the people who'd "validated" her. At least, not so much. They could sit quietly in the windowseat, holding hands, talking sometimes and sometimes not. Watching people on the street. Both of them perfectly happy. And he'd thought: Finally. I can stay with this one.

For twelve years, since he began dating at eighteen, he'd never had less than two girlfriends at once. It was a constant juggling act. And he was constantly on the look-out for more pins to juggle. Knowing all the time the performance was commanded by some undefined insecurity. Completely unable to fight it; and maybe having too much fun to want to fight it.

But, now and then, he felt the lack, too. No commitment meant no real closeness.

Amy's sheer intensity had overwhelmed his insulation. Maybe something more: some quality of underlying familiarity about her, as if she were someone he'd always known. It made him feel close to her at the roots of his personality.

And it felt good that she needed him *deeply*. He was a writer, a humourist, a freelancer, something of a rake, but compared to Amy he was as stable as the Rock of Gibralter.

It took time, though. The morning after that third date, Amy was resoundingly depressed. "It's not you," she said, huddled in a corner of her bedroom with a cup of coffee. "It just happens. It just comes. I'm up and then I'm down. It takes me a long time to talk myself back up again...

Prentice had talked Amy into seeing a psychiatrist. It wasn't easy; she wouldn't consider it at all when she was up – and when she was down she was sure that therapy would turn out to be a dead end, "Like all 'solutions'".

They gave her medication and it worked. She stabilized, without losing her vivacity. Prentice felt safer: he asked her to marry him. They moved in together; had a small, informal summer wedding on the roof of his apartment building. People in t-shirts, drinking wine on the roof of the adjacent building, applauded and yelled "Go for it!" when he kissed her. Amy had laughed and yelled at them to come over for champagne.

She stayed on the medication until the last three months of their marriage. Until then, everything went swimmingly. She was getting some work in an independent film production shooting in New York. He was riding high on the good box office for Fourth Base. Everything was great. Amy was growing up. She could go hours without talking about herself sometimes, and she wasn't compulsively competitive with other women. And then at the bottom of the emotional ninth inning, Prentice dropped the ball. He had an affair with Nina Spaulding, a rather pretentiously arty and very full-figured young dancer, and Amy found out. Maybe on purpose, Nina left an indiscreet message on the answering machine. Amy's fragile self esteem couldn't take it. She went off her meds and back on the wrong kind of drugs. Three months later, three months of near constant argument with Prentice, and she left him: and left New York for L.A. . . .

The ballgame on Jeff's TV was winding up. The Dodgers were doomed. With the fickleness of the L.A. sports fan, Jeff swore at them, gave the screen the finger, threw Doritios at a shot of the Dodger's pensive manager. "The hell with you lamebrains! You had the playoffs and you let the Padres, my God, the *Padres* take it from you, do you know what kind of average those guys have got? It's fucking humiliating."

Prentice got up to pee. All that beer. He called out from the bathroom, "You don't have to watch the game to the bitter · end, you know. Maybe there's some basketball on. Or, I don't know, backwards speed-skating or something. Check ESPN."

"No, I got to see how bad the humiliation is. Whether or not I should go so far as to wear a bag on my head for being a known Dodger fan."

Prentice came back into the living room and did a couple of kneebends. He'd been sitting down too long. Outside, twilight was whispering into evening. The noise from the pool was almost gone. There were other television sets faintly audible through the walls, mumbling softly to themselves in news anchor cadences.

Another beer commercial came on. Jeff stood up and went to the French doors, stared out at the frayed ends of the tangerine ribbon of sunset, visible above the opposite roof. It was a clay-tile roof, on the imitation-Spanish-style apartment building beyond the pool. Identical to his own building. "Goddamn that kid, too".

Prentice sighed. Okay, maybe if he listened to the latest on Mitch, it'd distract him from thinking about

Amy. "When was the last time you saw him, you say?"

"Six or seven weeks. I mean, I could've called the cops, do a missing persons thing, but he's not really missing, exactly, because he said he wanted to go off on his own, make his fortune, like, and he had a chance to sing in some rock band that was going to get a record deal . . ." He shrugged.

"He's too young to 'make his fortune, like', Jeff."

Jeff was a silhouette against the windows now, his back to Prentice. But Prentice could see his shoulders stiffen. "You telling me I shirked my responsibility?"

"I'm not really qualified to be selfrighteous about responsibility to people," Prentice said. Seeing a mummy in a file drawer.

"No, you're not. But maybe I did blow it, I don't know. You know what? I think I liked the kid looking up to me. I was mad when he thought he could do without me. So he moves out and – I just wanted him to come home on his own."

"With his tail between his legs."

"Sort of. It was stupid. I did call around, yesterday, to find him. Asked some people I knew he used to see. They hadn't seen him in a while. He's got this black girlfriend, Eurydice, I'd like to date her myself. Foxy. She claims she hasn't seen him. Kid could be dead in a culvert somewhere."

"He was doing drugs?" Prentice looked for a light switch. The room was getting darker and darker.

"Sometimes. Mostly not, around here. I don't tolerate it. But without me around . . ."

"He could be in jail, then. They've been doing a sweep for crack users"

Prentice switched on the light. Jeff turned to face him. Moving in slow motion, he brushed corn-chip

51

crumbs from his small, neatly trimmed black beard, then wiped his nose with the back of his hand. His eyes were glassy with unshed tears. "I'm gonna call the cops, the hospitals. See what I can find out." He went to the touch-tone phone on the end table beside the futon, put his hand on it – and froze. "I just thought of something. You know who was maybe the last person I know who saw Mitch? Your ex. Amy."

South Los Angeles

It wasn't a prison clinic, Mitch decided, after he'd been awake for a few minutes. It was a general kind of hospital, and it had the rundown, used look of the public hospital that poor people had to go to, and maybe they got turned away and maybe they didn't.

He felt okay till he tried to move. It felt like he was strapped down with barbed wire. Lay still and it didn't hurt much; move and it tore you up. And it felt, too, that his bones had turned to lead. They were that heavy to lift.

He just had a glimpse of his arm, all stitched with fine black thread, the stitched wound and the skin around it discoloured with orange-coloured disinfectant. He was sewn up like a badly made rag doll, with seams on his chest, his legs, his arm. Had he done his groin too? Had he done the thing he'd been thinking of when he'd lost consciousness: slashed up his own dick?

The More Man had wanted him to do it.

But he'd been drawn into unconsciousness, pulled down into it, and he'd lost the More Man and everything else. Until he woke up in this bed and in this hospital gown and in this pain.

Don't move. Just don't try to move. Because if it

hurts much more you'll vomit, and if you vomit you'll move your arms and legs with the convulsion of it, and the pain that would come, then – that was not something to even imagine.

So he lay there, floating in a septic pool of nausea, cotton-mouthed with dehydration, until a nurse came and looked him over, shaking her head with amazement. She asked him how he felt, and he said, "Hurts."

She looked like she was half-Indian, half-Hispanic. She had a Mexican accent. "Chure, I bet it hurts," she said, taking his pulse.

"Painkiller?" he rasped.

"We see what the doctor say."

"Water?"

"You not supposed to have any in the stomach yet but I give you some IV glucose water, you feel better." She set up an IV stand, put a needle in his right arm; she chewed her gum vigorously the whole time. She smelled like cigarette smoke. The glucose bottle fed by a rubber tube into a long needle that bit into the mainline vein of his right arm. She taped it down, and whisked out of the room without another word, probably to grab a quick cigarette in the nurse's lounge.

The bottle ticked out bubbles from its tube every so often, and coolness fed into his arm.

They'd put him in a loony ward, on medication. That's what'd happen, eventually.

He wondered if they'd posted a guard outside, or if the orderlies were supposed to keep an eye on him, or what.

He was sick, disfigured, and he was a prisoner too. They probably wouldn't even let him call his brother, without the juvenile hall authorities giving some kind of approval. His wounds were beginning to itch nastily, as well as burning and throbbing with pain. He couldn't scratch them.

He squeezed his eyes shut, as hard as he could, thinking that he was going to lay here and suffer for a long time.

Not if you don't want to.

"I have to."

You can come with us. We're sending someone to help you come back to us. They haven't got a guard on you right now. You're just a juvenile. You're not important enough. The orderlies are supposed to keep an eye on you, but they're not bothering to. We can get you away.

"Look what you've made me do to myself." Said with more disbelief than resentment. He didn't have the guts to be mad at the More Man. And the more he heared the More Man's voice, the better he felt.

That's right. If you hear me, if you really listen, you'll feel better.

He felt a trickle of the Head Syrup ooze through him, easing the pain a little.

That's all I can give you, until you come. The connection isn't quite there.

"I can't. I can't move."

We're coming to help you.

Terror and giddy anticipation. First one, and then the other. Wanting to yell for someone, ask them to get Jeff, and wanting to go with the More Man.

He knew he couldn't yell for help. He knew just where he was going. He had as much choice about it as a wad of phlegm going down a drain.

"I don't –" Try. "I don't want to –" Say it. "I can't –"

"Is he talking in his sleep?" A man's voice, asking it in a clinical way, almost as if thinking out loud.

Mitch opened his eyes, and saw a doctor, a dark little Paki or Indian dude, eyes just a bit too sunken. Coming in with the nurse. "I am Doctor Drandhu." Indian accent.

"Painkiller."

"I am not your doctor, so I can't prescribe it. Your doctor's up in the E.R., doing a little cutting and pasting on somebody else. He'll be here soon as he can. I came over from Culver City – I work at the Culver City Private Hospital – because Doctor Metzger – that's your doctor, Dr. Metzger, he said I might have a look at you..." He was talking distractedly as he looked at Mitch's wounds. "Very very nice sewing. Doctor Metzger does good work. It doesn't look like you lost a lot of muscle tissue, so if the nerves are well, you should recover, but you will have some scarring..."

"You got one like this one?" the nurse asked, surprised.

"Two, actually, correct. A young woman and a man about forty. We have just got the man in this morning. Were you taking a drug, Mitch? It's confidential."

"No."

"You are sure? We are not going to tell anyone about it, no."

Mitch just closed his eyes. Sure, right, just try and explain.

The doctor asked him another question. Mitch ignored him. He didn't even notice what the question was, at first. He was too busy trying not to throw up. He heard it when the doctor repeated it. "Mitch, who were you talking to when we came in? Are you hearing voices?" Mitch ignored that, too. After a few minutes he realized they had gone. But someone else was there. He could feel it.

He opened his eyes and saw the Handy Man. The More Man had sent him.

A little man with red cheeks and very big bright blue eyes and extra-big earlobes like that Senator with the bow tie who ran for president, and not much forehead, and a wide, yellow-toothed smile. He wore an old brown jacket, and a neatly pressed brown shirt, brown polyester pants. His hair was crewcut. He really didn't care much what he looked like, no, not the Handy Man. Just simple and clean, that was the Handy Man. Maybe that's why he didn't have any fingernails.

Panic. "No! I'm not going."

"There no one around," said the Handy Man, in his too-high voice, a midget's voice. He was only an inch or two taller than a midget. "And the ones out in the clinic, well, they're all busy, and I've brought something so you don't have to walk, and something so you don't have to feel any pain." He held up a syringe. "Morphine." He smiled apologetically. "We would prefer to use the connection instead, but it is broken, so . . ." He shrugged, and widened his smile.

"Morphine? Oh yes, please."

Let the Handy Man give him the painkiller, Mitch thought, and then he'd refuse to go with him. He'd buzz for the nurse. Yell for help.

But after the Handy Man shot the drug into the IV tube, a warm tide of indifference carried Mitch away and he let the Handy Man bundle him into some clothes and into the wheelchair.

On the way out, as the badly oiled wheelchair squeaked down the hall, he found himself staring hazily at the stitches in his arm. The black wiry stitches stuck out at the ends, where they were tied off, looking like insect legs, insect antennae. Insects burrowing in his skin.

56

He didn't care. He fell asleep, not caring.

Culver City, Los Angeles

"You sure you weren't sleeping with Amy?"

"I think I'd probably notice it if I was."

"That's not funny, Jeff. You know what I mean."

"I'm being honest. She came over and said she needed a place to stay for one night. Mitch was pretty dazzled by her. I think his respect for you quadrupled when I told him she was your wife."

They were sitting in Jeff's little office, Jeff on an orange crate and Prentice on Jeff's swivel chair. The orange crate would have collapsed under Prentice. He sat next to the PC workstation, with Jeff's collection of Playboy Calenders from the 1950s and early 60s on one wall, his Japanese robot monster toys, bookshelves made of cinder blocks and raw boards taking up another. They were untidy shelves, with magazines and graphic novels crammed in horizontally over the Penguin paperbacks and Jeff's pulp detective novel collection, each old yellowing paperback encased in a clear plastic envelope. In a closet was Jeff's small but startling gun collection . . .

They were waiting for the phone to ring.

"She stayed on the futon and Mitch slept on the floor in a sleeping bag. I knew you'd want to get all the sleeping arrangements clear. I tried to talk to her but she seemed really spooked. She said she was trying to make up her mind about something. Said she had a part, or anyway an offer, but she didn't know if she trusted the guy. I figured it was one of these casting couch situations."

"Shit."

"Yeah. Anyway, she didn't want to talk about it. She sat on the futon with her legs drawn up under her –"

"She always sits that way if there's room."

"– and stared at the TV. She watched like four sitcoms without hardly even *blinking* but she didn't laugh at any of the jokes. She was still on the futon, asleep, when I left for a meeting the next morning. I called home and Mitch said she'd left." He paused, staring reflectively into space as he remembered. "I think I... I was in a rotten mood so I argued with MItch, over the phone, about him finding a job or going back to school. And... when I came back he wasn't there. Left a note, didn't say much. I didn't connect his leaving with Amy. Maybe there's no connection. Probably not... "

"How come you didn't tell me before about Amy being here?"

"Because she asked me not to and because I know how you are. Irrationally jealous. I mean, I never laid a finger on her but I knew you'd grill me anyway if you knew she was here. You could be divorced or busted up with a girl for three years and still be possessive of her, Tom. Even if it was you that dumped her, which it usually was."

Prentice winced. "It's mostly if it's one of my friends. I can't stand the idea of one of my friends sleeping with my ex-girlfriends. I don't know why it should bother me, an ex should be an ex, but..."

The phone rang. Jeff dived for it. "Hello?"

A pause as he leaned vulture – like over the phone, one hand flat on the desk. "Where? Juvenile Detention? Jesus. Which one?" He reached for a pen and a yellow pad. "Got it. Thanks. Thanks Officer, I–" He shrugged, and hung up. "Cops don't waste time with amenities, just hang up when they're done. He's in JDH, possession of a controlled substance."

"He's in juvenile hall? They'd have to inform your mom or dad if they put him there, Jeff."

"They informed my mom, chances are, but she fucking lied to me about it. I guess she didn't want me to get him out, wanted to teach him a lesson or something."

"Or make sure he went through their drug rehab maybe."

"Maybe, if you want to believe she had decent motivations in lying to me. I doubt it. The bitch. Well, let's go see if they'll let us have him. Maybe I can get custody." Jeff seemed relieved, almost happy.

Jeff was almost out the door when the phone rang again.

It was the cob Jeff had just talked to. Jeff listened, and said, "Well why the hell didn't you –? Hello? Shit." Jeff went into his slow motion mode, moving as if in liquid wax as he hung up the phone, sat down and tugged at his beard. "He was taken to a hospital. He ran away from it. They don't know where he is."

Oakland, California

Constance was a virgin, certainly. In more ways than one, Ephram decided.

They were in a motel room Ephram had rented. The standard fifty dollar motel room. Ephram had decided it would be unwise to be seen bringing in another young girl to his condo. And the Pakistani people who ran the motel had not seen him bring the girl here. It was an "adult" motel, out near the Oakland airport, which meant that it had a pornography channel on its television. Constance and Ephram sat side by side on the bed, lazily drinking wine and watching the pornography channel. Actually, Ephram only pretended to drink wine. It dulled his control.

She watched the video-snowy close-ups of intersecting genitalia; watched it big eyed and with some confusion but happily, contentedly, because he'd pushed the appropriate buttons in her brain. She could watch a Roto Rooter man clean out a sewer, now, and find equal delight in it.

She was more deliciously innocent than Megan had been. Constance had never before watched pornography

– though she'd had an opportunity once to watch "a dirty video" at the house of a fiend, as she'd babblingly told Ephram on that first wave of the psychic high. She'd said no, wrinkled up her nose at the chance to watch movies of people rehearsing reproduction, till now. She thought about boys in terms of romance and dancing and dating and a little kissing, mostly, and read teenage romance novels which were so chaste there was scarcely even a kiss before the end of the book. And had never even masturbated. She had seen pictures of male genitals, and her dad told her anything about sex she wanted to know quite freely, in a clinical sort of way, and she knew how to have sex without getting pregnant or diseased. And she was curious about the act. Until now, only mildly curious.

Ah, he thought: Curiouser and curiouser, ha ha.

Being hardly more than a child, she'd never really had the *desire*, until Ephram rewired her for it. Using the associative technique he'd perfected with Numbers Nine through Fifteen.

It was ever so simple. You subjected the female to the pleasure-receiver stimulus, continued it as you subjected her to certain kinds of visual input, and then physical input. After receiving enough induced pleasure coupled with the sexual input, the subject associated *all* pleasure with that input, and her complicity became quite implacable and compulsive. Even frenzied – at least for a time, until the figures and sloughs of despond began to set in. Even then, one could always squeeze a few more drops from the sponge, if one was proficient . . .

The master switch supervened the other circuits of the brain. Supervened over choice, native character, self respect, self image or hope.

And then, of course, there was the punishment. An essential part of the programming and, lately, increasingly of interest to the jaded appetites, ha ha, of Ephram Pixie. And Ephram's friend; his unseen companion.

The "ghetto blaster" was playing certain Beethoven string quartets which had an astrological significance to Ephram – significance in the esoterica of the negative astrology – and the people on the little wall-mounted TV screen were copulating with energy, albeit no real enthusiam, when he at last began to fondle Constance.

She shied a bit at first, though grinning with the waves of pleasure he was sending through her. She made some tentative effort to escape him. But already her hips were making the involuntary humping motions, already the drugged look was so deep in her eyes all personality was drowned in it, and he knew he had his fingers on the strings of this pretty little marionette.

He made plans for her. He could make her love anything. He could make her love the bottom of his shoes. He could make her adore a German Shepard. He could make her plead to drink his piss and sigh with contentment when it was provided. He could make her as he had Number Twenty-one, who had been an enthusiast for the Humane Society – take delight in torturing small animals and then rolling naked in their half-vivisected bodies as they squealed and died. He could make her love a mouse trap, or a dead cat, or the taste of dog food; he could make her take pleasure in mutilating herself with scissors. She would beg him to let her mutilate herself with scissors a second time, if he gave her the pleasure waves when the first mutilation began. He could make her deeply desire to clip his toenails with her teeth. He could make her take joy in

masturbating in a bathtub full of earthworms ...
Or he could *force* her to do things, with the Punishment.
He could *force* her to eat a pigeon alive – and use
punishment to make her do it even when she had no
pleasure in it. Or, he could induce her to *love* eating a
pigeon alive. To experience bliss in it.

He could even make her want to kill her own father.

From the journal of Ephram Pixie, "9 May 1987"

It has always ruled us, of course, no matter what
we are doing. If we feel a little pleasure at having
cleaned out a file box, it is the brain rewarding
the pleasure receiver. If we feel a little regret at
having hurt someone – an emotional excrescence
I've trained out of myself – it is the punishment
receiver that experiences the regret as an inward
pang. If we feel a little happiness in the smell of
a breeze, or the fit of a new shoe, or the taste of
ice cream, or the thrill of taking part in an
athletic competition, or the sense of having done
a good day's work, or the good feeling that some
people experience on performing acts of charity –
the happiness is simply the brain rewarding the
animal as it has been programmed to do. It has
its sociobiological reasons for all of it. Sometimes
the rewards and punishments come in tiny little
increments, so small we're scarcely aware of
them ... we're constantly moving to the choreo-
graphy of reward and punishment ... Beyond it,
of course, is the audience at this grotesque ballet,
the invisible world. Through the invisible world,
and an understanding of the dark astrology, it is

quite possible to transcend the tyranny of the choreographer, the Great Programmer of Reward and Punishment. But this transcendance is given to only a few of us...

Garner had almost lost the Porsche at the traffic light on Fifteenth. He'd had to run the light, risk the police and a wreck and risk that whoever was in the Porsche would notice him.

A Porsche. Not something most teenage kids drove. Something a drug dealer might drive.

Now he sat in his '83 Toyota, outside the motel, trying to make up his mind about what to do. They'd gone into the motel and any doubts about what was up were banished. His daughter knew about birth control; maybe he shouldn't stop her from experimenting with sex. Maybe. But the guy was obviously fucking her judgement before Constance herself, with the drug. No way was Garner going to let that happen.

The Porsche was alone on the dark side of the motel parking lot, parked in front of the only room showing a light. That had to be the place. Constance must be in that room with the son of a bitch.

Garner considered calling the cops. Did he really want the police in on this? Constance could end up in custody. If he charged in without the cops, though, he could end up dead – and maybe Constance too. If the guy was a dealer he was probably armed. Garner wished he'd seen the driver of the Porsche more clearly – he hadn't pulled up in time to see them walk into the motel room together.

Garner felt a pang at having betrayed his daughter's trust. Turned into one of the Over Thirty monsters Abbie had warned him about. But on some other level, following her was the right thing to do. This was the only way to get the truth. And seeing Aleutia had made Garner determined on the truth.

Not my daughter. I won't have her trapped like that. Even If I have to be an asshole about it and follow her, just to be sure.

He'd almost had himself convinced it hadn't been drugs. You who talk about the mote in your friend's eye, take the beam out of your own, pal. He'd been hiding snugly in his own denial.

And then he'd awakened . . . heard that back door open. And knew instantly.

He made up his mind about what to do. He got out of the car and got the tyre iron from the trunk.

He walked around to the motel room and tried the knob. The door was unlocked. He took a deep breath and opened it. He stepped inside.

He stepped into glue. A world of glue. He couldn't move. He couldn't see.

Someone took the tyre iron from his hand. He heard the door close behind him. Then his senses closed down completely. He could hear nothing, feel nothing. Someone had hit him, was his last thought, as he slipped into a world where everything was gray and endlessly inert.

Constance was beginning to suspect that this wasn't a dream. As the waves of pleasure receded, she began to feel the rug under her bare feet. It scraped at her. She could feel the air on her skin. Sticky, foul. She could feel the weight of the metal rod in her hand. She could see, quite clearly now, the look on her father's face.

It was empty.

The one who'd called himself Michael had taken

control of her father's brain. Michael had a pinched look of concentration, as if he were having difficulty keeping a grip on both of them.

Maybe she could fight him now...

Pain like a rain of fire. Pain raining over her skull, burning down her spine. Malicious and all consuming and beyond screaming about.

"Please," she heard herself say.

"Raise the tyre iron over your father's head," Ephram told her. He sounded happy, though he had to grunt the words out through his concentration.

She obeyed instantly, hoping it would make the pain stop. The pain diminished a great deal, but didn't stop. Not quite.

"Drive the tyre iron through your father's right eye," Ephram said. She could tell he enjoyed saying *your father's right eye*.

"No," she said. It was all she could get out.

The pain last time was a campfire compared to the forest fire that now consumed her senses. Every last shred of her was looking for a way out.

It was easy to get out. Just push the tyre iron into...

But her father's face appeared through a veil of fire. No. No. No. *I'm not going to do it*.

The pain was unspeakable. She was knotted with nausea; she was wrung out by the hands of an ice giant.

She drew her arm back slowly and aimed the tyre iron, and struck.

It struck where she'd aimed it: at the side of her dad's head. She tried not to think about what she hoped to get away with...

Her father went down, blood splattering, coursing from the head wound. But he was alive.

She heard someone laugh. Two short monosyllables.

Like, Ha ha. "I'm not stupid, my dear. Do it for real this time. Bend over him..."

There were sirens in the distance. She waited. The man who called himself Michael waited.

The sirens warbled into a lower register, and faded away.

But the sirens had given Ephram pause. Who knew for sure this man hadn't alerted anyone? Perhaps they'd be along any minute. And find a corpse, here. Messy, as always. A problem.

If he killed the girl's father, and if the father had told the cops where he was going, perhaps just before coming in...

Well. They might get a description of Ephram from the Pakistanis. But of course when he'd registered he'd given them a phony license number and they hadn't checked. So that wouldn't be of any help to anyone.

If dad here didn't turn up dead, the cops would be less inclined to search out Ephram. And they wouldn't take the man seriously. After all, he'd seen nothing – he couldn't swear his daughter was in here. Evidently he'd seen her get into the car, though. Even so... she was old enough that the police would regard her as a probable runaway. There'd been no struggle, when she was taken. Not a visible one.

He had some new plans for this girl, after all. He planned to redesign her, with reward and punishment. Instead of killing her, he could make her into a happy and carnal accomplice. For a while. He'd hate to have to give her up now just to make escape more feasible.

Ephram sighed. "I will be magnanimous, girl. Your father will live. We will move him out to his car, and then we'll be going out to our own. I'll need to get rid of the Porsche soon. Bother..."

But, really, this was quite exciting. How much better it was, without the Akishra, diverting him from his divine inspirations.

Where would they go? He wondered, bending to lift the father up, make him look like a drunk supported between Ephram and the girl.

Someplace they could fit right in, he and the girl. Someplace it wouldn't look strange for an older man to have as companion a girl her age. Someplace corrupt enough to provide camouflage.

Wasn't it obvious? Los Angeles.

Alameda

Garner was sitting at his kitchen table by the phone, pressing an ice pack to his throbbing head, waiting for a police detective to call him back. But thinking the cops were probably a waste of time.

With his free hand, he touched the bandage around his head. It felt too tight. And it partly blocked the sight in his right eye.

He tried, once more, to remember the assault. He remembered opening the door. And then, *wham*. That was all. Next thing he remembered was paramedics bending over him. Someone had found him in the parking lot.

The phone rang and he answered before the first ring had finished. "Hello."

"Reverend Garner? This is Brent at Alameda General –"

Carrier sighed. He did a lot of counselling for the hospital. They knew him well in the Emergency room. He counselled recovering ODs; sometimes he comforted the AIDS patients. But just now all he wanted to do was start looking for Constance. "I'm really caught up in something now, Brent –"

"I know – I heard. But there's a girl dying here and she keeps asking for you. She's on the verge of a coma. Crack overdose. Some really massive amount. I guess her old man ripped off a dealer and they smoked all night . . . Girl named Berenson."

"Oh Hell." On the verge of a coma. With crack that probably meant Aleutia was dying . . .

He heard Aleutia's voice as soon as he stepped into the E.R. Whimpering, pleading.

Garner turned and saw her in one of the alcoves, lying on a hospital bed under heaps of ice.

He knew what the blanket of ice meant. It was a last ditch treatment to lower a soaring body temperature. A killing fever that came with crack overdose.

She was dying. And the baby . . .

Two nurses and a doctor worked over her. Machinery beeped softly as it monitored her vital signs. She lay there motionless, now. She'd stopped whimpering, stopped squirming.

"We're losing her again," the doctor said, his voice flat.

"Where's the obstetrician?" one of the nurses said, sounding like she was fighting hysteria.

Carrier wanted to go to Aleutia, hold her hand, try to reach her. But it was too late; she was unconscious, babbling in delirium, and he was afraid of getting in the way. He just stood there and prayed.

A slow minute later, as he stood riveted, watching, the heart monitor flatlined. The monitor made a single, empty tone, whistling into forever. A Code Blue. Her heart had stopped.

They tried CPR; they failed. They tried re-starting her heart with electrical jolts from a defibrillator. That hardly ever worked. It didn't work for Aleutia. She was gone.

"What about the caesarian?" a nurse said.

"We've lost the baby too," the surgeon said.

I prayed into a vacuum, Garner thought bitterly.

The cops. Go to the cops. Tell them about Constance. Find her.

Mouth dry, head thumping, Garner walked on wobbly legs to the exit. He just wanted to find Constance. *We've lost the baby too.*

"So did I," Garner said, aloud. "Lost my baby too..." He said it to no one in particular.

Or maybe he said it to God.

Los Angeles County Juvenile Detention

The visitors' room was painted white, overlit, and furnished with cheap orange plastic chairs, most of which were so bent they were a danger to sit on. There was a single decoration, a retouched photo of an autumn scene in New England. It was cemented to the wall. Some kid had scribbled on it with a ballpoint pen, drawing in a word balloon over the forest lake, which was reflective with sunset orange: *Get me out of here! I'm drowning in this orange shit!*

Prentice and Jeff sat alone in a corner, waiting for Lonny. The counsellor had said Lonny was Mitch's room-mate, and a friend of his from before the arrest. "A friend of his?" Jeff had said. "It's weird that I never met him."

"No it's not," the counsellor had said.

In the other corner of the room a Chicano boy talked

70

earnestly in Spanish with his mother. The boy was overweight, the skin of his face pocked, his hair puffed up in the sort of pompadour that's stylishly dimpled in the middle. It looked to Prentice like there was a hole going down into his head. The boy had a fake gold chain around his neck.

Jeff shifted uncomfortably in his chair. "You think that doctor was full of shit? Doctor Drandhu?"

"Christ, that name sounds like the villain of a Flash Gordon serial or something." Prentice shrugged. "That's something we can ask Lonny. If that shit was self mutilation."

"That's just not a Mitch thing to do. He might do all kinds of weird shit but Mitch hated pain. Hell, he hated any kind of discomfort, he was not your Spartan type, you know? And if he was into mutilating himself it would've showed up before now. I mean, he was never that fucked up."

"Yeah well. Amy was crazy but I never knew her to mutilate herself either. And she did it . . .

He broke off, embarrassed, as the Chicano boy and his mother bent their heads and began to pray together in Spanish. The counsellor had said, "Every single kid here is in a gang – for three exceptions, all of them white boys. Mitch was one of the exceptions."

There were tears rolling down the Chicano boy's cheeks as he prayed. This was not how Prentice pictured juvie gang members. But then, the kid's companeros weren't around to see this.

"You know," Jeff whispered, "they say the girl gangs are the worst. They've got these girl gangs out here now – they're sort a like Apache women were supposed to be. Torture the prisoners. Just mean as can be. They say you won't live if they get pissed at you and catch you – some

71

of the other gangs might let you live, after they beat you up, but never the girls."

"I'm glad this place isn't co-ed."

The door to lock-up buzzed and opened, and a boy came through. He looked half Oriental, maybe Vietnamese, half-Hispanic, some Cauc blood too. Long lank, black hair over his shoulders. He wore a *Metallica* t-shirt and jeans, high-top black Adidas. He swaggered just a little as he walked. His muscular arms were home-tattooed with snakes entwining cartoonish girls. Behind him came a potbellied black guard, his khaki uniform shirt popped open where his belly spilled over his shiny black belt, one hand on the butt of his holstered gun. "You got about ten minutes, Lonny," the guard said, "then you got Group."

"Group sucks," Lonny muttered, pausing to look awkwardly around.

"You axed for that group, homie," the wheezing guard said. He fished a cigarette from a shirt pocket, handed it over, lit it with an old Zippo, and left.

Jeff and Prentice crossed to Lonny. Shook his surprisingly soft hand. Introduced themselves. "Hi, howya doin'," Lonny said, politely but tonelessly. He stuck his free hand in a jeans pocket, the other one flicked the cigarette. He looked at Prentice and Jeff, then looked at the floor, then looked back at them. "So what you guys want?"

"I'm Mitch Teitelbaum's brother –"

"I know, you said that before. But whas'up, you know? I mean, I don't wanna be an asshole, but I got to check this shit out. Mitch was like my blood homie, you know?"

Jeff nodded. "Okay. Look – if you can answer some questions for us, we'll sign something for your lawyer, says you were helpful, it won't hurt when it's time to get out of here. We're trying to figure out where Mitch went. I'm not going to tell the cops anything you tell me – I want to go get him myself. You got any ideas?"

Lonny drew on the cigarette. He looked at them.

Prentice thought about offering him money. He had a sense, though, that offering money would have been taboo; Lonny's claim to close friendship for Mitch had the ring of truth about it.

"At the hospital," Jeff prompted, "they said someone saw him going out in a wheelchair, pushed by a funny looking kind of guy, older guy . . . Any idea who that might be?"

Lonny shrugged. "Maybe it's the More Man."

Prentice stared. Hadn't there been something in Amy's hospital evaluation papers about the More Man? Something she'd said more than once . . .

"I don't know who the fuckin' More Man is," Lonny said. "Mitch called the guy that, said someone at the Doublekey was going to help him break into recording. Mitch wanted to write songs and shit. All I know is, the More Man's hella rich."

"What's the Doublekey?" Jeff asked.

"It's this ranch, out by Malibu somewhere, people party out there a lot, girls go out and get free drugs an' shit. I heard that before, and Mitch told me about it too, you know."

"You ever tell the cops this?" Prentice asked.

"Fuck no." He snorted at the idea. He went to a chair that had a tin ashtray on its seat. He picked up the ashtray, brought it back, held it in one hand, tamped ashes into it with another. There was something curiously feminine about the way he did it.

73

"You ever see Mitch, uh... Jeff hesitated. "Hurt himself?"

Lonny grimaced, an expression fleeting as the lighting of a nervous fly. Then the impassivity returned. "Sure, yeah. I told him cut it out or I was going to kick his fucking ass for him."

Prentice waited for the boy to notice the irony in that. *Stop hurting yourself for I'll hurt you.* But he didn't. Maybe there was a reason...

Eyeing the cigarette to see whether there was a millimeter to smoke before the filter, Lonny said, "Yeah, shit, he dug this shiv into his arm down to the bone... plowed it all up... stickin' it real deep in himself all over... he was startin' to cut on his dick and shit too...

Jeff winced. Prentice's mouth went dry.

Lonny went on, "He didn't seem to feel no pain. I thought for a while he was bogartin' dope or something, to be doin' that, but I don't think so. He said it was spirits that did it, and I know there's spirits, I got an aunt, she can get spirits to come and take her over and she can put her hands in fire and it don't hurt her. I believe in spirits. Fuck, yeah."

For a moment, Lonny closed his eyes. His adam's apple bobbed. When he opened his eyes again they were moist. "I told him I'd kick his ass for him if he did that shit again." He said it this time with an odd kind of sentimentality. "He's like, my brother..." He gave Jeff a look that made him stiffen. "You probably find him out the Double-key. You go get his ass and bring him home, but don't be fucking telling the cops this shit. If they go out there and he gets busted and it's my fault, man..."

"I don't want him busted either," Jeff said. "Don't worry, Lonny."

"I'm not kidding man. Swear on your dick, you'll lose it if you tell the cops."

Jeff started to laugh, then saw that Lonny was completely serious. "On my . . ."

"You heard me. You swear or I'll tell some of my friends on the outside to go out that Ranch, tell Mitch to split before you get there. Swear on your fuckin' dick, dude."

Jeff swallowed. He shrugged. "Okay I swear. On my dick." Lonny looked at Prentice meaningfully. Prentice sighed. "I swear . . ." He glanced at the Mexican lady who was standing now, hugging the boy. Prentice lowered his voice to add, " . . . on my dick"

Los Angeles

"I've heard of the Doublekey ranch somewhere or other," Jeff said.

They were on the 101, in Jeff's Cabriolet, with the top down, but with no wind to cool them off. The traffic was backed up and desultory. The radio was playing, but low, Tom Petty was singing about good girls and bad boys, but Prentice couldn't make out much more than that. The sun made sundogs and quivery pools of light on the cars; it was slowly burning the crown of Prentice's head. He wondered if his hair was thinning up there. Male pattern balding, they called it. That'd be right in line with the rest of my luck, he thought.

Then he found himself looking at a black family with seven or eight sad-eyed kids packed into a battered old station wagon and just the way the clothes and odds and ends were crammed in around them made it clear they lived in that car . . .

And he thought: Prentice, stop feeling sorry for yourself.

"Jeff," Prentice murmured, "you ever wonder if there're things guiding us to see things... or not to see things? Influencing us? Like, if we're paying attention, we might be feeling sorry for ourselves and then something prompts us to notice someone worse off..."

"You mean, something guiding us like God? If you're guided, it's more likely being done by some part of your unconscious that knows self pity is dumb," Jeff said.

"I guess. Sometimes, though, I think..." He blew out his cheeks, feeling foolish. "Never mind. This fucking traffic sucks. Let's get off a here, get on the surface streets."

"If I can ever get to the goddamn exit."

The cars in front of them moved up a little; Jeff prodded his Cabriolet a few yards farther in the slow conga line, as Prentice asked, "You said you heard about this Doublekey ranch?"

"It's out near Malibu, like the boy said. I think... You know what it is, if I'm remembering right: It's Sam and Judy Denver's place."

"You say their names like I'm supposed to know who they are."

"Remember *Honolulu Hello?* That was their show. They produced that and *Gun City* and a couple of others and really cleaned up for a while which was pretty easy since their sponsor was —"

"Their sponsor was Horizon Soaps. Very funny. Stick to action writing, Jeff."

"Lighten up, man."

"Oh yeah, right," Prentice said, rankled. "Amy got chewed up and spit out by some asshole around here.

My career's in the dumpster. Then we hear all this depressing shit about Mitch. And the top of my head feels like you could fry an egg on it. And I'm supposed to lighten up?" Self pity again, he told himself. But it was hard not to take refuge in it. With Amy in a file drawer.

"So anyway," Jeff went on, "the Denvers used to host a very exclusive high powered little clique. They used to be quite fashionable. Then they sort of dropped out of sight. Supposed to be living quite comfortably off their residuals. *Honolulu Hello* is always in re-runs . . . I guess it was the molestation thing." Mitch grimaced. "The Denvers were accused of child molestation. The children of some maid they had for awhile . . ." His voice trailed off.

Prentice articulated what were probably Jeff's thoughts. "Child molestation? And Mitch is out there? He's not a kid but he's close enough . . ."

Jeff was chewing his lower lip. "I . . . don't know. Nothing was proven on them. But where there's smoke there's fire, or sometimes anyway. And there was lots of smoke."

"Well shit, then. Let's go to the cops, tell them that these accused child molesters have your teenage brother. They could be abusing him some way."

"I don't know, man. I promised Lonny –"

"You worried about your dick falling off, Jeff?"

"It's not my dick, it's my word, okay? But the other thing is – I don't want to give Mitch to the cops again. I mean, how much good were they doing for his 'rehabilitation' out in that place where he manages to carve himself up like a fucking turkey, you know?"

"You always hated cops anyway. How come?"

Jeff was silent for a minute or two. Then he said,

"I did some time when I was a kid too..."

Prentice nodded. His eyes had settled on Jeff's carphone. "Can I use your phone?"

"Sure. It's got kind of a crackly signal, but go for it, man."

"Thanks." Prentice took the phone off the cellular unit just under the dashboard and punched his agent's number.

Buddy kept him on hold for five minutes, but Prentice had nothing else to do as the car crawled toward the exit still a quarter mile away. Prentice glanced at Jeff...

And was surprised, and then not so surprised, to see that Jeff was crying. Silently crying; his bony cheeks coursing with tears. Thinking about his brother. Prentice looked away, gazed at the tract homes and *Denny's* restaurants and *Macdonalds* and *Burger Kings*, their toylike roofs visible down below the guard rail of the freeway. He tried to give Jeff some privacy, that way.

Finally he got Buddy on the line, shouting through the brassy pipe of the speaker phone. Buddy didn't palter with amenities. "Hey, Tom. How ya doin'. Say, I spoke to Athwright and he says he's giving your project 'serious consideration'. I don't know what that means except it's better than 'don't waste my time with that kind of shit' which is what he said about the last guy I sent over. But there's no guarantees. You know what you should do, if you want a break, dontcha? I mean, studios don't buy treatments much, they don't commission scripts too often anymore, nowdays they like to see that finished script. So they can make you rewrite it ten thousand times. But you know what I mean – a spec script, man –"

"Hey, I'm working on that." Which was a lie. Prentice had started half a dozen scripts but nothing came together in his head. It was like a locomotive with no steam pressure, it just wouldn't go, and he told himself *If I get the money for a commission I'll be motivated, I'll be financially relieved too, that'll loosen up the inspiration . . . I need the money first . . .* Some part of himself knowing he was making excuses. "But listen Buddy, it's still possible to get some money out front for, you know, people with a track record. I had a couple of misfires but I proved I can do it, I'm a Player, man, and if we act as if I'm not a Player then *they*'ll think I'm not."

"Look – a spec script gets you a *lot more money*. That's the bottom line."

"Like I said, I'm working on it. But that could take months. And in the meantime I need an advance. I got bills to pay."

"Well – I'm working on that. So. How ya doin', holdin' up okay? About Amy I mean. You feel okay?"

"Yeah I'm okay – uh –"

"Good, great, I'll call you if anything firms up, Okay? Ciao –"

"Buddy! Take a breath, pull your finger back from that button for onc second. Listen – I'm not just whining here. I need some work." He was aware, on some level, that he was saying this partly for Jeff's benefit. In the hopes that Jeff would pull some strings somewhere. Jeff was connected. "I mean: I really need work. Starting with an advance."

A moment of static. Some of Buddy's reply lost in interference. "– think, you're not? I tell you what – just to pay some bills – I do have something. You willing to do a slasher movie? This is not Guild work, you

79

understand, it's kind of under the board, you'd get maybe ten grand –"

"Are you serious?"

"I know it's piddly shit but hey if you need cash that badly, well . . . just to fill in, you could do it and forget about it. Do it under a pseudonym. It's going right to video – it's a made-for-video slasher film, see. It's called *Class Cut-Up.*"

"Cute." Prentice thought about it for about five seconds. Decided he'd rather go back to bartending. But he didn't want to fling the one effort Buddy had made for him back in the guy's face . . . "Let me sleep on that, okay, Buddy? And if anything else comes up"

"I'll get back to you. I got another call here –"

"Take it. Ciao."

Prentice hung up the phone. It seemed he was going to be twisting slowly in the wind of Arthwright's whim.

Anyway, they'd reached the exit. That was a start.

But when they drove down onto the surface street, major street repairs were going on, complete with ear battering jackhammers and backhoes jetting clouds of blue smoke. The traffic down here was even worse.

Near Malibu, California

Mitch was at the bottom of a swimming pool. An old concrete swimming pool filled with water so green it was almost black.

For some reason, he could breathe in here, under water.

Something big was shaking and quivering over in that green obsidian corner. The big shaking thing was coming closer to him now. A cloud of wiggling things. *Worms.*

Wriggling worms, glinting in the faint light from above. Closing around him. When he inhaled, he sucked them wriggling into his throat, trickling and slithering into his bronchial tubes, squirming with a kind of funnybone pain inside his lungs...

Worms in his lungs!

He thrashed about, trying to gag them up.

He fell off the bed with a bruising thump. Felt the hardwood floor under his hands. A swatch of bedclothes against his cheek. He'd been dreaming. In bed. The hospital. He was...

...not in the hospital, he saw, now, as he got painfully onto his knees.

He was raw with pain; grinding his teeth with the punishment that came every time he moved. As he looked around.

It was a room he'd never seen before. It was dark, and the colours of the room seemed to shift one into another when he didn't look directly at them. Old wallpaper, peeling in the corner; a pattern of hook-shapes alternating with drooping rosebuds. Could be this was where the hallucination of the worms had come from; a pattern in the wallpaper.

He had a sense, though, for a fleeting moment, that the cloud of wrigglers was there, just out of his line of sight, poised and sensitive to him. Then he shook himself, and the hallucination was gone.

The room had an old brass bed. A four poster, with scratch marks around their metal posts, near the mattress. There was one door.

He moved painfully to the door. He had laughed at old men, who moved the way he moved. *I won't laugh anymore*, he prayed, *if that's what this punishment's for.* He tried the brass knob of the old-fashioned darkwood door. Locked in two places; at the old skeleton-key lock and, he could feel, when he rattled the door, that there was a padlock on the outside, high up on the door.

He felt like crying, but he was incapable of it. It would take too much strength to cry. He took a deep breath. Told himself, it's okay, it's all right.

He sniffed the air. There was a cloying smell; a rotting flower stink. As if the rosebuds in the wallpaper were rotting.

There was also – somehow a function of the cloying stink of rotting petals – laughter, from somewhere; sticky, shrivelled laughter, and foreign-sounding music, sort of Arab and sort of Oriental and sort of American. Played on what sounded like a malfunctioning stereo.

The noise came through the room's single window. A big bay window all veiny with shadows and fragmented with light. It made him think of a biology class where he'd dissected a lizard and the teacher had him hold its bellyskin up to the light and you could see all the veins picked out in a rosy glow...

Roses. Big fat ones, he saw, as he hobbled up to the window. He'd never seen roses this big before. And the veiny shadows were made by thick rose vines, some as big around as his wrist, and all dinosaur-spiny with large thorns.

The window was nailed shut.

Bending to peer through a clear patch of window glass – and through a little rosebush cave of green and red – he could see, below, people moving twitchily across a twilit terrace strewn with trash. Most of them walked alone. Others stood singly in the shadows at the edge of the terrace. There was a big stone barbecue glowing with coals; on the grill were steaks, but they'd been allowed to curl and blacken. No one seemed to be eating. A woman moved erratically onto the flagstones, then stopped in the middle of the terrace, hunched over a little, hugging herself. Her shoulders began to shake. The others seemed to ignore her. Something fell from her hands: a large green wine bottle. It broke on the stones, splashing red wine and shards of green bottleglass. Then the woman collapsed, falling almost straight down, as if someone had kicked her knees from behind. She lay in a huddle. Still no one moved to help her, though a couple of people shuffled by, within a few feet of her. They didn't even look over at her.

After a few moments, the Handy Man came out onto the terrace, bent down, put his hands under her armpits, hoisted her upright. Strong guy for being so small. She got her footing, and he led her away. She seemed perfectly sure-footed now. (What was that music? Where was it from?)

The Handy Man, Mitch thought. The little dude from the hospital. Recognition brought back some memories, just flashes, images from a badly edited video: Darkness parting long enough to see out the window of a car, driving through a gate that rolled automatically aside. A black security guard holding a couple of snarling dogs back by their collars. A circular driveway. A big house. A wheelchair. The smell of roses and stale liquor. Another, smaller house. An old stone horse trough, and a stone jockey with a rusty iron ring in his hand. The hulk of a Mercedes, rusting on blocks in an overgrown yard to one side of the little house. Voices. Sobbing laughter. Darkness closing again.

The gate. Remembering the gate again he saw it was black metal, ornate along the top, with – painted in gold leaf – crossed skeleton keys as the centerpiece of the scrollwork.

Double keys. The Doublekey Ranch.

Down below, the music was suddenly switched off. A few seconds of silence, then raucous, jeering laughter. Then more silence. Then the sound of a dog barking. The dog yelped – and made a series of terrified, excruciating high pitched yips, and then that was silenced, too.

There were other voices, from the hall. A low, deep voice, whose resonance Mitch knew before he recognized the voice itself. It was the More Man. Mitch moved as fast as he could bear to, crossed the room, pressed an ear to the door. "This one doesn't party, we cultivate him in-board. Give him a . . ."

Give him what? Something inaudible. Had it been "bedpan"?

The More Man went on, "In a month or two he . . ." Inaudible. But knowing with a sinking, plunging certainty, that the More Man was talking about him, about Mitch. "No, no, he's not going to be . . ." Couldn't hear it. ". . . doesn't matter too much but he could surprise us. Pair him with the . . ." *Couldn't hear.* A murmur of someone, maybe the Handy Man, replying to the More Man. And then the More Man's voice: " . . . unless that asshole Ephram comes back . . ." Lost. The sound lost. Then: " . . . won't be looking for him, there's no need to –" He broke off speaking, suddenly.

He was aware of Mitch listening. Mitch backed away from the door.

Oh no oh no, said a scared little kid in Mitch's head. Just some part of Mitch himself going: Oh no, oh no, oh no.

Mitch told the little kid, *It's okay, I'm getting out of here. I'll get out.* But it was exactly like trying to comfort

84

a small child when the house is burning down around him. The kid was smart enough to know . . .

The More Man had lied, Mitch knew, with magnifying glass lucidity. The More Man had lied always and all along, about trading the body-play time for favours in the music business, for being here a little while and then going free.

Free? There was no way he was ever going to let Mitch go, never, not ever . . .

It was dark outside, when Mitch woke up again. He didn't remember lying down, or going to sleep.

Someone was at the door. He could hear them messing with the locks. He thought of waiting by the door, rushing whoever it was, knocking them down, sprinting for the stairs.

But just sitting up hurt like a bitch.

If raw hamburger could feel, he thought, it'd feel like this. I did this to myself, Mitch thought, looking at his arms. I cut myself.

He had to tell that to himself, again and again, to be able to think about it at all. It just didn't seem real.

The door opened, and the Handy Man came in, carrying a plastic tray holding a bottle of hydrogen peroxide, a sponge, bandages.

Bandy-legged and puppet-faced, the Handy Man. Smelling of hot dog grease and creosote. He ignored Mitch's rasped questions, whistling rather loudly and tunelessly as if to blot up anything Mitch said, and lay him back on the bed, bathing his wounds with foaming hydrogen peroxide. He smiled as, with nail-less hands, he bandaged Mitch, and smiled as he gathered up his supplies and left. "See you in the hot tub," the Handy Man said.

He didn't lock the door behind him. Mitch stared at the door, slightly ajar, hope rising like a feeble dog in his chest, and then the More Man came walking in, and the dog died.

"Hi Sam," Mitch said. Trying.

"Howdy Mitch," the More Man said. Mitch always thought of Sam Denver as the More Man. That's what the kids called him, on the street. The More Man was carrying a wooden tray containing a bowl of sprouts, wheatgrass and tomatoes. A few grainy looking vitamins lying beside the ceramic bowl. A wooden fork. A ceramic cup of what was probably carrot juice.

The More Man was a tanned, muscular man wearing a white linen jacket over a blazingly colourful tie-dyed t-shirt. Linen pants, white canvas shoes, no socks. He had a slight suggestion of wattles, a lot of lines around his foggy blue eyes, his collar-length, swept back blond hair receding a little. But he seemed to move about on a wave of youthful energy.

Mitch knew the More Man wasn't armed and he knew that didn't matter.

"Wheatgrass, Mitch," the More Man said, in his boyish, hearty voice. "Wheatgrass!" There was a sense of distraction about the voice as if the speaker was not really listening to himself, despite the heartiness. "Wheatgrass cleanses the blood, rebuilds the cells, revitalizes the chakras, energizes and feeds! Not too much, just enough, with a little alfalfa, some nice tomatoes. My dear Lord, Mitch, you're going to be shakin' the bacon and dancin' on air in no time!"

"Sure," Mitch said. He was sort of hungry. Queasy but hungry. "I'll eat it, Sam." All the questions were hiding just back of Mitch's teeth. Was it possible to ask this guy questions? Could a person even do it?

"And the vitamins!" the More Man said, setting the tray on Mitch's lap. "This one is Vitamin A. The carrot juice has a lot of A in it too! Good for healing! Needja strong! Got big happenins' comin down! The vibes are all there!"

"Great," Mitch said. What was he talking about? Songwriting?

"Record deals cookin'", the More Man said, winking. "Hang in there. Sufferin' builds character – you're almost there. Just hang loose and heal. Record companies snappin' at my heels."

Mitch knew, this time, with a bedrock certainty, that the More Man was lying. There never had been any career in the making. Not for Mitch.

But. Say anything. Just say anything, Mitch told himself. Anything he'll like. "Great, rad, I'm stoked, Sam!"

"Just let ol' Handy take care of you!" The More Man flashed a fluorescent grin at him and started for the door.

Panic. "Uh – Sam! Listen – the pain. I need, I dunno, something. To chill out behind. It . . ."

"I'll get you a painkiller, just a little, wouldn't want you to get hooked!" The More Man chattered, opening the door, bouncing his head a little on his shoulders like Ronald Reagan used to do when he was in a good mood. Sort of like an excited cockatoo.

Sometimes there was a squirming at the More Man's crotch. Sometimes his eyes dimmed with euphoria. Sometimes his smile became a rictus.

"I was thinking of the Head Syrup . . . I mean, the Reward." Mitch said. Heart pounding. Hooked? He was already fucking hooked.

The More Man's smile went out like a popped

lightbulb. He turned Mitch a look of sucking vagueness. "Rewards have to be earned," he said, lifelessly.

And Mitch was relieved when the More Man went out and shut the door behind him. Even though he locked it.

Mitch made himself eat the meal. Take the vitamins, washed down with carrot juice. The Handy Man came in and brought him a cap of something, maybe a "dilly", judging by the way Mitch was feeling after taking it. Feeling like he was melting into his bed. A dilaudid. The pain ebbed . . . the starved and beaten dog in his gut dreamed about being a happy and stupid puppy . . .

A noise outside the door. Sounded like it was down the hall a little, but coming closer.

Mitch opened his eyes and stared at the door and, after a minute, it came into focus. He listened.

It wasn't the Handy Man's padding footsteps. It was a dry, scraping sound, like something being dragged or . . . more like crawling. It kept going. After a while it was gone.

The Outskirts of

Bakersfield, California

The guy was kind of cute, Constance thought. He had a nice smile.

He's got a nice dick too, Ephram told her. Yes, she thought dutifully, he's got a nice dick.

When Ephram told her things, it didn't come like words in her head. Just little pushes of idea, maybe a picture or two. But Ephram was in there with her, all right.

She knew his name was Ephram, by now. She knew some other stuff about him, too. She knew that Ephram was a murderer. She had glimpsed it through the kaleidoscope strobing of mental ideation. He was a murderer, but he didn't let her care about that.

They were admiring the young man in a *Sizzler* steakhouse. The man was sitting across the aisle from them, a few booths up. He had long, wavy brown hair past his shoulders and a new-looking Levi jacket and a gold watch. There were some keys on the table with a little plastic BMW tab on them. He had a nice face that looked slightly Latin. *And probably a nice dick. A nice dick, A nice dick. A nice cock. A big fucking cock.*

Constance had eaten most of her steak, though she didn't feel like eating. But she was afraid of what Ephram would do if she didn't. This was the second night they'd stopped at a *Sizzler*. The time before they'd had the All You Can Eat Shrimp Dinner and Constance hadn't wanted much so Ephram had jolted her in the Rewards, gave her a flush of pleasure if she so much as looked at the Shrimp, and even more if she ate it, so she did, she ate it, and ate more of it and more of it, and he sat there silently laughing, his jowls shaking, watching her, jolting her with pain if she complained that her stomach was too full, jolting her with pleasure when she ate more, so that even the big guys in the restaurant who could polish off five platesful, even they stared at her when she went back for number seven, and she wanted to cry but Ephram wouldn't let her, he kept making her eat, Constance wolfing the stuff down noisily and rapidly, till she threw up, she projectile-vomited half-chewed shrimp across the table and then he made her eat some of that and enjoy it and everyone was afraid to come over and tell her to stop and then they left, Ephram pasting a hundred dollar bill to the cash register with some of her vomit, "just to pay for her disgusting mess", and she'd tried to run away again and he'd punished her terribly as they drove away . . .

So tonight she ate her steak.

She looked out the window. Headlights like stars going two by two fell horizontally along the horizon (what was up and what was down? Constance didn't know, she didn't think anyone knew) under a sky heavy with slate and indigo . . . Nearer were the motel signs, the gas stations and fast food places, this place so like the last town it was as if the day of slow driving hadn't happened, as if they hadn't travelled hundreds of miles.

"Come on, Constance," Ephram said aloud, as the young man Ephram had picked got up lithely and went to the door.

They followed him. Constance wanted to warn him but she didn't try, she knew Ephram wouldn't let her.

And why should she? (Was that her own thought or Ephram's? She wasn't sure). Why should she warn him? She had seen the world as she had never seen it before. Just watching TV with Ephram, she had seen it anew.

"Look there," Ephram had said. "Ethiopia, the government murdering thousands of its own people. Look there, our own government playing footsy with the Khmer Rouge after they murdered millions of innocent people. Look there, the industrialists are poisoning us – everyone knows they poison our air and water and people die as a result, but they feel no remorse, these men, and we are all too greedy for our economic comforts to truly punish them. Look there, how many thousands of rapes every week? How many murders? How many children are locked in closets or used for sex? How many *infants* used for sex? How many men have made how much money making nerve gas? Look there! The man who invented the Neutron bomb is on CNN, sweating with desire, urging that we use his toy on the enemy! How much murder are we considering, at his behest? Constance, did you hear that? Fifty thousand children die, every day, around the world, from famine! Think of the vast scale of the suffering! In Burma, in Ceylon, in Guatemala, people are murdered at the convenience of the government – but we are safe here, aren't we? Those of us free of persecution – what

91

do we have? If we're not beaten to death by men with baseball bats at our ATMs; if we are not dying of cancer on the fringe of some nuclear power plant, why... what do we have? What is our reward? Television and beer! Then: *death!* Or worse: abandonment to psychopathic strangers in nursing homes. Slow suffering! The horror of Death! *Annihilation!*

"Let us at least be ourselves, Constance! Let us at least prey before we are preyed on! Let us reward ourselves and take part in the slaughter instead of being the slaughtered! Let us not mouth the lie that the world was not made for murder!"

He'd said all that. She wasn't quite sure if he'd ever said it aloud.

"Hi," she said to the handsome young man in the Levi jacket. Walking up to him in the parking lot of his motel. "What's your name?"

He looked at her, and at Ephram, then back at her. He swallowed. "Darryl. And uh what's –"

"Eloise. And this is Benny. We're kind of bored – my friend just likes to watch..."

Darryl's eyes widened. Then he hemmed and hawed and flustered for a minute or two. Finally he said, "Wow. That'd be kind of weird..."

"Actually he doesn't have to watch. He could just listen, in the bathroom. People hear you anyway. In the next room."

"That's true. What the heck."

She could tell he was thinking that he'd have a good story to tell his friends, about the kinky old dude and his weird little mistress.

Darryl glanced at Ephram, who was standing a few paces away. Not looking at them, but staring up at a clutch of stars glimmering in a cloudbreak. Ephram stared at stars a lot and seemed to see things in them. Sometimes he talked to them.

"Uh . . ." Darryl said. "Your place, or . . .?"

"Yours," Ephram said, not taking his eyes from the shining stars.

Darryl led the way. Opened the door for both of them. Hemmed and hawed a bit more. Constance scarcely noticed, as Ephram was lacing up her brain with soft snakes of pleasure, making the feelings slither down her spine and through her groin and up again to nest thickly over the empty place that she used to call her Heart . . . so she couldn't feel the emptiness . . . and she simply took off her clothes and drank some of Darryl's Blue Nun and then let him play with her body for awhile and then she rolled over on top of him . . .

"Oh yeah," he said, "I like it when a girl's on top."

Constance not thinking, just doing, with Ephram's star-glimmery fingers inside her brain like a hand fitting perfectly into a glove; Constance slipping Darryl's penis inside her (rewarded with a blaze of pleasure that made her arch her back, which Darryl mistakenly took for something she got from him) and reached behind her to Ephram as he stepped from the bathroom to give her the knife . . .

The room was dark except for the pushy crowding motion of the TV light and a deader shine that came in through the white-curtained window. Not far away, outside, the freeway made noises. Different cars and trucks had their different pitches. Sometimes a big semi sent a faint shake through the building. The light from a *Pizza Hut* sign – one of the really amazingly high signs towering to be seen from the freeway – shone through the curtains in one corner of the window, and you could see wavery red outlines of some of the letters on the motel room wall. She could make out a *P* and a *Z* and an *H* and a *T*. Darryl had the wall-mounted colour TV on near the foot of the bed, MTV with the sound turned off, one of those fast-edited designer jeans commercials came on, and then Downtown Julie Brown with her hand on her hip, mincing and prancing, *wubba-wubba*, and then a Sting video (she wished she could watch it, she always thought Sting was cute... a flash of punishment for that... then a rewarding flush of pleasure as she thought: No, I'd rather fuck this guy and use the knife). And the noise of a crying baby and angry voices and slamming car doors from the parking lot and a thin honking from the freeway; a splinter of light from a truck flashing its highbeams, caught and spun through the Blue Nun bottle...

She cut off his nipples first. The knife was so sharp, they came off easily. The Niagara of pleasure that Ephram sent through him meshed with horror right in the middle of his face and the confusion was kind of funny (wasn't it?), a logjam of expressions and the blood welling prettily in the bluish TV light. Darryl, of course, briefly tried to escape but that was cut short by Ephram's ghost-hands working in the boy's brain, paralyzing him, then giving him a jolt of pleasure, making him giggle and making his face like The Joker, a horrible smile up to his ears almost, pasted there even when she starts to saw up the middle of his stomach with the knife, opening it up like with a can-opener (Next time, Ephram said, we *will* use a can-opener. and all the time her hips pumping on his cock which stayed hard because Ephram had control of that too, her vagina sucking, milking the semen out of him as the knife pulled the other lifebloods out of the belly and isn't it pretty inside, really, when you look at it just right and feel the molten wax of pleasure up your spine smothering your heart, and *Just get into it,* Constance told herself, it was the only way to get away from what you were doing, just nestle deep inside the pleasure that Ephram gave you . . .

Perhaps, Ephram thought, I'm going too far with her too soon . . . This is the third stupid young man in as many nights and Constance will be losing her brain's capacity for pleasure soon (remarkable how the brain never really lost the capacity for suffering: your delicious irony, my Lord) if he didn't ease up and give her time to restore herself . . . perhaps put her on some sort of tranquilizer for a few days . . . Ephram himself feeling the strain of controlling her and the men. Perhaps that strain making him careless, that and his greed for sensation. Three murders in three days along the same route. He really should get rid of the Porsche; he'd found himself putting it off, one gets attached to a fine car. Soon . . . With luck, the other two bodies hadn't been found yet. Yes, that's it girl, now put the knife in his hands and I'll make him suck on its wet blade so that the blade makes ribbons of his tongue . . .

Ephram, meanwhile, slipping up behind the girl and sliding his mercifully small member up into her anus.

Ha ha, if her father could see her now!

Ephram wondered briefly if the postcard he'd made her write had convinced the police she was just another runaway. It should have. He shouldn't have sent that one, though he'd made her cross out the signal she'd tried to send – and of course he'd punished her severely for that – but he'd been tired, feeling lazy, and they had no more stamps in the shop and he wanted to get it done so he'd sent it off instead of making another card. She'd

95

scribbled over it well, so it shouldn't be a problem. So, he asked himself, why are you letting it nag at you? Concentrate on the pleasures at hand.

But there was another distraction: Ephram saw something from the corner of his eye, that made him freeze. Was it some errant shadow from the TV set?

He turned and looked, and saw it clearly. His cock shrank inside the girl. No, no shadow, or not a shadow merely: it was the Akishra.

He saw them swarming in through the window, wriggling with hideous purpose, ectoplasmic and urgent with hunger, sending out squirming feelers, scouts trying to locate him. The Astral Protection he'd put on himself was fading or ... perhaps the girl had attracted them ... perhaps she had some latent Power ...

The Protection is not enough, at this close proximity, Ephram thought. They'll sense me. They'll know me.

I won't be enslaved again!

He drew back from the bed, doing up his pants, dragging the girl physically away from the dying man on the bed – and then jolting the man *hard* with a pleasure impulse, releasing the energy in him that would draw them over ...

There. The cloud of wrigglers had drifted through the air, were hovering over the bed, descending to feed. They were a young, blind Mass of Akishra and they hadn't sensed Ephram or the girl yet -- or anyway hadn't identified them. They were interested in the transmitter and the boy was transmitting beautifully now, his suffering and pleasure all murkily intermixed. The cloud of Akishra clothing him with their etheric maggotry. Oh Lord, the repulsiveness of their motion, how it ever sickened Ephram.

Now the boy's mind opened. He saw what had happened to him and he perceived the Akishra and his scream made the windows vibrate.

Ephram had got the girl roughly dressed and dragged her out the door. They fled across the parking lot. Behind them someone was shouting. The manager of the motel.

The police would find this particular stupid young man's body. Ephram had to get back to his motel and away before they came out to see who had left this horror . . . Too bad they couldn't see the Akishra, that'd cloud Ephram's trail, ha ha . . .

Well, it was not so grave, Ephram decided, when they'd got the car loaded and were away. No one had noticed them running away, evidently, for they were allowed to depart unmolested.

He put the girl to sleep, so that she slumped, snoring, in her seat, and he drove to the next cluster of generic motels and restaurants, for a rest before beginning again . . .

Alameda

Typical Bay Area weather, Garner thought irritably, as he locked up the house about ten-thirty in the morning, hunching his old brown leather jacket against the moist wind. He went hurriedly to the Econoline van – he'd traded in the Toyota for it, thinking he might need a free place to sleep when his money ran out. He sat behind the wheel, asking himself if there was anything else he should have packed. He kept himself busy that way, with details, so that he didn't think about Constance too much, because if he went crazy he could never hope to find her.

And it was all on him, finding her. It was obvious the police weren't going to be much help. Which was partly his fault: he hadn't written down the license number of that Porsche, when he had the chance. He thought he'd be able to confront the guy and take Constance back. It never occurred to him he'd be struck unconscious before he could utter a word; that Constance would be taken beyond his reach...

Stupid. He should have realized it might be abduction. He should have written the number down. You stupid son of a bitch, he told himself.

He leaned against the van, and took the post card out of his pocket. It was postmarked Fresno, the day before. A picture of the Sunken Gardens. Constance's handwriting on the other side. *Dad I'm okay, don't worry and don't look for me. Am with friends.* There was one line more that had been scribbled over. Then her signature. He had used a pen-eraser on the scribbled-over line. The result was hard to read, but after looking at it for a long time, he was pretty sure the line under the scribble had said, *Please take care of my doggie.* That was a code they'd set up when she'd been twelve and he'd got her fingerprints done and they'd talked about avoiding child-snatchers. She didn't *have* a dog. She didn't even like dogs. Whoever had her, had become suspicious, made her scribble out the signal line.

Of course, Garner had showed the cops the card, pointed out the message she'd tried to plant in it. The Oakland detective had squinted at it and made a wavering motion with his hand in the air. "Maybe, maybe not. Hard to say *what* it says. Can't really make it out. You think it was the signal line but to me it looks just as much like *Please take care of yourself.*"

"Why would she cross that out?"

"Who knows? Maybe she thought it would make you mad, like it was patronizing or something. This card seems to indicate to me that she left voluntarily..."

"Then why did they hit me on the head? My kid would never voluntarily leave me lying there on the ground..."

"Maybe she wasn't there, at that point. Maybe – and this is just as likely – you had the wrong room. And whoever it was, was getting loaded – that happens a lot in those motels – and they were tweaking out with crack paranoia and put out your lights because they thought you were busting in to rob them... We just don't have enough to assume she was kidnapped..."

He'd gone to the Alameda police, the Oakland police, and the FBI, and none of them seemed convinced it was definitely a case of abduction and not runaway. But they were "looking into it." Fuck.

And he'd gone to a couple of memorial societies for kidnapped youngsters. Her picture would appear on milk cartons. He'd stay in touch with them.

Now he was going to look for her himself and it was, maybe, as stupid as not writing down the Porsche's license number. It seemed likely they'd continue going south. The guy seemed less likely a drug-dealer, now. Drug dealers just don't up and leave their territory.

Garner looked up at the house. He had a kid from his therapy group house-sitting for him, an act of faith if ever there was one, and he had paid the rent for three months in advance out of the savings he had, and the rest he had with him in traveller's cheques...

Maybe she'd come back when he was gone. She'd need help and he wouldn't be here, he'd be out on some freeway with his face in a wild goose's ass.

James was going to be here. Give the kid some

responsibility, taking care of the place, and he'd be here watching the house if she came back. Garner would call the house every day.

James. Garner hoped the little son of a bitch didn't try to fuck Constance if she came back.

He slammed the side door of the '77 van. The door didn't latch, slid open again. He got more of a running start on its rollers this time and slammed it so hard the whole van shook and it stayed shut. He walked around to the driver's side and got in. The van started on the first try and he put himself in the stream of traffic for the freeway. Got onto the 880 headed South to San Jose. First step on the trip to Los Angeles. The sky was clumped with low grey clouds. A faint drizzle slipped across the road from time to time; filmy membranes of dirty water. Precipitation would slow traffic, but he almost wished it would really pour down rain.

He tried listening to the radio but every damn song seemed to have some sinister meaning for him, seemed to mock him about Constance. He remembered having read about the two human monsters who'd kidnapped a number of twelve and thirteen year old girls, tortured them to death, raping them in the intervals, and videotaped the whole thing... One of them had gleefully told the cops in his confession about having put an electric drill into the girl's ear and how she flopped about like a fish on a hook as he pushed it in and...

The tears came painfully out of Garner, coming out so hard and thick they hurt.

The motherfucker could be doing anything to her!

Pray, Garner counselled the drug addicts and the alcoholics. Even if you don't believe, pray. Its called *Fake It Till You Make It*, Garner'd tell them. Just pray whether or not you believe in God. You'll reach Something. It'll help.

But those little girls in the hands of those total assholes, those human monsters... You knew they'd prayed for help. But had God helped them? Hell, no.

The tears, achingly, ran dry. His face was sticky and hot. He kept driving. Just to make him feel as if he was doing something for Constance...

He thought about Aleutia and the baby, dead on that table. Just two more casualties to tick off on the endless list, two more taps of the calculator button.

The traffic was heavy. Crenellated rows of condos and ranch homes crowded the hills around the freeway, some of the projects with only a thin fence and thirty feet of dirt separating them from the roar of the freeway; many of them only half constructed. He was stuck for a while behind a double trailer semitruck emblazoned *Miracle Merchandizing*. He knew what that was, he'd seen something about it on the *Good Morning* show. A business that specialized in lighting manufacture and overnight delivery of hot, media-merchandizing, goods. Big money in Bart Simpson dolls, Bart Simpson keychains. Before that, Garfield – some of the cars around him still had the stuffed cartoon cat stuck to their windows trying to claw its way out, very funny. And lately it was *Chomper*, the *Simpsons'* clone show which had the cartoon toddler, Chomper, who ate and drank everything in sight and once, isn't it funny, smoked a whole carton of his alcoholic Mom's cigarettes ... Cut to a beer commercial.

And that semitruck trailer blocking his way was in all probability filled to the gills with Chomper dolls, Chomper keychains, Chomper posters, Chomper chewing gum.

101

Garner had to search for his little girl in this endless sea of irrelevancy and indifference and preoccupied people and deteriorating places. This is crazy, this is hopeless . . .

Not necessarily, Garner told himself He'd been on the streets himself for twelve years. A crank addict, then a downer addict and alcoholic. And there were ways to find people, down near the street level. If the guy was keeping Constance some kind of prisoner it might be that he'd have to hide himself and her in parts of town where he could get away with it easily. And if Garner was right, the son of a bitch would go to L.A . . .

Line up the *ifs* like toy soldiers, move them around the way you want, try to make yourself feel better. It's still just playing with *ifs*.

It's better than doing *nothing*.

He wanted a drink. If ever he had a reason to drink, he had one now. How long had it been? How many years?

He was *owed* a drink.

He laughed at himself, bitterly, and shook his head. Mentally changed the subject.

Suppose Constance *had* gone voluntarily. Who knew for sure what went on in her head? There was a lot more to her than the California airhead in the pump hairdo and the ankle bracelets and a greater interest in watching *Dynasty* re-runs than in reading. There had to be so much more under the surface. And in trying to give Constance "her space" all the time, he had maybe lost touch with her completely. They'd talked, they spent time together, but lately it had been superficial. The apparent shallowness of the girl was probably just a result of her being a teenager, with all the stresses of wanting to be liked.

Garner, himself, in high school, had been the school nonconformist, had worked strenuously on *not* being liked. Had been borderline pathological in his insistence on autonomy. Constance *wanted* to belong and his stupid prejudice had made him perceive that as shallow, kneejerk conformity. When in fact it was just healthy, human nature. Something the misfit in Garner was never comfortable with.

He ached, thinking about it. He'd lost her. It was easy to hate the bastard who'd taken her. It felt better to lay it all on the prick in the Porsche.

She hadn't run away. He just couldn't believe it. He knew – he *knew* – that she had been *taken*.

For no particular reason, he remembered when she was a toddler, the first time he'd taken her into a wading pool, a little plastic pool with the Flintstones in their caveman swimming togs printed all over it, the blue water a foot deep, and she'd been scared of the little pool at first. And why shouldn't she be? A toddler could drown in a foot of water, if she fell face down and panicked. If her Dad didn't watch over her all the time . . .

The guy might have his hands on her, right now.

To keep from screaming, Garner began a marathon of talking earnestly to God, praying for everything, everyone, as well as for Constance; for himself, he begged for strength and guidance and patience.

It took him another twenty minutes to get around that fucking truck.

Culver City, Los Angeles

"Where the hell did you get that?" Jeff asked, sitting at his breakfast bar next to Prentice. "Isn't it illegal for you to have that shit?"

"Maybe," Prentice said, distractedly, running his finger down the scribbled doctors' evaluations on the photocopies he'd fanned out on the table, "but I was married to her, right?"

"You bribe somebody?"

"Desk nurse. Gave him a hundred bucks which probably went to crack cocaine, from the look of him. It's pretty scary, what I hear about people in hospitals, nurses and doctors and orderlies, using hard drugs. They're gonna be pulling out your organs and selling them on the blackmarket to get drug money or something... Anyway, yeah, the guy photocopied Amy's files..." He tapped his finger on one copy-faded line. "Check it out."

Instead, Jeff got up to make capuccino. He had an espresso machine and a milk-steamer. He was going to be buying a house soon. Prentice felt resentment and jealousy chasing tails through him, and he stuffed it away, concentrated on the admissions form, reading aloud to Jeff: "Patient repeats certain phrases at intervals, eg: *The Morman won't let me come home*... patient is frequently labile..." Blah blah *blah*, the usual psychoguff... But check that out: 'The Morman'."

"The Morman?" Jeff said, over the hissing of the steamer. "Like... The More Man, you mean?"

"It says 'the Morman'. But yeah. She probably was saying, The More Man. Like Lonny said." Prentice waited for Jeff to react.

Bingo. Jeff turned, stared at him. "Come on. Mitch and Amy hooked up with the same guy? Bullshit."

"Hey – they both mutilated themselves, right? More or less the same way." Prentice smiled in quiet triumph. "I went to the Pinkertons, I was thinking of hiring them to investigate the whole shebang, but they're too fucking

104

expensive. But – they do traces on credit cards and stuff for a pretty reasonable fee. So I had 'em trace the account she had that Gold Card on – it came from Sam Denver."

"You're shitting me!"

"You know, that's a revolting expression. No, I'm not 'shitting you'."

"Who are you, Miss Manners? Listen, bro – let's go out to the Ranch. No more talking about it, let's do it. Denver's ranch. See if we can find Mitch. I mean, right fucking *now*. Just look into it. If it doesn't pan out, we go to the cops."

"Just go out there? Just us?"

"Hey – chances are the Denvers are like my old man used to say about spiders: 'They're more scared of you than you are of them.' They won't want any trouble." He sipped his capuccino. Sprinkled more chocolate on the foam. "And I got a gun, bro. I got a bunch a guns. I got a fuckin .357, they want to play games –"

'You been playing paintball too often, man. Spend too much time writing action pictures. *Dirty Harry*'s a fantasy, Jeff. But yeah. Let's go check it out. Only I want my capuccino first, with extra chocolate."

Near Malibu

Jeff was driving like a fucking lunatic, Prentice thought. There was a slate of thin cloud over the sky, but it was hot, the light suffused with an eerie sameness over the dry hills, the manzanita and stunted pine and purplish underbrush, the punky stands of yucca spears – all of it sometimes broken up by improbable squares of lushly green, manicured lawn where an irrigated estate or gated cluster of luxury condos wedged in between hills.

The Cabriolet made a razzing sound as it attacked the curves, fishtailing from time to time. Maybe Jeff's way of working up his nerve for the confrontation...

They had directions from Jeff's agent, who used to come out here, years earlier. But Jeff almost missed the dirt road. They were supposed to look for a redwood mailbox on a big, four sided post made of smooth quartz river stones. They saw the post at the last moment – Prentice spotted it and stamped an imaginary brake, yelling, "Shit – there it is!"

Jeff hit the brake and the tyres made crooked marks on the cracked white highway, Prentice grabbing the dashboard to keep from slamming his head into the windshield. "Coulda told me sooner," Jeff muttered.

"Not at those speeds, A.J. Foyt."

They backed up, turned onto the dirt road. There was a little gravel left in its deeper ruts. Jeff paused to look at the stone post. It was almost hidden in high fiddlehead ferns and sage. The wooden mailbox was gone. On the concrete post, the rounded quartz stones glowed faintly in the sunlight.

"Gotta be it," Jeff said. "They really let it go to seed." The car made a noise like a trumpeting baby elephant as he changed gears. They gunned up the road, pluming dust, tailbones banging on the seat springs as the car jounced in the ruts. The trees got higher nearer the top of the hill; there were hoary palm trees, here, transplanted long ago, looking over the shoulders of mistletoe-darkened oaks. Another curve and they came to a high, dust-coated hurricane fence, with a heavily padlocked gate made of the same stuff. Ten yards beyond it was a stone fence and a black, wrought iron gate figured with rusting cherubims holding a bullet-pocked sign that had once said, Welcome. Over the

106

cherubims was a wrought-iron figure of two crossed skeleton keys. The Doublekey Ranch.

Jeff pulled up in the shade of an overhanging bower of roses. Big roses, so red they were almost black. Looking closer, as the dust cloud parted around them, Prentice saw that the roses were overgrown up a dead oak tree; its trunk and lower branches a black, warped skeleton for the fleshy roses.

From the midst of the rose bush came a wet, throaty snarling. No. It wasn't from the bush – why had he thought it was? It was coming from beyond the hurricane fence. Two Dobermans with spiked collars were running alongside the fence, snarling, teeth bared. They jumped at the fence, making it ring like chain mail, throwing their full bodies against it; shaking dust loose with each clank and making both Prentice and Jeff twitch back in their seats.

Rose petals filtered down from above, pattering softly into the car.

The dogs threw themselves at the fence again. Rose petals rained once more. Prentice looked up and saw that vines of another rosebush clung to the top of the fence.

A black man, well over six feet and three hundred pounds, wearing a generic security guard's uniform, stepped from a small guardhouse at the iron gates and shouted at the dogs. They cringed back, wincing as if afraid of being whipped. The guard came striding up toward the fence, a shotgun aslant across his tubby middle, his eggplant pate shiny with sweat, dark glasses strobing. "Ya'll got an appointment?" he bellowed.

Jeff looked at the glove compartment, where his gun was hidden.

Prentice said softly, "Way too soon to even think about it, Jeff."

Jeff nodded. Prentice could see him gather his courage. He took a deep breath and got out of the Cabriolet. "Hi, how ya doin'!" he called, as the two men approached each other from opposite sides of the metal fence.

'Ya'll got an appointment?" the black man repeated.

Jeff shook his head. "I . . . I'm Jeff Teiltelbaum. I had word that my brother is here and I need to see him. I'm his legal guardian. His name's Mitch Teitelbaum."

'Mitch Tuttle . . .?"

"Teitelbaum."

'Lemme call up. I'm sorry about these damn dogs." He turned on his heel, slapping his thigh. "Come on, hounds, up wid me. Lesgo." The dogs trotted after him. Prentice could see a metal rod strapped into the man's belt that might be a cattle prod. He walked laboriously over to the guardhouse and reached in to a wallphone.

Prentice said, "This place is a paranoid's delight." Jeff nodded.

The guard came back three minutes later shaking his head. "Got no Mitch Teitelbaum here – hasn't been here neither. You maybe on the wrong road."

Prentice called, "This is the Denver place, right?"

The guard turned his mirror-glassed eyes toward him. "Surely. But your boy, he ain't here." He turned and walked away with an air of dismissal.

"Could we talk to someone from the house, the Denvers," Jeff began, "or –"

The guard turned back to them but kept walking, backwards. "No sir, not today. Mrs. Denver not feeling good. Can't have visitors. She's just not up to it. I already asked." He turned his back on them again.

At the guard house he hesitated, then turned toward them, raising the shotgun so its barrel rested casually

108

against his right shoulder. Not so casually, really.

Jeff hissed, "Shit, shit, *shit*," under his breath as he turned and got into the car. He started the car, backed it up, went slowly back down the road. Making a statement with his slowness: You didn't run us off, I'm leaving because I want to.

"Look, let's go to the cops," Prentice said, when they got to the edge of the highway. "Mitch was out of his gourd on something. Maybe these assholes are giving it to him. He could end up dead, like Amy."

Jeff stopped the car on the verge of the old concrete road. Sat there, staring at it. "Fuck the cops!"

"I know how you feel about them –"

"Especially LAPD. They're total fuckers. And I swore I wouldn't go to them. I swore to Lonny."

"That's just stupid, man. What is this, Tom Sawyer and Huck swearing on the bones of a pirate? For Mitch's sake, let's go to the cops."

Jeff made a long sigh. He coughed, spat dust over the side of the car. Finally, he changed gears so violently Prentice feared for the transmission, and the car bounced up onto the highway. "Okay. Okay, fuck it. Let's try the cops."

Near Malibu. The Doublekey Ranch.

Late afternoon. But it was shadowy in Mitch's room; no light on, and the rosebushes around the window took all the sun for themselves. It was quiet, except for the sounds of ripping wallpaper and, briefly, in the distance, the sound of a car – a sports car, by the sound of it changing gears and gunning away.

Mitch was peeling wallpaper. Starting it with a thumbnail, then peeling it away like the strips of skin he'd pulled from his own ribs, a few days before.

Fucking roses on the wallpaper. Drooping rosebuds between that spiky shape from European shields. Let's see what's under it . . .

He wasn't really seeing the wallpaper. His head was churning with pictures. Images of hurting himself, cutting himself, the nosing knife in his forearm. He tried to remember how it had started, how he'd got into something that sick. But it was like trying to see through a fogged window. It wouldn't come clear. Not quite.

Just bits and pieces. The More Man telling him, *Basically, it's a mystical discipline.* It had sounded heavy, then. Now the phrase sounded totally bogus to him. Mystical discipline, bullshit. That kind of talk was supposed to fake him into seeing himself as some messiah type guy. *Christ's scourging and crucifixion immediately preceded his exaltation*, The More Man had said. And he'd talked about fakirs who laid on beds of nails and saints who whipped themselves all day. *But the secret is, if you do it right, it's not painful! Mostly not. When it does hurt, it only hurts you for a while. Once you're in touch with that higher place, you can feel anything. Heal anything. The Spirit will heal you . . .*

They'd been on some terrace at a beachside condo. The More Man in shades, holding Mitch enthralled. *I want to make you a star, Mitch – but that takes a godlike transformatian. To be a real superstar takes total discipline. Discipline need not be painful. It need not hurt – it needs only the courage to explore . . . This body is not your true body, so what you do to it doesn't matter. Your true body is ectoplasmic, Mitch. It's ethereal, a higher thing that cannot be hurt . . .*

And then he'd given Mitch the Probe, just a big silvery knife. And when Mitch hesitated, this girl just sort of drifted out onto the terrace and, holy shit, it was Jeff's buddy Tom Prentice's wife, Amy, wearing a bikini, tanned but her body with all these mooncoloured marks on her, and she'd taken the knife (*Mitch peeled another long spiral of wallpaper away*) and knelt beside him and put her hand on Mitch's thigh – instant hard-on – and, with the other hand started carving her breasts with the knife.

Mitch wanted to vault over the terrace railing and run, when the blood started guttering along the edge of her bikini top, curling down the round sides of her breasts. He saw the look on her face, the most totally awesome ecstasy and he thought, *The bitch is sick . . .*

Until Sam Denver said, "Feel what she is feeling. Touch her arm, and it'll come through to you."

"She – no. I can't. She'll stab me."

"No. No she won't, Mitch. I promise you."

So Mitch reached out and touched her arm – and the feeling went into him like a hot wet tongue running over his nervous system. The feeling expanded from there; it encompassed him with a monstrous pleasure.

He was feeling what she was feeling, yes, he could even feel the hot, intense places where the knife dug in – where the pleasure was as intense as the flame of a welding torch, you couldn't look at it directly. He could feel her breasts (*peeling another strip of wallpaper away*) as if they were his own; could feel the blade slicing them an inch deep here and there . . .

Could feel his pussy getting wet between his legs.

He wrenched away from her, sick with gender disorientation. But wanting more of the pleasure. Immediately.

"Give me the knife," he said.

The next morning, he'd felt wrung out, used up,

111

depressed. The pleasures took their toll. The wounds? He couldn't feel them – not back then. He felt fear simmering slowly in a steel pot of emptiness.

But by the next night he was ready for more...

"Got some other little things I want you to do for me, first," Denver said. "Just to show us your devotion. Your dedication. There's a certain street..."

Now, Mitch wrenched another strip of paper from the wall and ground his teeth, shook himself, though the movement sent shards of pain spinning through him, to drive out the memory of what the More Man had made him do on that street.

But once you've felt the Head Syrup, *The Spirit's Reward*, the More Man called it, you'll do anything to get it back.

You want more, the More Man had said, *And it's all right to want more. They try to teach us that we should only want a little as it's doled out to us – but it's a lie, a conspiracy to make us slaves to Society, Mitch. The Spirit wants us to have more... and more and more...*

The slowed-down sound of electricity crackling. That's what tearing paper sounded like to Mitch, as he tore away another uneven strip of wallpaper. You could smell electricity, a kind of electrical burning smell, when the Reward was coming...

He'd cleared an area of the wall about a yard square, next to the head of his bed. Under it, was just more wallpaper. Another kind of rose pattern. Shit.

He wondered vaguely if they'd punish him for it. Probably not. They probably didn't expect him to be sane.

He had no idea why he wanted to strip away the wallpaper.

On the left side of the flame-shaped patch where

112

he'd stripped the outer layer of wallpaper away, the under-paper showed a long, drip-shaped brown stain.

His hands started to shake, as he tore away more paper on that side, revealing the old wallpaper beneath. More brown stain. Drippy brown stain. Where rainwater had seeped?

No . . . But he kept clearing it away till he was sure that it was a splash that had come from the bed. You could tell by the way it was splattered outward from the top right of the bed. He pinched a piece of the discoloured underpaper with his finger tips, and brought it to his nose. A smell of rot and iron. It was blood.

He thought, *What'd you expect, dumbshit?*

But he kept stripping away wallpaper, revealing more and more of the splash – and then a place where the underpaper had been breached. Clawmarks, four of them, ran down the wall here, to the plaster beneath. In one spot exposing a crack in the wall. As soon as he'd exposed it, he felt a little puff of cool air from the crack. And a moment later heard the voices.

And the edge of the crack was outlined in light.

He bent, and pressed his right eye to the crack (*an icepick, there'll be an icepick spike coming through the crack into his eye – no, shake that bullshit off . . .*) and squeezed his other eye shut. He could just make out pink shapes moving, in the next room . . . fleshy pink . . .

It took a moment for his eye to adjust. Then a piece of the neighbouring room came into focus. A man and a woman fucking on a bed. Fucking without rhythm on the bare mattress. He couldn't make out what they were saying. There was someone else, too, coming into Mitch's narrow field of vision for just a moment, moving to stand by the edge of the bed . . .

The More Man? He wasn't sure. He could only see an arm, a bit of his side. Then the guy moved back, into the shadows, and there were only the man and woman on the bed.

The couple on the bed were bleeding. They moved in sex like someone crawling across a desert. Like each movement was a fight with exhaustion. Each thrust a heave and a slump, a weak convulsion that was only technically sex. He could make out the knobs of the guy's vertebrae on his back. He looked so skinny, so used up. Blood runnelled down from a torn ear . . . the ear hanging by a flap . . .

They were crying, too. Weeping softly, the both of them. "Please," the man on the bed pleaded. "Let us stop. I can't . . . any more . . ."

"Yes please, please, please," the woman sobbed. "Just let us rest, we'll do a lot more later. A long, rasping, wracking sob. *"Please."*

"More," said the man watching from the shadows. "More. More. More. More."

Then the motion of the two on the bed changed. The whole quality of their movement changed. Mitch tasted burning electricity, shivered with lust for the Head Syrup, as the man and woman begin to giggle – hoarse, moronic giggles. Then they began to hump faster, writhing in puppeted semblance of sexual delight.

The woman's leg was twitching . . . spasming. Her arm flopping like a live fish dropped on hot coals. The man turned his face from her – Mitch couldn't quite see the guy's face but he could see and hear what was coming out of it: a thick vomit of blood.

Vomiting blood but still he humped into her.

Mitch felt the strength go out of his knees. He slid down the wallpaper to the floor.

114

Then he was up, lurching across the room, throwing himself at the window frame, smashing at it so that glass flew. But he couldn't get it open, it was completely blocked off...

He stared at the splintery geometries of broken glass on the floor by the wall. He could use a piece of glass to slash his jugular...

But then he felt the watcher. He turned, and no one was there, but he could feel the More Man watching him, and he could sense the hand of the Spirit poised over him. Waiting to punish.

They'd never let him kill himself. He'd never be able to get the glass to his throat. The More Man would never let him get away as easily as that...

Culver City, Los Angeles

"Hi – I'm Sargeant Sparks. I'm looking for Jeff Teitelbaum...?"

Even the cops here had the irritating California habit of making statements sound like questions, Prentice thought, looking up at the open living room door. *So, like, I'm going into therapy tomorrow? And I've got all these abandonment issues?*

Well, Prentice always wanted to ask, do you or don't you?

Prentice got up from his perch on the arm of the sofa and stood awkwardly trying to decide if he should let the guy in or wait for Jeff to come out of the bathroom. "Uh, yeah –"

But then the bathroom door banged open and Jeff crossed to the front door. "Yeah, officer, right here," Jeff said, opening the screen door for the cop who stood there. "C'mon in."

Officer Sparks was shaped like a bowling pin, narrow shoulders and wide hips. He wore thick-rimmed designer glasses and an air of weary authority. He had a sad, panda face. He came in carrying a clipboard.

Every so often the walkie-talkie clipped to his belt muttered to itself and cleared its throat of static.

"Have a seat, officer," Jeff said, rubbing his palms against the hips of his khaki shorts. He was nervous, working too hard at not actively hating the cop for being a cop.

"We've been looking into your report about your brother Mitch Teitelbaum?"

"Right," Jeff said "Mitch." He stood by the door as if ready to open it for the cop again as soon as possible.

"And we've gone out to talk to Mr. Denver?"

"You personally?" Prentice asked. He wasn't sure why it seemed important.

"Hm? Yes sir, I went myself. Me and another officer. We came to the conclusion that the boy is not there and Mr. Denver doesn't know where he is. But maybe I should ask – have you heard from him?" He smiled with one side of his mouth. "We're looking for him, too. He's supposed to be in Juvie Hall. For all know he's in the next room sleeping it off."

"He's not here and we haven't heard from him," Jeff said. His voice flat. "What do you mean, sleeping it off?"

"He was doing some time for –" He glanced at his clipboard. "Possession of cocaine. Chances are, he's on a run somewhere."

"He's not a drug addict, he's not 'on a run'." Jeff crossed his arms over his chest, then dropped them by his side, then crossed them over his chest again. "Did you guys search the Denver place?"

"No sir, we didn't have a warrant and we'd need a lot more to go on than the word of a kid you talked to in Juvie Hall."

Prentice considered bringing Amy into it. Her

117

turning up dead, her connection to Denver. The credit card. The stories of the More Man. But it would seem irrelevant to the cop. One thing at a time, please. Just the facts. And it sounded kind of silly to Prentice, now, when he imagined explaining the connection.

"That guy Denver is up to some weird shit," Jeff said. "I *know* he is."

"Seemed like a regular Malibu producer type to me," the cop said. "Which means he might *be* up to some weird shit, but probably not kidnapping. I get a feeling about these things, I learn to respect those feelings, you know? The kid is not out at the Ranch. That's my feeling... You have any evidence of kidnapping you haven't given us?"

Jeff chewed his lip. Finally he said, "No. But –"

Sparks scribbled on his clipboard, then glanced around, as if it had just occurred to him that they might be in "possession of cocaine" themselves, since Mitch had been. Thoughtfully, he said, "You have any evidence of kidnapping, best thing is to go to the FBI. One of their specialties." He looked at Jeff. "Do you think, sir, that Mitch could be hanging with some of his drug-using buddies? I mean – we have to assume, given his record –"

"That's all. Forget it, man. We should have known better," Jeff said sharply, opening the screen door so hard its hinges squealed.

The cop stood up, glancing around the apartment, stalling. "I was going to ask if I could use the phone –"

"They got one at the donut shop," Jeff said, gesturing toward the door.

The cop's jaws worked and his cheeks mottled. "This isn't a good way, sir, to get help from the police," he said, crossing the room.

118

"Nothing from nothing is nothing," Jeff said, slamming the door after the guy. "Christ!"

He and Prentice looked at each other. Then burst out laughing. Prentice's laughter more genuine. "'They got one at the donut shop!'" Prentice repeated, shaking his head, laughing.

Then he stopped laughing, and said, "Hey."

Jeff was crossing to the kitchen. He paused and looked over. "What?"

"He said, *The kid's not out at the Ranch*. That was the way that fat-ass cop put it. Like . . ."

Jeff nodded. "Familiar, calling it *the Ranch*. Like he was using a nickname for it. Like he knew the place pretty well . . ."

Los Angeles

Ephram was tired. But they were nearly there. It was eight p.m., just getting dark in the California summer, and the Porsche was flying along the Santa Monica Freeway, on its way to Venice. There were more palm trees, now, and the traffic had eased. The sky was going brown-violet at the horizon.

He glanced at Constance. He felt the ache, again, that had been plaguing him. Her eyes were sunken. Why did this bother him? He knew it would happen. It always happened. Her expression was composed and happy. The way she kept it.

Ephram shifted down as the traffic thickened, people up ahead rubbernecking a minor accident.

She hates me, he thought.

Then he thought: No, she doesn't. Because I have her soul in my hands, and I make it perform for me like a small, trained animal; I squeeze it and reshape it

119

like gelatin. She feels what she is commanded to feel. And it certainly wouldn't matter, if she did hate me.

The traffic slowed to a crawl; his attention was freed up. So he reached into her. Without even looking at her, no acknowledgement from him about what he was doing but a faint, smug smile on his lips; he reached into her brain with the 'plasmic fingers and squeezed her pleasure centre. She squirmed on her seat and moaned. He prompted her and, accordingly, she said: "I love you, Ephram."

He looked at her. No, she didn't love him.

He could make her mean it, though. He reached more deeply into her . . .

"I love you, Ephram," she said, turning to look at him, her eyes glazing with devotion, with sentiment. But her voice betraying a hint of desperation.

A black cloud swirled inside him. "No. you don't."

He reached over and grabbed her hand and began to squeeze her fingers together, hard. She whimpered with pain. "Now you love me?" he demanded. "When I do this to you?"

"Yes!"

He squeezed harder. Could feel the bones in her hand on the verge of cracking. She cried out.

He hissed, "*Now* you love me?"

"Yes. Yes." No pleasure in her now, just pain and fear and the steel corset of his command: *Tell me you love me*.

He let go of her hand, but reached under her skirt, grabbed her pubis, through the filmy panties and began to twist the soft handful of skin and flesh. "Now you love me?"

"Yes. Yes. Yes!"

She experienced no masochistic enjoyment of this whatsoever. He could see that clearly.

He twisted her crotch again. Harder. "You hate me."

"No, I love you."

"Hate me."

"Love you!"

He could let go of her mind and see what she said. She'd probably still say she loved him, out of fear.

"You disgust me," he said, letting go of her.

Then he gave her a charge of pleasure, to keep her quiet. She made a low, humming sound and nestled deeper into the leather of the bucket seats.

Maybe, he thought, if I spent enough time at it, I could make her really sincerely love me, giving her no option but that. Enough pressure on the mind would bend it into any shape at all. And that would be sincere love, wouldn't it? What sort of ridiculous contortions did people go though – and put others through – to make people love them, in ordinary relationships? This was more honest.

It would be real love. As much as there was such a thing as real love . . .

He wished it were night, so he could see the stars, look for guidance in the secret constellations. The sunset was taking its languorous, smog-blurred time. The lights of the city were glimmering brighter in the twilight. The drug dealers would be out on the street . . . And some of Denver's people, too, would be there . . .

Probably stupid to come to Denver's town. Could I be steering myself to self destruction, somehow? he wondered. Why did it matter so much what the girl felt today?

What was wrong with him?

He gave himself a small jolt of pleasure – something he was very cautious about doing, normally. Didn't want to bum himself out.

But he felt better, almost immediately. The evening took on a different cast. It went from tragedy to comedy.

When they drove up beside the traffic accident, they had a good long look It was worse than he'd imagined. There was blood and broken glass.

If he'd been here at the time, he could have made the victims of the traffic accident enjoy the crash, the mangling. Have to try that sometime. That'd be funny. A little auto-motive psychic tampering. That'd be a gas, ha ha.

The bitch hates me.

The San Fernando Valley

"I'm sorry, sir, we were told *invitations only*. You got to have a printed invite." He was a stocky, gum-chewing kid of about nineteen in a Burns Security uniform, with walkman earphones pulled down around his neck. He'd stopped them walking up the drive to Arthwright's place. It was a long, circular drive leading to a modern, jutting house with as many round windows as square ones. In the balmy evening, soft red and blue "Malibu" lighting painted blush and eyeshadow on the house's facade. The drive was ornamented with a cactus garden and miniature palms. Jags and Rolls-Royces and BMWs and Corvettes and the occasional Volvo lined the drive, nose to tail. "You can stay, sir," the security guard was saying to Jeff, "but –" He looked apologetically at Prentice and shrugged. "Sorry."

Jeff said, "This is bullshit, this guy is my partner and he's a good friend of Arthwright's –" Both exaggerations. "– and Arthwright's gonna be pissed if he doesn't get in. He didn't know Tom was in town –"

122

"Forget it, Jeff," Prentice said. This was typical of Jeff – and of Prentice. Jeff was a pusher, a don't-take-no hustler; Prentice was a more cautious angler.

The guard was squaring his shoulders and shaking his head, when Jeff spotted Arthwright stepping out the gate to say goodbye to someone. Arthwright's voice came to them distantly. "I just wished you coulda stayed longer, Sol – it's so great to see ya –"

"Hey Zack! *Zack!*" Jeff fairly shrieked it.

Prentice winced. "Christ, Jeff, forget it!"

Arthwright was about to go back through the gate – he looked up, spotted Jeff, and strolled over, one hand in a pocket of his casual dinner jacket – worn with jeans – the other scratching the back of his head. "What's the problem – um, you're Jeff, right?"

"Yeah, man. Jeff Teitelbaum. You know my buddy Tom Prentice here – we're having some trouble getting past the Gestapo –"

The guard heaved a theatrical sigh. "You told me no invite no entrance, Mr. Arthwright."

"That's okay, Billy, I got this one covered. Keep at it." Arthwright waved for Jeff and Prentice to follow him.

"Look, I don't mean to crash the place, Zack," Prentice began. "Jeff seemed to think since he had an invite it was for two –"

"Sure, sure, no prob," Arthwright said, leading them in through the wooden backyard gate. There was a TV camera mounted on a pole above the gate post. Prentice could feel its cold lens watching the back of his neck as they went in.

"Make yourself to home," Arthwright said, in a mimicry of a generic country accent, "and I'll get you a drink." He stepped up to a small, portable bar that

123

had been rolled in on casters, spoke to the bartenders, good-looking Mexican fellows in white tuxedos.

Prentice looked around. Jeff had said it was a Pool Party, but no one was in the pool. No one was even in a swimming suit. They milled about the ornamental-tile verge of the pool with cocktails and little plates of mesquite grill, or sprawled in aluminium loungers, in the soft rippling of reflected chlorine-tinted pool-lights. Soft Mexican music played from hidden speakers.

"Our special Sangria," Arthwright said, returning with a frosted glass in each hand. He passed them to Jeff and Prentice, winked, and said, "Party hearty." And vanished into the house.

"He wasn't pleased," Prentice said, feeling humiliated by the whole episode. "We probably pissed him off. And I'm trying to get a deal with him."

"He's probably embarrassed you didn't get an invitation," Jeff said. "Don't worry about it."

"Last thing you want to do is embarrass a guy like that." He forced himself to add, "But thanks for getting me in."

"You hungry?" Jeff asked. "I'm starved. But I don't like this mesquite stuff. Trendy bullshit. They had catered Dim Sum at the Studio's release party –"

"And Dim Sum's not trendy? You must be kidding. It's like Sushi. Most Americans can't stand that stuff but they choke it down –"

"Hey I fuckin' love Sushi, man. God, check out that platinum blonde. Holy shit. God, do the legs never stop on her? Be still, my heart."

"Your heart's not the organ in question."

"Oh, listen to Mr. Sensitive. Boy, you stupped so many of these bimbos –"

"Not *these*, I'm sorry to say. You think maybe

124

that one's had surgery? Her breasts are too perfect."

"Not necessarily. There're more beautiful girls – oh God look at that one, half Japanese and half black. That's, like, the most beautiful combination – uh, anyway," Jeff went on, after breathlessly gulping his Sangria, "there really are more beautiful girls in Los Angeles. It's the movies, they draw 'em like a magnet. For seventy some years now. All that money, all that glamour draws 'em, and they come here and get married and they have kids and there's a whole gene pool of incredible women here –"

"And guys who look like that one." Prentice nodded toward a tanned, muscled young Adonis in a muscle shirt and loose, fashionable, San Francisco tie-dye pants. He strolled by, talking about His New Project with an anorexic model-who's-really-an actress.

"Guys who look like that make me sick and they should all die," Jeff said, joking but with a spice of real envy.

"Half of these people probably had cosmetic surgery, man. Five years ago all these L.A. Jewish Princesses had their noses clipped and straightened – now it's *fashionable* to have a prominent nose with a little bump so they're having the bumps put back! I'm serious!"

Jeff and Prentice wandered slowly through the crowd, catching bits of conversations, checking out the Looks. A group of tanned, muscletoned people with elaborate razorcuts were passionately arguing about the benefits of free weights as compared to Nautilus machines. Another group advised one another on where to get Sushi without any worms in it. There were trendy punks too, the Beverly Hills variety with all their rebellion acquired in expensive Melrose shops; there were a great many people in white peon shirts, with raw crystals on thin gold around their necks. At least half the crowd drank Perrier and Calistoga instead of cocktails and Sangria and the Mexican beer. Only once did Prentice spot two people disappearing into the bathroom together. "Hardly anyone does cocaine anymore," Prentice said, "And that's good, and health is in so a lot of people don't drink, and that's okay, but it's like they all replaced it with Narcissism. Even the women are body builders."

Jeff nodded. "I'm getting back into working out myself. Hey, we sneer about it cause we're in bad shape. I'd love to look like Mr. Perfect over there, I admit it. But no way I'm gonna give up drinking. I'm gonna get that bartender to put a big shot of tequila in this thing."

"I'm with you, man."

They went to the bar, stiffened their drinks, and ran into a few of Jeff's friends and a line producer Prentice had worked with. A couple of drinks later, Prentice began to relax. The Mexican music was replaced by another trendy appurtenance, a House Music DJ who played mostly hip-hop mixed with 60s Motown classics. A dozen couples danced self-consciously beside the pool. Arthwright waved cheerily at Prentice as the producer threaded through the crowd. This time Arthwright seemed genuinely friendly. Maybe this was the moment to hit him up about commissioning the script. Or at least get some kind of feedback.

No. Chances were Arthwright hadn't read it yet and, though lots of Business was done at parties, it wasn't initiated by a guy lower on the pecking order. Talk of business at a social event had to be among equals, or initiated by the holder of power; the one clinging to the higher rung. Anyway, Arthwright had gone from view, now, sucked into the social vortex.

But he reappeared minutes later with the platinum blonde in tow. She was a tall, busty, blue-eyed woman, tanned and leggy, very much the California girl except for the black lace see through corset under her open red shorty jacket; the black lace corset was more of a New York club-scene look. She wasn't wearing any crystals, at least. She had ceramic Mexican Festival of the Dead ear-rings shaped like happy skulls, and figured-silver snake bracelets with little emerald chips for their eyes, and a rather cryptic tattoo on one shoulder. He couldn't quite make out the pattern . . .

"Tom, this is Lissa," Arthwright said, grinning like one of the Mexican skulls. "She wanted to meet you – she's a fan of *Broken Windows!*"

"Really? A woman of rare taste," Prentice said, "especially if you actually bought a ticket in the five minutes before it went to video." Trying for charming self deprecation.

She smiled. There was a ruby in her one of her incisors. "Oh yeah. I bought a ticket and everything."

Arthwright had drifted away and Prentice felt at a loss for a moment. She looked at him with finely tuned expectancy. He went for it. "You one of the 12-step crowd that only drinks mineral water, or can I get you a drink?"

"I'd really love a beer," she said. Her voice was husky, warm, its tone seeming to say, *Don't worry about it. Just take it easy and we'll be fine.*

He went hurriedly to the bar. Jeff was at the other end, hitting on a skinny girl with Mayan designs cut into the hair on the sides of her head. Ordering the beer, Prentice had a moment of uncertainty about whether to include the slice of lime; lime with beer had gone from hip know-how to unhip fad, lately, but she might expect it. He discarded the lime, and came back to her with the beer, and she smiled and said, "Dead on."

Prentice was feeling better about the party all the time. Sure, the girl was probably going to be a typical L.A. air-head, but what the hell. Take some time and live, man, he told himself. Maybe the sense of emergency that'd been dogging him was a phantom. Maybe Mitch's disappearance wasn't really his problem and it wasn't so important. Maybe it was time he put Amy out of his head too. Because there was nothing he could do about her. And as a lot of L.A. bumper stickers said, *Guilt sucks*.

"So – you work with Zack?" he asked. As if he were on a first name basis with Arthwright.

"Well, not yet. I'm a model. But really I'm an actress . . ."

He nodded mechanically – then she giggled behind her beer bottle. "You nod so gravely, but I saw the look in your eyes. I was kidding. I'm not a model or an actress. I'm a secretary at the studio. But Zack fucked me a couple of times and, in consequence, he feels like he has to invite me to parties so he doesn't feel like a shit."

He almost choked on his drink.

"I'm sorry," she went on. "Am I supposed to be less candid than that?"

"No, no – that's great –" He laughed. "You got me twice. Once with bullshit and once with the truth."

"Yeah. You're fun. Maybe I can say something to make you trip and fall into the pool."

"Have mercy, okay?"

"Oh, all right. I really did like *Broken Windows*.

I thought I saw that funny-and-sad middle period of Truffaut's in there."

"Yep. You got my influence on a platter. That period of Truffaut and – sometime I'd like to do an updating of Noel Coward."

"Noel Coward for the 90s – that's almost a high concept pitch. Except the illiterate MBA's that run things around here never read him or saw his plays."

"Good point," he admitted. "You like Kurosawa?"

The conversation veered between film makers and novelists and painters, and Prentice felt good about it. He felt he was coming off up to date and reasonably witty. Necessary groundwork for getting laid.

The innuendo flickered from time to time, the flirtation, the lingering moments of eye contact. Then she said, "Hey – let's go look at Arthwright's etchings. I wanta show you something . . ." She led him away by the wrist as Jeff watched, catching Prentice's eye to put on a comical look of disgusted envy.

Near Malibu

The same moment: another party. A flame-twisted shadow of the party at Arthwright's . . .

Mitch was watching it out the window, peering between rose-vines. There was music playing, that foreign sounding music with its slightly-warped record but an unwavering beat. There were people dancing but they had the look of extras dancing in a rehearsal for a movie, just going through the motions in an absent sort of way. There were knots of people talking with drinks in their hands, but they all seemed forced and furtive; and each one glanced, now and then, toward the doors of the guest house. Or toward the green, green darkness of the pool.

There was a wind; the roses nodded heavily on their vines. Trees at the edge of the backyard, their clutch of leaves scaly with the slippery sulfur light of the fire, swayed like stoned junkies. But despite the wind the surface of the pool was motionless, glassy as polished green-black obsidian. Perhaps the houses blocked the wind down there (did he hear a noise from the next room – something scraping across the floor? Weren't those two dead yet?) but no, he could see the breeze lift the lank blond hair of a sunken eyed hipster standing six feet from the water, and hustle a few brown leaves along the pool's edge. But the water remained motionless.

Maybe it just looked that way from this distance. (A drawn out scrape from the next room. Why didn't they . . .)

The light came from the moon, from a couple of table lamps brought out on extension cords, looking awkwardly out of place. Couldn't the dude afford better? Not one of his priorities.

And there was more light from a fire in an outdoor fireplace . . .

No, it was a bonfire, Mitch saw, looking closer. And it was made up of chairs. A couple of the wooden chairs that had been scattered around the terrace had been piled together. Someone had shoved rags under them and lit the whole thing on fire. The crumbling, burning frames of the chairs looked like the weird geometric structures you saw in your head when you hallucinated on drugs . . .

Thinking about drugs made him think about the Head Syrup. The painkillers weren't enough.

Someone came into the three intersecting circles of light – the larger wavery yellow circle from the fire, the

130

two smaller duller steady circles from the lamps at opposite corners of the terrace. It was a tall, thin woman with stooped shoulders and hanging, flattened breasts – he could see her tits clearly because she'd slipped out of the arm-loops of her gown and peeled it down to her waist so it hung like an apron. She was walking from the guest-house, carrying something that squirmed in her right hand. It was a thatchy yellow cat. She had it by the tail. She approached the fire and swung the cat underhand into the fullest depths of the flames. Completely engulfed, blinded and turning itself end over end in nerve-rioted confusion, the cat managed only one single high note of anguish before it went into shock.

Mitch looked away, muttering, "You fuckin' assholes."

No one reacted to the small, sadistic event. The woman only stayed to watch for a moment and then, expressionless, walked back toward the house.

Then, abruptly, she stopped walking. She turned, began walking in a new direction. Her feet suddenly uncertain of themselves, moving erratically, she walked a twisty line to a large white metal table around which sat six people. All of them men, one of them the More Man.

The woman pushed between them, shoulders twitching, and climbed onto the table. She flopped heavily onto her back, drew her knees up over her stomach like a surrendering dog, and began to claw herself, slowly and deeply.

Mitch wanted to look away but the More Man glanced up at his window. Seemed to see Mitch there, despite the shadows and the rosebushes. And Mitch found he was unable to look away from the scene.

How did she get the strength to do that to herself? Mitch wondered distantly, watching. Skin was really pretty strong stuff, after all. Peeling it away like that with your bare hands must be hard to do. Once she got the skin out of the way, though, the stuff underneath came more easily. It was much softer, most of it.

Someone got up from the table, walked to the pool. A middle aged man in one of those Mexican suits with the ruffled shirts and glowing lavender lapels. The guy in the pretty suit turned his back on the pool. He got down on his hands and knees, and then lowered himself, filly dressed, into the pool.

No ripples spread out from him as his body broke the surface. Just as his head vanished under the green, green waters, Mitch saw his expression change from indifference to terrified realization. Then he vanished without a ripple.

Mitch watched a while, expecting the guy to bob up again. Nothing.

He looked over at the table. The formerly white table was red, now. The men sitting at it had drawn their chairs back to avoid the pooling blood. The woman was steaming, faintly, from her wounds, and not moving any more. The More Man was looking up at Mitch's window.

Mitch was unable to leave the window. He looked away from the More Man, to the expiring bonfire of chairs where a greasy black twist of smoke screwed into the sky.

The Valley; Arthwright's Party

The first time he touched her, he was instantly twice as drunk.

132

They were in a large bedroom and there were indeed etchings on the wall, 20th Century work with an avante-garde look about them but also a sense of having been selected for interior decoration alone. There was an empty closet, and an open door leading to a small bathroom with a shower. They were perched on a large, circular bed with a golden spread, a brandy-coloured rug, and a wall to one side that was entirely mirror, the glass flecked with streaky black inlay, it functioned as a mirror for voyeuristic sex, but the black flecks attempted to disguise it as simple decoration.

As if in anticipation of their arrival, the overhead light had been already dialled low when they came in, and house-mix music pumped gently from some hidden stereo speaker. They could hear, through the curtained window, the muffled murmur of voices from the party still going on downstairs.

Prentice and Lissa, on the edge of the bed, made out with the economy of motion displayed by experienced adults. Prentice holding her slumped in his arms, their tongues swirling one another, mouths turning this way and that together as if seeking an unlocking combination that never quite turned up. Lissa undulating her torso, just enough to caress his pectorals with her breasts.

She pulled back and looked at him, amused. There was a faint flush around her mouth and her eyes were sleepy with arousal. "You look a little freaked out," she said. "You've got that, 'This is so sudden!' look."

The reply that came into his head was, *You're pretty familiar with that look, I take it?* But instead he said, "It's more like pleased surprise."

"Now there's a writer's expert escape. Let's see if..."

The rest of it went unsaid: she didn't want to intimidate him into a bad performance by saying

133

something challenging like, *Let's see if you have the same expertise in bed*.

He did feel off-centre. Not that it was the first time he'd snuck sex in an upstairs room of someone else's house during a party. He'd been working in Hollywood for a while. There were lots of rooms in this house and this one – being dusty and unused, its open closet displaying only empty hangers – was clearly a guest room where they weren't likely to be caught. But it was a little dismaying, being drawn so rapidly and seamlessly from the superficially friendly atmosphere of networking at an Industry party, to the seamy backroom perversity of a cheap porn video.

He told himself again relax and enjoy it. Question life too deeply and you miss its rewards. Who was that guru he'd liked when he was a teenager? Ram Dass? *Be Here Now*, Ram Dass had said. So, Prentice, be here now, he ordered.

He pulled her to him, a little roughly, and sought out her lips more hungrily – and he got that drunken feeling again, when they kissed. It was like the feeling poured out of her, into him. Like a drug that came from her touch. He'd felt strange, exquisite sensations passed to him in sex before, but never anything this intense. This distinct. This strange.

Was it being in love? That seemed . . . an inadequate explanation. Whatever it was, it coursed furiously through him, and changed him as it went. The misgivings melted away, as he and Lissa melted together, pulling off their clothing and wriggling up onto the middle of the bed.

They were nude atop the bedspread. He took time to say, "Maybe we should get under the covers. The sheets might be more comfortable –"

"No!" She said it rather sharply. "No. I like it out in the open." She turned to look at the two of them in the mirror. And then rolled out from under him, crouched beside him and began to lap expertly at his hard cock. She took it deeply into her mouth, after a while drawing back, almost letting go of the straining organ, running a kiss down its length... tracing the pulsing veins...

Glancing up at the mirror.

Ten minutes later they'd shifted again, and Prentice was pumping into her, distantly aware of the music, Steely Dan segued into some mindless but on-target Madonna number. He was kneeling between her legs, pulling her buttocks toward him as he thrust, feeling rush after rush of the druggy sensation ripple through him; she was playing with her breasts – for herself, for him, and for the mirror...

Prentice closed his eyes to savour the sensation – and somehow this narrowing off focus opened a new channel to him. He seemed to see himself as she saw him, rearing over her like a raging horse, mouth slack, eyes wild, the skin of his chest mottled with flush and glossy with sweat. And then he saw the two of them in the mirror, as she saw it. The mirror provided a voyeur's charge of objectivity that somehow tightened the concentration on the act, for some people; crystalized it in the mind. She was one of those people. Staring at the two of them, focused on the three of them in the mirror...

Three of them. The guy on the other side was the third.

A guy sitting in the dark, rocking slightly on his chair, watching them through the trick mirror. Face unseen, hidden by shadow and by turmoil. Something writhing in the air like a nest of transparent snakes...

But the vision faded and Prentice felt himself drawn, quite powerlessly, into the sucking void of orgasm.

★　　　★　　　★

Prentice stood in the guest room's shower, feeling unreal, and a little sick. Drained; still mildly buzzed. She'd said, "You use the shower first. You know how women are, it'll take me forever to get myself back together... There's a bathroom down the hall I can use. I'm just gonna slip into my dress for a second and run down there... the Back Room Sprint, it's called... Now gimme a kiss. And we'll meet downstairs at the pool." She'd been tender about the parting, after having mouthed the usual "God you must think I'm so cheap" stuff which neither of them believed even before he gave her the ritual reassurances. It was obvious to him that she had no real regrets or insecurities about the incident at all.

Now, in the shower, feeling the water but not feeling it, as if someone else were showering, he thought of the vision he'd had, the voyeur behind the mirror...

Bullshit, he told himself. You're just stressed out and a little drunk and way paranoid, God knows.

And then Prentice returned, feeling dislocated, to the party. He seemed to see everyone in a new light, now. He could see the various mating dances, now that he had less reason to perform one himself. What odd contortions they put themselves through...

God, he thought, what's odd is me. Seeing things. Feeling drugged without drugs. Something put into my drink? No. It wasn't like that.

Where was Lissa? He didn't see her. He saw Jeff, though, waving at him from a lounge chair by the pool.

Jeff didn't look happy. Standing near Jeff, smiling crookedly, was Arthwright. When Arthwright looked over, nodding at Prentice, continuing that tilted smile, Prentice knew he hadn't imagined the man behind the mirror, and he knew who it had been.

Near Malibu

Mitch was watching the heavy set woman being carried to the pool, but he was thinking about his Mom.

She had left Dad, she said, because he was a drunk, that was the weird thing. Hypocritical bitch. After the divorce she started to get drunk all the time.

He remembered when she'd come home and taken him into her lap and kissed him on the neck and there was something sick about that kiss . . .

Not just the smell of liquor, although that always made him sick No, it was a lingering kiss and there was something about it being on the neck, on the throat; a sense of being used for something. Like a sex toy, he realized now, though she'd never actually touched his dick or anything.

Why was he thinking about this now?

The woman was actively struggling now, as a group of five men dragged her to the pool; she was grinning with effort and hysteria. They were nearly there.

They'd changed the music. Now it was an old Madonna song, Christ, from years ago. *Material Girl.* But then somebody turned the record player's speed down, so it was playing it at 16 rpm, and Madonna was singing baritone, *I'm-m-m-m l-i-i-v-i-i-n-g i-i-i-n-n-n-n uhhhhhhhhh m-m-muhhh-t-earrr-i-i-www-urrrr-lll-dd . . .*

Mitch was still thinking about his Mom; how she'd have a few drinks and start whining, almost crying.

Using him for a sympathetic ear. But shit, he was only a kid. How was he supposed to help her? It made him feel all shrunk up inside.

Aaaa-nnnn-d l-i-i'm uhhhhh mmmm-uhhhhh-t-e-eerrr-i-i-i-uhhhh-lll guh-ernrrrllll . . .

Once in a while he'd try to get away from Mom by going to his Dad, asking could he move in with him. He wasn't really able to tell Dad how weird it felt living with Mom. But Dad was mostly into his guns, all he wanted to talk about was guns, and the one time they were going to "do something together" he'd got Mitch down to an NRA volunteer office to help stuff envelopes for some anti-gun control mailing. His Dad would change the subject when he tried to talk about how he didn't want to live with Mom any more, and changing the subject was a message to Mitch, told him that Dad didn't want to get around to the possibility of Mitch moving in with him so that meant he didn't want Mitch around . . . Didn't really want Mitch at all . . .

So big deal, Big, fucking deal.

Someone switched the record speed again, this time to 78 so Madonna was keening:

I'm living in a material world and I'm a material girl oh I'm living in a . . .

Now they were peeling off the big woman's clothes. Her rolls of fat and tits flopping free. Nearby, a few people were poking absently at the collapsing bonfire of chairs. Mitch could just make out the black filigree of the cat's skull and skeleton in the guttering coals.

The Handy Man was at the pool, forcing the woman in with the others. Where was the More Man? Nearby. Very near. Mitch heard a sound from the next room: it was a human sound, from a human throat, but it was not a cry, or a whimper, or a groan. It was a squeaky

138

kind of noise that said: *There are places underneath despair.*

Outside, the men had the woman half into the pool, holding her down, so her legs and torso were under the surface. Mitch could hear her screaming now, a thin faraway sound that might have been the happy squeal of a woman being teased by her friends, if you didn't know better, if you couldn't see her, now, fighting like a cat trying to get out of a tub of bathwater – that look on her round, childish face like a baby with its blankets on fire. And then her back arching, as something under the surface of the pool found her. As something happened to her, under the water, something you couldn't see. Her eyes popping and her mouth open wide as it would go but no sound coming out. And then . . .

It was hard to see from up here, but . . .

It looked like something was forcing its way out of her mouth. Something white and shiny and wet and quivering with strength.

The others crowded round her, holding her down into the pool, the men yellow in the firelight, looking like a cluster of wasps he'd seen once feeding in the wound of a roadkilled puppy.

A squeak from the next room.

A noise outside the door.

Mitch felt himself testing the waters of catatonia.

The San Fernando Valley

Jeff was simmering about something. Prentice thought maybe Jeff was pissed off at him because he'd deserted him at the party, but then, as Arthwright walked away from Jeff to say goodbye to some producer with a lousy

139

hair transplant who was taking his jiggly bimbo out to a white Rolls, Prentice saw the glare that Jeff sent at Arthwright's back. It was Arthwright Jeff was mad at.

"What's up?" Prentice said, trying not to look smug about Lissa as he sat down on the lounger next to Jeff.

Jeff looked him over irritably. "You just had a shower, looks like."

"Number one on the list of tell tale signs. Yeah. You look bummed."

"Arthwright's been hassling me to – Never mind, here he comes back."

Arthwright was strolling up with his hands in his pockets humming to himself along with the George Michael's tune the DJ was playing. *Father Figure*.

Arthwright stood a little too close, just between them. Prentice was still seated so Arthwright's crotch was level with Prentice's face. It made him vaguely uncomfortable.

"Can I have a quick word with you, Tom?" Arthwright said. It would have been more honest to say, despite the smile and light tone, *Get your ass over here, I want to talk to you*.

"Sure." Prentice got up, making a *What the hell is this?* expression at Jeff, though privately he was hoping it was about the script assignment. Prentice took his arm and led him away, toward the bar. The crowd was thinning out now. The bartenders wanted to knock off, were straining not to glare at people asking for drinks – some of the drinkers swaying, others casting deprecating glances at the drunks while asking for Calistoga.

Arthwright said, "Tom – I'm having a little tangle with Jeff Teitelbaum. I don't know, maybe it's because I'm not using him on the *Dagger* script, maybe it's

140

something else, but he's started this weird thing of getting at me through my friends. I *think* that's what he's doing. My friends, the Denvers – Sam Denver? Well, Jeff sent a lawyer up there to the Doublekey, threatening a court order for inspection of their premises or something – he's got it in his head that his little brother is up there. It's really pretty crazy stuff. I figure, hey, the Jeff's overworked, and he's got a bug up his ass because we couldn't use him, all right, I understand, we all have ego problems, we're all human. So uh . . ." They'd reached the bar. "Drink?"

"Uhhh . . . no, no we're taking off here in a minute." He wanted one badly but he also wanted to seem relatively sober and level headed.

"So anyway, I don't hold this against Jeff and I don't want to encourage my friends to countersue or anything, I'm telling them, hold off, we'll just talk to the guy, calm him down . . . I thought – maybe just to help Jeff out, keep him from getting his ass in a legal sling because of a paranoid trip he's on about his brother – maybe he's got some kind of guilt trip about his brother and he's projecting it on us, right? Anyway, I thought maybe you could talk to him for me. And – well, I'd feel better about you and me working together. After that. I mean, Jeff and you are friends and – I don't want to just lump you together, but . . . you know what I mean . . . ?"

Prentice had to snap his mouth shut. It had bobbed open when he'd realized just what Arthwright meant. It was as much in Arthwright's body language and tone as in the words. He meant: *Get Jeff to lay off the legal attack and the snooping and I'll consider giving you that break you need right now. If you don't do it, you're fucked.*

"Uh – sure," Prentice heard himself say. Felt a thrill

of horror as he said it. "I'll talk to him. See if I can straighten it out." His teeth felt heavy in his mouth. What a weird sensation.

"Great. And then we'll talk, we'll have a lunch meeting, do some business – Whoa! Here's the vanishing beauty, back again!" This last as he turned to greet Lissa who pushed up beside Arthwright, reached past him to squeeze Prentice's hand.

Arthwright stood between Prentice and Lissa as they held hands. Arthwright was smiling – laying a hand on Prentice's shoulder, and one on Lissa's. A holstered intimacy in that touch.

As Arthwright kissed Lissa on the cheek and walked away, Prentice tried not to think about the man in the bedroom mirror, upstairs.

East L.A.

Bugging out on the school bus wasn't hard. That was the easy part, Lonny thought. The bus that carried the work crew from Juvenile Hall to Griffith Park, where they were supposed to spend the day painting park benches, was a standard school bus with the emergency exit back-door. The emergency door wasn't locked and when the armed driver, halfway to the park, got in a shouting match with a UPS truck driver who was blocking two lanes with a sloppy double park, Lonny saw his chance and kicked open the back door and jumped down and dodged through traffic and climbed over a fence and skidded down the concrete embankment into the big culvert containing the skimpy stream that was called The Los Angeles River. He ran down the culvert a ways, then climbed up a drain pipe, went over another fence: crossing into East L.A., into a pretty fucked up barrio where he was going to find Eurydice and bring her out...

He found, instead, Orpheus. And all the time he was thinking of a third person. Mitch. Goddamn that little fucker. Mitch, his baby.

143

Sometimes you walk along without thinking where you're going; your body knows the way, your mind is someplace else. Lonny had glimpses of the neighbourhood drifting by after he climbed up out of the "river" and over the fence. Lots of little houses, some of them fanatically neat, with gardens and little fences; others strewn with hulks of cars and trash; clusters of small but noisy brown children who seemed to have been strewn themselves. The barrio cholos low-riding by, checking him out, seeing it was okay, that he had the right shoelaces and scarf for this neighbourhood, making with the power salute or just a nod. All the houses – neat or trashy – were small and cheap, hot little boxes cooking in the yellow brew of the Los Angeles air; most of them marked with graffiti.

He saw all this like a scattering of polaroids. In his mind he was seeing Mitch; was hunching with Mitch under the bedcovers with a flashlight, the two of them seven years old, giggling and talking about where babies come from and then Lonny touching Mitch's hairless groin, showing him things... No. That wasn't Mitch; he was misremembering. It was Gavin, the little boy under the covers, years ago; Gavin, who was a hustler now on Santa Monica Boulevard, the shit-whore giving his ass away for dope to motherfuckers with big cars and small dicks. But Lonny remembered the two of them coupled on the top of Gavin's bunkbed, Lonny thirteen and Gavin only just eleven, never thinking of it as fucking then. Instead it was "just trying some stuff out"; hard to think of it as fucking even later because, if he did, then Lonny would be a fag.

Mitch. More than once Mitch had let Lonny hold him, when he'd been hurting and needed comforting, or when he talked about his fucked-up parents, but

144

Mitch had never let him do anything else, had never let Lonny try stuff out with him, and Lonny hadn't forced him, had just that once put his hand . . .

Eurydice's place. He was here. Seeing the crackerbox plaster house with all the busted toys in the front yard where Eurydice and Orpheus and Aphrodite lived with their Holy-Roller aunt. She was an alcoholic, plus addicted to some kind of prescription cough syrup she got for "chronic bronchitis". Still, the woozy old aunt was better for Eurydice and Orpheus than their mom. They'd been moved in here by Children's Services because their mom had tried to sell their asses to get herself some hubba. Fucking crackpoofing cunt.

Their dad was doing twelve in the San Q.

Lonny walked up the concrete flagstones, paused at the bottom of the bowed wooden stairs to look at the yard. The toys in the dead grass and packed clay of the front yard were all grimy and busted, probably had been since the day after they came home from Toys-R-Us. Trucks with the wheels off; *Hot Wheels* cars embedded into the clay like fossils; splintered day-glo green and orange plastic squirtguns, and dried-up dogshit. And lying with a piece of yellow dried out dogshit nosing up to her head like some kind of giant killer worm, was a *Barbie* doll, with all its clothes gone and most of its hair ripped out and one arm missing. They were just dolls, but when he saw them like that they always made Lonny feel a little sick and sad.

One of the kids came out onto the slanty wooden porch, Aphrodite, an eight year old black girl in dusty shorts and a *Teenage Mutant Ninja Turtles* t-shirt stained with barbecue sauce; she was holding a black baby's hand, the baby just old enough to toddle around. A cousin. Baby with shit-filled cloth diapers pinned onto

145

her, nothing else. Lonny could smell the diapers from here, twenty or so feet away.

"Orphy!" Aphrodite called, into the house. "That boy's here that Eury used to mess wid."

Lonny winced in irritation. He'd never "messed wid" Eurydice. That was Mitch. It was Mitch in love with her, or told himself he was.

Orpheus came onto the porch, a raspberry Bartles & Jaymes wine-cooler in his hand. He nudged Aphrodite and the baby back inside. He was a tall, skinny black teenager with a basketball player's muscles. Reeboks and jogging pants and a Lakers muscle shirt and a fake diamond earring in his left ear and a gold chain around his neck with the big gold-plated letters *ORPHEUS* in the middle.

"Hey man, what'up," Lonny said.

"Yo, Lonny, where's Eury?"

"The fuck you askin' me?" Lonny said. "She's your sister. . ." Lonny felt a sinking in his gut. Eurydice was missing.

"Mitch's you homie, that why. Lonny, you got you ass thrown in Juvie so you can chill with Mitch. You know where Mitch is, don't tell me no shit. Eury with Mitch."

Lonny spat angrily at a wheel-less Tonka tractor. *You get you ass thrown in Juvie so you can chill with Mitch.* What was Orphy saying about him? "I came here lookin' for Mitch," Lonny admitted. "I thought maybe he'd be with Eury."

"Was Mitch got Eury fucking with that old dude. Out the ranch. You know where that place is?"

"The ranch? No. I thought maybe he went out there but then I thought, How'd he get out there? There's no bus out there. So I thought maybe he'd come here . . ."

146

"You on probation?"

"Yeah," Lonny lied.

"Who you got for a P.O.? Bentley?"

"No." He didn't want to talk about his Parole Officer. Because he didn't have one. "You think she's at that guy's place?"

"Yeah. Denver. She be goin out there yesterday night. I don't know where the fuck it is . . . Mitch, he know."

"Maybe. But he was in the hospital. Only he ain't there now, I heard. He cruised on it."

The Ranch. Eurydice, now. And Mitch.

Where was it? Where was the fucking place?

West Hollywood

Ephram had to bribe some guy fifty bucks at the door to get Constance in because she was underage but once inside it didn't seem to matter how old she was. A lot of the girls here, and most of the young gay boys, seemed like teenagers.

She'd never been in a disco, if that's what it was. That's what Ephram called it. It was just a long white room with coloured track-lighting and four wall-video screens. Just now the screens showed Janet Jackson – no, Janet's video was just finished, now it was Taylor Dayne. There was a long, curvy, transparent-plastic bar – by some trick of the light it looked as if the people at the far end of the bar were leaning on nothing, on thin air – and there were a lot of tables crammed together, and a small dance floor at the far end. Mirrors on two sides of the dance floor made the room seem to extend onward like another car in a train. On the third side of the dance floor was one of the video screens so

147

that a slightly larger-than-lifesize, two-dimensional Taylor Dayne was dancing with the half-dozen gay boys and hetero girls who rollicked on the dance floor.

Constance was occupying herself with all the details – even the splatter of colours mixed into the black floor tiles – in order to keep from feeling the panic, the fear that came like a swarm of mosquitos, the bad feelings that Ephram punished her for. In order to keep from thinking about Daddy. In order to keep from thinking about the men they'd murdered, her and Ephram.

Most of her mind, she knew, was locked away inside her, a mewling cat in a carrier-box. You had to ignore its muted yowling to get where you were going.

She wanted to go to the bathroom but she was afraid – *no, not afraid don't think that* . . . She wanted to go to the bathroom but Ephram would mentally follow her in, and it embarrassed her.

I have to follow you in. Otherwise you might wander off, out bathroom windows or back doors.

Escape? She laughed and sipped her Coca-Cola.

"We won't be taking any young men along with us, tonight, actually," Ephram remarked. "It happens that young ladies come here who work as rather expensive whores. They pick up the moneyed men at the bar here. We'll let one seem to pick us up. There are things I want to try. . . Best with a woman . . . A very young one preferably. . . Thank heaven for little girls, ha ha."

Constance nodded. (Don't think, don't think, don't think).

She sipped her Coca Cola. After a while, the video screen showed the band Poison, with their cockatoo hair and day-glo costumes and the cheap mystery of dry-ice clouds.

She had a thought and instantly hid it away.

From the Journal of Ephram Pixie
"for July the 22 199–":

It's not enough, anymore. My use of proxie neural pathways to experience pleasures is not entirely protecting me from being used up myself. I have a sense that there is some aspect of the negative astrology, some variant of the hidden constellations that is hidden to me as well as to ordinary men. Something veiled. Could someone be veiling it from me, setting me up for a fall? Who? Denver? The Akishra?

Could it be they've lured me to L.A...?

No. I am Ephram Pixie, master of my destiny as no man else is.

Still, I am feeling enervated. Or at least rather ragged in my enjoyments, sagging in my appetites. Perhaps it is at last time to attempt Wetbones again. If I do, it will attract the Akishra. And that could be fatal.

Or will it – in particular? This is Los Angeles. They feed so widely and so well here. It could well be that the Spirit brought me here so to give me a smokescreen, a place of concealment, where the Akishra will not notice me in the general background of suffering and decadence. So very many emissions here.

It could be that I have lost faith, that I should be trusting the guidance of the Spirit more. It could be that the Spirit plans to exalt me, at last, in this place and that is why I have been guided here. He does seem to be guiding me back to the Engorgement Ritual. But oh! That Ritual is so very taxing. But oh again! How very rewarding it is, once the labour is done, ha ha.

There could be another reason the Spirit is prompting me to Wetbones. It might well be the ideal way to stop any search for Constance in its tracks. When she was twelve her father had her fingerprints registered; there was a police drive on for it, a way to help locate children if they turn up missing, and to identify their bodies if they turn up dead... I saw it in her mind as a hope, back when I allowed her hope. She doesn't need all her fingers to be of use to me. Not really.

I have made my decision.

Wetbones.

Downtown Los Angeles

Garner had known what the police would say. The verbal shrug he would get. There were literally tens of thousands of missing teenagers in Los Angeles. Most of them were homeless addicts and prostitutes, living in cars and under freeways. Giving his report was just a way to get Constance's name on the LAPD computer.

Now he drove the van West, onto the freeway, glad he wasn't going East; traffic Southeast-bound, on the other side of the freeway divide, was thick as coagulated blood.

He'd spent five hundred bucks on a deposit for a detective agency, a cheap gumshoe who was just another warm body to go about asking have you seen this girl have you seen this girl have you seen this girl, anyplace she'd be likely to turn up.

Of course, he could be wrong about where Constance would likely turn up. And he could be wrong about it even being in this city. And even if it was in this city, the town was *so fucking big*.

But he'd learned to trust his intuition; he thought that maybe – along with the patterns of incidents and coincidences that made up the flow of life – pulses of intuition were God's Morse Code.

Or maybe he was kidding himself.

He had to stay busy. Had to. So he started on Hollywood Boulevard, showing a display cardboard taped with several pictures of Constance to anyone who'd talk to him. He wandered tirelessly but fruitlessly through Hollywood and the Fairfax and downtown L.A.. He talked especially to prostitutes, trying to get a handle on the local trade in chickens. Who was dealing in young flesh? Where were they?

It could be that the son of a bitch who had her would market her in those shadowy and seamy venues.

He walked the streets for two days, sleeping at night in his van to save money for bribes, before he began to hear the recurrent note. The rumours kept cropping up: *The More Man*. A rich movie industry sleaze who sometimes scattered largesse on compliant teenagers.

And then he began hearing about the murders. The kids on the street would try to sound knowledgeable about the murders. But all they really knew, apart from the condition of the corpses, was what to call them: Wetbones.

Culver City Los Angeles

Prentice was trying not to think A universal skill, a widely applied survival technique: Sometimes you have to just close your eyes and just do what you have to do.

"Jeff – you know where Mitch probably is?" *Careful,*

Prentice told himself, leaning back in the desk chair of Jeff's office. *You don't want to come off sounding like that cop that came over here. That'll turn Jeff against you in a hot second.*

Jeff was sitting pensively on the edge of the desk. Afternoon sunlight came in dusty stacks through the cantilevered blinds. "Do I know where Mitch probably is? If I knew where the fuck Mitch was we wouldn't be having this fucking discussion," Jeff said.

Prentice thought: I'm helping him, I really am. This whole paranoid thing is just making a wreck of our lives. Both of us feeding on it emotionally – me because of Amy, Jeff because he feels bad about not taking care of Mitch.

The dreams Prentice had been having about Amy were enough to convince him he had some kind of morbid entanglement with her memory. Best all that were jettisoned..

"Mitch is probably *deliberately* letting you stew, man," Prentice said. Everything he said was an attempt to convince himself as much as Jeff – an escape from culpability. From the sense of something precious inside him rotting away because he was trying to play along with Arthwright. "I mean, think about it – Mitch is into rock'n'roll. Wants to be a head-bangin' rockstar. Chances are he's hanging out with that crowd on Sunset Boulevard, down by the Whisky, the other clubs down there. I mean – he probably *was* at Denver's, and then that didn't come to anything, and he split for town."

But what about Amy? Prentice asked himself. Her connection to Denver. Her death.

He squashed the thought. Sometimes you have to just close your eyes and . . .

"Maybe you're right," Jeff said grudgingly. "But

that headbangin' crowd is *big*, man. How am I supposed to find him in it – if that's where he is.

"A private eye. Go on foot and ask people in the lines outside the clubs. Maybe even see Mitch there. I mean, if you . . ." He broke off. He was about to say, *If you tangle with the Denvers in court you could lose a lot of money – and and make an enemy of Arthwright.* But if he said that, Mitch might realize that Arthwright had put him up to this.

Prentice writhed inside. *Wrongwrongwrongwrong.* The word like a bell pealing in his mind. *Wrong.*

Jeff hugged himself wearily. "I'm fucking tired of thinking about this. I'll decide what to do tomorrow."

The desk phone rang. Jeff answered it in a monotone. "Yeah. Hello . . . Yeah, he's right here."

He passed the phone over to Prentice and left the room.

Prentice put the phone to his ear. "Tom Prentice here."

"Hi, 'Tom Prentice here.' It's Lissa."

Prentice's gut did another flip-flop. There was anticipation in it, and fear. "Hi. I'm glad you called."

"Listen – Zack wanted me to invite you to a party he's giving for some of his friends. He's giving it at their place, but he's setting it all up, I guess. Oh and I'm supposed to ask you – it was all very cryptic – how it's going 'with Jeff'? Whatever that's about."

"Uh. Fine." Could Jeff be listening on the extension? No, why would he? "It's taken care of."

"Good – I guess. I'm not in on that loop. Anyway – taking me to a party's a nice cheap date, don't you think?"

"I'd love to take you on the expensive kind." But he was glad he didn't have to, yet. He was veering

153

dangerously close to flat broke. God, he might have to write that video. "For that matter, I'd take a trip to Baghdad with you in an F-16."

"Good. I like an explosive date. But, in the meantime, Arthwright's party at the Denvers' is on Saturday —"

"It's *where?*" Unable to hide his startlement.

"At the Denvers'. You're supposed to *not* bring you know-who. Can you pick me up?" She gave him the time and her address and they exchanged a few more vague innuendoes and he hung up.

Telling himself, *This way I can clear up the question of Mitch being out there ...*

Then asking himself, *What are you so scared of?*

West Hollywood

"First time I saw a Wetbones body, I didn't want to believe it used to be people. If I believed that, shit, I'd have to puke," Blume said. "Eventually, I did have to puke." He was six inches taller than Garner, but slumped in his chair almost to the same height; he had bushy hair receding with clown-like frontal baldness. A tired, cynical face built around a long, thin nose; the nondescript clothes that private detectives wear. He took another long pull on his beer. "You sure you don't want a beer or something?" he asked Garner. "I don't like to drink alone."

Garner was tempted. He ached for a drink, sometimes, to put out the smoldering anguish of fear for Constance. But he wasn't going to throw away all those years of sobriety for anything so sickly as a mere temptation.

Garner shook his head. "Naw. I'll have a Seven-Up

154

though, if that helps." They sat in a corner booth under a buzzing Felix The Cat clock. Garner wished they'd sat nearer the door. The tavern stank of old beer and a piss-choked bathroom.

"How many of these bodies have you seen?" Garner asked.

"If you can even call 'em bodies . . . Two."

Blume heaved himself abruptly out of the booth and went to the bar. He came back moments later with a double tequila in one hand and a fizzing glass of soda in the other. He sat down, passing Garner the glass. "They didn't have Seven-Up. Sprite."

"Great. Fine. You were saying . . ."

Blume knocked back the double tequila in one swallow. Blew out his cheeks. Then shook his head sadly. "If there hadn't been a skull, you wouldn'ta been able to tell it was human. Too much of a mess. Just a lot of . . . wet bones. Broken up wet bones. Wet with blood and . . . gunk. Piss and phlegm I guess. Even shit from the busted intestines. Busted bones and guts in the middle of a puddle of blood. No clothes around. It didn't look like it was dug up, neither. Too fresh. Not like somebody'd messed with a grave. You could just see these bones were new. And in one there was this busted skull, and the eye – well, one of the eyes was intact. But no lids . . ."

Garner swallowed. His mouth was very dry. He took a long drink of the Sprite. His tissues seemed to soak it up like desert sand sucking a raindrop. "Seems to me it could still be . . . a hoax. Stolen bones from some medical school or . . . Were there organs?"

"Yeah. Some. What wasn't mushed into . . . gunk."

"And skin?"

"I didn't see it. But there was a lot of stuff I couldn't

155

quite make out what it was and I didn't wanna look that close."

It's a big city. it wouldn't be her.

"But – why do you bring this up . . . ?"

'They were all young girls, I heard, these bonepiles . . ." He shrugged. "I don't wanna be insensitive or nothin' but . . ."

"Any identification of the . . . ?" He waited, heart thudding so hard in his chest he thought that Blume must be able to hear it.

"Nope. That's part of why this thing hasn't really broken into the papers much because they're not connected to specific missing girls and the cops are taking the same tack that you did – that they're stolen bones . . . I.D.ing them's hard. There are so many missing kids in the L.A. area it's unbelievable."

"Yeah. I know." Garner fingered his soda glass. Stared at the slowly, slowly melting ice. "But you drive around in this town for a day or two – especially when you're from out of town – and you find the statistics about missing kids very believable indeed, Blume . . ."

"You got any kind of fingerprints on your little girl?"

"Yes. I left them at your office with your boss when I first came in. And I've given the police a stat of them. They should be in the police computer."

"As far as I know they haven't got any fingerprint I.D. on these Wetbones things yet. Hey, don't give me that look, it's a long shot – but we should push the cops into crosschecking it just to eliminate that longshot, when they've got some fingerprints on those bodies . . . If you can call 'em bodies . . ."

"You already said that," Garner pointed out, through grating teeth.

Suddenly he felt like he was going to vomit. The smell of the men's room, the stale beer, the reek of booze off Blume himself. He wanted to shout at Blume that he was killing himself with alcohol, an addictive drug that's sold on television to children, sold in advance through hundreds of thousands of beer and wine commercials, but then his automatic guard against self righteousness came into play, and he said nothing, except, "I need some air. Just keep looking for her, all right? I'll call you."

Garner lurched out of the booth, staggered outside, as so many drunks did, coming out of Blume's favourite low-cost boozery.

For a few moments Garner was staggering like a drunk but – he was horribly, terribly sober.

Santa Monica

She was beginning to see pictures in her head that seemed to come from nowhere at all. She knew where they were from, though – not from Ephram, not from God or the Devil. They were from her, the part of her that she couldn't stop from feeling.

Constance was sitting under a lemon tree in the backyard of the little condo that Ephram had rented, sitting in a lawn chair, wearing a white bikini that Ephram had picked for her, and sunglasses she wore as often as he'd let her. Ephram had pushed some buttons in her head and she felt no pain.

Ephram was in the house scribbling in that little book of his. It was the only time he left her alone and she was trying to enjoy it – though she knew he was still watching her in some way, and she mustn't even think fleetingly of climbing over that white wooden

157

fence and running. So instead she was sitting there quietly, seeing herself transfixed by steel poles.

It was a sharp, mental image, like a slide projection: Constance with three shiny steel rods, each an inch thick, thrust laterally through her breasts; another transfixing her neck; another through her temples, passing, presumably, through her brain. Constance smiling happily through it all, talking, chattering, saying nothing.

And then it would vanish, this picture, only to be replaced by another: Constance walking through a party, talking to people like she was the hostess, only she had a noose around her neck, already tightened, her face swollen and black, as if she'd already been choked to death, or – no, she wasn't quite dead, she was perpetually on the verge of choking to death, but never did, not quite, she just walked around chatting, shaking hands, hugging people, smiling as she said, *"Excuse the rope,"* in a strangled voice. No one seemed to mind.

And then she saw herself in a steel globe that was just a little bit too small for her body but big enough so that she could wriggle around looking for the escape hole that she knew must be there but she couldn't find She kept trying but still couldn't find it, and the globe was tightening, was getting smaller . . .

"Constance?"

She'd felt him coming before he'd spoken. "Yes?"

"We're going to go out tonight, we're meeting someone at a motel . . ."

She nodded. She tried to feel nothing. She was getting pretty good at it . . .

★   ★   ★

Lately, Ephram had got into this prostitute thing. First that girl they picked up at the disco, then call-girls chosen from classified ads in the *Los Angeles Swingles Guide*. Constance could see the logic, that the girls he picked weren't with pimps or madams, they were working alone, and they usually didn't tell anyone where they were going. Or so he assumed. But maybe he was wrong about that. Constance had pointed out that they'd know it was risky going out with all these strange men, maybe some would tell their boyfriends or whomever, have them waiting outside...

But no, Ephram said, they were complacent and too-confident, these girls, and besides he mentally frisked them for traces of accomplices. "These are girls," he said, "one can snip off at the stem – and no one will notice them missing in a tree already heavy with rotten fruit, ha ha."

None of the girls were surprised to see Constance with Ephram; with the trick. They were used to threesomes and foursomes.

Sitting with Ephram in a thickly padded blue vinyl booth in a dark corner of the Howard Johnson's cocktail bar, Constance felt a squeezing pleasure of anticipation and excitement. For a moment she thought that Ephram was prompting the sensations, but then she realized that, instead, those feelings were her own, were coming up out of her unbidden. And that meant, she thought with a surge of joy and relief, she was becoming what Ephram wanted her to be. There would be less punishment now – and she could be another person, a new person, so that the Constance she had been need no longer be responsible for the things she'd done; need not exist at all. The old Constance could die... on the vine. Like rotten fruit.

The latest girl was a little overweight, and Constance could see some anxiety in her eyes as she approached the booth, wobbling a little on her high pumps, carrying an overnight bag that would have her working lingerie in it. The girl was nervous the old man would reject her because she was overweight, and she'd lose the great wad of money he'd promised her. She had lots and lots of fake blond curls tumbling over her bulgingly exposed cleavage; she had a deep-dark tan and capped teeth and a tighter than-skintight short black dress. And a big butt.

Ephram beamed at her. "My dear! You must be Naomi! Sit down and I'll get you a drink..."

There were drinks and there was small talk and an envelope passed between Ephram and the hefty prostitute. Constance felt her pussy getting wet looking at the girl, imagining what Wetbones would do with all that flesh.

This was just getting better and better, Constance thought: now I'm responding. Getting excited thinking about it. That ought to please Ephram.

She could feel Ephram's glow of approval like a space heater in a cold room.

The girl made a few dumb, sexy remarks about Constance, stuff she probably just felt obligated to say. But Constance liked hearing it. She was beginning to enjoy female attention. It was something she'd never have thought herself capable of six months ago the very notion would have made her burst out, *"Gross!"*, but compared to most of the recent innovations in her appetites, it was minor.

After a couple of Margaritas, Naomi was animatedly talking about herself, on and on. Constance wondered if Ephram was already priming the girl's pleasure centres. "Oh anyway," Naomi was saying, "I met this *guy* you know? Who's, like, a movie producer? And he's, like, really into me? And he wants me to, um, audition for his next movie and I'm all, *Oh listen I wasn't born yesterday* but he's all, *No really, I'll get you an appointment right now let's call up my secretary* right? And, like, I knew it would happen eventually because I've always had this *higher destiny*. That's what the girl who does my charts says, *You have a higher destiny*."

Ephram smiled at that. "I'm quite sure you do, indeed, Naomi. Ha ha."

Naomi chattered on, "And, like, I always knew I'd be something special anyway, even without seeing it proved on my charts? You know? Because, um, like, I've always had this *talent* for acting stuff out – I always do it with my clients, they love it, I get in all these kind off like, *characters* the clients want and certain outfits – I have all these costumes – and I can just *be* like, these *people*, like I'll be Elvira – you know, Elvira from, like, on TV? And I'll pretend to be Elvira with a blackwig and a black dress and they ask me, *Come on, you really are Elvira and you do this on the side right?* And I say no, but I've always had this talent . . ."

Finally Ephram got a glazed look in his eyes that meant the girl was going to die soon. He paid the bill and took Naomi by her plump, silver-ringed hand and, still chattering, she followed Constance and Ephram out and across the parking lot and up to the second tier of the motel and into number 77 and Ephram put on the Adult channel. The girl didn't mind that at all, it just started her talking about how she'd acted in an adult video and knew some of those girls and how the director always said she was the one with real talent . . . she'd always had this talent, this knowledge of her special destiny . . .

161

Ephram toyed with her in the room for awhile, jolting the girl with pleasure, little jolts, which she attributed to Constance's touch. After a while Naomi stopped chattering, and they slipped into an unreal subworld, smoky with a pink fog that seemed to thicken out of nowhere, clouding the room with a fragrance that was both floral and epidermal; an insulated retreat where Naomi's black lace crotchless lingerie was the requisite uniform of simply existing here, and where the only window was the TV screen with its writhing pixel-patterned flesh and sodden connections and false sighs and cheap hip-hop soundtrack; and where the only constant beyond the probing of slick membranes and swollen clitoral nodes and Naomi's great bouncing and swirling breasts, was the dumpy little man masturbating in the corner; the little man was simply there, ever there in the background, as the two girls played on the bed – the prostitute, normally exactingly conscious of the ticking away of her mental taxicab meter – coasted with only a murmur of wonder down into a nautilus-shell retreat from the currents of time.

And the little man in the background was the source of nourishment and renewal, a ridiculous and divine fixture of this self-contained universe . . .

So it went until Ephram himself broke the spell by declaring that he wanted to do something special outside.

"Outside?" The girl seemed puzzled. She'd forgotten that Outside existed. Now the recollection of the outside world came back, because Ephram permitted it to. She nodded – and then frowned. She had mixed feelings about the proposition. She was intrigued, for financial reasons, because here was an excuse to ask a lot more money, but also dismayed because of the risk. "We could get busted for that. Now if it was off in the country somewhere... I did this video once, I was so good in it too, we were like naked cowgirls you know? And uh –"

As Naomi chattered, Constance, knowing Ephram's mind, was dressing the girl, smiling and nodding and tugging her dress onto her – grunting with the labour of it. At the same time Constance focused on the waves of pleasure Ephram sent through her, taking refuge in them. She needed refuge because at the mention of outside, the place for the Engorgement Ritual, her earlier mellowness began to slip away and she felt herself drying up inside, the familiar hollowness growing in her, the feeling that came when she was being used a little too much... being used up in the effort to insulate her from the monstrousness of her complicity...

Soon they were all dressed and it was the world that was naked around them, the exposed flank of the night making Naomi blink with confusion as they strolled up the alley. Naomi only vaguely articulating her misgivings, talking about "the shoot in the country" and how they did it and the "professional way to do outdoor stuff" but never really carping because Ephram wouldn't allow it, Ephram had his fingers on her control centre, giving only little punishments and big rewards.

The spot Ephram had picked out earlier in the day was in the parking lot of a healthfood bakery in a residential block of Venice just ten minutes stroll from the Howard Johnson's motel/bar/restaurant.

To either side, as they walked up the gravel alley, were houses with wooden backyard fences over which peered small palms and citrus trees and sunflowers. There was a faint scent of the sea from just three blocks to the West, and there was a rather cloying odour from some summery blossom calling out hopelessly in the darkness for fertilization. They heard a whisper of passing cars out on the street and, from the houses, the occasional murmur of voices as people on terraces drank beer over the remains of their charbroiled chicken. They heard them, but saw no one; and no one seemed to see them.

The bakery's parking lot was asphalt with a sprinkle of gravel and it was secluded by cinderblock walls on three sides. There was one yellow utility light burning over the empty lot, and no sound at all from the bakery. An odour of yeasty dough and molasses lingered. Constance found the smell sickening.

Ephram had brought along a buck-knife, this time. Constance wondered why; he'd never bothered with a knife on one of these expeditions. He was just unfolding it as they stepped into the lot. The girl hadn't noticed. Naomi was looking around, giggling nervously. "Oh wow. I guess this'll be .okay. Yeah, you know some people just kind of get off on doing it in weird places and I can, you know, get off on anything, I guess that's my ability as an actress —"

Constance nodded and smiled and undressed her, right here under the yellow, moth-haunted light, and under the few stars that could be seen through the smog. Ephram was speaking, now, droning to stars behind the stars, and to the Spirit, speaking in a language that sounded like something from India but wasn't quite. The girl looked at him in sheeplike puzzlement until her eyes lit on the knife in his hand. She opened her mouth. Then shut it and looked around for her clothes and bag. Constance could see she was planning to scoop up her clothes and run. The hollowness in Constance ached at this and she almost found herself warning the girl but then a stroke of deep pain and brutal nullity swept through her, Ephram punishing her, telling her, Say nothing. *It could be you and not her.*

Naomi went for it, grabbed at her clothes, started to run. Ephram tripped her, though he stood seven feet away. She stumbled and fell, making a cry like a little girl hurting a knee roller skating. Ephram let her get to her feet, then he called down the Spirit thing, whatever it was. You could *almost* see it, though it was invisible, it displaced the air and you could just make out a flailing tracery in the murk swarming over the girl, something almost like a translucent tube but, really, more like a great mouth and throat; a mouth with feelers furring its lips and no face or head to set the mouth in, just the cupping, the wet enclosure and the quavery lines . . .

Closing around the girl. Her heavy breasts and belly instantly compressing. The Spirit directed by Ephram to close invisibly around her. Encompassing Naomi head to foot. Flattening her breasts, her buttocks, her shoulders and thighs. Squeezing and twisting, like wringing a wet cloth. Squeezing the girl's insides out –

Out through her own mouth. Squeezing her insides out through her mouth.

Now it looked as if she was caught in some small tornado, and there was a paroxysm of movement in the air as Naomi turned inside out, bones and cartilage, soft tissues and hard, breaking and pulping and jetting out through her mouth, like some kind of perverse birthing labour, her mouth the vagina that squeezed out the fetus of her insides as if her guts had grown in the womb of her skin all these years –

Naomi imploding and then exploding, some of her

squeezed out through the ends of her fingers, niftily destroying the fingertips and their prints, each splayed finger shooting out its blood and bone like some fireworks effect before flying into red-rag flinders; some of her bursting out through the nipples, her breasts exploding from the sudden deepsea pressures Ephram had created in her body, the ripples flying off like champagne corks, the breasts emptying themselves into the air like foaming cherry-champagne bottles. Her womb expelling out through her vagina; other entrails blasting into confetti from her rectum. Most of the rest of her – including skull, brains and torso – shattered and forced out through her suddenly-flexible mouth. A hundred and sixty pounds of pulverized woman erupting, then funnelled downward by the Spirit membrane to the growing puddle on the tarmac . . .

And in the process *pulverizing* every nerve in Naomi's body, the implosion sending signals that were both monstrous and exquisite out to Ephram, sensations routed through Naomi's nervous system before it shattered, an explosion of feeling transmitted to Ephram, who absorbed most of it with a gasp of reeling ecstasy, before passing on a measured portion to Constance.

Constance felt it hit her in waves of liquid scintillations, sensations beyond pain and redefining pleasure, and she was, for a moment, satiated, her hollowness filled, the thundering and all encompassing pleasure beyond pleasure of drinking the crushed winelike essence of one complete entire human being, drinking psychically, so briefly and tantalizingly making herself whole by induction of someone else's wholeness . . . Naomi's whole body a swollen sexual organ crushed in the etheric vagina of Ephram's telekinetic bond with the Spirit . . . Crushed like a grape and like a grape squeezed from its skin, turned inside out and left in an oozing wreckage to make the asphalt wet and sticky. . .

A puddle of blood and broken bone and pulped flesh – and a garnish of blonde hair, like a pelt slashed from some fantastic fur bearing animal . . .

★   ★   ★

Constance had forgotten about the knife until Ephram made her kneel beside the wreckage of Naomi. Until Ephram took hold of Constance's left hand and flattened it out on the tarmac next to Naomi's steaming remains, so that Constance thought: At long last, he's going to kill me.

Constance was beyond struggling – especially now, in the aftermath of Wetbones, drunk on Naomi, stoned on the tsunami of sensation that had roared through her. She was pliant as a Gumby in Ephram's hands.

Let him kill her. It was a good time for it.

But instead he pressed the knife home on her ring finger, cutting it all the way through, below the second knuckle. Sawing away at the rubbery shred of skin remaining. Tossing the finger into the heap that had been Naomi – along with the gold C O N S T A N C E necklace he'd taken from her, weeks before.

Constance felt no pain through all this – he was pushing her cerebral buttons to prevent that, so she wouldn't thrash about – but the hideous crunch of the knife breaking through her finger bone reverberated through her, brought her horribly back to herself, and she seemed to see the wretched puddle of Naomi's pulverized flesh for the first time and thought she recognized the torn and flattened remains of a face in the midst of it, looking emptily back at her.

Near Malibu

There wasn't much in the girl's room. Just a bed and a window and a bathroom with a pile of paper towels for toilet paper. It was dark out, and the only light was from a naked bulb in the overhead bracket. It was a weak bulb. She could see light coming from under the locked hall door and a little coming through a crack in the wall from the next room.

She turned to look at the bed. It was bare except for a single clean white sheet, like a bed in an emergency room.

She stood in the middle of the room, hugging herself. They'd stripped her down to her underwear. They hadn't even given her a blanket.

She was pretty sure, now, that they weren't going to get her into the modeling business or the music business, either one.

★   ★   ★

Mitch had moved the dresser away from the wall, when he heard them bringing someone into the next room.

He had a feeling it would be someone new. Something about the way the voices murmured – by turns cheerful and smugly secretive. And then there was the confused quality of the girl's unanswered questions.

He could see her, in there, standing in the middle of the room, shivering though it was quite a warm night, hugging herself. A tall, slim black girl. Shifting her weight from foot to bare foot. Her long legs and small waist and the swell of her hips glossy with the meagre light.

It took him fifteen minutes with one eye pressed to the crack, shifting his head to try to see better, before he finally got a glimpse of her face.

Recognition went off like a firecracker in his head.

"Oh shit oh no! Eurydice."

Finally. He knew what they'd been saving him for.

Los Angeles

Garner understood the deadness in his feelings. He didn't begrudge it. He knew what it was, and he knew it wouldn't last.

The numbness made it possible for him to drive to police headquarters, where the main morgue was. It made it possible for him to park the van and to say to himself, from time to time, *It's not necessarily her, it doesn't have to be her*.

But it made him tunnel visioned and mechanical. He locked the van and walked to the front of the LAPD building but he didn't really see it. He had an impression that there was a metallic LAPD symbol on the front of the building somewhere. He was vaguely aware that it was drizzly out today, not raining out but the wind a

169

wet one, and he thought it was probably sometime in the interminable afternoon.

Inside there was a counter and, behind it, a black woman in uniform. Her face was a blur. It was like one of those TV reports where, for legal reasons, they'd used some kind of computer-video effect to block out someone's face with swatches of cubistic blurriness...

The sergeant who took his paperwork had a cloudy face, too. But the heavy set cop led Garner back to the morgue. There was the chattering of computer printers tattling on someone; there were squares of paper on bulletin boards with little black and white faces on them, and those, paradoxically, came into focus more readily than the faces of the flesh-and-blood cops around him: Wanted sheets displaying two grainy black and white views. Bland, ordinary faces. Many of them murderers. They all had a patient look about them. *You've got me now, and you're taking my picture, and you're going to put me in a cell, but I'll wait, I have only to wait...*

A blur who called himself a Morgue Orderly took him and the Sergeant into a cold room.

"You won't be called upon to identify the body, per se," the Sergeant said. "It's not really... identifiable. We're not even sure it's a..." *Not even sure it's a body*, he'd been about to say but decided that was unnecessarily gruesome, considering. "The hair was taken. We have only the necklace and the one finger to show you. We've identified the finger from the print but... The lieutenant wanted... well, if it were up to me you wouldn't have to..."

The cop's words phasing in and out of Garner's consciousness as a drawer was opened. There was a dark green bag of heavy plastic in it. It was a lumpy bag that,

170

from its lumpiness and shapelessness, might have been filled with garbage. There was no hint of a human body, except in the little freezer bag, next to it. A zip-lock bag. In the zip-lock bag was a small, slightly frosted human finger, with a distinct pink nail polish. A plump finger he knew quite well. As he stared at it, the Sargeant produced a Polaroid snapshot from his pocket. When Garner didn't turn away from his fixed stare at the finger in the freezer bag, the cop sighed and thrust the polaroid into Garner's field of vision. Garner had to make a world-wrenching effort to focus his eyes on the photo. It was a picture of a slightly bloodied necklace lying on a white paper towel. Her gold necklace. Spelling her name.

"Yes," Garner heard himself say. "Yes. Yes."

Garner followed himself out of the morgue, into the blurred hallway; the blurred chatter of the offices. It seemed that way: that he was following himself around. He could see himself walking with the cop. But he was not quite part of it. He was floating near the ceiling like a lost helium balloon. Bobbing along, detached, swept along in a slipstream by these strangers.

★   ★   ★

Another paradox: liquor brought a strange clarity to Garner's world. It dispelled the blurriness. He knew that was temporary, that booze would bring its own cloudiness, its own distancing, when alcoholism pulled him into the world of the bottle.

For the moment it had screwed him back into a definite point of view. He could see the big red X on the signpole in front of the adult bookstore complex across the street; he saw it with a new clarity. It was two stories high, that X, and its lower end was a good twenty yards over the parking lot. Just a big X on a pole. It seemed to signify more than just *dirty movies here*. It was like a hot-iron brand on the flank of the city. Or a cancel sign, a crossing-out of the city's dreamy ambitions.

It said, All this? It ain't shit. Cross it out. What was that line from Lou Reed? *Stick a fork in their asses and turn 'em over, they're done*.

Garner was in a weekly rates motel at the raw end of Hollywood Boulevard. He'd checked in, thirty-two minutes after leaving the police station. He was sitting at the grayed-out window looking at the boulevard, drinking *Early Times* Kentucky Bourbon from a plastic cup. He'd drunk his way down to the label on the fifth. Long way to go, yet. He remembered *Early Times*. It was cheap but it tasted pretty good.

He had seven hundred dollars left. He thought about that a lot. Used to be his savings. Might call that little putz James and tell him to sell everything in the house. Send the money, if the pimply motherfucker could be trusted.

The police thought that she had been put into some kind of machine. Maybe a crop thresher of some kind, or "some kind of processor" in some old factory somewhere. That would explain the Wetbones effect. The pulp and broken bone ends that had been his daughter. They'd taken her hair, like an Indian taking a scalp, and, presumably, it was displayed somewhere, in some basement room. Maybe the son of a bitch was jerking off over it, right now.

Your baby was put into a machine...

Your baby was probably raped and tortured and then put into a machine that...

172

And the fucking son of a bitch, *probably put her in alive!*

It was a fucking marvel how the world went on. How the cars continued to pass; how children continued to play Nintendo and talk about the Lakers; how Smurfs continued to gambol in cartoons for other children; how the President continued to lie in press conferences. All the usual shit went on. And someone had tortured his baby to death.

He looked out the window at the fibreglass dinginess of the monumental X sign; the razor brilliance of the points of coloured light coruscating the reptile-skin of the adult bookstore's parking lot: sunlight on broken glass. The dumb persistence of the Mexican crone with the aluminium walker, her back hunched with age, inching along the dirt path beside the curb, in one of the many ones of Los Angeles hostile to pedestrians.

"Give up and die," Garner told the crone with a mutter.

A jet, coming over the hills from the Burbank airport, seemed to shoulder sullenly against the sky as it veered West, probably for some unsuspecting tourist's nightmare sojourn in threadbare, polluted Hawaii.

The wall of the Mexican bar, beside its small gravel parking lot, was etched with the pathetic psychological watermark of Hispanic gang graffiti. Above it, something unfelt hung from the powerlines with the tennis shoes someone had tied together and tossed up there as a practical joke; something fell with a translucent blizzard of hydrocarbons from the smoggy sky.

Five years old, Constance came to him with her first Barbie. "I think Barbie's sick, Daddy." Constance had been morose, and unable to eat much, for weeks before.

He looked at the doll and there was nothing broken on it. He thought Constance wanted to play, so he said, "Uh oh. I'll be the doctor and you be the nurse and we'll –"

"No!" She was crying, now. "No, she's really hurt."

He stared at his daughter and somehow knew this was about her mom being dead. He had taken her into his arms and said, "How about you? Are you hurt?"

He'd coaxed her into talking about it and she'd begun to cry in earnest – and then to heal. There was no dramatic moment, no 'Barbie feels better Daddy!' But, as weeks passed and he stayed close to her and drew her out, he could see her begin to bloom, see her become interested in playing with other kids again, and he'd almost wept with relief. He had shown her – and himself – that he could be there for her. She's going to make it. We're going to make it. *We'll be all right* . . .

The police thought . . . a machine . . .

Now, in the hotel room on the downtown end of Hollywood Boulevard – well below the territory where Japanese tourists snapped photos of Marilyn Monroe's handprints in concrete and Bob Hope's star in the sidewalk – he said it aloud: "Grieving. What a fucking joke!" As if he deserved to grieve! Christ. Christ.

He was afraid to scream, or cry. He felt like a bug scrambling desperately to avoid the heel of some giant's shoe. Scrambling into a crevice in the floor, going to ground so as not to attract attention. So that the gargantuan, black, crushing weight of his criminal absence wouldn't flatten him to pulp . . . as she had been . . .

Surely she had screamed for him and he hadn't come. It didn't matter that he'd been unable to hear her, unable to come.

At least, now, he could be really, definitely punished.

But something in him rejoiced. It was a small thing he had starved and ignored and withered with contempt, for many years. A creature somewhere between plant and arachnid; a spider that started not as an egg but as a kind of seed; a crawling thing with roots. But now the liquor was irrigating it; now despair was revitalizing it. Its joy was unspeakable. A whole world of self destruction opened up for him, now. And it rejoiced.

It was the addict — and it had never really died.

The liquor, surely, was not going to be enough. Garner got up, staggered to the door. Went out to cop some dope.

Culver City, Los Angeles

More and more, Prentice was afraid of going to bed. Lately his pattern had been to lie there for at least an hour, his mind teeming and morbid, trying to think about anything but Jeff and Mitch, Amy and Arthwright; and thinking almost entirely about Jeff, Mitch, Amy and Arthwright.

He was staying at Jeff's now, which was probably a mistake. Sleeping on the couch in the office. It's back folded down so it made a pretty decent single bed, except for that valley down its middle, but he had some privacy here, and he was tired, so he should be able to sleep.

Should, but couldn't. Instead, he'd putter about the office, toying with Jeff's Japanese monster collection, looking at the hoard of comics and pulps; he'd pull out a book, flip through it, read a bit, put it back, and be unable to remember any of what he'd read.

175

It was dark out, and Prentice had the shades drawn. He was sitting on the edge of the sheet-covered couch in the dim room in his underwear, restless and worried. Thinking about Saturday. He'd be going out there Saturday. He'd be able to clear it all up then... And Arthwright would give him the break he needed...

But did he want to belong to Arthwright? After what he'd realized about the mirror in the guest bedroom? And then there was the way Arthwright had manipulated Prentice into doing his dirty work for him. Prentice had successfully talked Jeff into holding off on the court orders. They'd found a private detective referred by a cop – who was already looking for a missing teenager, a guy named Blume. That was a good start.

But still. It had been manipulation. Arthwright puppeting Prentice who puppeted Jeff. And then Arthwright prompting Lissa to check up on Prentice...

So what? Prentice told himself Arthwright was no more a sick manipulator than most producers in the business. It came with the territory.

Prentice glanced at Jeff's word-processor; in the gloom its monitor was a ghostly, square head propped on the desk. Jeff had been out taking meetings all day and he'd let Prentice use the computer for writing, in the hopes of getting a start on the spec script that Jeff and Buddy were counselling him to write. Prentice had produced exactly two pages of uninspired melodrama. Which he hadn't bothered to save.

On a shelf above the desk, the radio chattered to itself like a cancer patient trying to stay cheerful. The DJ finally finished blathering vacantly and put on a song. It was Iggy Pop's song, *"Butt Town."*

176

All over Butt Town
Values are thrown down . . .
But in Butt Town I'm learnin'
in Butt Town, I'm earnin'
in Butt Town I'm turnin'
into my
worst nightmare . . .

Prentice stared at the radio as if a hand had reached out of it and slapped him in the face. He stabbed a finger at the button, switched it off before Iggy could say it again.

"Fuck *you*, Iggy," Prentice muttered. He'd like to have flung the radio against the wall. But it was Jeff's.

Instead, hoping to ease some tension, he stretched out on the folded-down sofa and jerked off. It didn't help much. "Turning into my worst nightmare," Prentice muttered, stretching out on the sheets.

He couldn't quite bring himself to turn off the desk lamp.

Rest, he thought, and then get up, try to write some more, turn the restlessness into something productive.

He laid an arm over his eyes and stared into the dull flashes the pressure made on his eyeballs. It might have been an hour later when he went to sleep.

The dream, anyway, seemed to sidle up to him before he was truly asleep. Or was he dreaming about lying on the sofabed?

Amy was sitting on the arm of the sofa, near Prentice's feet. She looked good. Healthy. She wore blue jeans and a t-shirt, barefoot – *then* she wore lingerie and pumps. Then she wore blue jeans and a t-shirt again – it changed from second to second. She said, "That bitch is going to eat you alive, you know that don't you?"

177

"What?" he asked sleepily.

"You heard me."

They were walking through a shopping mall, now. Some generic shopping mall. He glanced at Amy and saw with a shock that she was desiccated and mangled again, as she had been in the morgue. She smelled of embalming fluid. A walking corpse, nude and mummy-like, but not shambling, walking perkily along with a purse on one arm, impatiently passing a troop of Girl Scouts selling cookies. She shook her head at them, No, she didn't want any cookies. They didn't react to her appearance. Lots of people in the mall were dead.

He looked away from her and said, "I don't want to see you like this. And don't say, 'Like what?'"

She said, "It's *your* dream. Make me something else. By taking me back to somewhere else . . ."

He put a hand over his eyes – and when he removed it he was in their Manhattan apartment, sitting with his arm around her, doing something she'd loved to do: watch a foreign film on videotape while drinking a bottle of red wine.

It was Fellini's *Juliet of the Spirits*. Prentice and Amy were cuddled comfortably on a big floor pillow, leaning back against the foot of her bed, watching the film. He felt warm and secure; he knew she felt the same way. For a moment or two.

Then he felt her go tense. "Nothing can stay like this," she said. "Why can't anything sustain for more than a few minutes? Or more than an hour at most? I could accept the downsides of life if there were more upsides. But there's an imbalance. It's mostly either downsides or dull gray areas, you know what I mean?"

"Yes," he said wearily. "I know what you mean." He was thinking that he was simply hearing the point of view that came when her depression hit her. She couldn't sustain simple warmth long, it was true. It was either a glittering *up* or a slide downward. There were few plateaus for Amy.

For the hundredth time he wondered how much of it was "a neurochemical imbalance" and how much was just the skew of her personality, her tendency to subvert happiness because of some childhood trauma. If it was the latter, it was something that could be overcome. But if he raised that point she'd get defensive...

Maybe he should just cut her loose. She was a basket-case and she didn't want to really do anything about it. He ought to let her basket drift like the baby Moses on the river. Trust that somebody would find her. He just couldn't take responsibility for another person's sanity.

"And that's what you did," Fellini's heroine said, on the TV screen, turning to look at him. "You cut Amy loose, didn't you Prentice?"

Prentice looked at Amy accusingly. "Don't put things in the movie. It's not respectful to the artist."

"You pushed me into leaving you," Amy said. "You wanted to get away from me. It was simple as that, wasn't it, Tommy? You had that affair and let me find out and then you acted as if you were sorry and wanted to go on but you were about as happy as a snail in a saltshaker –"

"A very colourful turn of phrase, Amy. I felt like a snail in a saltshaker. I felt like I was burning up with you. I had to babysit you constantly, and reassure you all the time, tell you it was all right ten thousand ways, and then endure your up moments – you were obnoxious when you were up as often as you were charming."

"So you cut me loose. Tom, how much is enough love? How much giving in love is too much? How do you tally it? You have units of love worked out on a calculator? How did you decide you were giving too much? You weren't the only one who gave. You could get pretty fucking moody yourself. You were really a pain in the ass when you were the aggrieved, sulking *artiste* because the screenplay was not going right or the critics had fucked you over."

"Yeah, probably. But it was a tempest in a teapot compared to your cyclone, Amy."

"To you. Anyway, I don't give up all that easily, Tommy. You're not really going to that party on Saturday, are you?"

He was staring at her. The golden reds and silky yellows with which Fellini had coloured his film were playing across her face, and the shadows seemed to run together in her eyesockets . . . to deepen in her cheeks and to etch out her breastbone . . .

She was sinking into herself. Shrivelling. Like the snail. Like the girl in the morgue.

He could smell the death on her.

He felt a purer fear, in that moment, than any he'd felt since early childhood. A four year old child was only four years and a few months from nullity – from the echoing void of pre-consciousness. That's why, he thought, small children could fear so deeply: in some visceral way, they remembered death.

Prentice shrank, too, from the blacklight, the negative shine of that fear truly pure and childlike fear of death.

He wrenched himself awake. Sat up on the sofa in Jeff's office, shaking and stupid with disorientation. That dream had been too well organized. It was far more coherent and thoughtful, in its argumentation and insights, than dreams ever were, in Prentice's experience. Dreams, if they meant anything, were metaphor. This one had been more like a goddamn essay . . .

And Amy was still with him. Her presence was almost palpable in the dim, cluttered office. He could taste Amy. He could smell her. He could feel her hair under his fingers.

He shook himself, muttering, "Cut it the fuck out," He went to get himself a drink, in the kitchen; some of Jeff's German stuff, *Jaegermeister*, chilled in the freezer! He poured himself a stiff one and drank it off. Amy drew away from him, a little. He poured himself another. Day after tomorrow was the party. Tomorrow, during the day, he'd try to get out of himself, enjoy himself. Give himself a chance to see things fresh . . .

★   ★   ★

Almost eleven-thirty, Friday morning. Prentice was strolling down Melrose Avenue. It was sunny but not yet too hot, and the street, on this block anyway, was reasonably clean. The exercise felt good, and the smog was mild. He was almost in a good mood.

He passed a newspaper vending machine, and glimpsed some headlines. *LAPD ADMITS "WET-BONES" IS HOMICIDE*. He ignored it, very deliberately. He didn't want to know about whatever it was.

Not today, anyway.

He checked out a few of the displays in the windows of the self-consciously arty boutiques. Glanced over a display of black rubber outfits for casual wear. He imagined hearing Amy comment: *How hot and sweaty and itchy are you willing to be for fashion?*

Farther on, a mannequin that had been spraypainted in gold and silver graffiti was posed like a fan of *Faith No More* in mid hiphop frenzy, wearing a black and red lace miniskirt and corset; it was dancing in a tangle of barbed wire. *Now that corset and skirt I love*, Prentice imagined Amy saying. *I'm such a sucker for underwear that can disguise itself as a dress... I wonder how much it is...*

The boutique was playing a song by The Cars that he remembered, called "You Wear Those Eyes." Amy had been enamoured of The Cars. Ric Ocasek was "just so grotesquely adorable". Prentice couldn't stand Ocasek's singing voice. Now he found himself singing along. Which was surprising – he was sure he'd never learned the lyrics to this one. The singing sounded better to him now.

He realized he was hungry and thirsty and his legs were hurting. I'm in rotten shape, he thought. He stopped in at a cafe that attempted to be a Parisian bistro, and ordered soup, bread, brie, and capuccino. Amy would have found the soup too thick with stock, but he liked it that way.

He ate and rested. Buzzing a little on the capuccino, he paid the check and continued down the street, stopping in at a couple of galleries. One of them was the sort that sell decorator art and impressionist prints to people who don't want to take chances on their own taste. He saw a couple of coloured etchings there by the same artist who'd done the pictures in Arthwright's guest room. He thought about calling Lissa, and asking her if she wanted to join him, take a turn about the galleries with him. No, don't be pushy.

He moved on to a gallery of local artists, paintings by gay neoexpressionists with frantic, guilt-edged images of copulation and self mutilation. He thought about Mitch's arms...

He hurried on to another artist: Gaudy paintings that were really arty political cartoons: Bush and Gorbacev jacking each other off on a heap of starving, suffering underclass.

These pictures, Amy said, are too didactic to last beyond the time. The curse of preachiness.

What Amy *would* have said, he reminded himself.

There was one painting that was more personal than political: A woman alone, on foot, on a freeway overpass, evidently despite all the painter's cartoonish hysteria – considering jumping off the bridge into the thick, brutish flow of traffic beneath.

Looking at it, Prentice felt a surge of reawakened memory. Memory of a feeling, mostly: what he'd felt when Amy had first left him. A sense of betrayal mixed with relief. Or was that what Amy had felt? He wasn't sure. He wanted her, suddenly, in his arms... He could almost feel her. could taste her lips, the distinctive flavour of her flesh and her favourite lipstick.

He began to feel something else, then. A suspicion.

All morning and into the afternoon, the feeling had been there. A sense of being dogged. Followed by Amy, of course. Not a feeling that she was in him... it wasn't like possession... more like she was looking over his shoulder, whispering in his ear, wreathing him with some lost essence.

He saw himself, then, as she'd seen him that day. The day they'd broken up. Tom Prentice with a refined sneer, a supercilious disdain at what he'd called her "childish over-reaction" at the affair he'd had. He saw clearly, beyond the unconvincing sneer, the fear and uncertainty briefly flickering in his face. The self loathing.

He *had* abandoned her. He had failed her and driven her away and she'd gone out into the urban-primeval outer darkness of Los Angeles and gone alone . . .

He wanted to put a fist through the painting of a woman alone on the overpass . . .

He turned and hurried out of the gallery, looking for a bar. He found a fern bar, with lots of brass and plants and abstract paintings – abstractions were more to his taste at the moment, they were safer – and he drank a double Jaegermeister. He cast about for a way to get his mind clear of Amy.

Found his way to the pay phone at the back of the bar. Jeff had given him permission to have messages left on his answering machine. He called up Jeff's number and pressed the appropriate touchtone buttons to get the machine to reel out its messages over the phone. He had to wait out three irrelevant messages for Jeff before there was one for him. It was Buddy. "Tom, this is Buddy – if I got it right, you're at this number – um, just wanted you to know that Arthwright called, he *is* interested in putting up a little money for your treatment . . ."

Prentice thought: *And Zack says thanks for the blow job*.

Buddy went on, "Um, I don't know how you pulled off that miracle but Zack says he's going to talk to you a little more about it at the party, whatever party that is – how come I'm not invited? – and I just wanted to tell you, don't accept any offers on your own, just smile and say, 'Sounds great – call Buddy!' Okay? Catchya later, pal. Hang in there."

A new record for Buddy on message length. Usually it was, "Hey I think we got a nibble, give me a call." Startled into loquacity, apparently, by Arthwright's willingness to cough up some cash.

Well. That was good, then. He should be happy about it.

He really should.

The Doublekey Ranch,
near Malibu

As Mitch's body healed, his mind began to flake away. Sometimes he heard a murmur of voices when he was sure the building and the grounds outside were empty. After a while he realized he was hearing the roses outside the window talking to one another.

When the Handy Man came into the room, Mitch didn't recognize him, at first. He looked the same as always, but somehow no identity clung to his familiar face. To Mitch this creature was just a moving module of flesh and purpose; an apotheosis of the minatory presence of this place. A thing that moved about the room like a videogame character, doing this and that; beeping now and then. Then he went away. Game Over.

Eurydice's voice brought Mitch back to himself. *"Mitch?"*

It came muffled through the wall.

"Come and talk to me!"

They'd spoken earlier, through the crack, but Mitch

hadn't been able to say much. "Oh we're just here, is all," he'd said. "I gotta lay down now. 'Bye."

How long ago had that been? Hours. He'd sat on the edge of the bed staring at the wallpaper, letting his eyes go in and out of focus. For how many hours? He shrugged, and got up from the bed, went to the wall, pushed the dresser out of the way, and crouched next to the crack.

"Mitch . . . Are you okay?"

Suddenly his pulse was pounding, his mouth was dry. "Eurydice," he said. "I'm geeking in here. I'm losin' it."

He could tell she was trying not to break down as she said, "How long you been there?"

"I don't know. Some days. Maybe some weeks. I'm not sure. They don't let me out at all. I go into some weird places in my head. I saw some shit in that room you're in. And outside. Eury, we gotta . . ."

They had to *what*? He wasn't really sure.

"Can't get out the window," she said. "Your room like that, too?"

"Yeah. There's no attic trap doors, there's nothing. No way to get out."

"The only way out is to jump somebody. When they come in the door."

He frowned. Did she really think that was possible? "They wouldn't let that happen. They know what you're doing. They know when you've been bad or good, so be good for goodness sake. They won't let us. No."

"There always be some way! Motherfuckers. Fucking motherfuckers lied, really trickin' us off, they . . ."

"We have to just *stay* here. Maybe they'll let us have lots of head syrup."

"Don't talk about that!" she hissed. He heard her thump the wall in her anger. "Goddamn it, why you such

187

a limp dick? We gone get out of here, Mitchie. We . . ."

"I was always in love with you," he said, suddenly.

She was silent for a minute. Then she said, "You tell me when we get out."

"We can't."

"Mitch – !"

"Don't get mad. We can't. Except . . . Um . . ."

"Except how?"

"Except if we . . . become like them. We got to learn to be what they are . . ."

Watts, Los Angeles

Garner found them, all of them, in the parking lot of a corner E-Z Check Cashing place, its windows cluttered with signs. *Any check cashed! Bus Passes; Money Orders; Food Stamp Pick-up; Western Union.*

On the opposite corner, across from the little parking lot, was Bubba's Discount Liquors. The crowd that hung out in the parking lot filtered back and forth between the check cashing business and the liquor store. They stood around laughing and arguing and hustling one another and ignoring one another and gossiping, their restless eyes watching the street. Now and then one of the girls, the toss-ups, would take a ride with one of the men who cruised by, looking for easy pussy. There were about forty of them in the Set, when they were all there; sometimes there were as few as ten, depending on what the Mix had given them. Garner had sat in his van and watched them for a while, sipping from his bottle until one of the girls approached him. A black girl – her skin the colour of coffee with a single spoonful of cream. She was short but quite pretty, despite being nearly emaciated. Big eyes, pointy tits in a t-shirt shortened to show her flat, muscular belly, brown jeans. It was the sort of t-shirt with a cat's face on it, traced out in gold and silver paint; its eyes were plastic fake emeralds glued on at the factory.

"How are you today?" she asked, putting it like that because he was a white guy.

He shrugged and said, 'What's your name?"

"Gretchen."

"I'm . . ." He thought back. When he was using, the time before, they'd called him Slim, on the streets. "I'm Slim."

"So. Slim – what's happening with you today?"

She was careful not to solicit him, and she was consciously speaking in mostly white English. She probably had an educated background. A fair number of addicts did. He'd met hardcore crack whores who had two degrees. They were usually black, though, even the educated ones. Going back to visit the old neighbourhood could be dangerous, if your life was going sour.

"What's happening?" Garner snorted. "My daughter's dead. She was murdered. I want to get fucked up. Really geeked-out fucked up on rock. And then I want some pussy."

She stared at him. Then laughed. "Well, you come right to the point anyway, don't you?"

★   ★   ★

They were in a dingy box that Gretchen's cousin, Hardwick, called "my crib". It was a studio apartment with the bathroom down the hall. It had nothing in it except a mattress where Garner and Gretchen and Hardwick sat with legs sprawled onto the floor; an aluminium chair missing the back; a pile of clothing in one corner. Even the fridge and the stove had been hauled out and sold somewhere, probably for less than fifty bucks each.

Garner knew it was stupid and dangerous to be here. He heard voices in the hall. From time to time people pounded on the door and asked, "What up?" Hardwick sent them away without opening the door but Garner knew that eventually they'd be back, and some of them would get in. And he knew that the more he was outnumbered, the more dangerous it was. Hardwick himself was a slender, muscular black man. Some weeks ago, after getting his back G.A. checks, he'd had his hair cut and shaped. There was a flat layer on top of his head, and his girlfriend's name, *TASHA*, was cut into the sides of his hair with calligraphic exactitude; but it had partly grown over as money went to crack instead of haircut maintenance. Hardwick wore a sleeveless, well-aged Lakers shirt, black work-out shorts and plastic sandals. Right now his yellowing eyes were focused on the crack pipe tilted off-centre and clamped between his lips.

Garner and Gretchen were staring at the pipe too. Waiting for their hits.

Garner had, of course, gotten off on the first two hits he'd taken, coached by Gretchen on how to melt the crack in the pipe with the lighter, how to draw the hit. Now, his hands shook where they clutched his knees as he struggled to keep from snatching the pipe from Hardwick.

That, he knew, would be very dangerous indeed. He hadn't seen any weapons on Hardwick but he'd seen the faded prison tattoo on the underside of his forearm, and he'd seen the old, black trackmarks on his veins from an earlier period of preferring the needle over the pipe, and, most important, he knew not a goddamn thing about

190

Hardwick. Nothing, except that he was Gretchen's cousin. And he knew scarcely anything about Gretchen. Except that she was a cocaine whore who had been a licensed RN who used to make 40K a year supervising a ward for a Chicago hospital before coming home on a vacation and getting hooked and subsequently forgetting her job, staying here for the next three years . . .

For all Garner knew, Hardwick was a murderer. For all Garner knew, so was Gretchen. Maybe they got white guys with money in here and got them fucked up and then rolled them. Or killed them.

Maybe not. Maybe she'd just wait till he was too loaded to think, and then steal his money and split. Maybe she had AIDS and syphilis which would be just too bad for him since, now that he was loaded, he had every intention of fucking her and that was understood to be part of the deal. He might be dead of AIDS in two years if he weren't beaten to death first.

All of it was possible and Garner was enjoying that possibility immensely.

With luck, he might get killed.

The pipe came around to Garner, at last. Fingers vibrating like tuning forks, he took his hit. He felt the rush; saw the room's colours drain and swirl around him; heard a humming in his ears. Then it was over.

He stared at the pipe in surprise as Gretchen pulled it from his hands. "Not mucha hit," he muttered.

"You gotta good hit," Hardwick said, absently picking at fuzz on the mattress, inspecting it between his yellowed fingers to see if it were a fleck of cocaine. Tweaking.

"No . . . I . . ." Garner shook his head. The rush had been brief and superficial. The next one, he knew, would be even less powerful. He'd never smoked crack before tonight, but in the old days he'd shot heroin and cocaine, slammed it into his mainline, and he knew what to expect from coke. A high, then a down, then a smaller high, then a deeper down, then a smaller high yet, then an even deeper down . . .

He wasn't feeling great, now, but still, he was stoned. Stoned and numb, which was right where he wanted to be. Constance seemed like a strange dream. An aberration in his life. Constance and the years of ministry. He had taken up the past seamlessly; he was back where he belonged, on the streets, burning himself up like a smoldering cigarette butt.

He waited impatiently for the next hit. It finally came but it wasn't much and he said so.

"What it is, we don't have the good shit," Hardwick said. "I can git it though. You front me two hunnerd, I bring you somethin' like a quarter ozzie."

Gretchen was shaking her head at Garner, but he fingered two hundred dollars out of a shirt pocket – he had the rest of his money tucked into his shoe – and passed it tremblingly to Hardwick. "Just do it fast."

"Need to borrow your van, bro," Hardwick said, shooting Gretchen a warning look.

Garner stared at Hardwick. The room swam around him. "My van? I don't know, man . . ."

"Hey – I leave you my I.D., and you in my place here, this is where I *live*, man, so you *know* for sure I'm comin' back."

"Oh yeah." That seemed to make sense. Sure. Yeah. He passed over his car keys and Hardwick was up and out the door.

"Motherfucker," Gretchen said. "I hope that wasn't all your money."

It came to Constance suddenly, on a balmy early evening, with the sunlight turning the smog into a sluggish light-show at the horizon.

She *could* run away from Ephram. All she had to do was suffer enough. And what would that mean? Misery. He'd shoot her full of hurt.

So what? She looked at her maimed hand; the bandages over the stump of her missing finger. He'd cut off her finger and she hardly felt it. She was disfigured, and she didn't care. She could take it. Anyway, what could be worse than this seesawing between ecstasy and the steel rods?

She was sitting on the back stoop of the place he'd rented, looking at the wasps making dabbing motions with their bodies at the rotting lemons in the corner of the backyard. They didn't seem to want the lemons but couldn't quite leave them alone.

Maybe they get sweeter when they're rotten. She looked at the fence. The gate in it.

Ephram was in the shower. He'd be distracted, though she knew he was monitoring her somehow. But he couldn't be following her too closely. He hadn't punished her for these thoughts . . .

"Go on," she said. "Let him."

She stood up and started toward the gate. It was just across the yard but it seemed to take a long time to get there. Then she'd reached it, fumbled at the latch, pulled it open, stepped into the alley –

It came like black lightning. Negative lightning from the negative constellations, from the hidden cracks in the sky, searing through a thousand light years to seek out the mote that was Constance, smashing into her head, scorching down her spine, exploding in her gut. She felt as if her intestines had exploded and blasted shit throughout her.

She screamed and staggered but kept going.

Constance!

She was in a gravel alley. The mouth of the alley and the street were about forty yards to the left. She staggered that way – and then her legs stopped working. She fell, paralyzed.

He'd reached into the motor-controls of her brain. He'd stopped her cold. She was lying on her face, with the lower half of her body turned into a granite statue, shivering with sickness and pain.

Then it lifted. It was as if the wing of an angel had come between her and the pain. It was gone. The feeling in her legs returned. She felt no hurt but for the sting of a scrape where the gravel had dug her knee.

All right, Constance. You dirty little whore. Go. You don't love me anyway. You never loved me. Go. Run away. Enjoy...

The words echoed in her head – and then faded. She got to her feet. Was he really going to let her go? She jogged off down the alley. She got to the corner. She had no money – wait, she had a dollar in change, in her jeans.

A dollar was enough for the city bus that came trundling along the boulevard toward her, as if eager for a long-anticipated rendezvous.

Hollywood

She knew this was the Sunset Strip, in Hollywood, and that the crowd standing in line outside the rock club was there to hear some headbangers. She could hear some band inside thundering away. It was about eleven p.m.

and getting dark, and she was hungry and tired. That's about all she knew. She'd called her dad's house, using his credit card number, and some boy answered, "Garner residence." And she'd asked, "Who're you?" He said his name was James and he was house-sitting for Mr. Garner and she told him, "This is Constance. I just wanted to tell dad I'm okay and uh, I'm . . . Uh . . ."

Then she'd hung up. She wasn't sure why. Why didn't she tell him where to find her? Why didn't she *want* her dad to find her?

She thought about the cops, again. But she was a murderer. Even though Ephram had forced her, she had murdered people, she had cut them up and tortured them to death, and if she turned Ephram in the cops would get her too. They'd never believe she had been forced to do all those things. They'd never believe her about how Ephram had done it. And how could she prove it? She couldn't.

Of course, she should at least turn Ephram in anonymously. Stop the killing. They'd be looking for any lead at all on the Wetbones killings. They'd check out the call.

Why couldn't she do that? She could make the report for free, by calling 911. What was stopping her?

She churned inside. Her emotions in such turmoil she couldn't move, couldn't turn this way or that. But one feeling came up, more stridently than any other. It took her a while to recognize it.

"No," she said aloud. "No, forget it, no."

She shook herself out of the stuck feeling, and walked up the line of headbangers. Not sure what she was looking for.

She found it, though: she picked them out easily. Three boys, who'd clearly come here without girlfriends.

Boys with fantastic, feathery, multicoloured haircuts and leather jackets; badges pinned between the spikes on the black lapels, military insignia, anything official-looking enough to be both glittery and out of place. "Hi you guys," she said, stopping near them as if she'd been about to walk by but had only just noticed them. "Didn't I meet you, like, somewhere in the Valley at that girl's party? What was her name?" She kept her maimed hand in her jacket pocket.

"Oh – Olivia?" one of the boys said. He wore dark glasses and fingerless black leather gauntlets. Spiked belt, like the others, and spiked straps slung around his snakeskin cowboy boots.

"Yeah," Constance said. "I think her name was something like that. Olivia. I was kind of drunk."

"Oh *wow*," the taller, blond one with the big adam's apple said. Buying the lie completely. "I think I remember you. Are you, like, the chick that fell into the pool?"

"Yeah. That was me."

"Oh dudette," said the smallest and, judging from his slack mouth and dull eyes, the stupidest one of the three. He had black hair and zits and eyebrows that grew together. "You don't rully get stoned unless you like fall over, you know?" He said *stoned* so it sounded like *stooned* and *know* so it came out knoo. "An' why fuckin bother to get stooned if you don't rully get stooned you know?"

"I know," she said, making herself smile. The line shuffled toward the door; she went with the three boys, peering anxiously at the burly doorman. "I'm not 21 – do you think I could get in this place?"

"Oh yeah dudette," the small, stupid one said. "They got it fixed so if you don't order no drinks at the bar, you can be under 21 and still get in the club, you know? You just chill in the main room. Hey, you wanna smoke a number?"

★   ★   ★

The small, stupid one paid her way in and snuck drinks to her, hovered close, touching her arm from time to time, checking out her tits, thinking he was getting over and he was finally going to get laid. The other two tried to bird-dog her too, when they could, but she stuck close to the stupidest one. She could handle him.

The place was dark but fragmented with coloured light, pierced by the small spotlights striking at the stage in perfectly straight-edged shafts of whirling cigarette smoke; the walls reverberated with the roar of the Marshall stacks behind four air-humping rockers on a beer-sticky stage. Once she saw a handful of sweat from the capering lead singer fall onto the footlight next to the monitor speakers and sizzle back up in oily steam. The bass player was kind of cute.

Huge waves of metallic sound rolled out of the Marshalls and over the crowd, so that most of the time Constance didn't have to make conversation, since it couldn't be heard anyway. The club was only a four-hundred-seater and the noise of the band would have filled an auditorium.

She felt strange. Confused, hungry but not hungry, tired but wired, teetering on the crumbling edge of a cliff unseen in the darkness of her inner world. She had been stuffing her feelings into the cat-carrier for so long, guarding her thoughts so endlessly, she couldn't quite make sense of freedom from Ephram's super-vision. Every so often, she asked herself, again: Why don't I call

197

the cops? Why don't I try harder to find dad? Why don't I try to get home to Alameda?

She felt no guilt, not really, but a dull ache of disgust at having participated in the killings. It was like stepping in dogshit. She really hadn't had any choice. She'd tried refusing, three times, letting Ephram punish her – he could leave her lying on the floor paralyzed for hours, or move her limbs around like a puppet. Could make her part of it whether it was voluntary or not. And when he pushed her pleasure buttons, she responded automatically to do whatever was necessary to keep it going. There was no choice about that, not at those levels of pleasure. It was . . . programmed. Something she knew about from her dad.

Oh God. Now *there* was some guilt: Thinking about her dad. How could she go on like this without getting in touch with him? He must think she was dead or something . . .

Dead. What difference did it make who was dead, and who was briefly alive? Everyone, Ephram had pointed out, was dying: they were in a waiting room called life. When they were done waiting, their number was called and they were hustled through the door into death. Into nothingness. She'd seen so much death. It seemed so near and so easy. What did it matter if her father thought she was dead? She was near enough to it.

She hugged herself, wincing as the guitar player went into another sonic tirade. She could make out the music in the wall of sound, but it was some kind of speed-metal thing, and she didn't relate. She liked Bon Jovi and Whitesnake because those guys had something sweet about them, even if they did act like hard-rock types sometimes.

No matter what she thought about, that *one feeling*

wouldn't go away. It was this painful pulling sensation in her gut. Like there was a crab in there, pulling on her innards with its serrated pincers, trying to get her to *go* somewhere. The discomfort was getting worse and worse.

She felt something else, now, and sharply. A hollow aching. A big black hole of depression. The drinks and the pot hardly helped at all. It ached *deeply* in her, from her stomach down into her uterus. She thought she might collapse inward on herself...

She imagined Ephram, smiling at her in an avuncular kind of way. His semi-erect little pee-pee radiating solace and waves of Reward...

Now the stupid one with the single long eyebrow was yelling something in her ear. Something about did she want to go get loaded, somewhere. He was making his move.

She had to get away from him, hanging around him just made her want to give in to that aching hunger...

Made her want to kill him. It would feel good. It would be such a relief to kill him.

She shouted in his ear: "Do you have any condoms?"

His eyes lit up, hearing that. He shook his head. "No! But –"

"They have some in the girl's bathroom here, I think. There's a condom machine. They cost a couple of dollars. Could you give me the money?"

He nodded, trying not to grin, and gave her a small wad of cash. She squeezed his arm, smiled at him, and headed for the girl's bathroom. Once camouflaged by the crowd, she broke for the exit door.

★　　　★　　　★

Ephram wasn't surprised to see her come back. He had known, and that was the only reason he had let her go. The inevitability of her return was almost tiresome.

He took her hand and smiled, to show he held no rancor for her, and led her into the living room. They sat down on the leased couch. "I had to come back," she said mechanically. "Did you do something to . . . ?"

"Did I make you come back with my mind? Not at all. You were well out of my reach. No, my dear. You came back on your own, wagging your tail behind you, ha ha." He smiled at her, trying to make it a sad smile, hoping she'd feel sorry she'd hurt him. Not wanting to force it on her psychically, if he didn't have to. "You see, your brain has been somewhat re-ordered. You are an addict now. What you felt was withdrawal. It would have gotten worse. It would have killed you." This last was a lie, of course, but a necessary one.

"I'm an addict? Addicted to the Reward?"

"Yes. I know you don't love me – but I hold no grudges, my dear. After all – only a short time ago, you were forced to submit while I cut off one of your fingers. No doubt a bit traumatic, but a necessary sacrifice, for our protection. No, I will not punish you this time. In fact –" He put his arm around her, and with it gave her a burst of Reward. She slumped against him with relief. "Did you call anyone?" he asked.

"No," she said absently, humming to herself. "No. Well – I tried to call my dad once but he wasn't home and I didn't try again . . . I didn't call the cops or anyone either . . ."

"Good. Lovely." He wondered in passing why he hadn't been more worried about that possibility. In the interim between her rebellion and her withdrawal, she might well have turned him in. It occurred to him, not for the first time, that he had been behaving with a sort of recklessness lately.

He shrugged and went on, "Well now – I have some news for you. I have made a decision. I have, you see, been chewing your fate over in my mind, this last couple of weeks. Wondering if I should send you into Wetbones and have done with you, or go on as we have been – or, the third possibility. I have decided on the third recourse. That other step. I seem to have . . . to have become very attached to you.

"And I would like to see you feel the same about me. I know you don't, despite your pretenses. I'd rather not simply program you to be attached to me. I want something deeper. So . . . I thought perhaps – and this may be foolish – if I taught you what I know, up to a point, you might see me as I really am, underneath, recognize the Nameless Spirit that guides me. Understand me better. And learn some of these disciplines yourself." He hesitated, licking his lips. His mouth had suddenly become dry; the palms of his hands damp. He felt strangely off-balance – he was used to simply commanding her. He sighed, and went on, "You could become an initiate. I've never shown you my diary but . . . well, ah, all in good time. Understand, anyway, that this is an honour I have shared with no one else. The others are all dead. Only you have been chosen for this Knowledge . . ."

"I know it's an honour Ephram. I do," she mumbled into his breastbone.

"But you must promise me to be very close-mouthed about whatever you learn. Look at this . . ." He took a newspaper clipping from his shirt pocket and unfolded it for her; it showed a photo of three cops standing around awkwardly in the trapezoid of a yellow-tape police barricade, as a plainclothes morgue technician squatted with

201

a bodybag. There was a row of onlookers behind the tape. Ephram tapped the image of a faintly-smiling man in sunglasses. "This is a certain Samuel Denver, my dear. Some of his followers call him The More Man." Ephram paused to read a paragraph under the photo: *The remains left by a fourth "Wetbones" killing prompted Angela Herman, Assistant District Attorney to issue this statement, "We are bearing down on 'Wetbones' with all we have, and so far getting nowhere. But we won't ease up – this killer has taken the final step that only the Nazis equalled. He's taken women victims beyond even reducing them to murdered sex objects, or hunted ar mals – he's turned them into unrecognizable mounds of w ecked flesh and bone. It's the ultimate dehumanization and I'm sorry to say it doesn't surprise me – that's the logical next step in our deterioration as a society...*" Ephram chuckled, and went on, "Denver's been talking to people around the investigation. He has to be – because they're calling it 'Wetbones'. That's my term and he is one of the few who knows it. I don't think he's giving them a line on me – that'd be dangerous for him. He's playing games, is what he's doing, the rogue. He got into this photo on purpose, expecting I'd see it ... He paused to give her another jolt of Reward, so as to seal her attentiveness. "And you see, Constance, I do not wish to be located either by the police or by dear old Samuel..." Odd, he thought, how he'd come to think of her so much more personally than the other girls. She was not a number in his journal the way they were, not any more. She was Constance. Very reckless indeed. "We must be careful, Constance, even of a small slip. Well, ha ha, a small slip can lead to a big slap, my dear. Oh yes."

"Tell me," she said, snuggling against him. "Tell me about the Spirit..."

"The Nameless Spirit? In time, my little one" Ephram said. "Not yet. First you must know the behind of it all ...

"In 1923, a group of people came together in Hollywood at the house of a woman named Elma Juda Stutgart. She was a wealthy German immigrant – though perhaps immigrant is not the word. Citizen of the nation called Wealth, is closer. She maintained houses in several countries, and often returned to her lovely home in Berlin. Mrs. Stutgart was recently widowed; her husband had been rather mysteriously lost overboard in the course of a transAtlantic voyage. She had a servant who was a rather sturdy Bavarian peasant from the Black Forest and she called him Thandy, although I think this was some sort of corruption of his real name.

"Mrs. Stutgart was fascinated with the relatively new art of the motion picture – to generously grace that business by calling it an art.

"Actually, Mrs. Stutgart's true fascination was with a certain silent film star. She gave a number of extravagant parties for her pet star. The parties began as glamorous, and soon became sordid. Valentino and William S. Hart and Fatty Arbuckle were regulars at her bacchanals. Mrs. Stutgart was a morphine addict and once in America, increasingly infatuated with cocaine. Cocaine was quite a popular drug, in certain circles, even back then. Its addictive qualities were not understood in those days, and it was not illegal. Bowls of it were set out at parties and the revellers indulged with wild abandon. This, along with drink and his native stupidity, is what got Fatty Arbuckle in trouble.

"The director James Whale, the auteur behind the films *Frankenstein* and *The Invisible Man*, was a cocaine addict and, in the '30s, one of Mrs. Stutgart's most frequent guests. Sometimes Whale was her lover, but so was nearly everyone else, after her film-star sweetheart refused to have anything to do with her. Apparently she'd gone mad with jealousy at a party, on seeing her pet flirt openly with Rudolph Valentino, and tried to kill him with an ice pick. She continued the parties spitefully without him, throwing herself ever more into perversity. There were, for example, the young boys, not yet teen-agers, whom she hired from the local fagens; a baker's dozen of dough-soft young things who were forced to act out an obscene play Mrs. Stutgart had written, buggering one another while declaiming bad verse. Must have been quite amusing.

"Are you paying attention, Constance?"

"Oh yes, I am, Ephram, really, I'm listening!"

"There were more exotic visitors to Mrs. Stutgart's late-night circle," Ephram continued. "There was Madame Blavatsky, the Spiritualist and architect of Theosophy, and Aleister Crowley, a drug addict himself. He was largely a fraud as a sorceror, was Crowley; but a fraud of great power, strangely enough. Mrs. Stutgart learned some interesting things from Crowley and Blavatsky. Certain things that neither of them spoke about in public or in print, except to hint at it. Mrs. Stutgart experimented with some of these things, and Crowley and Blavatsky, alarmed at her successes, soon departed for the continent. But Mrs. Stutgart was undaunted. She went on and down, ha ha . . .

"She was a driven woman, our Mrs. Stutgart. Cocaine users, and users of methedrine – whether they inject it, smoke it or snort it – inevitably discover, my pet, that after the first few strong doses of cocaine or amphetamine, there's very little pleasure left in the drug. There's only the compulsion to get high. The pleasure

204

centre of the brain – and this you and I know only too well, Constance – has only so many cells and can only bear a certain amount of unnatural stimulation before it's necrotic. Burnt out, you would call it. So what is left? What next?

"The drug-maddened Mrs. Stutgart and a few of her grasping, leechlike friends found a way to bridge the gap, to pass beyond the barrier. They found that, having learned certain psychic disciplines, and having contacted certain . . . well, certain creatures of the Ether World, and having made arrangements with those creatures, whom we call the Akishra, they could use *other people's* brains for pleasure. They could pirate that pleasure. First, one takes control of those people with the proper manipulation of the reward and punishment centres of the brain – then one stimulates them, whether through pleasure or pain, rerouting all sensations through the pleasure centre. Once the pleasure stimulus is used up, the pain sensors can be used and the impulses altered. And one can experience a portion of what goes on in that other brain by proxy. If one has control of five such people, one can feed off five brains– without damaging one's own brain. It is the soul, ultimately, my dear Constance, that experiences pleasure or pain – the brain is only the fragile circuit that translates the sensations.

"Now, Mrs. Stutgart became more and more reclusive. Many of her circle were murdered, or very sensibly committed suicide. She became more psychically powerful still – and her 'arrangements' with the Akishra, the creatures who make this parasitism possible, became more involved. They maintained her in a degree of good health, while others aged around her. They fed, through her, on the shattered souls of those who were her prey. She took the senses, the minds of her victims; the

Akishra sucked instead at their spirits. She had become symbiotic with them.

"Eventually..." Here Ephram paused to sigh, and chew a nail in sudden anxiety, wondering: What was he risking, with these revelations?

But he found he could not prevent himself from continuing...

"Eventually, little Constance, Mrs. Stutgart developed a new circle of friends around her. A whole new generation. This was in the 1940s, and on into the early '60s. There was, for example, a young producer named Sam Denver. Whom she eventually married. She changed both her first and last names – she goes, now, by Judy Denver. Also in this circle were other luminaries of film and the arts. There was the actor Lou Kenson; there was the painter Gebhardt who claimed to do portraits of one's aura as well as one's physical person. And there were –"

"I remember Lou Kenson!" Constance exclaimed. "He was a big star when I was little. He was in that TV show *Honolulu Hello*."

"Yes, yes, quite. Ah, also in this new circle were many who didn't seem to belong – such as myself. I had written an essay on Nietzsche that 'Judy Denver' enthused over, so she contacted me, and wired me a ticket to visit her at the Doublekey Ranch. Some intuition prompted me to accept. There, at the Ranch, I was initiated. I had a rather spectacular talent, you see – a talent the others did not have – which set me apart, and made me a valuable resource to the Denvers.

"The blossoming of this Divine Vision, as I think of it, this special talent, made me realize I was above the repugnant miscegenation that the Denvers and their set indulged in...

"What's miscegenation?" Constance asked.

"Interbreeding between races, my dear. In this case it went farther, really – it was interbreeding between species. Well, perhaps what they were doing was not exactly breeding, not sex – but it was a hideous congress of animal and man. The Akishra are thinking creatures, in a sense, but they are not highly evolved beings – they are really a kind of animal. An etheric animal. They are not in the same class as the Nameless Spirit . . .

"I did not wish to belong to the Akishra. So, I broke away. I found the Nameless Spirit, and with it, my own direction . . .

"Pleasure is important, but – despite what I may have told you for my earlier convenience – it is not enough alone. There must also be exaltation. True dominance and transcendence! Otherwise I would be only what the Denvers are: pleasure vampires. Vampires of the pleasure-centre of the brain, something they are absorbed in so fully they are no longer able to think beyond it. It is their *raison d'etre*. Pleasure – and pain in others that becomes pleasure in the Akishra.

"Pleasure can be taken to levels the Akishra cannot comprehend, when one becomes the superman, the man who is more than man. And we simply cannot achieve real dominance with the damn worms haunting us day and night . . ."

"Ephram?" she asked. "Could you give me a little more Reward now?"

"Oh yes, my dear. Here's a little. That's all for now.

"We'll talk more of this later. We'll talk of the Nameless Spirit. First, let me play some Mozart for you, and let us have a bite to eat. I know how you like pizza, and I ordered one for you in anticipation of your return. I'll just put some in the microwave. Then we'll drink in

207

more Reward, and contemplate, together, a fine and elegant murder . . ."

Sherman Oaks, Los Angeles

It was a relief when Lissa opened the door. Though the sunny afternoon seemed to make a joke of his fears, Prentice had been irrationally certain that Arthwright would be waiting at Lissa's place, smirkingly poised behind the door. "I should have been cool and waited to see you at the party," Prentice said. "But –" He shrugged ruefully and hoped he was coming off charmingly smitten. "I just had to see you."

She smiled. "I can live with that." She was wearing a sky-blue Japanese robe, embroidered with red dragons, open in the front to show only a white string bikini. "You wanted to see me – and you can see me pretty well, in this thing. I was out back getting a tan. Come on in."

He'd been hoping that coming here would drive the burden of Amy's imagined presence from him. He'd felt dogged by memories of her, almost by a sense of her nearness, for days. It was wearing on him. Sometimes it very nearly terrified him.

But the nagging intrusiveness, the taint of Amy's point of view, stuck with him as he followed Lissa into the house. *Tacky robe she's wearing*, he imagined Amy saying. *And these paintings. What is she, a Hare Krishna?*

The wall was adorned with framed prints of Hindu deities, scenes from the *Uppanishads*; brilliant-hued panoplies of spirits from the tormented fertility of India.

They stepped into a modern living room with a flagstone floor scattered with sheepskin rugs, and a tinted glass back wall; out back, a cinderblock fence enclosed a kidney-shaped pool, a redwood hot tub, and immaculately gardened strips of Bird of Paradise, gardenia bushes and yucca. The back door was open and the heavy odor of gardenias hung almost cloyingly in the air.

"You live rather well," Prentice began, pausing to look around. He had almost finished by saying, *For a secretary*. But that would have been rude. Still, it was odd. This place was large and expensive.

"The place is left over from a former marriage; he got the cash and I got the house," Lissa said; she said it rather glibly, Prentice thought. She looked at him thoughtfully a moment, then went on, "I was just going to have a light beer. You want one?"

"Sure. Thanks."

Beers in hand, they settled on the white couch. "You look kind of tense," she said.

"Do I? I guess I am. It's a couple of things. Not knowing how to act today with you – how much of what happened at the party was a fluke of your mood or . . . or what. And I've been bothered by . . . Well. Maybe I should tell you about Amy."

She raised a casual hand. "Hey. You're under no obligation to apologize for having girlfriends and wives or whatever."

Prentice imagined Amy remarking, *You might know the slut would take that attitude.*

He took a long pull at the beer, and then said, "You misunderstand, Lissa. Amy's dead. She was my ex-wife. I identified her body not that long ago . . . I'm still a little freaked out by it."

He expected the ritual noises of sympathy from her. But she only nodded slowly, and squeezed his arm. And said, "Look– the only thing you can do is *let go*. Just let go of her. And feeling responsible – I see that in you, that you feel responsible. But we're not responsible for how other people end their lives. You know? You get out of yourself you'll feel better. I've got an idea . . ."

She disappeared into a side hall, past the kitchen area, and he wondered if he were supposed to follow her back to the bedroom. He imagined Amy saying, *God what a bitch. 'Just let go of her' she says. That's easy for this slut to say* . . .

"Stop it," he muttered to himself

Lissa came back with something cupped in one hand. She sat down and opened her hand; in it were two large gel capsules of white powder. Prentice stared at it, then shook his head hastily. "No. No thanks. I don't indulge. Too many of my friends have taken the big plunge behind drugs . . ."

"This isn't anything addictive. It's MDMA. *You* know – Ecstasy."

He knew. He remembered Amy had taken it . . .

She went on, "With a little demerol mixed in, just a little, to take the edge off because these are pretty big hits."

"Uhhh . . ."

"It's a great aphrodisiac."

She knows your weakness, all right.

"Sold," he said defiantly, taking a capsule. He downed it with beer, and she took hers as she walked to the CD player. She put on some George Benson. Then crooked a finger at him, opened her arms. He stood and walked to her, and he thought he could hear Amy saying, *You've done it now, dumbshit. She's completely –*

But then Lissa slipped into his arms. And with that contact, the imaginary voice cut off. The stifling memory of Amy, the presence that had dogged him – simply vanished. Instantly.

Prentice and Lissa danced. By the end of the third tune, there was an electricity flickering between his teeth and along his spine, his nerve ends sang along with the music, his dick was hard, and he was convinced Lissa was the finest girl in the world.

Watts, Los Angeles

"Yeah right," Garner said irritably. "I'm supposed to give you my —" He broke off not wanting to let her know he was down to his last fifty dollars. It was amazing his money had stretched this far, considering the night of smearing his lungs with crack residue.

"Your cousin steals my van and a big roll of my money and you want me to give you *more* money?"

"That was Hardwick, shit, I'm not Hardwick. Anyway what I trust you for either? You ran out on me."

"I went to look for that asshole. Shit, why should I stay? You weren't living up to your side of the bargain."

Meaning, she hadn't put out. The crack had affected him with an outrageous sexual desire, and it was a tacit part of the deal that she come across for her share of the stuff. She'd kept inching away from him, saying, "Just hold on now, it's worth waiting for, we going get real here in a minute, lemme see that motherfuckin' pipe first." Slipping into something closer to ghetto English now that she was fucked up and tired.

Tired. Both of them, now, on the street corner, staggering through the conversational wrangling like zombies, sagging from their bones. That's how Garner felt, anyway. Gretchen looked tired but a little fresher than him. She's used to this shit, he thought. Probably got herself tuned to sleep for two days once a week.

About seven a.m. Hardwick's room had become a shrinking box. Garner had gone out to see if he could catch sight of Hardwick, improbable as that was. Any loony move could seem like a good idea, loaded on this shit, he reflected. You got stoned and everyone could see it: could see your highbeams on, your eyes and mouth gaping, your exposed brain with a smoking hole in it. They could chuck anything they wanted into that hole in your skull. They saw you coming and they *took* you. It was a street skill they had: picking out the ones stoned enough to be stupidly tunnel-visioned but not yet stoned enough to be dangerously paranoid.

Whatever indignity crack left him open for – *every* indignity, ultimately – it did one thing for him in exchange: Crack totally and entirely occupied his mind. It pushed out even visions of Constance shoved alive into a crushing machine . . .

Take another hit

He'd found a place down the street that'd rent him a room for a few hours, and he'd holed up there, knocking back a bottle of wine and six Ibuprofen, which combination, he'd heard, would shoehorn him into sleep. It worked for a while; something close enough to sleep descended on him in the roachy hotel, until a pain in his gut woke him; it was a pain that eventually resolved into a rusty-knife forged out of depression and sheer self-hated, gouging and torquing into him till he had thrashed himself off the bed and back down onto the street.

Here on the street, in the pitiless sunlight, he immediately encountered Gretchen, dressed in the same clothes, eating one of those mushy popsicles pushed out of a plastic envelope. That would be breakfast for Gretchen.

Ten paces away a white hooker stood on the sidewalk, next to a parking meter. She was the kind who did her best to compensate for being butt-ugly by wearing layers of make up and having her hair immaculately coifed. She was a big stocky, scowling girl. He thought for a moment she might be a transvestite but, looking closer, he could see she was simply an apeish looking woman. Even from here he could see the rash of track marks on the backs of her hands. She was pretty hard core, using her veins up to that point. She was jonesing bad, too; she couldn't get comfortable, where she stood. She'd shift from one foot to another; then walk a few feet, around the parking meter; then walk back; toy with the meter's lever idly. Then she'd look nervously up and down the street. Shift from foot to foot. Her hands twitchily clutching and unclutching. Straightening the hem of her dress. Three times.

She was pretty sick from heroin withdrawal, poor thing. She wouldn't be out here this time of day, shifting twitchy like that, if she weren't.

Garner once had a jones on heroin himself, in earlier years, and he remembered the insistent discomfort that just got worse and worse and worse till you were like a plucked but still-living turkey turning on a spit over a slow fire.

Have to see if he could cop some of that, later.

"What you staring at that bitch for?" Gretchen asked.

"Maybe I get my money's worth, I go to her," Garner said, though he had no such intention.

"You think I should've put out for you last night? You think you'd've been able to get it up then? No way, that stoned. You think so, you don't know rock. But you had some sleep, you could do it now – we could get a rock and, before you lose your hard-on, we could get down together . . ."

Garner shrugged. He felt like shit. He felt like an old, old man; he felt wrung out and vastly depressed; his brain scorched and his self-disgust an inflamed, pustulant sore in his gut. And that was from smoking the stuff she was now proposing he buy for them once more. Already, the stuff was killing him.

But he could almost taste it in his mouth. He could picture melting the crack, the smoke; he could picture inhaling it. He could imagine the rush – which his addict mind told him would be good again, though deep down he knew it wouldn't.

There was really no choice about his decision at all; none that he could perceive.

So this is what Aleutia went through, he thought, as he followed Gretchen down the street, and into the Projects, where only the stupidest white drug users venture without an armed guard. Here, there was no thinking about Constance. Not while he was being crushed alive himself.

Near Malibu

"This fence a motherfucker," Orphy grunted, pulling himself up onto the top.

"Just keep going," Lonny whispered. He was already waiting on the other side of the fence. He'd scratched his right arm and one thigh rather badly, going over the top where the sharp wire-ends of the fence-weave stuck up; the wounds burned, and his heart thumped. They still had another fence to go over: the smaller, black iron fence.

It was a pretty dark night out, Lonny noticed, now, looking around. It hadn't seemed so dark up on the road. Maybe they should have done what Orphy had suggested: drive the ripped-off truck right through the gate, bash it in, bash into the next gate, then right up to the house, guns blazing, yelling for Mitch and Eurydice. But that kind of shit, he was fairly sure, only worked in movies.

There was only a sliver of moon, and the stars seemed interested but didn't shed much light. The stars just wanted to watch.

Oak trees and some pines and little Manzanita grew around the borders of the place; there was a sickeningly strong smell of roses from where they overgrew the front fence. There was a guard over there, so they'd snuck around, outside the fence, to the flank of the place. Here, between the two fences, was sage and yucca and thatches of dry yellow grass and grotesquely twisty manzanita that seemed to shift and hunch toward him . . . No, that was the breeze that had been coming up. One of those Santa Ana winds. Warm and kind of weird. It picked up again, skirling dust around his ankles and making tree branches scratch out off-key notes against the chainlinks.

The inner fence should be easier. But they had to hurry, a place like this would probably have . . .

He heard their running feet, coming through the brush, before they started barking: Guard dogs. Probably *attack* dogs.

"Get your ass down here, Orpheus, goddamn it!" Lonny yelled. "The fuckin dogs are comin'!"

Orpheus was just lowering himself to drop when he heard the dogs snarling and Lonny yelling, "Look out here come the fuckin dogs!"

"No way man I'm goin' back over!" Orphy shouted,

his voice panicky. He tried to scramble up the fence again, his shoes ringing the links, as the dogs bounded into view. Sleek, dark animals, streamlined as sharks.

Lonny drew the .45 from under his coat, as the bigger dog went for him, the other one bounding to leap at Orphy's legs where he dangled from the fence. Orphy screamed as Lonny fired – and for a moment Lonny thought he'd somehow shot Orphy but then the bigger dog folded up in mid-leap and fell at his feet, convulsing, jaws frothing blood. He couldn't see where he'd shot it.

Orphy was screaming *"Shit shit shit motherfucker!"* as the other sleek, slick-furred attack dog tugged at his ankle, gnawing and pulling with nasty jerkings of its whole body, putting its weight into jerking him off the fence – he fell onto his butt, and the dog lunged for his throat.

Lonny had spent the last ten seconds aiming carefully, for fear of hitting Orphy. He fired, putting a round into the back of the dog's head, and it collapsed with a single yelp on Orphy's legs. It lay there, splayed and quivering, like a cartoon of a dog sleeping contentedly on its master.

Orphy gave a grunt of disgust and rolled the dog off him, then peeled his bloody socks away from his ankle. It was rent in three places but not deeply. "Fuck! I hope that shit-eating hound wasn't rabid, man!"

"They ain't gonna keep no fuckin' rabid dogs to guard their place, dude," Lonny said. "Oh fuck– here comes the guard now."

He was a big, dark silhouette with a blaze of light at his gut like the light of an oncoming train bearing down on them. Orphy scrambled to his feet and followed Lonny, sprinting into the brush between the chainlink fence and the black iron one.

They expected the guard to follow – Lonny could see the shotgun in the guy's other hand, a black bar in the dimness – but the dude ran to the dogs, babbling and bawling. Lonny couldn't make out what he was saying. "Dude sounds fucked up on something, to me," Lonny said.

"Maybe he just crazy for those dogs."

"Maybe both. Come on . . ." He crept in a halfcrouch back out the way they'd come, coming from behind and one side of the security guard. By the time the guard heard Lonny coming and looked around, Lonny had the muzzle of his gun three inches from the corner of the dude's jaw. "Drop that shotgun, motherfucker, or you are dead meat in two seconds." He didn't hear Orphy behind him. He wondered if the son of a bitch was backing him up like he ought to be.

Clunk, the shotgun fell to the ground. The guard said, "You ain't gettin over on shit! You try to rob these people, it just ain't gonna happen, these people here, you illin to fuck wid em. I know, I seen some shit, bro –"

In the backlight off the flashlight, Lonny could see the guy's eyes, the pupils small, for it being so dark out, and his face glistening with sweat. Maybe it was just because of the gun in his face, but something about the dude, like he was going to go off like a hand grenade, made Lonny think there was more happening here. "What you loaded on?"

"Dust," the guy blurted. "Or you wouldn't a got the drop on me."

Great. PCP. This guy was still dangerous. "Sittin up here smoking dust joints all night? We ain't here to rob shit. There's a boy in there, his name Mitch?"

"Up at the house? You the third people to ask about him. Was his brother up here, then a private detective,

217

I told em I don't think he's here. Denvers say he's not here – but what I know? I never even been to the house."

"Bullshit!"

"It's true! I never been up there! That's part of the deal. I never cross that inside fence – I'm not supposed to, unless I see someone climb over it. You the first to get past the outside fence." The dude's voice getting higher-pitched, babbling faster, like he was working himself up to something, "Fuck yeah I see it, I know some shit, I seen some shit, but I never ask nobody nothin. They pay me three times what I get working in town, then you motherfuckers come and murder my poor hounds and you – now you *fucking up my motherfuckin JOB!*"

A blaze of light blinded Lonny as the flashlight swung and thunked hard into the back of his gunhand and he felt the .45 fly from his fingers and then the guy was reaching for him –

Crack, crack. Two red fingers of light and two shots: the guard staggered back, Orphy's .38 smacking him in the gut. The guard groaned and dropped the flashlight. Lonny grabbed it up, swung the beam to find the .45 as the guard went stumbling off wailing something about "Now you fucked up, you done hurt me –"

Blood singing in his ears, dizzy from hyperventilation, Lonny pointed the .45 at the guard's back, in a sudden panicky need to blow somebody away. But Orphy stepped up, shoved Lonny's gun-hand down, and hissed, "No forget it, let him go. He don't matter. With the shooting, the people at the house probably already call the cops by now – if they going to. Let's get over the fucking fence."

The guard had gone ahead of them, stumbling through the gate up toward the house, looking for help. They could hear him cursing as he crashed through bushes.

Orphy and Lonny were within sight of the house. Looked like two houses, a smaller one in back; you could just see a corner of it from this angle. They saw no lights.

Orphy muttered, "I think my ankle's swelling up."

"Can you walk?"

"Yeah. You know what? It looks to me like nobody's home."

"Bullshit. They switched off the front lights when they heard those shots, so we'd think so."

"I don't know, man, that don't –"

"Just come on, Orphy. Let's hurry and get it done. We doing all right. I watched your back, got that dog; you came in for me with that asshole, we doing okay. We got the juice on, so fuck it, let's do it."

With the flashlight doused they followed a path toward the house; it was an old brick path, the cracks between the bricks lumpy with moss; Manzanita and miniature palms and a riot of bird of paradise crowded in thickly on both sides.

About fifty yards from the darkened columns of the main house, the trees and brush were cleared for a lawn that had gone to seed; the yellowish grass was knee-high now, and clumped with thistles. The brick path skirted the lawn on this side – on the far side of the lawn was a gravel driveway, thatchy with weeds beside it, an old, stone watering trough and a plaster jockey lawn ornament. Lonny saw no cars and wondered where they kept them.

To Lonny's right was a passageway of trellis, heavily coated with rose vines and morning glory. There was a statue of a woman that had become overgrown with the rose vines. He found himself staring at it.

Then the statue moved. It *was* a woman. A woman stuck in the vines.

Orphy saw her first. "Jesus Christ..." Lonny followed him up to the woman and switched on the flashlight. Thinking it would show she wasn't real; was some kind of dummy.

When the light hit her she squirmed and chuckled miserably to herself. "Fuck!" Lonny breathed. She was nude except for a tattered, brown-stained bra. She looked like she'd been wedged into the vines, but some of them seemed to have grown in around her. Which was almost possible; she was so emaciated – her skin more blue-gray than pink, her skeleton pushing through – she might have been there for weeks or months, if someone was feeding her. The thorns had dug permanent pockets into her skin, which was streaked brown with old blood. When she squirmed, fresh blood runnelled down...

Lonny shone the light on her face. It wasn't Eurydice. It was some white woman, who had maybe once been blonde. Her hair was mostly gone now, and her right eye was scratched out. A shiny green-black centipede ran from the light back into its home in one of her nostrils. She shuddered and sneezed.

Orphy was cursing him. "Get the fuck away from her, man..."

Lonny lowered the light; it pooled at her crotch. One of the thicker vines ran up between her legs, wedged deeply in her crotch...

"Jesus, lady!" Lonny burst out, trying to pull a vine free from her.

"Don't!" she rasped. With that sound giving out a smell of supreme rot. "Go...way."

Orpheus took Lonny's arm. His tone humbled now

220

as he said, "Let's go. We get her out later. Police or ambulance or something."

Lenny let Orphy pull him onto the path. "These people are fucking illin', Orphy." His voice breaking; tears burning his eyes. What he'd seen was only just beginning to sink in. "They're sick motherfuckers."

But fear gave way to repugnance when he saw, only a few steps farther on, the men on the other side of the trellis. He couldn't see much more than their silhouettes, dappled with starlight and twisty with vine-shadow. Most of them wore clothing but at least two of them were naked. All of them were men – no, there, a woman moved into view. She wore a dress but no underwear. She stood with her legs well apart, her hips thrust forward, the skirt lifted, her gray pussy caught in a patch of thin moonlight. Like the others, she was masturbating.

"Fuck!" Orphy burst out. "They're all . . ."

They all were. Jerking off.

Lenny shone the flashlight on them just enough to be sure that none of them were Mitch or Eurydice. The woman had her hand in a hole dug in a tall, hollow-eyed man's side; he was standing there wobbly and shaky as she worked her hand around in the wound up to the wrist . . .

Lenny quickly took the light off them. They whispered to Lonny. He wasn't sure if he was hearing the voices, imagining them – or if they were just coming into his mind from somewhere . . .

"Some of this . . .?" The woman asked, in a whisper.

"Hey little boys, have you ever wanted to see the roots of your own penis?" A man's voice.

"You guys like to party down, right? That's what you party animals like, huh? Party party party party party . . ." Another man's voice.

221

"Hello, hello, how are you today, taking a walk, taking a walk, come to visit, come to visit? Look at this, look at this!"

No human voice.

Lonny pointed the gun, fired convulsively through the trellis. A fully bloomed rose became a fireworks burst of petals as the bullet passed through it and someone whispered, *"Good. Again!"*

Orphy was dragging Lonny along, then, in a run down the path toward the house. Lonny's palpitating heart telling him, This is the wrong way, you should be running to get the fuck out of here!

But they kept going. They almost stumbled over the security guard lying half in the grass, his legs sprawled across the walkway. They made the mistake of pausing to look. There was a woman squatting over the guard's face . . .

There was a man playing with the guard's cock. He'd twisted wire around its base to keep blood in it, force an erection. In the darkness it was a moment before Lonny saw the other people crouching in the long grass. Waiting.

Then the dark figures were up out of the grass and coming at them. Hands outstretched. Laughing.

"Shiiiiiit!" Lonny wasn't sure if it was him or Orphy who screamed this as he fired the gun impulsively at the dark shapes. Heard a grunt and then a giggle and they kept coming and he turned to run toward the fence but there were others on the walk back there, coming after them, the illin fuckers jerking off as they came. He fired at them, too, and then the gun was empty and there was no time to reload so he sprinted toward the house, his lips drawn back in the rigidity of total fear, babbling, "Orphy come on goddamn come *on* and –" Gun shots

behind him. "And don't waste no bullets we gotta get over here we gotta – we gotta – we gotta –" Not sure what they had to do. And then he stumbled, going down on his hands and knees, grinding his teeth at the pain as a brick-corner smacked into his right kneecap, cursing when the flashlight glass shattered on another brick. His little totem of light snuffed out. He tossed the dead flashlight away as he heard running footsteps behind him, someone calling to him mixed up with a moron's giggles. Lonny jumped to his feet and took off again, chest heaving, thinking he should try to load the gun. But these people (the house was looming up in front of him now, dark and motionless) didn't seem to care if they were shot and *oh no where was Orpheus?*

As he reached the front steps he paused, panting, looked back for Orphy – and didn't see him.

A whisper in his head. *"Hey kid, wait up, we wanna parrrrrtay!"*

And then he heard Orpheus's voice. Yeah. For sure. It was him. How could a dude as hard as Orpheus make noises like that? Screaming piteously, from somewhere in the darkness behind the screen of rose trellises.

Culver City, Los Angeles

"When's that party you're going to?" Jeff asked, coming into his office. He seemed agitated, Prentice noticed, looking up from the word processor's display. Jeff was putting his hands in his back jeans pockets, taking them out, crossing them over his chest; the lines of his narrow face were tauter than ever.

"Tomorrow night, Jeff. What's got you so . . .?"

"My brother is still fucking *missing* man, that's what!" He chewed at his upper lip; it gave him a bulldog look.

"I talked to that fucking detective. Blume. He doesn't know shit except that kids are turning up dead. Teenagers, young women. One man so far – his body was all crushed –"

"Oh, that. Yeah, I read about it."

"– so they don't know much about him except they're pretty sure he was in his mid-twenties or so which means it wasn't Mitch."

"Why should it be Mitch? Kids go missing all the time, Jeff – if they were all murdered there'd be bodies everywhere –"

"Now you sound like that fucking cop. This detective was your idea. Blume went out to Doublekey and just gave up at the gate, the way we did."

"He didn't circle around the place?"

"He did. With binoculars. He said he didn't see anything but trash on the ground and a couple of drunk older guys sitting by a dirty swimming pool. He watched for a long time – he claims. From different angles. Waste of time. If they've got Mitch he's in the house."

Prentice felt a twinge of guilt. What if Mitch really was out there?

He thought about Lissa. He had mixed feelings about her. He couldn't get over the feeling that she'd manipulated him. He still felt sort of spaced out and odd after the drugs. It'd felt good at the time but since then he'd been prone to brief, bizarre anxiety attacks. Sudden fears of – nothing at all. Still, he hadn't been bothered by a sense of Amy's nearness, since then. The drunken rapture of Lissa's touch had driven it out of him. At times, though, he could *almost* sense Amy, not quite but almost, just on the periphery of his awareness . . .

"I'm going to the fucking Feds," Jeff was saying,

"much as I hate to. And I'm gonna start in with the lawyer again."

"Tell you what," Prentice said. "Hold off on that just three days. I'm going to talk to this detective, and do a little research on the Denvers." Maybe he could get Arthwright to sign him after Monday. And then Jeff could sue to his heart's content.

"Three days?" Jeff took a deep breath. "Yeah. Okay, three days. Keep me posted, man." He turned to go, then paused at the door, remembering to be civil. "How's the script?"

"Finally starting to happen. But slow."

"Slow is all right as long as it's steady. How's that pussy you been getting?"

"You're so sensitive, Jeff. A real modern, 'sensitive' man."

Jeff laughed, paradoxically pleased by the dig, as Prentice had known he'd be, and went back into the living room to catch CNN's Sports Update. After a few minutes of pretending to work, Prentice joined him.

Near Malibu

The gunshots had given Eurydice hope, for a few minutes. She'd thought maybe it was the police. But now they'd stopped and there was only distant laughter and a scream from out there, and no sounds of sirens. It hadn't been the police. It had been the More Man and friends – playing.

There were other sounds, now – from the room beneath hers.

There was a hole in the floor, near the bed. It was too convenient, this hole being there, looking accidental but somehow punched through two layers of floor. She was pretty sure this hole and the one in the wall were put there for her and Mitch to find.

So she told herself she shouldn't play along; she shouldn't listen to what was going on downstairs. Shouldn't try to see down there.

She put her fingers in her ears and kept out most of it. Still, she heard the mesh of laughter and wailing, like roses and thorns on the same vine, and she heard someone whimpering, *"Don't let it get on me don't let it get on me don't let it – !"* and then she heard someone else say in a calm voice, "Plant them in his wounds." And then there was a panting . . . and then a pissing sound . . .

The crackle of bones slowly breaking. A bubbling wail.

She started yelling, just a lot of wordless noise to cover up the sounds. She dragged the mattress from the bed and dumped it over the hole in the floor. She could still hear it, faintly. She clapped her hands over her ears and paced around the room feeling she was going to rip open from the razor-sharp unfairness of it.

Her gaze came to rest on the crack in the wall. She hurried to it and squatted on the floor, thumped on the wall with the flat of her hand. Sometimes he didn't answer.

This time he answered. "Eury?" Mitch's voice. Sounding far away and unattached, like a voice heard from a TV in the next apartment.

She flattened herself against the wall, her ear pressed to the crack, head tilted down so she could talk into it. "Did you hear those gunshots? Do you think it's anything . . .?"

"I've seen them play with guns before."

She choked on a sob. She wasn't going to be rescued. Why should she be? It was always the same. She knew that from when she'd worked out that her mama saw her as a way to get G.A. and extra foodstamps and then money from white assholes. She was just a lump of flesh that moved around and waited to be used for something. She always had been. Why should anybody come to get her out of here?

But something in her hissed like an angry cat, made her keep looking for a way out; made her ask, "You talk to that Handy Man like you said, Mitch?"

"Yeah. Yeah. I asked him. Told him I didn't want to be –" He sniggered idiotically. "– to be, like, a hodad around here. He said maybe I'd be like the More Man someday, and maybe not, and it was something you have or you don't have . . . and we'd know when the time came and . . . I think he was just playing with me . . . He doesn't seem like he's even really here . . . Like in his head he's always someplace else . . . He started talking German to me, once, but dude must know I can't speak German . . ."

"Mitch . . . You ask him about me?"

"He wouldn't say anything. But they're going to use us soon. I know it. There's a rhythm here . . ."

"They give you Reward?"

"Head Syrup? Not for a long time now. They're saving us . . ."

There was another way out, she thought. "Mitch – if they busy, it might be somebody could kill theyself, you think, before they git on it?"

"Maybe. I wish we could kill each other. Wouldn't that be good?"

"What?"

He went on with a hoarse excitement, "We could strangle each other and try to do it so that we each killed the other at exactly the same second. It'd be tricky, because one would tend to fall over before the other but

227

– well, maybe something sharp would be better . . . I've got some broken glass . . ."

"Mitch, what the fuck you talking about? You trying to get into they heads? Is that why you saying this?"

"We could break through the walls so we could get to each other and then we could –"

"Mitch, shut up! Just fucking shut up!"

He was quiet for a moment. Then he said, "I'll wait over here on my bed till you feel better."

She heard him move; and the creak of the bedsprings. Then she heard a plaintive keening from the room below. She thought she could feel the cry vibrate in the boards under her hands.

Watts, Los Angeles

It was somebody's apartment, he had no idea whose. He was being herded about by Gretchen, just now, and she'd herded him here, and he was so stoned he hardly noticed anything about it, except that it was almost as bare as Hardwick's. And it was a little bigger and the stove was still there.

There were also four children in it. Garner noticed them only abstractedly at first. Four black kids, one of them about three years old, sleeping – or trying to – on the bare floor mattress, as Garner and Gretchen and the kids' father, if that's who he was, took hits off the pipe in the kitchen area of the apartment. Little details slipped through to Garner from time to time, when he wasn't hitting the pipe: the floor sagged; the walls were yellow; the light from the kitchen glared onto the dull faces of the black children sharing a single blanket.

Garner had used his Visa card, the only credit card he had, to get cash, and they were going through that now. He was almost out of money again. How long had he been on this run? How long had he been chasing the high? It was late at night. He could hardly feel his arms and legs. He had made a few tentative tries at getting Gretchen alone, ended up looking like a jackass as he tried to fuck her standing in a bathroom; couldn't even get it up. Hadn't tried to argue with her when she said they didn't have time for this, they had to get some more crack.

And now, once more, the stuff wasn't working. It was just making him antsy for the next hit. He was almost assed out: busted, wasted, unable to buy more. How much money did he have left? Twenty bucks maybe? Maybe if he could get away from these two parasite – this babbling, yellow-eyed, middle-aged man who sometimes sputtered into a non sequitur of cursing like a victim of Tourette's Syndrome, and sallow, shrivelling Gretchen with her darting fingers. He hadn't been able to go ten feet without them following him. That motherfucker Hardwick had his van... was either stripping it or ferrying people around for money and selling everything in it piece by piece...

The last of the high seeped away from him, leaving him only tweaky rigidity in his nerves, lust for the pipe no matter how empty its reward, and the aching pit of depression that made him feel cold and hollow as a brass statue.

Why wasn't he dead yet? Constance was dead...

"You hear dat?" the guy said. What was his name? Charlie? "That de rollers?"

Gretchen shook her head. "They no cops here. You tweakin."

Charlie forgot about it, hunched down to pick at flecks of ceiling plaster that had fallen into the cracks between the floorboards. Tweaking them up between thumb and forefinger. Tasting them. Spitting them out. Garner had to fight the urge to do the same.

Thing to do was find a dealer, Garner thought; find a dealer maybe on his way to the set, smash his head with a bottle or something, take his dope and take his gun. That way he'd either get killed or he'd get some cash. Get some dope. Another hit. And then another hit.

He felt like he was dying the way Constance had died. He was being slowly crushed and cut up, too. By dope and the projects.

Maybe it was working out.

"We assed out," Gretchen said, scraping the last of the resin from the pipe with a coat hanger wire.

It struck Garner again how easily he'd slipped back into the street mix. Years of being away, being clean, teaching others to stay clean. But who could blame him, after what had happened to Constance?

Oh yes. The addict in Garner had seen its opportunity. And Garner was back out on the street and all the years working in the ministry might not have existed at all. He knew with a calloused certainty now that he had become a drug counsellor to keep himself clean; he had preached at himself by preaching at other people. Now he had come full circle, dumped from the butt-end of the night. A familiar feeling: being a human ashtray; burnt out and choked. Soon, inexorably, he'd be broke. Shot to the curb. This was the way it always happened, of course, for everyone. He could think: *I knew it would end this way. It always does.* Sure he'd known, and he could say he'd come in with his eyes open . . .

But it just didn't help much.

The crack was gone – except, doubtless, for the little bumps of rock that both Gretchen and Charlie had

230

craftily pocketed at some point. No use trying to pry that out of them. There was simply no more crack. There was just the pipe and the room and the two parasites calling themselves Gretchen and Charlie and the four children on the floor.

He saw them now. The kids. He seemed to *feel* the sight of them lying there in the same room with strangers smoking crack in the middle of the night. None of them asleep but knowing from experience it was best to fake sleep or the crazy motherfucker Charlie with his spluttering curses would kick the shit out of them . . .

It smacked into Gamer then like a baseball bat: The realization. *He* was doing this to the kids. He, *Reverend* Garner. He was contributing. He had paid for the cloud of secondary crack smoke that descended now over that three year old.

"I wonder can you get you C.A. check now?" Charlie was saying. He was talking to Gretchen. "I mean in the fuckin mo'ning, can you get one, if you show you pregnant."

Garner looked at her. She didn't look . . .

He looked at her harder. She was pregnant. The 2nd trimester, maybe. Of course he'd known it. She was emaciated but . . . in the bathroom when she'd tugged those pants down . . .

She *was* pregnant. He was giving crack to the baby in her womb. He. Garner. Was helping funnel crack to the baby in Gretchen's womb; was merchandizing the misery of the kids on the mattress.

Gretchen was watching him. Saw the panic on his face.

"Let's go get a hit," she said, trying to head him off. "I'm fi'in to find this girl you going to like, she do somethin' for you fo' a ten rock –"

231

But he lumbered for the door. Pausing long enough to babble, "I'm sorry – I'm – I'm sorry –" at the children. Before fumbling the lock open, bolting out into the hall.

Gretchen and Charlie came trotting up behind him as he plunged down the stairwell. Into darkness.

Oh shit. He was in a dark stairway in the Projects. A fucking maze the cops wouldn't come into unless they were forced to.

Feet and heart clattering, he descended into the stink of urine; of rotten chicken from a garbage bag someone had left on the stairs. He nearly lost his footing, stumbling over the bag, but found the cold iron of the railing as he fell, caught himself. A light came wobbling behind: Gretchen and Charlie – who was muttering "Motherfucking motherfucker tryin gaff me off, owes me some shit I done let him use my place, I fittin to kick his mo'fuckin ass," – coming down after him, using a Bic to light the way.

Then Garner found a doorway, was out in the open air. But in the midst of the Projects. He stood there gasping, pulse hammering in his ears, thinking he might have a heart attack. Trying to look for the street, but the concrete walls seem to melt into dead ends of graffiti and trash, wherever he looked.

Four men were standing together ten feet away, staring at him. They were all wearing baseball caps turned backwards on their heads and identical gold coloured suit jackets and fake gold chains and red laces in their sneakers. Project gangsters. "Who he wid?" one of them said.

"He ain't wid shit."

They started moving toward him.

Gretchen stepped out of the door behind him, and Charlie. "He wid me."

"Bullshit. He ain nobody. Fuck him."

One of them moved around behind Garner, as he was trying to decide which way to run, and grabbed his hair. That was first. Garner shouted in pain, and yelled, "Gretchen!" The gangster dragged him by the hair back into the stairway. Garner struggled, but it only made the pain worse.

The others had vise-grips on his arms, were all dragging him along now, though Gretchen was yelling in the background somewhere. Something about how he was hers, she'd found him, they had to give her some of this . . .

In the ephemeral flare of a Bic he glimpsed the place they dragged him to. It was a basement of the Projects. A furnace room, strewn with trash. Something moved sinuously in one corner. All thoughts of self destruction vanished in the prospect opening before him: He wanted to get away before they did what this room and this time and these people promised they could do.

It would go on and on . . .

He screamed and tried to wrench free but someone smashed an elbow into his nose; he felt it pop like a smashed grape. Someone kicked his feet out from under him. He could hear Gretchen yelling something; felt hands pawing his wallet from his pocket. Other hands skinning off his pants. A low pitched grinding as someone kicked him in the ribs; a squealing sound as someone kicked him in the head. The flicker of a lighter.

"What he got? He got rock? Lemme see that fuckin' wallet, bitch. He got —"

"He think he goin somewhere." They started again. Starbursts, flashes of light that were the kicks to his head. Tasting the floor through blood and smelling hot piss splashing around him and hearing Gretchen laugh . . .

And it did: He'd been right. It went on and on.

Near Malibu

Lonny wasn't sure how long he'd been crouching in the old cactus garden between the main house and the smaller one out back. He'd crawled in on his hands and knees and nestled among the yucca spears and he had only been jabbed once or twice. He held the gun lovingly as a kitten in his hand as he peered through the bushes, wishing he'd never come, feeling sure that Mitch was dead. Not wanting to find what they'd done to Orphy.

How could people like this hang out in the world at all? Why was it allowed?

There was a light in the window of the guest house, downstairs. Once, he thought he heard Orphy's voice from over there. Some of the others came and went – just shapes in the darkness, some of them nude, some of them in sloppy clothes – and now here came four more, so he scrunched down lower, biting off a shout when he accidently drove a cactus needle into his right arm near the elbow. Grimacing, he felt for the broken-off needle and plucked it out. He was going to lose an eye in here next. Had to get out.

But he was safe in the cacti. Maybe he should stay till daylight. These sick fuckers probably slept during the day. Or maybe they never slept. That wouldn't surprise him, either.

Two more of them went by, carrying something long and sodden that dripped onto bricks. What they were carrying didn't have to be a man's severed arm. Not necessarily.

They paused a moment, next to the pool. One of them bent and seemed to tease the surface of the water with the drippy end of the thing he carried in his hand. Lonny thought he saw something sparkle, faintly, in the pool, then, but he wasn't sure. The two laughed. Were they men? Yes, now, seeing them pass across the open area of the terrace where more starlight reached them, he could see they were white men, both clothed but one of them with his dick hanging out his fly – from here it looked like a little white worm.

They paused at the door to the back house – and both glanced over their shoulders at the cactus garden. A flash of teeth as they grinned. Then they went into the house.

Holy shit, Lonny thought. The fuckers knew he was there. They'd known it all along.

They wouldn't leave things like this.

Lonny crouched lower, got down under the curve of the yucca spears, and squirmed like a soldier moving under barbed wire, pulling himself with his elbows, till he got free of the cactus garden. Then he got to his feet and ran in a crouch across the big terrace.

He still had the gun, anyway.

And he had to know. He scurried up to the lower window of the guest house. The windows were curtained. He heard voices. One of them was Orphy. Sounding delirious. He had a drunk, disbelieving quality about his

235

voice and Lonny couldn't work out exactly what Orphy was saying.

He made up his mind. He went toward the door, circling the treetrunk-thick stem of the huge rose bush growing up the side of the place – looking quickly away from the yellow bony thing wired into the roses. (Bones with only the grease of a human body left on them.) Gun at the ready, Lonny walked through the front door of the guest house. There was a hallway, strewn with trash and rose petals. Beyond it, a sickly gray light from the hall corner.

The trash moved. Lonny stared. There was a man among the bottles and cans and old rags. He looked like a rag himself. He was crawling through the trash toward Lonny. He wore only bloodstained diapers. Baby's disposable diapers. Scabby rips all over his gray skin. He was . . . Lonny shook his head with amazement. He'd never seen anyone that skinny except on TV commercials about those starving kids overseas. A skeleton with skin shrunk-wrapped on it.

"Don't . . ." the guy rasped. No hair on his head. His eyes looking two different directions. "Don't . . ." The voice like a rustle of paper, barely audible. His body made a dry scraping on the floor when he moved a few inches closer. Saying, *"Don't let them do this to you."*

Lonny's mouth went dry. Instantly. He turned to run – then he heard Orphy yell his name. *"Lonny ya fucking . . . Jeez motherfucker . . . Don't . . . Lonny . . . !"* Something skewed wrong in his voice – the words were pleadings, protests – but the tone was childishly happy.

"I've got the gun," Lonny murmured. And maybe they had Mitch with Orphy.

He forced himself to go around the corner and look through the door into the room.

236

There was one dirty white bulb directly in the middle of the ceiling. Under it was a kind of platform, about bed-height from the floor. It took him several seconds of staring to be sure that the platform and the chairs around it were made of human arms and legs. The bone-ends, the bits of meat at the join, showed it was real. They'd preserved it and crudely stitched it together and tied it up with strips of skin; clunky and haphazard looking, but it held together as Orphy thrashed on it.

Orpheus was strapped spread eagled, naked on the bed with the Feasters – so Lonny thought of them – crouched around him, or sitting in bodypart chairs. They were connected to him. Something like stretched-out bits of glue ran from their mouths and exposed genitals, into Orpheus. The stretched-out bits quivered and flowed, and Lonny could see that they were alive, that they were something . . .

Something like worms. And they were part of the people around the bed, half a dozen people including the guy who called himself the More Man and the little guy, the Handy Man, and a woman whose eyes seemed to shine . . . you couldn't see her face at all, there was a kind of gas mask effect because the transparent slick white stuff had erupted from her mouth to cover most of her face. The other worm things squirmed into the wounds on Orpheus's throat . . . Another woman crouched over his genitals, chewing them up, as a worm thrashed whitely next to her pink tongue . . . A fat man crouched next to Orpheus's foot; the ankle had been broken, a bone end sheering out through the breached skin and the guy was licking marrow from it. Orpheus looked down at the guy and made a sound of pleasure.

Orpheus made that sound?

They'd done something to him. He was writhing,

Lonny saw now, not in pain but in ecstasy . . . as the More Man used the severed arm of the security guard to fuck a wound in Orphy's side, the arm a dildo. Orphy writing in repugnant happiness. Feeling no pain while they snapped his bones. He looked invitingly at Lonny. Mucous bubbling from his mouth as he urged: "Git on, Lon!" he said wetly. "Take a hit!"

The worms thrashing and squirming over this feast. Not eating flesh but taking something – taking what? The woman looking up at Lonny with eyes that were glossy with sensation but something imploring in them too.

Use the gun on me, boy. Use it on me

Was that *her* voice?

Use it on me, Mein Schönes jung. The head. Shoot me in the head

Orpheus's belly was humping up with the movement of the things probing in him and he was way beyond yelling now, he was just staring deep into the lightbulb and going "*Ack . . . ack . . . kuh . . . ack . . .*" as they probed into him, his eyes bulging, the joy in his face worse than anything else. All of them smiling through the wormstuff at Lonny. Reaching out . . .

Lonny felt a buzz in his head. A flush of pleasure.

"NO FUCKING WAY!" Shouted so hard he could feel something rip in his throat. And the gun came up –

Me, herrliches boy . . .

– but he wrenched the .45 away from the target it wanted, and pointed it at Orpheus. Fired. Felt it jump in his hand, glimpsed Orphy's brains splash. He fired it wildly at the others till it expended its magazine – with the last round, the light bulb exploded and the room went dark.

He threw the gun into the darkness and spun, careened into the hall. Sprinted for the front door.

He stumbled through the trash. Bottles and cans rebounded from his feet; he felt his heels crunch something that was probably a spine. A fading murmur of gratitude came from underfoot. Then he was outdoors and racing across the terrace. Someone lunged from the shadows under an oak tree and he felt a hand close around his wrist and he shrieked his best approximation of a karate yell and slammed a fist into a soft part of whoever it was. They went flailing down and he kept going, tearing through brush and feeling it tear through his skin, until he got to the black metal fence. He was over it in seconds, wailing one long note like a siren the whole way over. Dropped to the other side, ignored the pain in his ankles and ran on. Another fence. It was nothing. He went up it like a cat up a treetrunk. Dropped into the sand on the other side. Thought he heard a really pissed-off yell behind him. They hadn't expected him to get away.

He just kept going, shouting hoarsely, "Not me you fuckers!" He kept going, running at random into the brittle, aromatic brush of the countryside, until his legs stopped working. He fell into sand and rocks.

After a spinning while, the sobbing started. With that, came strength to crawl.

It didn't matter how he went. He just had to keep going.

Culver City, Los Angeles

Prentice had been sitting with a stack of books at the table in the Los Angeles main library since eleven a.m. It was almost two. His butt hurt from the chair and his stomach growled, but something kept him there. He imagined Amy saying, *You always did give up too easily, Tom. Like with me...*

He shook himself, and focused on the book. It wouldn't do to let the Amy obsession haunt him again. He turned the page, and then he saw them. Sam and Judy Denver.

The book was called *Those Fabulous Hollywood Parties*. The Denvers had been known for their parties. Prentice was looking for anything he could find about them – he wanted to get some kind of impression of them, and judge how likely it was that Mitch was actually being held out there . . .

He'd just about given up on finding them in this book – it seemed to focus on the old *Hollywood Babylon* sort of parties from the days of silent movies. Too early for the Denvers.

But here they were – there names caught his eye, first, in boldface under the photo. Not the names "Sam and Judy Denver." It said *"Mrs. Stutgart and Future Husband, Mr. Samuel Denver."* The date was 1929. Here was a middle aged woman and an older man in Roaring Twenties fashions, Denver holding eight champagne glasses clutched together at the stems like a bouquet in his hands, Mrs. Stutgart slopping champagne over them as if to fill all eight at once. Both of them laughing. Oliver Hardy looking on, making a comical face of mock astonishment; Faye Wray drunkenly leaning on Hardy with one of her dainty feet cocked up behind her. Another man stood rather stiffly in the background in an immaculate black tux. Denver's bowtie was undone and his salt and pepper hair rumpled.

Prentice stared. Maybe it was a misprint. This man was far too old, here, to be the man who later made his mark in Hollywood as a television producer. That would be thirty years later. This man was at least sixty. The producer of *Honolulu Hello* must have been this man's son.

But to the right – under the caption *The Merry Widow*, and after a rather sensationalistic description of the widowed Mrs. Stutgart's ribald, cocaine-dusted parties – the text related, "...born Elma Hoch, she married the industrialist Albert Stutgart; their relationship was said to be stormy and it was, in fact, during a storm that poor Albert was mysteriously lost overboard during a transatlantic crossing to New York. It was some years later before she married Sam Denver and became Mrs. 'Judy' Denver. Sam was later to become a successful television producer.

"In the late '30s and early '40s the parties at the Doublekey Ranch faded noticeably after nasty remarks by L.A. columnists regarding certain of Elma's visitors who were alleged to be high functionaries in Germany's Nazi party. The man shown in the background behind Faye Wray and Oliver Hardy has been identified only as a 'Mr. Heingeman, a follower of the German firebrand Mr. Adolf Hitler'.

"Sam and 'Judy' were childless but for a time ran a 'charitable' summer camp for disadvantaged youth at their Malibu ranch. Accusations of child molestation, which were never prosecuted, caused the closing of the 'charitable summer camp' in 1976..."

So it was the same guy. But how old had he been, as a TV producer? Ninety? A hundred?

Prentice got up, stretched, and went to the microfiche stacks. His body begged him for food and his brain implored him for coffee. But he had to know immediately...

In minutes he was at another chair, reading the old newspaper accounts from a fiche projector screen, shadowed over, in spots, with magnified dust particles and what appeared to be the leg of a fly. *Variety*, early

'70s. A photo of Sam Denver giving an award for documentary film production at a dinner for the Producer's Guild. Maybe the guy's last public appearance, from what Prentice had been able to find out. The picture showed a man in a leisure suit, his hair dark blond. He looked about 40. He looked *younger* than the picture in the *Those Fabulous Hollywood Parties* book. But it was unquestionably the same guy.

Unless – it was a son by another wife. That *must* be it.

It took Prentice another ten minutes to locate an encyclopedia of Television History in the nostalgia section. Denver had one brief paragraph. It didn't give a birth date for him. It was the only entry he could find with that omission. It simply said *"Born –?"* The last remark about him was, "Denver married the widow of industrialist Albert Stutgart in 1946. He has no children as of this writing."

It *was* him.

So what? The guy was probably into health foods and plastic surgery. Maybe he looked older in that photo from the 20s than he really was. But looking at the picture, he had a nasty feeling of recognition. An ugly certainty.

Prentice decided to check the microfiche files one more time. There might be an article about the child molestation incident . . .

★   ★   ★

The house was only a mile from the library. It was a small, stucco house with Spanish tile roof and a row of sickly geraniums in a red wooden box on the porch railing. Prentice pressed the buzzer for the third time.

A raucous voice inside said, "Awright, keep your pants on!" It was followed by mimicry in a weird little cartoon voice, *"Awright, keepapantin!"* The door opened and a woman with a parrot on her shoulder scowled at him from the other side of the screen. She was somewhere in her sixties, probably, her hair puffed out with the odd shade of blue-silver that some old ladies affect, her face jowly, her hooded eyes as green as the parrot. She wore a mu-mu with scarlet and blue flowers; the bright green parrot crapped on the print of a nasturtium on the old woman's right shoulder, and shifted its footing, torquing its head to peer at Prentice with one hostile eye. "All I can say is, you better not be selling anything," the woman snapped. "I needed that nap, boy."

"Actually –" Well what *was* he going to tell her? How was he going to get her to open up about it? With an inward sigh, he chose the one route that would probably work. Lies mixed with the truth. "I'm a writer. A screenwriter. My name's Tom Prentice. I have been, uh, researching a story about Wendy Forrester –"

"She's dead. Did your research tell you that?"

"Well – no. Uh – when did she die?"

"A year after her lovely little summer vacation. That much you can find out yourself. I'm not stupid enough to tell you anything more without a contract."

"What? A . . . ?"

"You heard me. You want the story, you people have to buy it. I owe it to that poor child to get a little something for her story."

Prentice almost laughed aloud at this pretzeled logic. But managed instead to say, "I see. Story rights for the film. Well, it's not that far along. We don't know if there's enough of interest . . ."

"A twelve-year-old child driven to suicide by the filthy molesting of a TV producer? If you want to believe the suicide part of it."

Prentice held in his surprise. He hadn't seen anything in the article about the suicide. But then, it had happened much later. "What do you mean, if you want to believe that part of it?"

"I think those bastards killed them both."

"Both . . . ?"

"My sister and my daughter, obviously."

"Obviously! Obviously!" the parrot squawked.

Prentice could smell vodka on the woman now. She leaned against the doorframe, cocked her head the way her parrot did, and sharpened her glare. "Wendy was my niece. And I don't believe this business about Susan killing herself after she found Wendy dead. I can't imagine Wendy loading and shooting her father's shotgun at herself. A little girl like that! She didn't know how to load a shotgun. Killed herself with a shotgun! The police will believe anything if they're paid enough," she added, sniffing loudly.

"You think she was murdered."

"Surely! She was in therapy and she was beginning to talk about those Denver people!"

"Do you know what exactly they did to her? I mean – nothing was proved. Did a doctor –"

She aimed a mottled finger at him. "I am *not* telling you another goddamned thing without a contract. You think I don't know your business? Of course I do. Why, I've written a screenplay! Part of one anyway. I have it in a notebook. I can get an agent and a lawyer – " She snapped her fingers. "Just like that, my fine boy!"

Prentice nodded. Everyone in L.A. who spoke English, and some who didn't, had a screenplay somewhere. He deserved this harangue, he supposed. He'd lied to her about his interest.

244

"If you want to come in and have a drink we can talk over a deal —"

"No, uh, no thanks. I'll — I'll send a representative around." Maybe he'd send Blume over to talk to her. "Your name is . . . ?"

"Griswald, Lottie Griswald. I don't mean to be rude, now, but a story like this —"

"I understand. You're, uh, perfectly within your rights." He decided he'd learned enough. What sounded superficially like a morose and isolated old woman's paranoia might well be true. Maybe it hadn't been a double suicide. "I'll be in touch . . ."

"You sure you wouldn't like a drink?"

"No, no really, thanks." He backed away, smiling, almost stumbled off the porch but caught a railing and steadied himself, turned and hurried down. He heard the old lady mutter something, but he couldn't make it out, till the bird echoed it for her:

"Asshole!"

Downtown Los Angeles

The codeine was making Garner woozy, but he was grateful for it. It was the only thing that had got him through the morning at the General Assistance office. The hours at the combined food stamp and welfare office were humiliating; the stories were true: they treated you like a dog. No wonder there were so many welfare cheats – it was the only revenge. And the place was foul-smelling enough to make William F. Buckley sneer knowingly. But Garner had gotten emergency food-stamps; he'd eaten and kept most of it down.

Now he stood in the smoggy late afternoon on a barren streetcorner under a freeway overpass. The street echoed with the shriek of the big trucks shaking dust down from the monolithic slabs of concrete above him. He was standing at a payphone next to a hotdog stand, waiting for James to call him back. He thought about the freeway that had collapsed in Oakland, during the October 17th earthquake; he thought about how, at first, the media had rosily reported that people were "heroically pitching in to help" until it was learned that more of them were looting the bodies; he thought about a woman he'd counselled who'd been pinned, by the collapse, in an overturned car. Two men had come from the Oakland slums, clambered over her to rob the bodies of her friends, then jerked her purse from her hands and crawled away – one of them stepping on her broken leg as he went. He thought about all this with Olympian disdain, through the fuzzy filter of the codeine they'd given him at the hospital.

The payphone rang. It was James. "Mr. Garner? Hi! Um – I couldn't get the guy Sykes on the line. But I left a message that you need him to wire you some money at Western Union and all that."

"Try him again. And I want him to see about selling my things. Tell him he can take forty per cent." Garner was pretty sure Sykes would come through. Sykes owed him favours. He mentally went down the list of the other people he could siphon money from. His brother, though he hardly ever saw him, ought to be good for a hundred or two. His friend Larry – but he'd have to be careful about that, Larry was a reformed addict too, he might suss out that Garner was going to use the money for drugs.

No. Probably not. Garner had been clean a long time, so far as Larry knew. But it was best he didn't talk to Larry himself, he'd hear the slur in his voice from the codeine.

"You gonna be okay, Mr. Garner?" James asked.

"Sure." Okay? What a fucking joke. "Sure, I'm just . . . mild concussion, some fractured ribs, busted nose, a few bandages. What happens if you're lucky when you get rolled down here. I was looking for Constance in a rough neighbourhood –"

"Oh shit!"

"Hm?"

"I forgot to tell you she called! Constance called. How could I forget that? Jesus!"

Garner snorted. "She called." Just like the postcard. The scumbag had her call, sometime before he killed her, to try and keep them from looking for her. "And she said she was okay and all that and not to look for her?"

"Um – not exactly. She said she was alive. That's about it. Then she just sort of hung up. Oh and your brother called the same day to say happy birthday."

"Yeah. Great." The depression rolled over him like a tidal wave of sludge. "Listen – I really need that money." He had it all figured out. He'd just avoid the toss-ups, the strawberries, the coke whores, the other users. He'd buy himself a case of whisky and a double handful of crack cocaine and lock himself in his room and burn himself out that way.

"Sure thing, Mr. Garner. You got it."

"Okay. I'll check Western Union in the morning." He could get through the night without crack. He had the codeine. He could trade some foodstamps for liquor. Of course, he could also trade foodstamps for crack. It was done all the time. Crack or heroin. He could get fifty dollars worth of rock for a hundred dollars worth of food stamps. It was something to think about. "Thanks James. See you . . ."

He reached out to hang up the phone. His hand

stopped over the hook. What was wrong? Why couldn't he hang it up?

The codeine mists were parting...

Your brother called to tell you, happy birthday.

His hand started to shake. He put the receiver to his ear. "James!"

The infinite buzz of a dial tone, like his own neurological drone behind codeine. Fingers shaking, he stabbed the buttons again, calling Alameda collect. Waited impatiently as the operator languidly asked James if he'd take a collect call...

"Mr. Garner? You forget something?"

"James – when did you say my brother called?"

"On your birthday. He said it was your birthday."

"James – no think, get this right – was it the same day Constance called?"

"Yeah. It's right here on the note pad. And I remember because her call interrupted your brother's call. She came in on call waiting. And when I came back he'd hung up –"

"Two days ago? She called two days ago?"

"Yeah."

His birthday. A day *after* he'd I.D.'d her body. He remembered the cop, on the way out, saying something about how her body was the only one with a finger intact. Lucky they could get an I.D. this time...

The son of a bitch. The motherfucker. The *bastard* had cut off his daughter's finger and dropped it in with somebody else's body but JESUS FUCKING CHRIST SHE WAS ALIVE!

Ephram was in the lawn chair, in the back yard, in that same smoggy late afternoon, a Panama hat and yellow tinted sunglasses shading his eyes from the westerly tilt of the sun as he scrivened busily in his notebook Constance was in the chair beside him, dozing.

Ephram wrote,

I can't get over the feeling that I am playing some odd sort of game with myself, a game which as yet has no name. Could it be that I came here out of a sense of destiny? A realization that here – or more precisely in that snakepit out by Malibu – waits those who should be, and will be, my followers? Is it not possible that the stars have turned to facilitate my domination over them? The Dark Constellations are beginning to yield up their secrets; the Negative Signs are beginning to speak. Once more I turn to Nietzsche at his most inspired, and this I write purely from memory, demonstrating how well I know his gorgeous *Ecce Homo*: "...I know my fate. One day there will associated with my name the recollection... of a crisis like no other before on earth ... of a decision evoked *against* everything that until then had been believed in, demanded, sanctified. I am not a man, I am dynamite... For when truth steps into battle with the lie of millennia we shall have convulsions, an earthquake spasm, a transposition of valley and mountain such as has never been dreamed of ..."

There was a noise at the back gate, making Ephram glance up from his notebook. His blood seemed to arrest in his veins.

Sam Denver pushed the gate open and, smiling, stepped into the back yard.

"Hello, Ephram."

Ephram took a deep breath and put on his courtliest persona. "Why Sam. This is an unexpected pleasure."

Constance was just sitting up, blinking sleepily at Denver. Shading her eyes against the glare of the sagging sun. Ephram could feel the fear rise in her, as she looked at Denver.

"Constance dear, why don't you go into the house and get a chair for Mr. Denver."

"All right." She got up and hurried into the house.

He hoped she wouldn't take this opportunity to run anywhere. It would be most embarrassing to have to drag her back here by the brains in front of Denver.

"You seem to have her well trained," the More Man said. "It's kind of sweet, really."

"How did you . . . find your way here?" Ephram asked, glancing at the back fence. There were several large men back there; difficult to see them clearly in the glare of the westering sun. There would be one or two others around the front. He wondered if they were Denver's followers from the Ranch, or if they were hired muscle. He could paralyze one or two, of course, but the Akishra protected Denver from him, at least up to a point, and Denver would surely be armed . . .

"How did we find you?" Denver raised his eyebrows in mock astonishment. "You advertised for us, of course! The Wetbones killings. That could only have been you. You left your calling card all over town, Ephram. It made things a bit hot for us. But I assume you wanted us to

250

find you. The Akishra led us straight here, of course."

Ephram felt dizzy. "The Akishra?"

"Yes. You really thought you wouldn't attract them? After all those engorgements? Or perhaps you thought you had eluded them each time? They are here. But your . . . 'friend' has kept them somewhat at bay. The one you call the 'Spirit' . . ."

Ephram crossed his arms over his chest to cover the trembling in his hands. They are here.

Denver sighed and went on, "Judy's out in the limo – she's become rather . . . well, your prediction has come true, I'm afraid. They've overwhelmed her. They've externalized. It's rather a disgusting sight. Oh, thanks – Constance, was it?"

Denver sat in the kitchen chair Constance had brought out for him. She resumed her seat in the lawn chair next to Ephram. He was gratified to feel her clutch his arm – she clearly preferred him to Denver, it seemed, despite all.

Denver was staring at her. She lowered her eyes. He nodded to himself. "Yes. I believe so. I saw this girl in the paper. Her picture. They found her body, or so they thought . . ." He looked at the bandage, where her finger had been removed. She covered it with the intact hand. He grunted. "Oh, I see. Very clever." He looked back at Ephram. "Are you ready?"

Ephram knew precisely what Denver meant. But he said, "Ready for what, dear fellow?"

"Why, to come out to the Ranch, of course. We can't let you roar about town like a loose cannon anymore. And you've got to help Judy."

"I hardly think I can do anything for her."

"You can get Reward without the Akishra. Or at least – you used to. You can repel them, you can muddle them

251

– you've demonstrated very handily that you can do that, or you wouldn't have gotten this far without an Attachment. You can, ah, delouse her for us. You can save her."

"What utter nonsense. She's made her bed, now she must lie in it – with whatever's in it, ha ha. I can do nothing. If you want to help her, put a bullet through her brains."

Denver turned to look once more at Constance. It was a look of bloodless longing and desiccated lust. She turned to bury her face in Ephram's pudgy arm.

Denver laughed. "To make her prefer you – over *anyone* – oh yes, you must have her very much in hand. Well, we'll soon see if she has any juice left in her. She'll be coming along too, of course." He stood up. "And it's time to go. Now."

Perhaps, Ephram thought, if one of the men at the back fence were armed, he could take control, manipulate the man. Make him shoot Denver in the back of the head.

He reached out with his mind . . .

And drew back The men at the back fence were Denver's followers. They were clouded with the Akishra. Slimy to the mental touch.

Ephram composed himself for the inevitable. He stood up, and drew Constance to her feet beside him. He bowed, ever so slightly, to Denver. "We are, of course, gratified by your kind invitation."

Culver City

Prentice decided to take a long, hot bath, relax for half an hour before trying to finish writing the first scene of his screenplay. He was tense, lately; probably because he kept waking up at night. Every hour or two after he'd

252

gone to bed he'd sit bolt upright, suddenly and completely awake, with Amy's voice fading in his ears. But no memory of what she'd said.

It took him a long time to get back to sleep and now the tension and fatigue was catching up with him. He got up from the desk, went down the hall to the bathroom. He ran the bath, undressed, sat on the toilet lid waiting for the tub to fill. There was a distant noise from people having an early evening swim in the complex's pool; otherwise the place was dead quiet. Jeff had gone for another one of his endless strings of meetings...

The tub overflowed on Prentice's foot. He jumped a little, then reached down and hastily let some water out. Have to sop up the floor later... He replugged the tub and dumped a little bubble bath in, ran the water just enough to make it foam up. He got in; the water slippery with liquid soap and hot enough to bring sweat to his forehead. He lay back, feet toward the faucet, and tried to relax. *Don't go to sleep – just relax for a minute...*

Something was bumping against his leg. He opened his eyes and looked at it. It was a woman's hand, severed redly at the wrist, floating between his knees. There was a ring on it, a gold band with an opal, which he recognized. It was Amy's. Blood swirled from the wrist stump, pink with the dilution of steaming water. Strangely enough, he felt no particular surprise or disgust.

Other parts of her began to bob up from under the soap-milky water. A middle section of leg, with one dimpled knee. A neatly snipped out segment of torso complete with breast. A healthy, unscarred breast, he noticed with casual objectivity. The body parts bled freely and the water went red and redder yet ... and then Amy's head bobbed up, by his feet. Her neck had been sawed neatly through. Her hair was plastered to her head with water and blood. The lips on her decapitated head moved soundlessly. He could read the lips a little. *Help me. They have me . . . they have a lot of us . . . help us . . . That girl . . .*

"Oh shut up, Amy!" he interrupted.

Her lips drew back in a snarl. The head straightened, bobbed vertically in the water. It moved toward him, its lower half sunken in the water, only the eyes showing above the red, bubble-castled surface. Coming at him the way an alligator does, only its eyes and the top of its head showing. But you knew its mouth was opening under the water . . .

That's when the fear broke free in him and he kicked out, screaming, thrashing –

And woke in the tub. Woke to hear the echo of his own scream in the confined bathroom spaces.

The severed body parts were gone. But the tub was filled with blood. He scrambled to stand up, mewling with repugnance, thinking: *Amy's blood Amy's blood . . .*

But then he noticed the gash on his left hand. During the nightmare he'd flailed out and smashed a shampoo bottle against the wall and cut himself on the broken glass. Panting, standing in the tub, he kicked at the water and saw the scum of red part. He hadn't actually lost much blood . . .

He pressed his right hand against the gash in the other and with one toe pried up the drain plug. The blood in the tub began to move amoebically toward the drain as the pipes made an echoey sucking growl and the cleaner water welled up. Tenuous shapes formed there, around the little whirlpool where blood and water spiraled. For a moment, one of the shapes was Amy's face. The red lips mouthing *Help me . . . Help us . . .* And then it melted swiftly away in down-whirling water and was gone.

The Hills near Malibu

The first thing Lonny noticed when he woke was the smell. He thought: They caught me and they threw me in some stinking pit of rotting dead people under the ranch. Maybe he should just lie here and let himself die.

He decided he had to face it anyway. He sat up – the movement made his head swim with pain – and opened his eyes a crack.

"Oh fuck," he said. Now he knew what the smell was from. He had been captured by a hippie.

He was in a shack, unevenly lit with greasy yellow light from three kerosene lamps hanging from three different walls. The reek of unwashed man and dog overcame even the oily stink of kerosene. Sitting in an old rocking chair at the foot of the bed, watching him fixedly, smoking a briar pipe that reeked of pot, was an old hippie. At least, that's how he looked to Lonny. He wore kerchief-patched, age-shiny jeans and, yes: they were bell-bottoms. His horny, dirt crusted feet in homemade leather sandals. He wore an ancient Grateful Dead t-shirt, the one with the skull crowned in roses...

Roses...

The girl in the rose vines.

"Look like ya seen a ghost, brother," the old hippie rasped. Sniggering to himself. "You come off the Cocksucker Ranch?"

"I . . ." He couldn't seem to pull up any words.

"Devil's Cocksuckers is what them fuckers are. The Devil's Cocksuckers." He sniggered again, this time showing his few rotting, mossy teeth. His gaunt face was leathery and sun-reddened. His eyelids budded with benign growths; his eyes were the faded blue of his jeans. His receding, waist-length black hair and beard were streaked with gray and clumped with dust. His mustache had grown over his mouth and was stained with food and pot-smoke. His fingernails were two inches long and crusty with dirt. He reached over to a worktable next to the squawky rocking chair and found a box of wooden matches. Meditatively, with one hand, he relit his pipe, never taking his eyes off Lonny. Leaning against the wall next to the worktable – within reach of the rocking chair – was a twelve gauge shotgun. Lonny never forgot it was there and neither did the old hippie.

In a corner, behind the rickety, multi-padlocked door, a mongrel dog got to its feet in a nest of foul rags, stretching, shaking itself, its long brown fur matted, the inevitable grimy kerchief around its neck. It came trotting over, claws clicking on the flattened tin-cans nailed down over most of the floor, and laid its muzzle on the old hippie's lap, casting sideways glances at Lonny. The hippie put his hand absently on the dog's head; somehow, its blind trust in the guy put Lonny more at ease.

He looked around; there were shelves of rusted tools; from nails on the shelves and ceiling dangled little dolls made of coloured wires and bits of junk. Between the rickety, unmatched shelves, the walls were covered with odds and ends: a cobwebbed poster of a babyfaced Mick Jagger and a startlingly human Keith Richards posing in costumes of Asian potentates against a psychedelic backdrop; randomly nailed up road signs pocked with bullet holes; and lots and lots of glued-on newspaper clippings, gone the colour of aged ivory, scribbled with notations and multiple exclamation points.

Sure. The dude was a paranoid old hippie. "You . . . find me?" Lonny managed.

"About a mile west. Me'n'Jerry here watched you for a while, crawling and talkin' to yourself." He exhaled an aromatic plume of marijuana smoke. "You crawled right through one of my fields and never looked twice at the buds. You either don't like pot or don't know it – well I expect you was spaced pretty bad. I knowed you was one that got away. First one I know about except for the movie star. And I helped him too. Lots of graves out in them hills, around the Ranch . . . You want some of this?"

He offered Lonny the pipe. Lonny shook his head. It was the last thing he wanted. "You . . ." He struggled with his mouth. "Hard to talk . . ."

"You're dehydrated is one reason. And maybe you're trying not to think about some things, and that keeps your brain busy. You got to deal with it sometime, brother, but maybe now ain't a good time. You did, though, dincha, see some pretty bad stuff in there, dincha. Devil's cocksuckers. Suckin' them worms. Dincha?"

Lonny didn't want to even acknowledge the memories with a *yes*. But he nodded, once. Forced out: "You got any coffee?"

The hippie stopped rocking and leaned forwards so suddenly toward him Lonny thought he was going to bite him in rage. But the old dude grinned and cackled, "Hell fucking *yes!* It's the only thing I go into town for, that an' aspirin. I go in twice a year, regular as the bad wind! Sure, Hell yeah, I got some coffee that'll make your hair stand up on your head and go, *Holy shit!*"

★   ★   ★

Turned out his name was Drax. Mike Drax. The coffee was everything he'd said it would be and, though Lonny'd knocked back two cups only after drinking three pints of water and eating beans and tortillas, he was buzzing so intensely he was barely able to hold himself quiet on the edge of the foul-smelling bunk. He tried to relax and asked, "How'd you come to be out here?"

Drax looked at him with a bald suspicion. "I like it out here, is all."

"Look – I told you what happened to me. Come on. Straight up. You know all about the Ranch. Why didn't you tell the cops?"

"Now what the hell would the pigs do? Some of them over there at the Cocksucker Ranch *is* cops. They in it up to their old piggy snouts." He sniggered and muttered, "It's all there, I seen it all." He waved toward the newspaper clippings. "I got the proof right there. You can check 'er out. That Mideast oil thing, it's there too. They suck on that just the same. Yeah, brother. Dobbs knows and Jerry here knows and I know." He turned to the cluttered, paint-spattered work bench that served for all the table the shack had, and sorted through a mound of tarry, golden marijuana, began to crush pot-buds between his thumb and forefinger with practiced exactitude, winnowing out the seeds.

258

The old dude smokes too much fucking pot, Lonny thought. No wonder he's half cracked.

"Your friends might still be alive," Drax said. "Sometimes the Cocksuckers save 'em for a long time." Abruptly he shot a narrow eyed look at Lonny and said, conspiratorially, "I *will* tell ya." His lingers kept crushing and winnowing the pot as he looked at Lonny, and went on, "It was my dad. He was a singer. Well he started out a rancher – we had a *real* ranch I mean, down in New Mexico. Worked it ourselves too. My mama was long dead. My dad, he was a real singin' cowboy. Not much of a rancher. About the time I was ten somebody heard him in a honky-tonk, signed him to records, two years later he was singin in big concerts. That led to movies. He was in two westerns. Then he was in television. Well sure, he was a good looking fella.

"I was a boy, I thought he was a god. Goodest-hearted man you ever want to meet. Took me everywhere with him, right to the nightclub concerts, near everywhere he went. Never left me somewhere so he could play with those pretty-pussy girls. He loved me! And then, when I was fourteen, *bang*, he forgot I was alive! He left me to knock around by myself. He knew I was alone in that big old house and he . . ."

The anger shook its way out through Drax's voice; showed in his white knuckled grip on the armrest of his rocking chair. The dog whined and put a paw on his lap. Lonny sat very still. The old fuck was crazy and he might grab one of the oily tools on the desk and brain him on a whim, for all Lonny knew.

Drax's shoulders slumped. He went on, a little subdued. ". . . they did it to him. Sam Denver, he took my old man up to that place and they played with his head and made him one of them and started soaking up his money and his talent and everything he had. They wanted me, too. They came to get me one day and I went over to that ranch and I saw what they were doin' to them kids and I went over the fuckin wall, brother, you bet your fuckin' ass! Got myself up to San Francisco. Got myself a ticket to the other world, from Mr. Owsley himself, who I knew personally. Hell, I fucked his old lady and with his blessing, too. It wasn't no perverted thing, either. And then I drifted down to Santa Cruz. And I read about they found my old man dead in a car, all wasted up. I think he was trying to get away and they crashed his fuckin' car is what they did . . . Well, I knew a few things by then, I seen that other world and I knew some Peyote eaters, they showed me a few things . . ." He gestured toward the fetish dolls hanging from the shelves.

There was only one window, with a wooden, padlocked shutter over it. Drax got up, crossed to the window – only three paces, his every step seeming to bring out a creak in each board of the little one-room shack. He took a thickly clustered ring of keys from his pocket and opened the padlock on the shutter, tilted it back and propped it up with a stick. Lonny blessed the infusion of clean air coming through the broken-out window panes, as Drax pointed through the window at the ground in front of the shack It was all packed earth, enclosed in a circle of waist-high wooden posts. Hanging from each post was a trio of the fetish dolls – made from bright pieces of radio wire, bits of transistors, feathers and dried seeds and strips of cloth; they seemed to glow golden-red in the light of the setting sun. "You see that? They guard us! They guard us here. The More Man is scareda me, brother, you know he is. I know some things and I got some friends. He knows I'm going to get him

260

sometime soon. The solstices swing around: with the stars you can see and the stars you can't, they tell the story. I'm going to get the son of a bitch, and I'm here practically on his front porch, waiting for the chance . . ."

Lonny was intrigued. But the coffee having worked its way through him, he had more urgent concerns. "You got a bathroom here?"

Tongue trapped mischievously between his snaggled teeth, Drax whirled on him, sniggering. "Well, I guess I sure as hell do! I got a bathroom maybe forty square miles wide! Just be careful there ain't no snakes laughin at the pimples on your butt."

East Los Angeles

Garner got off the bus a few blocks from Blume's apartment building. The city was supposedly trying to cut back on air pollution but the buses gouted black smoke and this one blew a toxic cloud directly onto Garner as he looked around the street corner. Choking, stomach bucking with nausea, he hurried across the street. On the other side was a liquor store and a row of tenements, most of them draped in the evening shadow; the streetlights had been shot out at both ends of the block. In front of the tenements the Set roiled with men and women, blacks and *cholos* mostly, and a few skinny white girls. Most of the steady customers for crack were white, middle-class men, Garner knew, and he watched them drive up in their Camrys and Ford Tauruses and buy crack through the car windows.

Garner had been to the Western Union; he had some money on him now, himself . . .

And he realized he had crossed to this corner only because he'd glimpsed the drug-dealing Set happening

261

down here. This wasn't the way to Blume's place. He should've turned down the Boulevard.

Goddamn, he thought, it's got me already. Two lousy runs and it's got me.

Well, it asked him, so what? I mean, what's the use? Constance probably isn't really alive. The guy probably had some other girl call and say she was okay so we'd stop looking for him. But that didn't make sense – they'd expect someone on the other line to know her voice. Okay – so she was alive that day. His birthday... He's probably killed her by now...

But it didn't seem as if he planned to. Not right away.

Suppose she *is* alive? What of it? You'll never find her. He can torture her to his sick heart's content – might be cutting off more of her fingers right now – and you could be within a block of her and never know and probably never see her.

So you might as well give up. You give that money to Blume to continue the investigation, it'll be thrown away. He's a waste of time. He's hopeless. It's all hopeless. Might as well use the money to get loaded...

Thinking all this, he'd drifted into the Set.

No one crowded around him, as they would a white guy who looked like he had money, because, instead, he was bandaged and dirty and dishevelled. And he thought for a moment he might get through without buying. He was walking a razor edge; horror on one side and drug lust on the other. He wanted to buy; his bowels felt like they'd let go with the excitement of it. And he very much *didn't* want to but his hands were clammy, his heart thumped with fear.

Are you crazy, man? What happened last time? Beat to shit in a basement!

But the addict in him superimposed images of the

262

pipe over that, and soothed him: *Don't worry. Not this time. This time you'll do it differently. You won't get hurt. You won't get ripped off. This time . . .*

"You lookin' for something, man?" A hispanic guy with wrap-around sunglasses and a red kerchief headband. It was so dark out here, how did the guy see with sunglasses on?

"What you got?" Garner heard himself say.

"Doves. Choo want it or not, this ain't cool we stan' around an' chit."

Constance . . .

But Garner nodded and fished four twenties out of his pocket. The guy swept them from his hand and with the other dropped four irregular white pellets in his palm. Drifted quickly into the Set.

Garner turned around, walked back toward the liquor store, frowning. Something about that exchange . . .

In the light of a neon beer sign in the store window, he examined his purchase. It looked a little too white and crumbly. He tasted it. Aspirin and baking soda.

He stared into his palm. He'd been gaffel'd. Ripped off.

He tossed the white pellets into the gutter. A weight slipped from his heart.

"You look pretty happy about it," said a deep voice, just in front of him. He looked up and saw a tall black man in a turtleneck sweater. Gold watch on his wrist. He was somewhere between forty and sixty. Hard to say in this light . . .

But somehow Garner knew the guy was a minister.

"They gaffel you?" the man asked. When Garner nodded the man said, "You were smiling. How much money you lose?"

"Eighty bucks." He noticed two women standing a

263

little behind the man. They had stacks of leaflets in their hands. Smiling black ladies. They seemed amused. The man they worked with just stood there, rocking slightly on his loafers, hands in his pockets, looking at Garner casually but with an irritating knowingness.

"You a minister?" Garner asked.

"Pastor Ray Brick, First Congregational." They shook hands.

"I was a Methodist pastor, if you can believe that. Still am officially, I guess."

"I can believe it. Man, we lose 'em all the time. You used to be a drug counsellor – in recovery yourself?"

"You guessed it."

"Uh huh. That's a pattern. One in four long term addicts-in-recovery relapse years later. Most of 'em don't make it back. What was your excuse?"

"My daughter was kidnapped. Probably murdered."

He looked impressed. "That's a pretty good one. You had enough, out here?"

Garner stared. His guts knotted.

Don't waste your time, the addict said. You can be more careful next time you buy.

"Let me ask you something," Brick said, seeing his hesitation. "You think it was a coincidence, you getting ripped off and me coming along like that? Well, it was. But you should know – God's the only one can arrange coincidences. You were happy you hadn't got real crack. You don't really want it."

Garner nodded, slowly. "I – was on my way to meet a man . . . might help me find my daughter."

"That's pretty important. How about we walk you a ways in that direction – till you get out of this neighbourhood. Can we do that?"

Garner nodded, enormously relieved. "I'd appreciate it." He felt tears welling. "I really would."

★ ★ ★

Blume's door was open about two inches. Typical of a drunk to space out something basic like closing your door behind you. The guy was probably useless as a detective, this far into alcoholism. But then, Garner thought, I've been pretty useless as a pastor lately.

He knocked and waited. No reply. No sound of movement from inside. A little lamplight spilled through the door and the angry mutter of a TV set.

The agency had said Blume hadn't been in for three days; hadn't been answering his phone. "He goes on these drunks from time to time," his supervisor said. "I don't know why we never get around to firing him"

Garner pushed the door open and went in. It was a cluttered studio apartment, smelling powerfully of a catbox and some hidden rot. The cabinets and drawers had been opened, their junky contents dumped on the floor. A half empty bottle of Jack Daniels on the floor beside him, Blume sat facing Garner in a green cloth easy chair in the very centre of the room. He was in his underwear, sitting in front of an old black and white TV set currently showing a wonky double image of Barbara Walters interviewing another "reclusive" movie star. Blume was staring at it, motionlessly, unblinking. Garner could see the gray and white TV screen reflected in both Blume's eyes in nearly perfect miniature. Beyond him, above the crap-lumpy cat box, was a half open window onto a fire escape. No sign of the cat. The cat had abandoned ship.

There was a book held in Blume's hands. A biography. There was something about the way it was set up in his hands that made Garner feel sure it had been put there by someone else, set up like a prop. The title of the book was *Remembering Trotsky*

Garner didn't bother saying anything. He took a moment to decide if he wanted to walk around behind Blume. He hated to give them the satisfaction. But in the end, he did it. He stepped behind Blume and saw the ice pick stuck to the handle in the back of Blume's skull. Just one small trickle of blood dried on the bald scalp beneath the handle.

Garner turned away, grimacing, thinking it would have been a better effect if they'd turned off the TV. He caught a tiny blinking red light in a far corner, next to a huge heap of old *Los Angeles Times*. It was a call-recorded light on a Sears answering machine, the phone on top of it.

He circled Blume widely and went to the phone, hit the answering machine's play button. There was a message from the agency, telling Blume if he didn't at least call in before midnight he was fired. And then there was a message from another of Blume's clients.

A petulant, phone-fuzzed voice said, "Blume? You there? No? Okay. This is Jeff Teitelbaum. I get this cryptic phone message from you saying that Sam Denver was seen at the sites of three Wetbones murders – if I'm hearing this slurred-up mumbling of yours right it says 'not long after killings'... What the fuck? You trying to give me a heart attack with this cryptic shit? If you think my brother is one of those Wetbones victims just fucking come out and say so and get your ass over here. You can't leave me messages like this and just... Shit! I'm at the Culver City hospital right now but I'll be home in a half hour or so... I want you over here personally.

My address in case you're too blitzed to find your fucking rolodex is . . ."

Garner dug through Blume's things for a pen, finally located a stub of a pencil and scribbled the address down on the back of a tract for Brick's drug recovery program. He folded it up and carefully put it in his pocket, then looked around for notes or tape recordings or photos – anything pertaining to Blume's investigation.

He found nothing relevant. They'd have taken anything like that, of course.

He made a quick, anonymous call to the LAPD to report the body, then hurried out, keeping his mind focused on his errand so as not to think about crack. Hurrying to find a bus that would take him to Jeff Teitelbaum's part of town.

Los Angeles

"You're really not going to that party?" Jeff asked again, as they walked into the overlit, almost empty lobby of the hospital. The one Mitch had run away from. "I mean, Christ, you got a deal trembling on the verge with Arthwright. Not a good time to snub his party."

"Arthwright." Prentice grimaced. "I don't think I want to know Arthwright all that well."

"It's your career."

Prentice shrugged. What was he supposed to tell Jeff? That he kept hearing Amy in his head warning him away from Arthwright and Lissa? That he was afraid of Lissa – for no clear reason at all? That he didn't quite believe there was a party to go to – and he wasn't sure why? And he hadn't yet told Jeff where the party was. The Doublekey Ranch. After what the old lady with the parrot had told him about her niece's death, he didn't much want to go out to the ranch...

Jeff went on, "So, did the doctor tell you what he wanted?"

"You can ask him yourself," Prentice said, nodding toward the small white-coated brown-skinned man coming through the double doors into the lobby. Doctor Drandhu.

Drandhu advanced, one hand extended for shaking, smiling nervously. "Mr. Prentice! Mr. Teitelbaum! Correct?" His accent was native Indian, but his English was otherwise controlled with a brittle formality as he shook both their hands with fingers that felt like they were made of bird-bones, and said, "I am thankful you were able to come. Oh you have hurt yourself, Mr. Prentice?" He was looking at the bandage on Prentice's left hand. The cut still smarted dully.

"Yeah. On a busted bottle in the tub." He still felt strange after the dream in the tub. He wanted to run out and get a drink

"Not a very professional bandage, Mr. Prentice, would you like me to...?"

"No, no thanks. What's up? You said it was something about Mitch?"

"It is related, yes, yes. Please. There is someone I must show to you." He led the way through the double doors, down the antiseptic-reeking halls. "I asked you to come because your brother, Mr. Teitelbaum, was one of my first ES patients..."

"ES?" Jeff asked. "You've got a name for it?"

Drandhu smiled shyly. "Emaciation Syndrome. This is my term. When I find out more about it I will write a paper. But there is so little I understand now, I am sad to say. So very little. I am a little frightened, to be frank, and feeling very much alone. When I try to interest

268

my colleagues they say I am mistaking AIDS or drug-induced emaciation for something distinct. But I don't think so, no. The patients are negative for AIDS and . . . no, there are no drug indications. But the wasting and the self mutilation . . ."

"My ex-wife had the same thing. If it *is* a disease," Prentice said.

Drandhu looked at him with interest. "Oh yes really? That is very interesting. They knew each other, the boy and your wife?"

"A little. But . . ." He shrugged. He didn't want to get into it that far, yet. "Anyway, yeah: it occurred to me and Jeff that it's just too big a coincidence, Mitch and Amy having the same kind of sickness. Mitch had just started to lose weight but the rest of it was there."

"I will talk to you about that just a little later if you do not mind. I would like to take some notes. But now there is a man here with ES – he asked to speak to you. He said he knew what was causing his problem but didn't want to tell me. I think he is afraid . . . Oh, yes, here he is, here is – Mr. Kenson?"

They'd stepped into a private room; a generic hospital room. Kenson was lying on a white hospital bed. He was strapped onto the bed, under the sheet, its mattress cranked up so he was near sitting position. The straps weren't psycho-restraints, Prentice judged – they were to keep him from falling off the bed. And Kenson looked as if he could fall off, quite easily: he was a shrunken caricature of the man Prentice had watched on TV years before. His eyes were sunken and unaligned, looking at separate parts of the room. His lips were flattened onto his few remaining teeth. His arms were bandaged wrist to shoulders. A bottle of glucose water hung from a portable stand, feeding into a tube that bit with a steel needle into a vein on the back of Kenson's bony hands. "It must have hurt like a bitch when they put that IV needle in," Jeff said softly, as they came to stand beside the bed.

Kenson nodded. "Did."

Drandhu seemed flustered by the lack of introductions. "I should perhaps say, this is Mr. Louis Kenson, and this is Mr. Teitelbaum and Mr. Prentice his friend. Mr. Teitelbaum's brother was the one I told you about, Mr. Kenson —" Drandhu turned hastily to Jeff. "I do not mean to lapse confidentiality, no, but it seemed so important to find the connections —"

"Don't worry about it," Jeff said. He drew a chair from the opposite wall and sat down by the bed. "You wanted to talk to us, Kenson, I think?"

"Yeah." His voice a croak. "I thought maybe you'd seen some things. I mean . . . You know what your brother was into? See, if I tell the doctor here, he's going to think . . ." He paused to wet the scraps that were his lips. "He's going to call in the psychiatrists . . . I figure if I have somebody else here who knows . . . I was hoping you might have found the kid. Brought him here too. I guess not huh?"

Jeff shook his head. Prentice looked around for a chair. There wasn't another one. He was suddenly very tired. He hadn't been sleeping much. And looking at Kenson made him feel drained himself

"Well — maybe we shouldn't talk about this," Kenson went on hoarsely. His voice drifting to join his gaze which was lost somewhere in the middle distance. "Maybe not. No I don't think so. If you haven't talked to the kid."

Goddamn it, Prentice thought, *I want to know.* "We haven't talked to Mitch lately. But I know what really happened to a little girl named Wendy and her mother, for example." That was mostly a bluff.

Jeff looked over with puzzled surprise. One of Kenson's eyes stopped its roving on Prentice. "Do you? Well then. Okay. Let's talk."

"Drandhu to Pediatrics . . ." A nurse's voice from some distant intercom speaker.

"Oh my gosh," Dr. Drandhu muttered. "They are calling me." He took a tape recorder from his pocket, no bigger than the kind of transistor-radio that mental patients carry about with them, and hung it on its little leather strap from the IV stand, just under the bottle of glucose water. "Please – I have to go upstairs and check in. But it is I think all right if I record this?"

Kenson gave a leathery sigh. "Fuck I don't know. I guess so. I don't know why I'm bein' so careful. I guess it's habit. Thirty years of hiding things . . ."

Drandhu switched on the tape recorder, then fluttered around Kenson for a few moments, writing down his pulse and temperature.

After the doctor had gone, Kenson told them about Mrs. Stutgart, and the Akishra. Jeff listened with polite amusement. Obviously not believing a word of it. But Prentice felt the rightness of the story. And he could almost hear Amy, somewhere, saying, *I suppose you know your girlfriend is one of them. A pleasure vampire, in more ways than one.*

"I was one of them for a long time," Kenson was saying. "But after a while, see, it's not enough for the Akishra just to be there to take their share of stuff psychically. They move in on your body. They get to be part of you. *Physically.* And I couldn't hang with that. So I started backing off – and then Denver started holding me prisoner. Using me for their games. Which

271

sure, I deserved, I can see that. It's karma energy, you know? But I waited for a chance, and I stole a car. Denver's toy-boys came chasing after me and I took off into the desert and the car died under me and then this crazy old desert rat came along. He says he was watching us the whole time, following along. He puts me in his pick up and takes me to his place and the toy-boys leave off the chase. They're kind of scared of this old guy for some reason. Denver says the old guy's an unknown quantity and he's protected so they stay away from him. His name's Drax. So anyway, Drax brings me to town and leaves me at a doctor and they send me here."

"The Akishra..." Prentice said. He could almost visualize them. Why? Why did it seem familiar?

"You have to understand about the Akishra, man, or you don't understand anything. I mean, the real nitty gritty about these fuckers. Hand me that water glass, will you, I need to wet my...thanks." He paused to sip the water. Took a deep, weary breath and went on, "The name Akishra, see, is from Hindu mythology," Kenson was saying. "People in the Orient, they know all about 'em. They're astral parasites.They're...they look like worms, big transparent worms. Sorta silvery. Bunches of them. Never only one, except the Slabfathers. The Akishra Prime. You can't see Akishra with the naked eye. Your hand goes right through 'em without feeling a thing. But they're there. They seem immaterial, like less than fog, but they're material in a way. Some kind of subatomic particle stuff they're made out of, Judy says. And yeah, they're here. They're all around people. Especially addicted people. Mythical! Shit. I wish to fuck they were, fellas."

There was just a touch of theatrical delivery left in Kenson. The actor in him seemed to enjoy telling the story, despite his wretchedness. "You have to get this clear: the *Akishra are everywhere and always have been.* Everybody – and I mean *everybody* – who is addicted to anything, well, the Akishra's involved. Cigarettes? Right. The ones we call the Alpha Flutters are there. The smaller Astral worms. If you could see a cigarette smoker the way a trained eye can see him –" He laughed bitterly. "– cigarette addict has this . . . it looks sort of like an Indian chiefs head-dress made out of these floating astral worms. They're stickin' out of the smoker's head, see. Attached to him at one end – their bodies floating up there like seaweed.

"Your moderate drinker, he's generally free from astral parasites. But real alcoholics, they got a bigger kind of worm looks sort of like a tapeworm. A line of 'em running up their spine to their heads, streamin' back there. Cocaine addicts got another variety, looks like a big corkscrew. Mean, manipulative little fuckers. Heroin addicts get another kind look like leeches. You can have two or three different kinds at once of course. A whole fur of 'em. Barely see some people for the worms on 'em. Walk through a crowd downtown, it's enough to make you puke, once you learn to see 'em.

"The addict see, is losing life-force. He's basically using up his life energy on his addiction – little bit by little bit. The Akishra suck that run-off. They get developed enough, they can encourage the addict to go farther and farther. Mostly, though, the Lower Akishra just ride along and stay quiet, take what they can get. Now, the Akishra come in lots of varieties, and there's the Prime Akishra – got one of those hatin' me and suckin' at me right now. They're coiled around you, those Primes. Any of the worms get big enough, they do that: twist around you like pythons. Now the Primes, they're the ones that we know how to communicate with, we can make deals with them, and they can have a lotta psychic influence on people. Those you got to sort of invite in – they're special. They got to be brought in on you with ritual, see.

"And – we make these deals with 'em. What we do is, we bring in fresh people and put the plaything, as we used to call the people, through all kinds of sick fun and hell that releases the life-energy run-off. The Akishra suck that up and then re-route some of the pleasure-impulses back to us. And they addict us, and pick one of us out to follow around, start drainin' off of us too. You followin' me? And if we let them actually move into our bodies, well, they regenerate the cells. On the outside, anyway. They keep an old body running. But the price for that's nasty to see, when it goes too far. Judy . . ."

He shook his head and paused to rest, panting slightly. He reached up to a rack behind the bed and drew down an oxygen mask, making a "wait a minute" gesture with his free hand. He inhaled oxygen for a full minute, while Jeff fidgeted on his chair, embarrassed by Kenson's ravings, and Prentice shifted from foot to foot, wanting a drink. And feeling strange about wanting a drink, in light of what Kenson had been saying . . .

Kenson put the oxygen mask aside and said. "I'm sorry. I'm so tired."

"Maybe we should split," Jeff said. "Let you rest."

"No! No, let me get this out. It's been years I've been wanting to . . . part of me wanting to tell someone . . ." He swallowed a little water and went on, "Now, some of the Akishra will let the victims wander out into the city in search of, well, sensation I guess you'd say. Just . . . sensation. Stimulation. They get to be sucked dry – like me."

Like Amy, Prentice thought.

Jeff heaved a sigh of aggravation. Kenson didn't seem to notice. He continued, "The Akishra withdraw after the victims are used up and too far gone to be helped. And not coherent enough to be listened to. They become withered up street people, if they live that long, you see'em dying in vacant lots, babblin'...It's kind of funny, though. I mean, it's not as if every kind of pleasure attracts the Akishra. Only the kind that's...like a sickness in you. That's the kind that uses up bits of your soul, y'know. Sometimes if you change direction you can break away from them...the addict voice they plant in you gets fainter and fainter, like, and they give up and leave. But if you were one of us, with the real psychic communication – well, eventually you come back to 'em. And that's because you're addicted to the Akishra connection itself. Addicted to the ecstasy. The Reward. It's...more than you can imagine, when you play along with the Primes. That's all I can say in my defense – some of the things I took part in, man, with no hesitation and no thinking, it's sickening to remember and it's easy to judge me but once your pleasure buttons are pushed like that, you're fucked. You get programmed. You get addicted. And the fuckin' Akishra take advantage of that. So it's like it's this addict part of your brain conspirin' with the fuckin' worms..."

"That's it," Jeff said, standing up suddenly. "That's all of this bullshit I can handle. I'm sorry, Mr. Kenson. You were great, by the way, in *The Bishop's Daughter*. Now I gotta hit the road." He turned to Prentice. "I'm gonna call Blume again. You won't believe this message he left on my machine. He's playing with my head, the fucking drunk."

"You like prostitutes, Mr. Teitelbaum?" Kenson

asked, pausing to cough afterwards. "It's hookers, right? Maybe two a day sometimes."

Jeff turned to gape at him. "What?"

"I can see the sex addict worms on you, man. And it's a kind people get from using women in a professional way. Sick sex. Impersonal and nasty in your car. They give you head, most of the time, probably, right there in the car. Lots of guys with dough are addicted to it. The women are so *accessible* and some of them are surprisingly good lookin'. Sometimes you like to go to those brothels where they line up for you and you pick 'em, I bet. That's the part you really like – you point and say *that one* and she gives it up. And it's an addictive charge you get outta that. Your worms are real thick around your –"

"Shut the fuck up, Kenson!" Jeff said dangerously. His face mottled red.

"It's true, isn't it? And how'd I know? You going to tell me I had you followed?"

Jeff looked at Prentice who was careful not to look back at him or smile. Prentice had been wondering how one guy could take so many "meetings".

Jeff was breathing hard. He spun on his heel and shoved past Prentice, storming out the door. Prentice went to the chair and sank into it with a thump. "Kenson – you too tired to answer a couple of questions?"

"You don't think I'm full of shit, too?"

"I – don't think you're full of shit. No. Is there some way that . . . well, suppose I was having sex with a girl and she had an arrangement with these Akishra prime, could she, uh, enhance the experience through them to kind of draw me in and uh . . . ?"

"Sure. That's Lissa's favourite thing. You know her?"

Prentice's limbs suddenly felt leaden on his bones, as

if truth had tripled gravity. In a small voice, he said. "Yeah. I do."

Kenson nodded. He reached up and took another long hit of oxygen. Then he held the mask on his lap and said, "If you can crank my bed down a little I could go on for a few minutes more maybe . . ."

Prentice was sitting within reach of the two control buttons, on a box just out of Kenson's reach. He pressed the lower button and the bed whined to itself as it lowered the top end of the mattress almost to horizontal. "That's good," Kenson said. "Right there. I need a little elevation . . . Well, now. What you want to know?"

"Besides the Akishra – are there other creatures on the Astral Plane, or whatever you call it? Maybe something more . . ."

"Benevolent? Sure." He scowled. "But they're haughty bastards. The higher spirits. The Akishra are just a kind of animal. Etheric animals. But the higher ones . . . some of them are things that only help you if they bother to take any notice of you, and some of them are nasty fucks that are always fighting. They're always playing a kind of game . . . well, Judy called it a 'dance' . . . the dance of the ones who construct, who grow things, with the ones who destroy things . . . I don't pretend to understand all that very much. All I know is, the so-called 'good' ones are there, but they never did shit for me. They're hard to get in touch with and what I heard it gets harder all the time.

"See, the Akishra, and the other predators, all your garden variety demons, they reproduce in cycles. And they got going with this really big reproduction cycle a couple of times in this century – most recently in the middle 1970s. Started to spread through the world, usually showing their works through your serial killers,

277

your child molesters, your Republican Secretaries of the Interior, vicious assholes of all kinds. Usually they aren't so – what's that word. Uh . . . symbiotic. They're usually not so symbiotic as they are with Denver and his toyboys. Well anyway, the Akishra are gearin' up for another big repro cycle." He chuckled creakily. "You think there's a lot of murderous lunatics out there now? They cultivate those fuckers . . . Just wait a few days till the cycle's complete. Denver's got the incubator out there at . . . oh God." He lapsed into silence, his eyes closed, hands clenching.

"You want a doctor?" Prentice asked.

Kenson shook his head. His shoulders quivered. After a few moments his eyes fluttered open. He lay there looking into nowhere, murmuring, "One thing, Jeff . . ."

Prentice didn't correct his confusion about who he was talking to. He could see Kenson was drifting.

". . . one thing to . . . get clear . . . the human hosts of Akishra . . . they always . . . always offer themselves up *willingly*. Whether or not they know it . . . know it consciously . . . they always . . ." He shook his head and made a shooing gesture with his hand.

Feeling unreal, Prentice got up to look for Jeff.

★   ★   ★

He saw Jeff on the phone in the lobby, trying to reach Blume. Prentice called to him, "Hey Jeff – I'm gonna wait for you in the parking lot."

Jeff nodded and said, into the phone, "He's what? When? So who am I talking to? Sergeant what?"

Prentice thought, *Now what?* He didn't want to know, quite yet. The story Kenson had told him was too much to deal with already. If it were true. Now, stepping

out into a chilly evening the blotted sky promising rain–
Kenson's tale once more seemed like raving. He probably
had some disease and some kind of occult hobbyhorse
and he'd slung all this together in a paranoid fantasy to
explain his illness.

But he knew Lissa. And he'd said –

"Hello, Tom."

She was there. Lissa, just getting out of a convertible
BMW. Prentice felt his legs weaken, looking at her. He
thought he felt Amy somewhere in the background,
trying to tell him something. But he ignored the fantasy
and walked over to Lissa. She wore black jeans, a red
halter-top, red spike heels. The heels looked particularly
sexy with the jeans, somehow. He stopped just out of her
reach. "Hi! How'd you track me down!"

She glanced past him at the hospital. He started to
turn, to see what she was looking at, or who but she came
closer and touched his arm as if to hold his gaze. "Hey
– are you standing me up? Weren't you supposed to pick
me up about an hour ago? For the party?"

"*Is* there a party?"

She looked at him in a fair reading of hurt surprise.
"Why would I say there was if there wasn't?"

"I don't know." He exhaled windily, suddenly feeling
stupid. Why would she lie??

He took a step back, looking at her in the indirect
light of the parking lot's streetlamp. Was it there? A kind
of tell-tale sheen in the air around her, that seemed to
squirm a little?

He shook himself and looked away. She stepped in
and threw her arms around him, drew him close. And
instantly he felt the warm, drunken sweetness pass from
her to him. He found himself putting his arms around
her, returning the embrace, as she said, "Listen –

279

something's bothering you. Aren't we close enough we can talk about it?"

"I don't know – for some stupid reason I feel responsible for Amy. What happened to her. And now I just talked to this guy who was sick with the same thing as Amy . . . If that's what it was . . ."

It all seemed murky and distant, now that he held her again. This was real; this feeling. *This* was important.

"Look – I want you to come to this party," Lissa was murmuring. "Because I want you to meet the people who saved my life."

"How'd they do that?"

"They got me off drugs. They've been sort of weaning me off them. I shouldn't have taken that X, the other day. I wasn't supposed to. See – there's a new drug going around town." She drew back and looked at him earnestly. "You heard of Xedrine?"

"No . . ." He felt pleasantly sleepy but somehow glowing, his loins, his sexuality shining with a soft light.

"Well – Xedrine is this new designer drug. I was hung up on it and – I thought I could get off it by taking Ecstasy as a substitute. But no go. A lot of people are hung up on this stuff, and other drugs, and the Denvers help them get clean. They have a drug detox clinic out there."

"Yeah . . . that might explain all the secrecy . . ."

"Sure. The celebrities. And listen – I just realized today I knew your ex-wife! Amy! Only a little – she was out at the clinic. She was a Xedrine addict. She and Lou Kenson got into it."

Kenson? His attention came back from the plane of pleasure for a moment. "Lou Kenson . . ."

"Yeah, Lou was really gone on the stuff. And Amy. It can leave you wasted, make you prone to self mutilation.

And it'll give you paranoid fantasies . . . hallucinations of monsters crawling on you, that kind of thing. Like the way cocaine overdose makes you see bugs on your skin. Kenson and Amy back-slid into the drugs but I stayed off Xedrine and the Denvers are the ones who helped me. They and Zack Arthwright . . ."

He felt grounded, then, and enormously relieved. It all came together. It made sense. He smiled. "God – I needed to hear that. Wait'll I tell you what . . . Well – later. Let's head out there. I came in Jeff's car –"

"Not a problem. Let's go in mine."

"Okay – let me just go in and talk to Jeff."

She made a something-smells-bad face. "I'd rather you didn't. That guy's kind of crazy. I don't want him to know I'm here. Couldn't we just go?"

Prentice shrugged. Jeff was a big boy. He could call him later and explain. "Sure. Let's head for Malibu."

★   ★   ★

Jeff was just coming back in from the parking lot when Drandhu bustled up, stethoscope in hand. "Ah, Mr. Teitelbaum, there you are! Do you mind if we go and talk to Mr. Kenson a little more?"

"Sure, whatever. I got some questions for him. If he can be reasonably civil for about five minutes."

"He said something . . . disturbing?"

"He pissed me off is what he did. But come on. Probably Tom went back to Kenson's room."

Just outside Kenson's room Jeff noticed a short, stocky guy with a kind of Howdy Doody look about him, and big earlobes, walking along toward them carrying a canvas bag. He smiled sunnily at them and continued on past.

There were shouts and curses from Kenson's room. Inside, they found a fat, mustached male nurse trying to hold Kenson down. "Doctors orders, you're supposed to take it easy, pal –"

But Kenson was going into convulsions, moving with an energy that Jeff would have thought impossible, given Kenson's condition. Coming closer, Jeff was sickened, seeing Kenson was foaming at the mouth, jaws snapping open and shut clack-clack-clack, arms flailing, legs randomly kicking. His bowels letting go, judging from the stink and the stain spreading down the sheet. And the tape recorder was gone from the IV stand.

"Who put that bandage on his head?" Drandhu snapped. "No one was to have put any bandages there – had no need at all . . . !"

Kenson gave a final shudder and lay back, gasping, eyes rolling wildly, rigid now. The nurse stepped back, protesting, "Look I didn't touch his head, I just heard him flapping around in here and –"

"Yes, yes, just get out of the way –" Drandhu snapped, moving around behind Kenson. He unwound the bandage.

Not knowing why, Jeff was drawn to stand behind Drandhu when he removed the bandage entirely . . .

The top of Kenson's skull had been freshly sawed away. And his brain exposed. And his brain was squirming.

Someone had taken the top of his head off and introduced vermin into his brain. Real maggots – not the ethereal variety. Spiders. Centipedes. Large black and red ants. Dozens of them, thrashing and chewing their way through his brain.

Kenson gave a final spasm and died, as Jeff turned away and threw up on the male nurse.

Near Malibu

Mitch tried to remember coming here, and couldn't.

As far as he knew, he'd always been in the fog room. There was just a bed, and there was Eurydice, and that was all. There were no walls. Just the fog around the bed. If he looked up from Eury's heaving, sweat and blood-sticky breasts, and if he stared at the fog for a moment, it resolved into shadows that fanned out like shapes in a kaleidoscope; they were man-shaped shadows, and they were caressing themselves and dancing in a stupid sort of way. And then they were fog again as a jolt of punishment pushed his attention back to Eury and he pumped into her and the Reward came and he knew the things on the other side of the fog were feeding but it felt good, it felt very good so it was not to be argued with, you were not to notice the suffering on Eury's face, the look of a terrified lost child, you just got into the pain and then you didn't have to notice the other hurt, the one that couldn't be expressed, the final pain, the pain at the root of whatever it was that made Mitch himself . . .

Just keep at it and after a while maybe it would end.

But he was pretty sure it wasn't going to end till they were both dead . . .

A Highway Near Malibu

The BMW took the curves at fifty, but Lissa was a better driver than Jeff. Nothing much was bothering Prentice, anyway. He felt dreamy. Even the pain in his hand from the gash was gone, completely faded. He was strapped into a bucket seat, letting the damp wind lick his ears and stream his hair, looking up at the few stars visible through knot-holes in the ceiling of clouds.

Lissa was amazing. She had only to touch him and he was transported. Maybe it was being in love. Hadn't Kenson said something about her? He couldn't remember what it was, now.

"Oh Hell," Lissa said.

He looked at the road ahead. A wispy gray broom of rain swept down the highway toward them. And they still had the top down on the car.

In seconds the rain was on them, even as Lissa reached back to unsnap the accordion top, and hit the switch to close it over them. It came up a little too high and caught the wind, didn't clasp properly. Lissa cursed, trying to close the convertible top with one hand as she drove with the other.

"Maybe we'd better pull over," Prentice said vaguely, as the chilly rain off the sea began to patter down over them. He tried to help her with the top.

But she snapped, "Don't touch it! It's cranky, it has to be done just right ... goddamn it ... And we don't have time to pull over ..."

What was the hurry, he wondered. It was as if she were trying to get him there before ...

Before what? And what had put that thought into his head?

The rain splashed down his face now, and he felt odd,

as if he were just waking up out here in her car. He remembered getting in with her and driving out here but till now it hadn't seemed quite real.

What *was* real? Suddenly he found himself thinking that maybe some of what Kenson had told them was real. And just as suddenly the story Lissa had told him about "Xedrine" seemed improbable. Contrived.

It was as if the dash of cold rain water and Lissa's distraction had slipped him from a noose he hadn't been aware of till he was free of it.

How did I get here? he wondered. He'd been determined to avoid Lissa and Arthwright. How could he have believed that bogus story about the drug treatment centre? How could he have got in her car after all that Kenson had said about her?

And why, he wondered, was Lissa the one who was to bring him – and not Arthwright?

Lissa had been assigned to him, he thought. (*Did* he think it? Or was it Amy's thought?) He was a natural for Lissa. He was the type that went for her specialized bait.

He was the type. That seemed a key, somehow. A *type* is compulsive about something.

It had started long before Lissa's effortless seduction of him. He seemed to see an unbroken linkage of cause and effect stretching back to his days living with Amy, in New York.

It began with his need to blindly chase girls. Why had he started cheating on Amy? Was it just her sickness? Or had that been a handy rationale? Some of the time he'd been happy with her – and he'd been frightened by his happiness with Amy.

The car swerved on the newly slick road, threatening to spin, but Lissa kept it on track, and now they'd come to a straight stretch. She used the opportunity to close the convertible roof the rest of the way. Absently, Prentice helped her lock it in place.

There'd been something missing in his life with Amy – something more than the stability sacrificed to her erratic behavior. He'd missed the sense of validation that came from new seductions, new relationships. He remembered something a male character in one of his scripts had said:

JACK
Women to me are doorways. They're a way
into another would – an alien country where
the landscape is made up of each woman's
distinctive personality, her tastes, her
desires, the way she feels under my hands
and the way she feels about my hands...
And me, I'm an explorer, is all. I can't be
satisfied with exploring only one frontier...

He remembered, too, what Amy's reaction had been, reading that. "An explorer? That's a comfortable euphemism for it."

Euphemism for philanderer. For a guy who needed to have affairs. Who needed that periodic input of reassurance that he got from making a new girl. But there was something else, underlying the urge. A concealed anger against all women.

Riding passively along in the BMW, distantly aware that Lissa was saying something to him, trying to snag his attention once more, he was nearly overwhelmed with a sudden and infinitely tragic yearning for Amy.

And that seemed to pierce a membrane of some kind...

When he turned to see Lissa, all filters were – for one

moment – quite gone. He saw Lissa as she really was. Seeing her spiritually and, in some etheric sense, physically.

The sickly, silvery-grey protoplasm of wormstuff had grown out of her mouth and eyes and out from psychic pressure points in the throat and temple – the worm had taken her over and grown to surround her, its great lamprey mouth, ringed and razored, turning toward him when she looked his way... its body, thick as a primed firehose, sliding through her body like a maggot through rot. Sliding through her. Squirming. A part of her and independent from her, as she calmly drove the car...

The worm had clusters of polyps for eyes. They could convey no human expression, but he saw clearly its longing and hunger as it looked at him.

Prentice shrieked like an infant stepping on a scorpion.

He flailed, and his hand closed over the steering wheel. He wrenched it toward the brush to one side of the road. Anything to get out of the car.

The BMW squealed and Lissa shouted in furious surprise. A flash of a concrete post pebbled with tiny round stones and then the car shuddered into a stand of Manzanita, the trees' load of rainwater shell-bursting over the windshield. A sickening thump as Lissa struck the windshield at the same moment; some of her blood splashing across its inside. The car jerked back with finality, the engine dying. Prentice was distantly aware that he'd thumped his own forehead on something; that Lissa had been badly hurt. He clawed at the door, scarcely able to see for the blinding pain. Lissa clutched at his elbow, hissing. He didn't want to look at her. He wrenched free of her weak grip and jerked the door open, flung himself from the car. Head pain grinding with every step, he ran into the brush and up into the hills. She was yelling something after him, but it didn't sound as if she was following.

After perhaps a quarter mile, his breath coming in panting stabs, he stopped and looked around. He had to clear his eyes of the lashing rain, before he could quite focus – it was dark out here, though a little light came from up the hill. A house up there. The Ranch? It was too dark and rainy to tell. He was standing on the edge of a gravel road. It forked, a little ways to his left. He stepped onto the road, and walked unsteadily up to the fork. He could taste blood mixed with rainwater, running down from his forehead.

He stood there, blinking stupidly at the fork in the road. Should he go up one of these forks, or go back down the road the other way?

Go up the hill, and then to the right, Amy told him. Quite clearly. *Look for a red pick up truck . . .*

Prentice staggered up the right-hand fork, feeling gingerly at the ragged lump on his forehead. He kept on, more or less blindly, thinking about Lissa. Wondering if the thing could pull free of her and come slithering up the road behind him.

The rain slackened to a mist, but he was already soaked to the skin, his clothes rasping and heavy. Up ahead, off the road to the right, was a soft, yellow light. In the oily shine from a small square of window, he could just make out the outline of a one-room shack, and to one side of it, a pickup truck.

Culver City

Garner found the apartment easily enough. But it was locked and dark and no one answered the door. He stood on the dark landing, trying to decide what course to take now. Get something to eat and come back, maybe. He still had a little money. He was getting hungry, and his fractured ribs were aching; his nose and head, too. He needed more codeine, and some food. The codeine would upset his stomach, though. And he probably didn't deserve to eat. For all he knew the bastard motherfucker who had Constance was starving her in some basement.

Once more the sludge-wave of post-cocaine depression rose up around him . . .

He forgot about it, for a moment, when someone pushed the muzzle of a gun against the back of his head. All he could think of to say was probably the wrong thing, but he said it anyway. "You sure move quietly, man. I didn't hear you comin'."

"I saw you up here trying my door knob, went to my car and got my gun and came back real quiet. It worked out."

Garner could see the guy out of the corner of his eye. Gangly, narrow face, big nose. A glitter of honed intelligence. An expression of triumph. He was the kind of guy who liked guns and had been just waiting for the opportunity to use his . . . "How many other places here you break into?" the guy asked.

Garner said. "I don't know why I tried the knob. Not even thinking. I'm on codeine, it makes me fuzzy. You're Jeff Teitelbaum?"

He looked startled for a second, then smiled. "So you can read names off mailboxes."

"I guess I look pretty bad, huh? Haven't shaved. Hair all fucked up with bandages. Like a street person. Probably smell like one too. Shit, I *feel* like one —"

"Bandages . . ." Something seemed to occur to

Teitelbaum. "Jesus Christ. You're with those lunatics who murdered Kenson!"

"I don't know any Kenson. But I came here partly because of a murder. Detective named Blume. I found Blume's body over in his place...and uh..."

Teitelbaum's jaw had dropped. He took a step back and slowly lowered the gun. Garner turned and looked at it more closely. Holy shit. It was a .357.

"You really need that thing?" Garner asked. "A gun like that the bullet would probably keep going through my head and right through somebody's window. Must be frustrating to be a gun freak and not get a chance to use it much."

Teitelbaum scowled. "What the fuck you know about Blume?"

"I hired him to find my kid. You lost a child? A boy – Mitch, isn't it? I heard your answering machine message to him..."

"So that's it..."

Garner tried to ignore the gun and spoke fast. "Whoever's been doing the Wetbones killings took my daughter and left her finger with somebody else's bloody bones. Blume thought there was a connection between them and somebody named Denver?"

"There's a kind of cult..." Jeff broke off, shaking his head in exasperation. "I can't believe I'm discussing this stuff with a..."

"A street bum? I got rolled, is all. I screwed up, and then I got rolled. I haven't had a chance to clean up. They've got my daughter, man. And I want to know what you know."

290

She was skilled at hiding it. But Constance hated Ephram deeply and profoundly.

Even so, she wished she could be with him now. And not just for the Reward. He was safer than these people. This place. This dimly-lit room with its infrastructure of purest grotesquerie. Besides, Ephram wouldn't make her watch a thing like this, not for so long. He'd have stopped it by now, for all the wrong reasons. He'd have regarded it as "esthetically gauche" or something.

The bed. It was made of people. Pieces of people. Pieces of legs for posts, bones for frames, most of it looking brown and old. But the skin over the mattress (what was the mattress stuffed with?) looked new. It was made from a black man; maybe not much more than a boy. She could see his face upside down on the side of the mattress. The eyes were sewn crudely shut.

The room stank.

The teenagers, a white boy and a black girl, were humping listlessly in the middle of the bed, and clawing at one another. It was making Constance sick, because she wasn't getting any Reward, and some of her natural feelings of repugnance were coming back. But the More Man and Thandy, the Handy Man, and the woman with the white thing growing from her face – they wanted her here, they wanted her to watch. They were standing on the other side of the bed. Playing. She supposed they were preparing her for something. She didn't care. She just wanted to get back to Ephram and hide behind him.

On the bed, abruptly as the fall of a house of cards, the boy collapsed. "Lost too much blood," the Handy Man said, examining him. "He's dead."

"Now," the More Man said, "is the time, Constance.

291

Go to them. Mitch's dead and Prime will pass to you — you will become one of us."

"No, thanks," Constance said.

The More Man laughed. "A good semblance of winning ingenuousness."

Something glimmered around the More Man's head. She could see that he had the thing that looked like an undersea-crawler on his head, too, like his wife — only his was less substantial looking. It reached out, though, to Constance, stretching like phlegm, reaching for her. She backed away. The door was locked behind her.

"Time to par-*tayyyy* . . ." the More Man said softly, mockingly.

The Handy Man said something in German. The woman with the big sea snail thing on her head answered in German, something muted and bubbly under the stuff, and sobbed, and lifted up her dress and . . .

Constance looked away. The slim black girl on the bed of body parts was crying softly, rasping. "Mitch . . ." The boy was dead. The black girl was trying to heave his body off her and couldn't. She was crying with crusted, dried out eyes and cracked lips, trying to roll the boy off her. Constance looked away from her too. She didn't want to feel bad for anyone. If she let herself feel anything, it'd open a can of . . .

The yellow-silvery tendril reached out to her.

A rattling in the lock Then the door opened behind her.

She turned and saw Ephram there.

But Ephram looked defeated. "That's enough . . ." He tossed the key onto the floor. "I . . . will cooperate, Samuel."

"You *have* become peculiar lately," Sam Denver chuckled. "Very well, Constance." The tendril slunk back to him like the gelatinous antenna of a snail pulling into itself.

Denver drew the Handy Man aside, away from his wife. "What can you do for her, then, Ephram?"

Seeing they'd lost interest in her, Constance edged toward the bed. She wasn't sure why – but she had to do this. Maybe some door in her had been left open a slit. She pulled the white boy off the black girl, rolled him toward Denver's side of the murdered bed. The girl turned on her side to try to crawl off the bed – and found herself staring, three inches away, into the mummified face of the boy they'd made into a mattress cover. She screamed in recognition: and Constance saw the family resemblance between the two faces. The girl's brother.

The girl covered her face with her hands, screaming uncontrollably into her bloody palms. Constance helped her to stand, and drew her aside. The girl fell silent, shaking. Constance wondered if Denver would let the two of them get out the door.

Ephram was staring at the woman. That'd be Mrs. Denver, Judy, from what he'd told her. Once Mrs. Stutgart. Ephram was doing something to her with his mind. Ephram grimaced and shook his head. "I haven't got the strength. They're too firmly a part of her."

Denver nodded grimly. "Then get the hell out of here. And leave the girl."

Ephram hesitated. Then he started mumbling. He was chanting, Constance knew, calling up the . . .

"No," Denver said. "If you can't do it alone, don't do it."

"It's the only way," Ephram said, pausing in a distracted kind of way. "The Spirit can draw them off from her. I don't have enough strength."

"The Spirit!" Denver laughed bitterly. "What the

293

Bloody Hell do you think the Spirit *is*, Pixie? Don't you know what it'd do to her? Or is that what you want?"

Ephram stopped his murmuring. He blinked at Denver. "What do you mean – what it is?"

Denver shook his head. "Do you really have that much of a blind spot? But of course, it's kept you that way... Ephram, your spirit is just another Akishra. A Magnus. The most powerful Akishra – but it is still just an Akishra."

"No!"

Constance had never heard Ephram sound so off balance. And so afraid. She looked at the door. The girl beside her – God, she smelled bad, of rotting blood and shit and worse stuff – was sinking to her knees, unable to walk by herself. Constance couldn't carry her and couldn't bring herself to leave the girl here. What am I *doing*? she wondered. Maybe she'd been too long without Reward, and this was withdrawal. This feeling...

"You don't think I'd perceive such a thing?" Ephram said, with a trumped-up sneer. "I'd *know*."

"You really can't see them?" Denver said. "The control lines? I suppose it doesn't want you to. See for yourself. Here, with our influence, you should be able to see them..."

Ephram looked up, and shocked Constance by whimpering. Constance followed his gaze. Shimmying into view like puppet strings over Ephram's head were dozens of fine, translucent tendrils. Now, as they began to move around, billowing and gleaming, they didn't look like puppet strings so much as the little trailing stingers that dangle from big jelly fish...

They were sunken into his head. Grown right into it. They stretched from Ephram up into, and through, the ceiling. And through this world into another. They were not *quite* physical things – you could see that, looking at them. But they were there.

"You pretentious old bastard," Denver said. "You thought you were better than the rest of us – because of your overblown talent? That you were in touch with some glorious God of the dark dimensions? You perfect ass! It was just the biggest Akishra; the Magnus itself. The greatest of them, playing games with you, letting you play on the line, reeling you out then, reeling you in now. It brought you here, for this. Manipulated you into coming to L.A. Oh, yeah. The thing you called down for Wetbones. And – you want to bring that here? Now? You're out of your pompous little skull."

"Yes," Ephram croaked. His face gone white. "Yes. Having come this far: yes. To cure us all." And he spoke three more words.

The ceiling seemed to vanish. It turned transparent and then faded completely. Smoke replaced it, a living smoke made up of ten thousand restless, microscopic eyes. Constance thought she glimpsed people there, too, whirling, caught like the birds in a tornado. The rectangle that had been the ceiling was now an infinite reach of crowded and living sky. And then the iridescent bulk of the creature who'd masqueraded as the "Great Spirit", the Akishra Magnus, descended slowly toward them. What Constance could see of it made her think of a house-sized plasticine squid; its upper parts tapering into the boiling smokes of staring, black-light space; reeling in on some tendrils, seeking with others, its vast sticky, glimmer-edged, polyp-bearded mouth opening...

A great wind raged through the room, roaring, smelling like an overheated electric train; and static electricity invested the air, making Constance's hair crackle out, as the "Spirit", the etheric animal that had kept Ephram for its toy, lowered itself over Mrs. Stutgart, taking her into its translucent, feeler-furred envelope. They could see her inside it, through the foggy membrane. And for an instant, within it, she was freed – the husk of Akishra was drawn off her head, and the old woman beneath wept with gratitude. Then the woman's own face was peeled off her skull, sucked cleanly off her, upward, and her eyes remained in her skull for a moment staring in naked realization. Until the skull exploded, and Elma Stutgart disintegrated into a pulp of flesh and bone...

Denver was all this time moving away from her, pushing the Handy Man ahead of him...

The bed, the cobbled body parts of the furniture, were leaping in the electric galvanization pervading the air, tearing free of one another, twitching with the damaged reflexes of some half-rotted nervous system. A spasmodic tarantel of dis-juncted body parts.

Constance stood near the door, unable to move, paralyzed with the immense psychological gravitation of what she was seeing.

She saw Ephram rigid, shaking, his eyes rolling back in his head. The Magnus reeled him toward it. He staggered its way. Shouting over the roaring wind something Constance recognized from one of the evenings he'd made her read to him from Nietzsche: *"The beauty of the superman..."* He paused to gasp for air, then went on, *"...came to me as a shadow..."* He paused to clutch at the twitching, preserved leg that had been part of the disassembling bedframe. Then seemed to make a decision and deliberately let go, shouting, finishing the quote: *"...what are the gods to me now!"*

Ephram was sucked slowly toward the Magnus, as blood ran down from new wounds opening on his skull and neck, a hundred little rifts giving up brain and blood to accompany soul through the feeding tendrils of the Akishra Magnus...

As the great one tilted toward him, its mouth opening.

Constance thought she caught a glimpse of a single opalescent eye in the writhing tendrils of its lower parts; maybe even a fragment of a desperate face; a visage that might once have been human, millennia ago, the remains of something that now suffered enormously in the aching, interstellar void of hugely imbecilic hungers.

Ephram glimpsed this face too, and seemed to sense its implications. Now he tried to hold back, shrieking. She could see his face contorting as he attempted to use his talent to disentangle himself from it. But it drew him nearer, with little effort. Constance almost felt pity for Ephram...

And she felt herself drawn after him. She felt a jolt of Reward as she staggered toward the Magnus, transmitted through Ephram but originating in this Lord of Akishra itself. She was connected to Ephram – she had to go with him. It was that simple. It was not to be questioned...

No. Go your way, my dear. More than me, it wants you. Go. Ephram's voice, from nowhere. *Let us take some comfort in frustrating it, a little.*

And then she felt Ephram withdraw from her. His psychic fingers slipping out of their sockets in her brain. She felt cold and strange and sick and relieved.

Ephram tried once more to hold himself back. Shouting: "Ich bin der Ubermensch!" (Hearing that, the Handy Man laughed).

Then Ephram was drawn up inside the Spirit –

Constance found her will to move again; she turned and jerked the black girl to her feet. Denver and the Handy Man had gone ahead of her, fled from the room.

Constance pulled the sagging girl along with her, out into the hall.

The wind roared through the door, behind them, banging it open and closed, open and closed, and open again. Denver and his wife's servant were waiting for her, the Handy Man weeping now, calling softly, "Elma . . . Elma . . ."

Constance felt it when Ephram exploded. She felt it as a release of hatred: her own. And suffering: his. Her own buried hatred; his buried suffering. She screamed like a vivisected cat. She bared her teeth at Denver – preparing to lunge at him. Sink her teeth into him.

Then a mountainous pressure vanished completely. It was just gone.

There were two sickening squelching sounds. Out of sight, in the room behind them: Two bodies pulverized to lumps of mush, dropping from mid-air to splash over the remains of the bed and the dead boy. Constance looked through the open door. The room was empty, except for the absurd tumble of body parts and the fresher, steaming, unrecognizably pulped heaps of what had been two human bodies. The ceiling was in place again, with the same cobwebs.

I ought to be happy Ephram's dead, Constance thought. She smiled wearily. *And I sure as Hell am.*

The Spirit – he Magnus, the Akishra, the godsized predator of Astral places – was gone, for now. It had withdrawn.

Constance's rage floundered and lay sodden in her. She swayed, feeling as if the floor were rocking under her, though in fact the house had settled to a new quietude.

Slowly, she turned toward the front door. It was very easy to figure out, she told herself. You just go away. Just walk away...

"No," the More Man told her. He took a gun from his coat pocket. The tendrils, the thing on his head, were no longer visible. But she knew it was there, too, cocked as much as the gun.

"No," the More Man said. "You will stay with us. And play."

The Hills Near Malibu

"He's out there, talkin' to nothin' again," Lonny said.

"He do that a lot?" Prentice asked, wearily. He was pressing an old towel soaked in cold water against his battered head. "I did some of that myself, lately."

He and Lonny were sitting in the best-lit corner of the old shack. Prentice propped up on the bed, Lonny sitting on the rocking chair next to it. The dog paced restively near the closed wooden door, growling softly to itself.

"It's almost dawn, too," Lonny went on. "Fuckin Drax's been out there since midnight. Smokin' weed and chewing those cactus buttons and talking to those dolls on their posts out there. It's trippin' me out. Like he might geek out and come in here and smoke *us* with that shotgun. You sure you can't sleep? You oughta."

"Sure, like I can sleep when you talk about how this fuckin' crazy old hippy is going to come in and waste me while I'm sawing logs. Shit! Anyway, I think I remember something about how you're not supposed to sleep for a while if you get a concussion. If that's what this is."

"So let's get you to a doctor, dude."

"No. Drax says he's got a way to beat them. Let's check him out."

"If he's not just, like, hallucinatin' it."

Wincing, Prentice got up and walked to the window, and peered out at Drax. He was squatting between two of his kerosene lamps. Small white insects flung themselves at the lamp, drew back, and flung themselves again. The dawn was just adding aluminium filings to the blue steel of the sky. Drax said something inaudible, then cocked his head to listen. He rocked back on his heels, laughing, reacting to something that was said. By no one visible. Then he stood up, and stretched. Looked at the horizon. He stared into the white crescent of sun that showed over the hills. Then he turned, picked up a kerosene lamp in one hand and the shotgun in the other, and strode back to the shack.

Drax shouldered through the door, hands laden with gun and lamp – and paused to glare at Prentice as if he'd never seen him before. Then he seemed to remember, and grinned. "Yore wife got a great sense of humour. Says some damn funny things." He stalked past Prentice to the woodstove in the corner, hung the lamp on a nail, and dumped water from a bucket into a coffee pot sitting on the stove's white upper shelf. Some of the water spilled onto the stove griddle, and it sizzled into steam.

Prentice stared at him. After a moment, not caring much about the shotgun that Drax had leaned against the wall near the stove, said, "You're full of shit."

Drax nodded, his beard wagging. "Her name's Amy, am I right?"

Prentice shivered. "You found that out from someone else."

Lonny snorted. "You never told *me* her name. He be

talking to Orphy, too, and he came back with some shit only Orphy know about."

It wasn't that Prentice disbelieved in the supernatural. Not after what he'd seen in the car. But he didn't want to believe Amy was . . . so close.

Drax took a brown sack of coffee from one of six stacked crates, all of them containing coffee, and dumped an unconscionable amount in the coffee pot. "Fuck you if you don't believe it, pal," he said cheerfully. "But how you think you found your way here? Luck? No more'n this boy did. I've been working on these here friendships for a while . . ."

They drank coffee and Prentice ate a plate of stale Oreo cookies, which Drax also bought by the crate. He declined marijuana. After drinking a cup of acrid coffee with a thoughtful look on his face, Drax hurried to the door, ran outside, and vomited explosively. Then he came back in, wiping his beard with the back of his hand, muttering, "Damn peyote do it to me most every time, when I drink coffee." And to Prentice's amazement poured himself another cup of coffee.

After they'd eaten, they went outside to pee. Prentice was feeling better. He pissed toward Denver's house, though it was hidden by the swell of a hill and trees and distance, and pissed toward Lissa's wrecked car, and spat once in that direction too. It did him good.

Then Drax said, "I want to show you what I got to kill them things with. If we got time to do it."

"What's this about 'time to do it'?" Prentice asked, walking with Drax and Lonny through the blue light of early morning, around the side of the shack.

"They going to reproduce like a motherfucker, so to speak," Drax said, "and if they get too far along we're dead meat. Awright. Here we go. What do you think?"

He flapped a hand in the general direction of the battered red '59 Ford pick-up. It was scored with rusty dents. Its front window had been knocked out. Its crooked hood was wired down. It had oversized tyres with big, stand-out tread. Some sort of old tractor tyres, never meant for a pick-up.

"What do I think of *what*?" Prentice asked, his headache beginning to pound again.

"The truck!" Drax said, impatiently, eyes wild. "That's how I'm gonna git 'em! What do you think?"

A Highway near Malibu

Garner was tired. He thought he could feel his bones bending with each wrenching turn the Cabriolet made as it shot along the freeway. Now and then the rising sun strobed in the hollows between hills and caught him a blinding flash in the eyes. He turned toward the west. His eyes were tired. His ribs ached. He was a mess.

But he was psyched, too. He might be close to Constance. Jeff Teitelbaum, at the wheel, was fresher than Garner. But Garner was less afraid. Garner was afraid of nothing but his addict.

"You know, Jeff," Garner said, "they might not be there. Your Mitch. My Constance. You could be wrong. Blume could be wrong. We could get trigger happy and kill some people who have nothing to do with this."

"Who killed Kenson?" Jeff demanded. "He mentioned the More Man. Denver *is* the More Man. Blume connected the More Man to Wetbones. It's that simple."

"I hope it is simple," Garner said. "But I doubt it will be. I really do doubt it."

If they were wrong, Garner thought, someone innocent could get killed. But he had a feeling – and it

303

was something he hadn't felt so assuredly in years. A sense of guidance. Even the return to using cocaine had been guided, he suspected. He had to hit bottom again and see the true horror of it again. He had to come face to face with his own shrivelled faith, side by side with his bloating addict. He had been guided through that particular circle of Hades, through the Projects, through its punishment, and brought out again, and when he'd nearly stumbled back into the pit, he'd been saved first by a rip-off artist, who'd done him the favour of selling him bunk crack, and then the presence of another pastor out doing street work. And hearing the phone message at Blume's.

You should know, Brick had said, *God's the only one who can arrange coincidences* . . .

He was being guided here. He was sure of it. But he knew that being guided here was no guarantee of success, or safety.

The sad truth was, God was not all powerful. Not in Garner's estimation. God just did the best He could. And lots of the time it wasn't enough.

The Doublekey Ranch, Near Malibu

It was neither day nor night, here. It was dark, but not dark as true night. It was dark as the dirty fog . . .

A thick, oily fog had gathered around the Ranch. Constance hadn't noticed it coming. Now, she watched it thicken as she sat on the wooden lawn chair, near the brick barbecue. Near the pool. The black girl, Eurydice, sat on the terrace beside her, nude and shivering, hugging her knees. Constance hadn't been able to get her to say much except her name. That was okay, too.

She wondered at the fog. She knew it was no natural

304

fog. She could feel it on her skin, sliding over her with exquisite subtlety. A slithering feeling. And it was so thick and so dark overhead.

She saw, now, where it came from. It seeped upward from the pool. The glossy surface of the pool, so green it was black. Something seethed just beneath that surface. It was getting impatient. It was getting near time. It was nearly there . . .

There were others. Two women and three men, standing around near the door. They were just gray-black silhouettes in the fog. One of the men was playing with the buttocks of the shorter of the two women; another man was playing with himself. She thought they were looking her way, but she wasn't sure.

Music started up behind her, making her jump a little. She turned and saw the More Man and the Handy Man standing by Ephram's old ghetto blaster. Thudding, foreign sounding music. The two men had been standing there for awhile, she decided. Staring at her from behind.

What were they planning to do with her?

She had been thinking about killing herself, off and on, in the hours since Ephram's death. She was free of him. Denver had certain psychic powers, but nothing to compare with Ephram. He didn't have Ephram's power to paralyze her with a look. She could find something, something sharp perhaps, and kill herself before they began to use her. The More Man frowned, looking at her, as if he guessed her thinking. She spoke quickly, to distract him, said the first thing that came into her head. "This . . . this fog. What is it?"

"It's to keep the daylight from irritating the incubation," he said, nodding toward the pool. "Not that daylight would hurt them. It just irritates them, might spoil the timing a little."

She tried to remember what Ephram had said about the Akishra. "How come . . . how come they're, um, incubating here? I mean – they're not exactly from . . . from this world. Are they?"

"Oh but they are," Denver said. "They live in two worlds at once. Till now, though, they've been more physical in the Astral plane." He looked down at her maimed hand. Stared directly at the stump of her missing finger as he said, distractedly, "That's changing, little Constance. The Akishra's rootedness in the farther world. After this, they'll be quite physical here." He said it with wistful resignation. "And they'll be everywhere . . . ." Adding softly, to himself, "Just everywhere . . ."

She supposed that ought to frighten her, but she couldn't see how anything mattered, except getting away for a little while. She tried to think of something else to say. And wished that Ephram had showed her something. Taught her something. But there just hadn't been time.

Now and then, she could see the worms. She saw them now, around Denver and the Handy Man, a wriggling corona picked out against the fog.

She grimaced and turned from them, to Eurydice. Said to Denver over her shoulder, "Can Eurydice have a blanket or something?"

"No," Denver said. "I think not."

"Oh, don't be stupid," someone else said, strolling up to them. "Give the plaything a blanket."

Constance turned to look, and didn't recognize the man.

"Constance," Denver said, "This is our friend Mr. Arthwright. Mr. Zack Arthwright."

"Such thorough introductions are really not necessary," Arthwright said, looking annoyed.

"She's not going anywhere. Where's Lissa?"

"I was hoping you knew."

Denver shook his head. "Haven't heard from her. And the others?"

"They're in the front house. Getting fucked up. Dilettantes! They'll be here, in a few minutes."

"Good," Denver said. He looked at Constance. "It's almost time."

★　　★　　★

The ladder was made of roughly-sawn, irregular tree-branches. Trying to climb it, Prentice felt like one of the silent movie comedians he'd seen in the book about Hollywood parties. He slipped and tumbled his way up the ladder, at last achieving its top, and the top of the fence, as Lonny trudged up pulling the cable. *I got it all worked out,* Drax had said. Prentice snorted. If he'd thought this thing through the way he'd put this ladder together, badly lashed, of twine and pine branches and two by fours, they were in deep shit.

"We're in deep shit no matter *how* you look at it," Prentice muttered.

He thought he heard Amy say, *You're doing the right thing.*

He'd imagined her at his elbow for an hour now, urging him to do as Drax said . . .

Now, looking over the fence into the mist around the Doublekey Ranch, listening to the eerie, wailing, alien music from beyond the trees, Prentice thought: Maybe, after all, he ought to get down the road to a phone. Call Jeff. Call the cops . . .

But, no. Not after what Lonny had told him. There was no time to talk the cops into getting a search warrant.

And Lonny hadn't been making any of it up, Prentice knew. Kenson had told him. Lissa had shown him. And Amy whispered to him. There was no turning back.

Prentice paused a moment at the top, balancing precariously on a crooked branch, peering into the foggy underbrush. "There's . . . some kind of smoke around the house . . ." He whispered down to Lonny. "Maybe it's on fire. But . . . actually it doesn't look like smoke."

"The sick fuckers are probably barbecuing some poor asshole," Lonny said, a little too loud. "Yo, go on over and take this fucking cable, I can't hold it no more. It's heavy."

Prentice winced. Go over? He wasn't looking forward to it. "Maybe they hired a new security guard."

"I don't think they got it that much together. They're too caught up in their own weird shit, man. Let's get it *over* with."

Prentice sighed and took a moment to bend the wire ends at the top of the fence downward, so he wouldn't snag on them. Then he slung a leg over, braced, slung the other leg over, cursing under his breath. He was using muscles he'd forgotten about.

He lowered himself to the end of his arms and then dropped to the dirt, half expecting to be shot in the back or to feel a dog's jaws close over his throat. But nothing happened, and there was no sound, except the distant, dissonant music. He turned and looked at Lonny; he was hoping Lonny wasn't as scared as he was. The kid's expression was controlled, but his fear was there, in the tension of his hunched shoulders. He wanted to bolt, too.

Instead, Lonny pushed the cable through. It was an old, rusty cable four inches in diameter, thickly coated in rubber insulation, its nearer end covered with a homemade cap of rubber and black electrical tape. Touching the cable, Prentice could sense the electrical field around it; the suppressed power coursing through it. It ran twenty yards back behind Lonny to a spindle that Drax had set up, an hour earlier, that acted as a roller; there was another one in the brush, and from there it stretched to the electrical tower Drax had patched into.

If the old man couldn't open the front gate, Prentice thought, all this is for nothing.

It was going to be a hot day. Some insect in the undergrowth made the sound of a monomaniacal marraca player; a lizard zig-zagged over a rock on the other side of the fence. Lonny's face was streaked with dust and sweat. He was angry and scared. Prentice found himself admiring the boy. "You're a pretty tough kid," he said. He had a need to say something sentimental to someone, now. Before going on with it. And probably getting his ass blown away.

Lonny glared toward the Doublekey Ranch. He put his hand on the old Colt .36 six-shot revolver that Drax had given him, stuck now in his belt. "Mitch is dead. You should've seen the look on Orphy's face, too."

"How you know Mitch is dead?"

"Drax said so. After a while, you get to believe him."

"You've probably done enough here, Lonny," Prentice said dutifully. He hoped the kid wouldn't take his advice, as he went on, "You could split now. Make your way back to town."

Lonny turned the glare on Prentice. The look was one unceasing outpour, unwavering as a cop's flashlight. "Mitch . . ." He wasn't capable of saying the rest without breaking down – or bursting into a screaming rage.

Prentice nodded. "Yeah. Well. Come on over. It's almost time."

★   ★   ★

It was daytime, but it was night. Garner felt the hair rise on the back of his neck when they stepped into the fog. The stuff was almost as dark as smoke, but it wasn't smoke. You could breathe it, though you were sorry to; it left a faintly repugnant taste on the palate. Garner now carried the pistol that had been pointed at him a few hours before. Jeff Teitelbaum carried an Uzi – but not quite a real Uzi. It was a semi-automatic variety that gun-lovers could buy legally through the mail. Each trigger pull let go a round, but it didn't spray bullets. "I always knew they should ban these fuckers," Teitelbaum had said, getting it out of the trunk of his car. "I'll vote for a ban. But I wanted to get mine before the ban came down. For once, I'm glad I'm that kind of sicko. It'll be useful, today, seems to me..."

They'd found the front gate unguarded – Teitelbaum had seemed surprised at this – and they'd popped it with a crowbar, then climbed over the black iron inner gate. Now, prowling through the brush not far inside the iron fence, inside the cloud of dirty fog, they could no longer see the main house. There was only a thirty-yard visibility here, in the shadow of the trees and brush, and the closer they got to the house the thicker the fog seemed, the darker it got.

"Maybe this fog shit is some kind of toxic leak from somewhere," Teitelbaum said, as they moved slowly along the brick path.

"It's not making us cough," Garner pointed out. "And if it is, we've had such a thorough dose by now..." He shrugged.

Was Constance here? Was she alive? It might be better not to find out...

Up ahead, to one side, was a sort of tunnel of roses. Climbing vines from rose bushes had crawled thickly

310

over a trellis passageway. Through a gap in the roses, Garner glimpsed something moving.

Garner had used a gun, in his pre-pastoral years on the street, but mostly for bluff. Once, he'd shot a guy in the leg. He hadn't wanted to kill him. But this time . . .

Am I really going to be able to kill someone? Garner wondered. It was the last time he wondered that.

They'd walked up close beside the trellis. The smell of roses was cloying and mixed revoltingly with the fishy stink of the fog.

A hand darted through a gap in vines and closed around Teitelbaum's neck, jerked him against the trellis so that rose petals showered and his Uzi barked into the ground before he lost his grip on it. The gun fell clattering on the brick as Teitelbaum shouted a name – it sounded like *"Lissa!"* – and Garner rushed to his side.

He saw their attacker through the gap in the roses. It was a woman. Lissa, he assumed.

Her head had been smashed open, just above the left temple. The crack in the skull could be clearly seen, splintery and deeply gashed into the tissue beneath. There was nothing in her eyes. And as Garner struggled to pry her hand free of Teitelbaum's throat and struggled with his own rising terror, he was pretty sure that she was dead.

Teitelbaum had told Garner about the Akishra. Had repeated Kenson's story. Which Teitelbaum had come to half-believe himself. So Garner knew about the worms. And he *believed* – in some intuitive way he'd always known about them. And somehow Garner knew, without doubt, that the blow on her skull had killed this woman.

And he knew that only the worms were keeping her going.

They were moving through her easily, through this

311

once beautiful woman, like snakes through water, weaving in and out of her. Leaving her skin bruised but unbroken where they'd gone. Others waved around her head like the ring of slippery stingers bristling from a sea anemone. Somehow, in taking her over, becoming more corporeal. Operating her. Moving her about. It was something you could see in her unnaturally sinuous movements; the animalistic suddenness of her attack.

Garner, trying to yank the flailing, bubbling Teitelbaum free now, felt something wet winding itself around his wrist. He let out a childish yell of revulsion and jerked away, slapping the thing off him, then jerking the gun from his waist band. He thrust it through the gap at the woman, and pulled the trigger. It was harder to pull than he expected. The gun boomed and recoiled, knocking Garner's hands up to impale on inch-long rosebush thorns. He hissed between clenched teeth in pain and pulled his hands off the thorns, drew back from the bush. The woman had fallen back; Teitelbaum was kneeling, clutching his gun to him, making hacksaw sounds as he gasped for air.

Garner forced himself to move toward the entrance to the rose tunnel. Just at the edge, he saw the woman woven into the vines. The dark fog slithered past her in wisps that were like the ghosts of the vines that held her. She spoke hoarsely, barely audible, *"Kill me kill me kill me kill me kill me and fuck you fuck you forever"*

Garner acted instinctively. Whispering, "Go with God," as he pointed the gun at the woman's head, and blew her brains out.

She slumped in the vines. Then the worms started to show themselves . . . She began to wriggle free . . .

He heard Jeff Teitelbaum calling hoarsely to him but he moved on, around the corner. . .

Someone was running up the alley of roses, with a gun in his hand. Nearer, the woman was getting to her feet. No: The worms were raising her body to stand. Using the meat of her, collectively driving her remains. Beyond her, a man was coming toward them; he wore a yellow shirt and yellow pants and a gold chain.

And spun around, smashed by bullets, when Teitelbaum fired three rounds at him in two seconds, firing through the bushes. "Dammit!" Garner shouted. 'You don't know who –"

"It's fucking Sam Denver!" Teitelbaum shouted. "He's –"

He didn't finish saying it, maybe seeing Denver get up – though the top of his head was shot away. Walking toward them with a side to side swish that might have been funny except for the blood masking Denver's face and the worms emerging from him, far more than in Lissa, coming out like a carnation blossoming in fast-action, the thin petals writhing with urgency. The fog – looking gray green, now, as if moving into some new stage – patterning itself in the air around Denver, responding to the changes in him, creating an etheric, vermiform aureole around him like the mandala behind some tusked Hindu deathgod.

Five more licks of fire and five *cracks* from the *faux* Uzi, and Denver danced backwards and fell flat. Then began to get up once more, springy and eager.

Lissa was missing most of her face, but she was reaching, now, for Garner. He fired once more into her neck, hoping that if he snapped the spine...

She went down. And immediately began to get up again.

God – had they done this to Constance?

Garner turned and ran after Teitelbaum, who was

trotting toward the main house, crying like a child – and waving the gun around like a small boy playing Army.

Garner tried to remember a prayer from the Bible. And couldn't.

Somewhere behind them, he heard the rumble of an old vehicle, a big engine that coughed and missed and sounded as if its engine would give out at any moment.

★   ★   ★

The gunshots had come from the West, Prentice thought, near the front of the place. He and Lonny were off to the South. "Probably just playing with guns and whoever they got now," Lonny said calmly. 'It's too soon for it to be Drax."

They were dragging the cable like a firehose, Lonny taking the head of it, working their way through the brush to the inner fence. They'd moved deep into the fog, though the stuff reeked wrongness, and they could make out the bulk of the main house beyond the fence and the screen of trees . . .

"Oh God," Lonny said, pausing with the cable hitched up on his hip, pointing at something to one side.

Dogs. Parts of the dead guard dogs he'd told Prentice about.

"You do that to their bodies?" Prentice asked, without thinking.

"Dude, you think I'd mess with them like that?" Lonny replied, disgusted by the suggestion.

The dogs had been gutted; their entrails hung like Christmas ornaments from the branches of the small pine standing close by; the purplish, dried-out guts dripped with maggots. The remaining corpses of the dogs, on the ground, had their backs broken, were twisted into

Oroborous circles of rotting flesh; still attached to the necks, their heads were shoved down under their ribs and back between the hind legs, snouts forced up and out through ripped rectums, the entire head crammed through to the ears. Through his disgust, Prentice marvelled. It had taken someone considerable time and effort and it seemed supremely pointless. The fog swarmed almost imperceptibly around the wrecked carcasses. The sight made Prentice's stomach feel as if it were turning inside out, too.

He turned away and they stumbled on, dragging the cable to the black iron fence. It was lower than the other; Lonny scrambled easily over it, dropped to the other side, and pulled the cable through. Prentice made the climb, with significantly more difficulty, and dropped to the other side just as the old Ford pick-up, its one working headlight making a tunnel of dull light through the fog, jounced through the brush, its tractor wheels finding purchase in the thick mesquite and grinding through. Old Drax grinned in the cab of the truck as he pulled up with the rear of the truck close by them. Looking closer Prentice saw that the grin was more a rictus of fear. The old hippie was as scared as they were. Wearing overalls now, Drax came huffing out of the idling truck, hands shaking, and ran to the back . . .

"I saw some of 'em, saw some of 'em, had to run one of 'em over," he chattered as he dropped the tailgate of the truck and reached for the cable. He and Lonny muscled it up to the spool fixed to the pick-up bed.

It was a wooden spool with another, similar length of cable attached to it. The spool was bolted down onto the bed of the truck. He ripped away the black tape on the cable end, glancing over his shoulder, obviously expecting someone to come after them at any moment. "You

315

do that shooting?" he asked Lonny, as he worked. He took hold of the cable on an insulated section and with the other hand unscrewed the cap. The exposed copper spat fine sparks into the fog.

Lonny said, "Uh uh. We thought it was you . . ."

There was a noise from under the truck. A very soft noise. Prentice thought maybe it was just Drax's foot scraping something.

Drax took the end of the cable on the truck's spool, and attached it to the cable coming through the fence, screwing an insulated clamp down onto it. "I hope to Mescalito that holds," Drax said. Shadows in the fog moved over his pale face as he dropped the cable –

Something jerked him off his feet. Prentice jumped back and looked at the ground. Lissa!

Oh God it was Lissa, just enough of her face left to recognize, and a deep tyre tread printed into her back, one arm tangled up with the axle like a piece of bloody rope. Her free hand clutching the fallen Drax's ankles as he scrabbled back from her his face twitchy with horror.

For a long moment Prentice felt a profound pity go through him – and then a veil of fog drifted away and he saw the worms fluttering around her head . . .

Lonny's gun banged and echoed and most of Lissa's head exploded. Drax was up, running back from the cab of the truck with a shotgun. "Get back! Ricochets!" He yelled. They scurried back as he fired, the shotgun smashing her tangled arm off at the shoulder, freeing the truck of her. Lissa's body tried to climb from under the truck but seemed to have difficulty organizing its few working parts . . .

Prentice looked away. As Drax ran to the cab of the truck and climbed in, threw it in gear, Prentice tried to tell Lonny he'd had enough, he was leaving. But he couldn't quite say it. His tongue seemed numb in his mouth. He felt as if he was going altogether numb inside. He wanted to go back but he was not at all sure he had the strength to climb over the fence. And then Lonny swung his gun around to kill Jeff, as Jeff loomed up in the fog, a bearded stranger at his heels.

★   ★   ★

Constance lay passively under Arthwright as he rammed into her, each thrust of his hips driving her a few inches farther along the terrace, to the edge of the pool. Now the top of her head thrust out over the vitreous, secretive surface. She heard things moving down there. She could sense them, all of them, and she sensed more: all the worms moving excitedly in the soil, under the surface of the earth. Nothing like the Akishra, but somehow communing with them; she sensed things hovering in the air around her, unseen; she sensed the huge psychic gravitation of the Magnus lowering itself over the pool. It hadn't gone far; it had only withdrawn to wait.

She saw shapes unfold and fold and reshape again in the fog overhead; intricate geometrical designs, like Mayan carvings; ugly variations of mandalas; constellations forming and reforming: one shaped like a scorpion, another like a spider, a third like a hangman.

She watched all this only distantly – her hair dangling in the wet surface now, sucked slowly through the waxy ooze over the pool as Arthwright fucked her along the slippery ground. Now her shoulders were over the stuff and soon her torso would dip into it, her head upside down in the water, her eyes greeted by the swarm that waited down there . . .

They were neatly detached, these perceptions,

capering beyond a druggy haze. She barely felt Arthwright's penis in her; she felt mostly the swelling boil, the pustulent buboe, of her own pleasure: the Reward they were jolting into her, using up the last of her ability to feel as they shot it into her in time with his triphammer thrusts.

If she just concentrated on the glow of Reward . . .

And didn't pay attention to the hallucinations, the signs. The tarantula with a body shining like a hairy lightbulb; the corkscrews of blue fire pursuing one another endlessly through the fog; the imploring faces of Ephram and Elma Stutgart Denver and the boy who'd died on the bed: these she could see scribbled in the air to one side, sketched in shadowy fog. In the background: the far away screaming of Eurydice where someone was raping her by the old fireplace, pushing her head into the fire as they raped her. The Madonna record they were playing at a speed freaked Minnie Mouse 78 RPM. The vagina lined with seeking worms that opened in the sky: inside it, a window into Hell that opened with the squeal of tortured glass . . .

Arthwright's detonating head.

It blew up, his head, she saw through slitted eyes. It shattered upward and outward, close in front of her, taking most of his face with it. Then she heard a familiar voice cursing and ending with a sob: *"Oh shit I shouldn't have done it that way –"* the voice said. The voice was very familiar but she couldn't quite make out who it was.

Then Arthwright's corpse was flipped summarily away from her and she was dragged back from the edge of the pool and a man was pulling her to her feet and she sagged down on knees weak from disorientation and the sudden, vicious cessation of Reward . . .

"No, no, no, don't," she told the man. A bearded

man, who looked a little familiar. Who was he? It didn't matter who he was. 'No don't, you stopped it, you stopped the Reward I have to find it again...' She turned and ran to the edge of the pool.

He caught her by the wrist and dragged her back, just as a big ugly red machine roared around the corner of the main house, smashing through a corner of the cactus garden as it came toward the terrace, its one eye shining...

Something vast screamed with frustration.

A drain opened up inside Constance and she want down it.

★   ★   ★

Garner caught Constance as she fell. He tossed the gun onto the terrace next to the shaking body of the man who'd been raping her. Then he picked her up in his arms and carried her out of the way of the crazy old man with the truck. He had a three second sweeping vision of the scene on the terrace before the truck hit its objective.

He saw Jeff Teitelbaum shooting a gun at someone who was holding a girl's head over a fire at a stone barbecue, as the one they called the More Man glided around the corner of the house, moving in that oozy walk that meant the worms were guiding what was left of him; something flopped out the door of the back house and it was too late to warn Jeff as the thing moved onto his back – a shapeless wreckage of probably-human flesh that was furred with worm-heads, tendrils that flittered around its broken bone-ends and torn tissue, muscle and flesh mixed – Wetbones, Garner knew. Reanimated, guided by the tendrils... tendrils that reached up from it to the thing that manifested in the churning fog over the pool:

319

A vast thing, up there, at first looking like a partly-filled hot air balloon, then a tapering head, its nearer end bifurcated into a worm-edged mouth opening to show a terrified remnant of face – its tendrils reaching out to puppet the starfish of smashed human flesh that closed around Jeff Teitelbaum and broke his neck –

Reaching out with other tendrils to embrace the six men and two women who stood naked and blood-spattered around the body of a woman near the back of the main house –

Reaching out to Prentice – it must be Prentice – who was running open mouthed and glaze-eyed to pull the girl from the fire; stretching out to the boy Lonny who'd nearly shot Teitelbaum and Garner two minutes earlier. Lonny now reflexively shooting at the More Man who had one hand in his own guts and another on his purplish, exposed dick, as a worm grew arm-thick from his mouth, the worm reaching for Lonny. . .

As the thing over the pool reached for them all. Reached for Garner.

Three seconds were up. The cable on the spool unreeling behind it, the truck roared up to the pool. The crazy old hippie in the driver's seat, screaming triumphantly at the top of his lungs, drove the truck deliberately head-on into the water. The exposed strip of wire on the spool-attached end of the cable struck the water with all the voltage that could be stolen from a high power line as the truck broke through the waxy protective skin over the pool and nosed down, crackling with sparks. It sank into the surging, boiling, green-black waters. Watching, Garner understood. He could see the colony of tens of thousands of tiny astral worms outlined in violet fire, deep-frying in the pool, as electricity arced and crackled in small lightning bolts across its tortured surface. Like

320

randomly aimed particle accelerators, the seething electrons shattered the plasmic; Astral skeins of the Akishra – and travelled along the circuits of etheric relationship, conducting up through the tendrils of the Lord of Akishra hovering over the pool, passing into the Magnus and through it into the others on the terrace and in the house.

Violent streams of electricity roared down from the Akishra Magnus and into the More Man; into the wreckage of Jeff and his murderer by the doorway to the back house; into the weave of rose bushes up the outer walls of the guest house. The rose bushes writhed like a nest of neon snakes, wailing in despair. The vast currents of electricity crackled into the eight Followers and Feasters standing back of the fireplace, and into two worm-driven corpses – the ragged remains of Lissa and Arthwright – crawling along the stone flags. Fingers of electricity dabbed like the fingers of a blind man at Garner, and seemed to find him not to their taste; they moved on to Constance, pausing over her so that she went momentarily rigid, and glowed faintly in his arms as a starburst of worms fled from her, disintegrating in the air. The charge left her, and passed over Lonny and Prentice and the black girl; and went on.

The electricity crackled more powerfully yet into the More Man, into the worm-haunted hamburger that had taken Jeff Teitelbaum, into the More Man's followers – and they shook and screamed, electrocuting physically and spiritually, each surrounded by a spark-spitting corona of brilliant blue-white discharge, human fireworks displays; they ran spasmodically to one another and, as if galvanized to act out the archetypes of their compulsions, they lunged at whoever was nearest. The Handy Man tearing into the body of the More Man with

321

his bare hand – the rest crowding together, doing the same to each other, a crowd of about ten of them closely clumped, tearing one another to pieces with teeth and bare hands, so that rags and gobbets of flesh flew through the halos of sparks, each flying handful of bloody flesh itself flaring with electrical discharge and exploding in sparks; the More Man and companions bodily burrowing into one another, a woman thrusting her head into her partner's guts and emerging beside the shattered spine as someone else, electrified into superhuman strength, ripped her leg out of its socket and then thrust his hand into the wound to yank out her intestines, and someone else sank teeth into the side of the face of the one who'd torn the leg away and someone else popped out the eyes and then the brains of the one who bit the woman who...

It took five seconds, as the old red truck boiled like a lobster in the pool. The human hosts of the Akishra tore one another to pieces, faster and faster till it was too fast for the eye to follow and then they – and the worms that motivated them – were lost in a seething cloud of exploding flesh –

Garner turned away to see a raging ball of electricity double back from this hand-made Wetbones and up the connective tendrils into the Akishra Magnus, which detonated like a sobbing and suffering roman candle, expelling a hundred thousand trapped spirits that spiralled away into void and...

The Akishra burned in the air, ten thousand thousand worms fluttered up and burned out. Or burned out of this world, Garner supposed. There was no exterminating them, not completely.

And then the fog dispersed. Sunlight expanded around the pool. The apparitions vanished from the sky. The Magnus was no more. The More Man and companions were steaming heaps of burnt flesh, without the Akishra to animate them. Lonny was helping Prentice carry the poor, charred, black girl away.

Garner was abruptly aware that he was dizzy, in danger of falling over with Constance in his arms. His heart was playing a drum roll, his mouth as dry and foul as a road kill. But he had to see one more thing. He turned to glance into the pool . . .

In the pool, Drax was, of course, quite dead. The pool had lost its colour, was now crystal clear, illuminated with an inner glow. The truck was glowing with violet fire; and inside it, like a filament in a bulb, Drax glowed with a psychedelic coruscation all his own, his shining corpse grinning in triumph.

14

Berkeley, California . . .

One Year Later

Garner was glad he'd thought to bring flowers. There were none in Constance's room. She was wearing shorts and a rather old *The Simpsons* t-shirt and no shoes. She'd put on weight, a little too much. Earlier in the year, in the months after the Ranch, she'd barely eaten at all. Now she was eating too much. He wasn't sure if that was good or bad.

She sat by the window, at her desk, with a copy of *Cosmopolitan* open in front of her. She was looking at the pictures. Next to her was a broad window looking out on the hospital's Activities Lawn, a sort of commons where sports were played and picnics held and catatonics wheeled about. The sky was overcast; the light that came in through the window was muted. The trees sheltering the sanitarium from the world were beginning to streak with russet and yellow.

He stood looking at her a moment, readying himself. She was better, he told himself. She'd really gotten better. The months of withdrawal symptoms were over. She had stopped trying to slash her arms up; she'd long since stopped attacking people.

"Hey dudette," he said, putting the flowers on the table across from her bed. He put the sack of cookies down next to them. "Smell anything good? Not me and not the food around here. Not even the cookies. I mean the flowers. You like carnations?"

"Sure." She looked out the window. "You gonna watch TV with us again tonight?"

Something about the question hinted a gray continuum of hopelessness. It dug a hole through him. But he said, "That's the plan. I brought cookies for the whole floor."

"Next time bring candy for Marcia. She doesn't like cookies. She's weird about cookies. Somebody choked her by forcing 'em down her once. Her mom said she was over-eating so she tried to teach her a lesson and she almost died. From cookies."

Her voice was a monotone.

He wanted to hug her. He knew better.

She turned a page of the magazine. He carefully didn't stare at the stump where she'd lost a finger. After a moment, she asked, "You been going to meetings?"

"Sure. I got a year clean and sober next week. I didn't tell you, I was elected secretary of a Narcotics Anonymous meeting over in the city."

"That's good." Her voice was as flat as the line on Aleutia's EKG.

"So –" He was afraid to ask it. It might push her into one of her screaming fits, and he found those hard to bear up under. But it was September and her therapist said he was supposed to ask her around the beginning of every month. He took a deep breath and plunged in. "How about it? You want to come home for a weekend? Get you back here bright and early on Monday. I was thinking this Friday —"

"No."

"We could talk about it."

"No."

Floundering, he blurted, "Constance — why not?"

"I lived in that house." She was still looking out the window. Her voice was still a monotone but now it seemed an octave lower.

He waited. She didn't say anything else. He prompted, "Go on — please."

She shook her head. He wanted to go to her, to put his arms around her, at least touch her on the shoulder. But he knew she didn't like that.

Still — he *had* told him something. *I lived in that house.*

She'd lived in that house, their house when she'd met Ephram Pixie.

"Why didn't you tell me before, it was the house? The reason you didn't want to do home visits . . . I thought it was me . . ."

She shrugged.

He said, "Want to come and stay with me someplace else? Um . . . How about we visit your aunt in Portland?"

He waited on tenterhooks for twenty seconds. Then she nodded. Relief flooded through him. He remembered a Barbie doll. He wondered how her therapy was going, but didn't want to ask her. "Sooner or later," he said, "you have to look at what you went through. I know it's hard here, because they don't believe a lot of it. But *I* know what happened. And I'm willing to listen as much as you need."

She covered up her maimed hand with the intact one. He knew that as a warning.

He thought about confronting her. Talking her through it. *He made you murder people. Only you and I know it wasn't you who did it – that he had the power to make you do that. Only I believe you. But God knows and you know and I know and the police don't know and it's okay now to feel the pain and sadness that you couldn't feel then. You have to just feel it and let it go, just feel it and tell yourself yes my body was a murderer, my hands helped torture people to death, but it wasn't really me, that wasn't me, it was him. You know it rationally and you know it emotionally and now you've got to say it, you've got to –*

But he was afraid of it, himself. It might shatter her completely. . .

"I liked it," she said. "He made me like it."

Something took off and soared inside him. *She was taking about it!*

"It wasn't you, Constance! He pushed a button that made you feel pleasure. He punished you when you didn't play along. He paralyzed you when you tried to run. Sometimes he manipulated your limbs. He raped you a dozen ways." He was trying not to cry. It was hard; it was really hard not to cry. "Anyone would have done what you did because –"

"But *I* did. It wasn't 'anyone'. It was me."

"No! It wasn't really you. You were trapped in the body he was using. You were trapped inside. He was moving you around like a puppet."

She shook her head. She opened her mouth and shut it again. Her shoulders shook and for a long moment he prayed she would cry.

She didn't. She pushed it back down, again.

But Garner wanted to dance around the room. *She had talked about it!* For the first time in a year. She'd talked – just a little bit. It wasn't even the light at the end

327

of the tunnel. But it was a little gray patch hinting that the far-away light was closer.

"I got three kinds of cookies," he said. "Better tell me what kind you want before we go down and put on the Disney channel. I'll put some aside for you. You know how Alice is. She'll eat a whole box by herself."

"Then she goes in the bathroom and throws it up," Constance said matter of factly. But she got up and went to look in the cookie bag . . .

The Hills Near Malibu

Lonny drove the old Datsun off the highway, and up onto the dirt road. The road led through the horse pasturage, over the hill, down into the brushland, and up another hill to Drax's shack. Eurydice grabbed onto the dashboard to steady herself as the car bounced from rut to rut.

It was about ten in the morning. Lonny came early, so there was no chance they could be caught out here after dark. It was safe after dark, it wasn't that. But Eurydice couldn't handle it here at night. And neither could he.

Lonny glanced at her, checking out the work the surgeon had done on the side of her face. The burn scars weren't so bad, but she still looked patchy. He wondered if he should tell her she looked better, since she'd just come out of the second round of plastic surgery. Might make her feel better. But it might just make her think about the scars that were still there.

Better keep his mouth shut about the scars. The idea in bringing her out here was to heal a few wounds, not open old ones.

He stopped at the wooden gate to the horse pasture and got out, opened the gate, swung it to one side for the car. Hurriedly got back in the car and moved it through. Have to close the gate before the horses decided to check out the big world.

But the horses were more interested in the car. Eurydice smiled when he pulled the car up, and the three apaloosas trotted up to the Datsun. "They hoping for a treat," she said reaching out a window to pat a soft muzzle.

"Next time we'll bring an apple or something," he said. He got out again and closed the gate before the horses could get out. This is stupid, he thought, I should have asked her to get out and close the gate after I drove through.

But you felt like never asking her to do anything. That's the way it was with her now.

They drove on along the tracks that passed for a road, then down the other hillside. From here they could just make out, about a half mile away, the hilltop where the burnt-out ruins of the Doublekey ranch stood. Lonny had come back and torched it, in the wet season when it wouldn't start a big wild fire. It was probably unnecessary, but it made him feel better. It had been funny to watch the cops scurry around there, after the fire: The second time they'd been out there in droves and had gone away completely confused.

Lonny glanced at Eurydice to see if she were staring at the Doublekey. She was looking somewhere else.

They drove down and over the hills, and then up to Drax's place. He wasn't there anymore, of course. Not exactly.

They pulled up out front, near the ring of posts and the fetish dolls, which had been carefully maintained.

Lonny cut the engine and waited, the metal under the Datsun's hood ticking as it cooled. Eury looked at him and he made a "wait a minute" gesture. She shrugged and settled back in her seat to wait.

Lonny could feel him watching them from inside the house. After a full ten minutes, the door of the shack opened and Prentice came out.

"Okay," Lonny told Eurydice. "We can get out now."

They climbed out of the Datsun. Lonny shook Prentice's hand. Prentice smiled at Eury and patted her arm. His hair and beard was almost as long as Drax's had been, after only a year. His face was haggard; his eyes hidden in sunglasses. He wore a pair of Drax's old overalls and boots, an Iggy Pop t-shirt. Jerry, Drax's dog, snuffled up from behind Prentice, looking them over. Jerry looked around as if hoping they'd brought Drax with them.

"How you doin', dude?" Lonny asked.

Prentice nodded. "Good, good. Real good. Good. You bring my stuff?"

"Sure."

They went to the trunk and pulled out the crate of coffee, another with some groceries. Lonny carried them to warping planks that passed for a porch. He knew that Prentice didn't like anyone to come inside. They stood in the shade of the perilous porch roof for a few minutes. Prentice glanced nervously at Eury, then looked quickly away; looked at her again.

Lonny took an envelope from the pocket of his Levi jacket. Passed it and a pen to Prentice. Eury watched with a frown as Prentice opened the unsealed envelope, took out the cheque, signed the back, and gave it all back to Lonny. Prentice hadn't even looked at the amount. Lonny put the cheque and pen back in his pocket.

"You need anything else?" Lonny asked.

"No, no, not right now, no. I'm good. Good."

Prentice glanced at Eury. She hadn't been out to the shack before and he seemed to think she wanted something of him.

Lonny prodded her gently, "Anything you want to ask, Eury?"

She licked the scarred flap that was the remains of her lower lip. "I . . . " She looked at the hilltop, some distance away but always looming over them, where the blackened bones of the Doublekey stood.

"Nothing," Prentice said. Nodding reassurance to her. "Nothing there. Nothing's come out, and nothing's there."

She smiled with relief, then went to sit in the car.

"You sure you don't want anything else?" Lonny asked.

Prentice shook his head. "I got electricity here now. I'm good. Great." He looked at the car. "Listen. Half that money – she gets it."

Lonny smiled. "Okay" He took his car keys out of his pocket. "Well . . ."

"Sure." Prentice smiled back at him. "See you next time."

He waved once, shyly, at Eurydice, and went back into the shack, the dog trotting behind him.

Lonny got back in the car and drove back the way he'd come. Eury closed the car windows against the dust.

After they'd got to the highway, Eurydice asked, "What that cheque about?"

"Money from the movie. They started shooting it, so he gets more money. He doesn't want to mess with postmen."

'But how come he signed it for you?"

"He doesn't like banks any more either. And he trusts me. I never take anything except what we agreed on to do his errands and shit."

"He sold a movie, huh?"

"A horror movie. I guess he got some inspiration somewhere. I don't know where."

She laughed, as she was supposed to, and that was good. But then she said, "They should put me in the movie. A horror movie. I wouldn't need no makeup."

"Hey! Come on. No *way*."

Her mouth buckled and he thought she'd cry, but she didn't, not quite. Instead she changed the subject. "He going to build a house out there, now he got money?"

"I don't know. Seems to like it the way Drax had it. He got a *lot* of money for that horror movie. They seemed to be sure it was gonna hit big I guess. He bought the land the shack is on, you know. And the Ranch land too. He owns it."

"No shit? He – how come you do this job, Lonny? Just to be nice?"

He was a little embarrassed that she'd figured him out. "No. I like to help him out, but – I need to go out there, too. I don't sleep too good, if I don't see him out there now and then." He thought he'd take her someplace to eat. It was good to have someone to go to dinner with. He liked being with Eury because she knew the things he knew, and because she didn't expect him to touch her, the way some other girls did. Like him, she didn't like to be touched any more.

And at dinner he'd tell her about the money Prentice gave her. Money for a better place to live. And better plastic surgery.

They were silent for awhile. Then she said, "Yeah. I'm glad he's there. But I feel bad for him. He's . . . just him and that odd dog. He must be lonely, all by himself out there."

Lonny shook his head. "Oh, no. He's not lonely out there. Not at all. He's got Amy with him . . ."

332

SHADOWS

Kimberly Rangel

WHERE TERROR RULES...

In the distant past, in a far-off land, the spell is cast, damning the family to an eternity of blood hunger. Over countless centuries, in the dark of night, they are doomed to assume the shape of savage beasts, deadly black panthers driven by a maddening fever to quench their unspeakable thirst. Then Selene DeMarco finds herself the last female of her line, and she has to mate with a descendent of the man who has plunged her family into the endless agony.

_4054-9 $4.99 US/$5.99 CAN

WHEN SHADOWS FALL

BRIAN SCOTT SMITH

Martin doesn't believe his aunt's death is an accident, and he and a couple of buddies are determined to find the truth. But when he starts sneaking around the house of his aunt's new "friends," he never expects to witness a blood-drenched satanic ritual. But he does see it, and more important, the witches see him!

Suddenly Martin is in a horrifying race for his life. He has to stop the witches before they stop him for good. And he has to do it before Halloween night, the night of the final sacrifice, the night when the demons of hell will be unleashed on the Earth, the night when shadows fall.

___4313-0 $4.99 US/$5.99 CAN

ALONE WITH THE DEAD

ROBERT J. RANDISI

New York City is in the grip of a nightmare. A twisted serial killer called the Lover is stalking young women, leaving his calling card with their dead bodies—a single rose. And there's a copycat out there too, determined to do his idol one better. But the Lover isn't flattered. He's furious that some rank amateur is muddying his good name. As the nightmare grows ever more intense, one detective begins to suspect the truth. As his superiors close ranks on him, he realizes that his only ally may be the Lover himself.

___4435-8 $4.99 US/$5.99 CAN

Dorchester Publishing Co., Inc.
P.O. Box 6640
Wayne, PA 19087-8640

Please add $1.75 for shipping and handling for the first book and $.50 for each book thereafter. NY, NYC, and PA residents, please add appropriate sales tax. No cash, stamps, or C.O.D.s. All orders shipped within 6 weeks via postal service book rate. Canadian orders require $2.00 extra postage and must be paid in U.S. dollars through a U.S. banking facility.

Name_____
Address_____
City_____State_____Zip_____
I have enclosed $_____ in payment for the checked book(s).
Payment <u>must</u> accompany all orders. ❑ Please send a free catalog.
CHECK OUT OUR WEBSITE! www.dorchesterpub.com

DRAWN TO THE GRAVE
MARY ANN MITCHELL

"A tight, taut dark fantasy with surprising plot twists and a lot of spooky atmosphere."
—Ed Gorman

Beverly thinks that she has found something special with Carl, until she realizes that he has stolen from her. But he doesn't just steal her money and her property—he steals her very life. Suddenly she is helpless and alone, able only to watch in growing despair as her flesh begins to decay and each day transforms her more and more into a corpse—a corpse without the release of death.

But Beverly is not truly alone, for Carl is always nearby, watching her and waiting. He knows that soon he will need another unknowing victim, another beautiful woman he can seduce...and destroy. And when lovely young Megan walks into his web, he knows he has found his next lover. For what can possibly go wrong with his plan, a plan he has practiced to perfection so many times before?

___4290-8 $4.99 US/$5.99 CAN

Dorchester Publishing Co., Inc.
P.O. Box 6640
Wayne, PA 19087-8640

Please add $1.75 for shipping and handling for the first book and $.50 for each book thereafter. NY, NYC, and PA residents, please add appropriate sales tax. No cash, stamps, or C.O.D.s. All orders shipped within 6 weeks via postal service book rate. Canadian orders require $2.00 extra postage and must be paid in U.S. dollars through a U.S. banking facility.

Name_____
Address_____
City_____ State_____ Zip_____
I have enclosed $_____ in payment for the checked book(s).
Payment <u>must</u> accompany all orders. ☐ Please send a free catalog.

CHARLES WILSON

NIGHTWATCHER

"A striking book. Quite an achievement."
—Los Angeles Times

The staff of the state hospital for the criminally insane in Davis County, Mississippi, has seen a lot in their time—but nothing like the savage killing of Judith Salter, one of their nurses. And with three escaped inmates on the loose, there is no telling which of them is the butcher—or who the next victim will be. Even worse, as the danger and terror grow apace, the only eyewitness to the nurse's death—a psychopathic mass murderer—begins to reveal a fearsome agenda of his own.

___4275-4 $4.99 US/$5.99 CAN

BLOODLINES

J. N. WILLIAMSON

Marshall Madison disappeared the night his wife committed suicide. She saw the horrible things Madison did to their son, Thad, and couldn't deal with the knowledge that their daughter, Caroline, was next. Caroline is taken in by a kind, hardworking family, and Thad runs off to live by his wits on the streets of New York. But Madison means to make good on his promise to come for his children. And as he gets closer and closer, the trail of bodies in his wake gets longer and longer. No one will keep him from his flesh and blood.

___4468-4 $4.99 US/$5.99 CAN

DOUGLAS

HALLOWEEN

THE

MAN

CLEGG

The New England coastal town of Stonehaven has a history
of nightmares—and dark secrets. When Stony Crawford
becomes a pawn in a game of horror and darkness, he finds
that he alone holds the key to the mystery of Stonehaven,
and to the power of the unspeakable creature trapped within
a summer mansion.

___4439-0 $5.50 US/$6.50 CAN

Dorchester Publishing Co., Inc.
P.O. Box 6640
Wayne, PA 19087-8640

Please add $1.75 for shipping and handling for the first book and
$.50 for each book thereafter. NY, NYC, and PA residents,
please add appropriate sales tax. No cash, stamps, or C.O.D.s. All
orders shipped within 6 weeks via postal service book rate.
Canadian orders require $2.00 extra postage and must be paid in
U.S. dollars through a U.S. banking facility.

Name_____
Address_____
City_____ State_____ Zip_____
I have enclosed $_____ in payment for the checked book(s).
Payment <u>must</u> accompany all orders. ❏ Please send a free catalog.
CHECK OUT OUR WEBSITE! www.dorchesterpub.com